Carl Werner,
An Imaginative Story

Available from the Simms Initiatives and the
University of South Carolina Press

Carl Werner,
An Imaginative Story

With Other Tales of Imagination

―⸙―

William Gilmore Simms

Critical Introduction by Sam Lackey
With a Biographical Overview by David Moltke–Hansen

The University of South Carolina Press

New material © 2016 University of South Carolina

Cloth original published by George Adlard, 1838
Paperback published by the University of South Carolina Press
Columbia, South Carolina 29208

www.sc.edu/uscpress

Manufactured in the United States of America

25 24 23 22 21 20 19 18 17 16
10 9 8 7 6 5 4 3 2 1

ISBN 978-1-61117-685-8 (pbk)

Published in cooperation with the Simms Initiatives, a project of the University of South
Carolina Libraries with the generous support of the Watson-Brown Foundation.

William Gilmore Simms: A Biographical Overview

David Moltke-Hansen

Introduction

Harper's Weekly put it succinctly in its July 2, 1870, issue: "In the death of Mr. Simms, on the 11th of June, at Charleston, the country has lost one more of its time-honored band of authors, and the South the most consistent and devoted of her literary sons" (qtd. In Butterworth and Kibler 125–26). Indeed no mid-nineteenth-century writer and editor did more than William Gilmore Simms to frame white southern self-identity and nationalism, shape southern historical consciousness, or foster the South's participation and recognition in the broader American literary culture. No southern writer enjoyed more contemporary esteem and attention, at least after Edgar Allan Poe moved north. Among American romancers (or writers of prose epics), only New Yorker James Fenimore Cooper was as successful by the 1840s. In those same years, Simms was the South's most influential editor of cultural journals. He also was the region's most prolific cultural journalist and poet, publishing an average of one book review and one poem per week for forty-five years.

Before his death Simms saw his national reputation fall along with the Confederacy he had vigorously supported and with the slave regime that many in the North had come to despise. Nevertheless reprints of most of the twenty titles in the selected edition of his works, first published between 1853 and 1860, appeared up until World War I. Thereafter only *The Yemassee*, an early romance about an Indian war in South Carolina, continued in print. The tide began to turn in the 1950s, when five volumes of Simms's letters appeared and a growing number of his works were issued in new editions. Publication in 1992 of the first literary biography, by John C. Guilds, and establishment of the William Gilmore Simms Society and the *Simms Review* the next year at once reflected and fostered this revived interest. Yet not until the 2011 launch of the digital Simms edition of the South Caroliniana Library of the University of South Carolina did scholars of southern, American, and nineteenth-century culture have the prospect of ready access to all of Simms's separately published works. With the University of South Carolina Press's cooperation, readers also will have access to sixty works in paperback editions by the end of 2014. Simms himself never saw nearly so many of his works in print at one time.

Clearly the decline in the critical standing of, and historical attention to, Simms and his oeuvre in the century after his death has reversed in the years since. The last three decades of the twentieth century saw more published on Simms than the previous hundred years (Butterworth and Kibler 126–200; MLA International). The last decade of the twentieth and first decade of the twenty-first centuries saw more dissertations and theses on him (forty-one) than had appeared in all the years before. This is not to say that Simms is yet given the attention directed to some of his contemporaries. For the first decade of the twenty-first century, the Modern Language Association International Bibliography lists roughly four times as many scholarly publications on James Fenimore Cooper, more than ten times as many on Nathaniel Hawthorne, and sixteen times as many on Edgar Allan Poe. Not surprisingly, therefore, Simms is not yet included in most anthologies of American literature, although he is a subject or a source in an expanding and ever more diverse body of scholarship.

To prepare to read Simms, it is important to see his writings in multiple contexts. He rarely wrote about himself outside of his more personal poems and his letters (some fifteen hundred of the many thousands of which survive). Yet he systematically drew on his background, personal experience, and relationships in his work. He also shaped that work through a progressively developed poetics and philosophy of life, history, and art. He did so in the context of his very broad reading of both contemporary and earlier Western literature and in the midst of multiple professional engagements and responsibilities. The richness and variety of these writings and involvements make Simms a key figure for future understanding of the literary culture, issues, and networks in mid-nineteenth-century America.

Background

Simms's family history reflected the dynamics that fueled the spread southward and westward of the populations, plantation economy, and society of the South Atlantic states. Simms's ancestry also reflected the Scots-Irish and English roots of what became identified as southern culture by the 1830s, a generation after the end of most immigration to the region. Two of Simms's grandparents, William and Elisabeth Sims, were Scots-Irish and migrated to South Carolina from Ulster. One, John Singleton, was an American-born son of putatively English immigrants, who had come to South Carolina from Virginia. The fourth, Jane Miller, was daughter of two Scots-Irish and Irish descended people—John Miller, of North and then South Carolina, and Jane Ross. Ross's family also migrated to South Carolina from western Virginia, where members lived cheek by jowl with other Scots-Irish families, who migrated to the Carolinas (White, *Ross*). Simms's father and Uncle James migrated in 1808 from Charleston to Tennessee, then to Mississippi. This was after the bankruptcy of the elder William's business and the deaths of his wife and their other two sons. Following the last of these losses, the elder Simms's hair turned white in a week. To his anguished eyes, Charleston appeared "a place of tombs" (qtd. in Guilds 6, 12).

For the son, however, Charleston was home—so much so that he refused to leave his maternal grandmother and move to Mississippi when his uncle came to get him in 1816. Then the fifth largest and by far the wealthiest city, as well as one of the greatest ports, in America, Charleston was at the peak of its influence (Moltke-Hansen, "Expansion" 25–31; Rogers). Cotton culture on the sea islands to the south, begun in 1790, and rice culture in impounded lowcountry tidal marshes meant that the port was filled not only with sailors of many lands and languages, but also with enslaved people of many African and Creole cultures and speech ways (slaves continued to be imported legally in large numbers until 1808). This street life made vivid the transnational nature of plantation agriculture and the fact that the developing region's dramatically expanding borders "were not just geographic; they also were human, historical, and intellectual" (Moltke-Hansen, "Southern" 19).

Even more important for the future author, the expanding region's borders and nature were taking imaginative shape. The West of the senior William Gilmore Simms and the first Creek War in which he fought, the Revolutionary War of the young Simms's maternal grandfather, the backcountry of many related Scots-Irish settlers, all these became grist for a lonely, energetic boy, who spent as much time with books as he could (Simms, *Letters* 1:161). The possibilities of such settings, incidents, and characters were not confined to history alone. Simms reported that he "used to glow and shiver in turn over 'The Pilgrim's Progress,'" while "Moses' adventures in 'The Vicar of Wakefield' threw [him] into paroxysms of laughter" (Hayne 261–62). Sir Walter Scott's Border and medieval romances and James Fenimore Cooper's Leatherstocking tales also deeply colored his imagination (Simms, *Views* 1:248, and Moltke-Hansen, "Southern" 6–15). As affecting were the ghost stories and Revolutionary War tales of his grandmother and the verses sent, and tales told, by his father.

These diverse tales became reasons to explore—in books, but also on the ground. As a boy, Simms ranged through the city and along the banks of the Ashley River, which fed into Charleston Harbor. He did so in search of scenes of colonial and Revolutionary battles and incidents (*Letters* 1:lxii). He first heard his uncle's and father's many Irish and frontier stories when they visited in Charleston in 1816 and 1818, respectively. He heard more on his trips to Mississippi during the winter of 1824 through the spring of 1825 and again in 1826. The first trip took him through Georgia and Alabama, where he saw elements of the Creek and Cherokee nations. At the time, Simms later reported, he was a boy "cumbered with fragmentary materials of thought, . . . choked by the tangled vines of erroneous speculation, and haunted by passions, which, like so many wolves, lurked, in ready waiting, for their unsuspecting prey" (*Social* 6). When he first got to Mississippi, traveling partly by stage, partly by riverboat, and partly by horse, Simms learned that his father had just come back from "a trip of three hundred miles into the heart of the Indian country" (Trent 15). Later father and son "rode together on horseback to various settlements on the frontier of Alabama and Mississippi" (Guilds 10–11, 17–18). Simms recalled as well "having traveled 150 miles beyond the Mississippi" (Shillingsburg, "Literary Grist" 120). The next year he returned to the Southwest by ship. "During this [second] trip he carried a 'note book.'" There he jotted episodes, encounters, stories heard, characters seen, and descriptions of the landscapes unfolding around him. He also wrote "at least sixteen poems" (Kibler, "First"; Shillingsburg, "Literary Grist" 123).

Simms took a third western trip five years later, writing letters back to the newspaper that by then he was editing (*Letters* 1:10–38). Together these three trips provided materials for his writings over more than forty years. "The first . . . produced mainly short fiction; the second inspired much poetry; . . . the first and third . . . yielded three novels written in the 1830s" (Shillingsburg, "Literary Grist" 119). This was, in part, because of the trips' timing. Sixteen years after the first trip, Simms told students at the University of Alabama that in the interval their world had changed from a howling wilderness into a place of growing civilization (Simms, *Social* 5–6). Had he not gone when he did, he would have been too late to see the frontier. Later travels took him many other places and also provided much grist for his writing. Never again, however, did he experience the frontier firsthand. Furthermore, on these later trips Simms was a practiced professional writer, no longer that boy haunted by passions.

Personal Life

After the ten-year-old boy's momentous refusal to leave Charleston, his grandmother sent Simms for two years to the grammar school taught on the campus and by the faculty of the nearly moribund College of Charleston. By then he already was "versifying the events of the war [of 1812]," just concluded, publishing "doggerel" in the local papers, and learning to read in several languages (*Letters* 1:285). His trip west a decade later helped him decide to pursue both literature and a career in law, but back in Charleston—this despite his father's urging that he stay in Mississippi. Upon his return home, he began to read law and also launched a literary weekly, the *Album*, which ran for a year. He became engaged as well to Anna Malcolm Giles, daughter of a grocer and former state coroner.

A year later the young couple married. This was six months before Simms was admitted to the South Carolina bar, on his twenty-first birthday, not long before he was appointed as a city magistrate. Although living up the Ashley River in the more healthful, less expensive village of Summerville, Simms kept a law office in the city. Shortly after using his maternal inheritance to buy the *City Gazette* at the end of 1829 and moving down to Charleston Neck, just north of the city limits where he had lived as a boy, Simms lost both his father and his maternal grandmother. He also found himself attacked because of his Unionist stance in the Nullification crisis resulting from South Carolina's rejection of a federal tariff. Then, in early 1832, Simms's wife died. Soon after, he took his four-year-old daughter back to Summerville to live and determined to sell his newspaper and leave the state for a literary life in the North.

Fueling his ambition was the correspondence Simms had begun several years earlier with an accountant whom he had published in his *City Gazette* but not yet met—Scots immigrant James Lawson. At the time Lawson, seven years Simms's senior, edited a New York City newspaper and, in addition to writing plays and poetry, was a friend (and, later, informal literary agent) to a wide circle (McHaney, "An Early"). Simms's trip north in the summer of 1832 saw the two begin a lifelong friendship, cemented as they squired ladies about and interacted with Lawson's literary circle. In subsequent years Simms multiplied the number of his friendships, in both the North and the South, making them in some measure a replacement for the family that he had lost. Lawson remained the closest of his northern friends, while James Henry Hammond, a future governor and U.S. senator, became his closest friend in South Carolina.

Late in 1833, after his Summerville house burned, Simms wrote Lawson to say that he was enamored of "a certain fair one" (*Letters* 1:73). Seventeen-year-old Chevillette Eliza Roach was the daughter of "a literary-minded aristocrat of English descent" with two plantations on the banks of the Edisto River in Barnwell District (later County) (Guilds 70). The courtship was protracted, as Simms felt it necessary first to clear debts that friends had bought up on his behalf. He also was determined "to marry no woman" before he was "perfectly independent of her resources, and her friends" (*Letters* 1:78). Therefore he did not propose until the spring of 1836. The nuptials took place seven months later, and as a result, Simms came to call the four thousand acres of Woodlands Plantation, with its seventy slaves, home. It was twenty years, however, before he took over management of the plantation and, then, only in the wake of his father-in-law's final sickness and death. Five years after that, he lost his wife, the mother of fourteen of his fifteen children. Nine of the children Chevillette bore him had already died, devastating Simms repeatedly. Five were still living (three sons and two daughters), as was Simms's daughter by his first marriage, who helped raise the youngest of her siblings. Those remaining children—even Gilly, who fought in the Confederate army—all outlived their father. Gilly and a brother-in-law ran Woodlands after the war, when Simms, though dying of cancer, was earning what he could by writing again for publications in the North and editing one or another South Carolina newspaper.

Career

The trip north in 1832 did not result in Simms moving there. Except during the Civil War, however, he returned almost every year. This was because the contacts he made, and the exposure to literary culture that he enjoyed, helped him define his future as an author. Earlier he had written fiction and criticism as well as journalism, filling the pages of several short-lived cultural journals and his newspaper, but between the ages of nine and twenty-six Simms had focused his literary efforts primarily on poetry. Beginning with his first book of verse in 1825, he had published five small volumes in Charleston. A couple had received positive notice in New York, and in the fall of 1832, J. & J. Harper issued the sixth anonymously from there, *Atalantis: A Story of the Sea*. Coming back the following summer, Simms had in hand for the Harpers a gothic novella, *Martin Faber*, and after his return south, he also would send the manuscript of his first two-volume border romance, *Guy Rivers: A Tale of Georgia*.

The reception of these and the romances and short stories that followed quickly made Simms one of the nation's most successful fictionists. He continued to issue poetry as well—roughly a collection every three years over the thirty-seven years that he worked as a professional author. But this output was dwarfed by the fiction—on average a title every year (counting several serialized works but not counting the many revised editions). Then there were the two dozen separately published orations, histories, and biographies as well as edited collections of documents and dramas and a geography of South Carolina. Add to these the revised editions and the further printings and issues of his own works and it appears that Simms saw a title coming off the presses at the rate of one every three months or so. Making that figure all the more astounding is the fact that, during more than a dozen of those years (the early-to-mid 1840s, the late 1840s-to-early 1850s, and the mid-to-late 1860s), he also was editing a cultural journal or newspaper. Furthermore he contributed reams of reviews and poems, hundreds of op-ed pieces and columns, and dozens of short stories and public addresses, which were never collected and published in volume form.

His career mapped an arc. It ascended meteorically in the 1830s and peaked in the early-to-mid 1840s, before beginning to descend. One reason was the popularity of the historical fiction that Simms began to write. When he left behind the law, his first newspaper, and the Nullification controversy, as well as his sadness, historical fiction was all the rage. Sir Walter Scott had fueled the craze, beginning with the publication of his first Border romance in 1814. He died in September 1832. Seventeen years Simms's senior, James Fenimore Cooper, the closest America had to a Scott at the time, was at the peak of his reputation and success, having started publishing his romances in 1820. Thus the way had been prepared for a writer of Simms's historical imagination and preoccupations. Within five years of his first trip north, moreover, Lawson's (and now his) circle became loosely affiliated with a nationalistic and Democratic group, self-styled Young America, this after Young Italy and similar ethnic, nationalist, European, cultural and political movements (Moltke-Hansen, "Southern"). Edgar Allan Poe and other members gave Simms's first fictions positive, if not uncritical, attention.

By the end of the 1830s, paradoxically, Simms, like Cooper, found his success attracting unauthorized editions of his works because Britain and America did not have an international copyright agreement. Further, in the wake of the panic of 1837, Americans bought fewer books. Simms's response was to diversify his portfolio. He turned to biography and history, including his hugely successful *Life of Francis Marion* (1844). He also returned to the editor's chair, overseeing one and then another cultural journal. These were unlike the ones he had edited in the 1820s: they included contributions by numerous authors, not just those from Charleston, but from the region and also the North. The ambition motivating the journals was to connect and promote Charleston intellectually. Consequently the journals more closely resembled metropolitan quarterly reviews in their offerings.

The mid-1840s saw Simms involved in politics, even serving a term in the South Carolina legislature. By the middle of the Mexican-American War in 1847, he had concluded that the South needed to become an independent nation. Thereafter, although he maintained ties with many in the Young America circle, he no longer promoted his writings as fostering Americanism in literature (*Views*). Instead he increasingly emphasized the ways in which his three romance series — the colonial, the Revolutionary, and the border — were making tangible and meaningful the origins and development of the future southern nation and the sad but inevitable consequences for Native Americans (Watson, *From Nationalism*; compare Nakamura).

Sectional politics colored more and more of Simms's perceptions, speeches, and private communications. The rising tide of abolitionism had him aghast. It also fed his growing sense that his position in American letters was slipping. He returned to editing, and his poetry, which was more often explicitly about the South, became increasingly patriotic in tone. Although his first biographer, William Peterfield Trent, insisted that Simms's declining standing reflected the change in literary fashion from historical romances to realistic novels, Simms in fact wrote more and more as a social realist in the 1850s (Wimsatt, "Realism").

The Civil War consumed Simms. As he wrote Lawson, "Literature, especially poetry, is effectually overwhelmed by the drums, & the cavalry, and the shouting" (*Letters* 4:369–70). He did manage to editorialize often and to rework and finish things long on his desk, including poems, a novel, and a dramatic treatment of Benedict Arnold, the northern traitor in the Revolutionary War. Then, in the wake of the Confederacy's loss and the failure of his vision for the South, he found himself recording the loss in a new newspaper, dealing with the trauma in his poetry, and becoming more existential and psychological in his fictional treatments. Simms's old New York friends tried to help. He did edit and see through publication a volume of Confederate war poetry. Yet it is a measure of his reduced stature that the several new romances he published appeared only in serial form. In part this may have been because he was in a sense competing with himself. Publishers were beginning to reprint volumes out of the selected edition of his writings. Many of Simms's works were available in book form, just not new works.

Associations

As the *Letters* testify, Simms had complex, overlapping networks of friends and colleagues. As a boy and young man, he received the friendship, patronage, and commendation of a variety of well-placed people in Charleston, including Charles Rivers Carroll. It was Carroll with whom he read law, to whom he dedicated his first romance, and after whom he named a son. Both men were Unionists during the Nullification controversy. So were Hugh Swinton Legare (later U.S. attorney general) and the considerably older William Drayton, as well as lawyer and editor Richard Yeadon and Greenville, South Carolina, newspaper editor Benjamin Franklin Perry. Also considerably older was James Wright Simmons, who had joined with Simms to launch the *Southern Literary Gazette* in 1828, when Simms was twenty-two. Through him Simms had direct contact with such British literary figures as Leigh Hunt and Byron (Kibler, *Poetry* 15).

The next group of influential friends and collaborators that Simms acquired were members of the Lawson circle and included such figures as Edwin

Forrest, the Shakespearean actor, and Evert Duyckinck, who published several of Simms's volumes in Wiley and Putnam's series Library of American Books, which he edited. Among the many others were poets and editors William Cullen Bryant and Fitz-Greene Halleck. Simms also made nonliterary friends in New York and Philadelphia, such as John Jacob Bockee and William Hawkins Ferris, the cashier at the U.S. Treasury office in New York who, after the war, helped Simms, Henry Timrod (poet laureate of the Confederacy), and others.

As a Barnwell planter, Simms met a widening circle of South Carolina's leaders and literati. For instance his acquaintance with James Henry Hammond began in the late 1830s and deepened into a friendship in the early 1840s. It was in the early 1840s, too, when he again was editing cultural journals, that Simms became friends with many southern writers. He regarded several of them, including Virginians George Frederick Holmes, Edmund Ruffin, and Nathaniel Beverley Tucker as members, together with Hammond and himself, in a "sacred circle." Uniting the circle were members' devotion to the South and a shared sense of the marginal status and critical importance of the life of the mind in a largely rural and unintellectual region (Faust, *Sacred*). Others of Simms's wide connections in the region did not interact as much with each other, but Simms long corresponded with Maryland novelist and lawyer John Pendleton Kennedy, Irish-born Georgia poet Richard Henry Wilde, Alabama lawyer and writer Alexander Beaufort Meek, and Louisiana historian and assistant attorney general Charles Gayarré, among others. By the 1850s, when Simms once more returned to editing a cultural journal, many of the writers whom he recruited were members of a younger generation. Poets Paul Hamilton Hayne and Henry Timrod were two. Often they and a half dozen others of Simms's and their generations met in John Russell's Charleston Book Shop and adjourned to dinner at Simms's Smith Street home, "dubbed 'The Wigwam'" (*Letters* 1:cxxxvi). Shortly before his death fifteen or so years later, Simms wrote Hayne, "I am rapidly passing from the stage, where you young men are to succeed me" (*Letters* 5:287).

Thought

The welter of Simms's works disguises unities and dynamics of the thought underlying them. From early on Simms was convinced that art ennobles or transforms, as well as gives voice to individuals and societies; therefore it must be cultivated assiduously. Without the potential for high artistic attainment, he insisted, societies are not ready for the independence and regard of free peoples. This is where Simms the historian joined Simms the poet. Societies develop, he argued (using the stadialism of the Scottish historical school), from imitation through self-assertion to achievement and also from savagery through strife to settled agricultural communities and, ultimately, to a hierarchical civilization supporting a rich artistic life. It was the job of the artist to help envision the goal, inspire the pursuit, and inform the process. That process was at once progressive and dialectical. Order, without dynamism, stifled development, as did the obverse—the dominance by ungoverned impulses or uncontrolled license. This was true in the individual, but also in societies as a whole. War was necessary for civilization, but its success was measured in the securities of the home, the center of cultural production and reproduction.

Whether in the public or in the domestic arena, "the true governor, as [Thomas] Carlyle call[ed] him—the king man—" guided rather than impeded the forces of change and progress (Simms, "Guizot's" 122). There were few such men with the capacity to lead. The same was true of nations. Neither all people nor all peoples were equal in either capacity or attainment. That was why Native Americans were overrun and Africans had been enslaved by European peoples in the New World. Indeed, Simms argued, "slavery in all ages has been found the greatest and most admirable agent of Civilization," giving education and examples to less evolved peoples (*Letters* 3:174). The degree to which a people had evolved mattered. That was why, he held, Americans had won independence from the most powerful empire in the world. They had done so through their Revolution, led by an elite that felt correctly its time had come (Simms, "Ellet's" 328). By mid-1847 that also was Simms's judgment for the South: the region had evolved enough to become independent (*Letters* 2:332). The hope inspired and then failed him and the people he sought to lead.

While not all men could rise to the highest rank, they all had the same responsibility at home. There the father was patriarch, protector, and head, while the mother was nurturer, moral instructor, and heart. There, too, children's characters and minds were formed by age twelve ("Ellet's"). Children's upbringing was critical to citizenship, and it was through her sons and the support of her husband, father, and brothers that a woman shaped the public sphere. The culture and character instilled in the child expressed and informed not just the household, but the larger society—the people.

"The history of peoples and their embodiments in institutions, states, and artistic productions—these were the great subjects" in Simms's view (Moltke-Hansen, "Southern" 120). Yet "poets were the only class of philosophers who had recognized" this until his own day, when at last "we now read human histories. We now ask after the affections as well as the ceremonies of society" ("Ellet's" 319–20). Peoples or races—that is, ethnic groups—were not unchanging any more than were their politics and their cultures. They either advanced or were overrun by history. Further, new peoples emerged, and old identities were submerged. The Spanish conquistadors were the creation of centuries of conflict with the Moors: their motivation was the glory of conquest, not the routine of trade or the plow. On the other hand, the English settlements in North America reflected the impulse to transform the wilderness into verdant farms and build society (*Views* 64, 178–85; *Social* 8). The same impulse drove Americans westward in Simms's own day and gave Americans their Manifest Destiny.

To explore these facts of the South's settlement and its place in international conflicts, Simms wrote all together, between 1833 and 1863, two romances set in eighth-century Spain, two set during the Spanish exploration and conquest of the Americas and two during the later English colonization of South Carolina, seven set during the American Revolution, and—depending on how one counts—perhaps eight set on the borders of the nineteenth-century South. After the war he published one more Revolutionary romance and two more that, like it, were set beyond the boundaries of civilization. He also left two unfinished romances, also set beyond society's normal reach. These late works, however, no longer had as their framing justification the cultivation of the South's future and civilization.

White southerners had their independence foreclosed by the war. In his last works, therefore, Simms found himself exploring the psychological, philosophical, and historical impulses that led to the Confederacy's demise and what, in the aftermath, it meant to be a good man and to build for the future, however impoverished. On the first score, he argued that the impulse to idealism behind abolitionism ignored historical realities, becoming inhuman in its consequences. On the latter score, he affirmed responsibility for one's dependents and the virtues of stoicism, as well as a continued commitment to the beauty and truth of art and the impulses to the cultivated life and fields. Therefore, in the face of the burning of his Woodlands home and library in February 1865—during Sherman's march and in the midst of desperate circumstances—he insisted that home, or the ideals and past characterizing its potential, still was at the center of true civilization, but only if elevated by art (*Sense* 8, 17). It was wrong to measure civilization by the getting, spending, and mad dashing, or material progress and utilitarianism, characteristic of both a capitalistic North and also many southerners. These traits he often had attacked even before the war, insisting that "the work of the Imagination, which is the Genius of a race, is only begun when its material progress is supposed to be complete" (*Poetry* 12).

Writings

Simms expressed many of his ideas most personally in letters and most cogently in essays, speeches, and occasional introductions to his books. But he illustrated them most fully in his fiction and poetry. By the time he arrived in New

York in 1832, he had formed many of the core ideals and beliefs that would shape his work. His application of them, however, modified his understanding over time. Growing as a writer and growing in knowledge and experience, he also grew as a thinker.

In his hierarchy of values, poetry came first. It was a prophetic calling as well as evocative of the deeply felt (or, sometimes, the fleeting) and thus testimony to the perdurance and transcendence of the beautiful and the human spirit. Yet, as Simms often ruefully reflected, prose spoke to many more people. That was a principal reason why he turned to writing prose epics or romances. He gave his most concerted consideration of poetry's value and roles in three lectures in Charleston in 1854. Over the prior three years he had given portions of them in Augusta, Georgia, Washington, D.C., and Richmond and Petersburg, Virginia. Entitled *Poetry and the Practical*, they did not see print until 1996, as Simms never found the time to expand them as he wanted. On the other hand, his last address on the same themes, *The Sense of the Beautiful*, was issued soon after he delivered it, also in Charleston.

Many of his important reviews have not yet been gathered, but Simms collected some in 1845–46, and *Views and Reviews in American Literature, History and Fiction* came out in 1846 and 1847 in two "series." Beginning with a consideration of "Americanism" in literature, the first series explored the themes and periods of American history for treatment by the novelist. Simms argued there, and in forewords to several of his romances, that fiction rendered the past more truthfully, interestingly, and tellingly than histories and biographies could because fiction—like poetry—required imagination to look beyond what is not known or expressed. The second series examined additional American writers and what distinguished them, for instance, in their humor.

Despite their early success, Simms's romances, novellas, and stories provoked mixed reviews. Poe eventually concluded that Simms had become "the best novelist which this country has, on the whole, produced" but also insisted that "he should never have written 'The Partisan,' nor 'The Yemassee.'" This was in a review of *Confession*. That novel, like the gothic *Martin Faber*, demonstrated, Poe contended, that Simms's "genius [did] not lie in the outward so much as in the inner world." Yet he nevertheless wrote of Simms's short-story collection *The Wigwam and the Cabin* that "in invention, in vigor, in movement, in the power of exciting interest, and in the artistical management of his themes, he has surpassed, we think, any of his countrymen." Other critics, especially in the genteel and Whiggish Knickerbocker circle, joined Poe in condemning what they considered to be the excessively graphic and vulgar qualities of many characters and scenes, and Simms's prolixity and sententiousness, in his romances (Butterworth and Kibler 64, 50).

The violent realism and earthiness of the romances did not result in realistic novels. Although Simms received early praise for his characterizations (particularly of women), he used the romance formula, with its stereotypic heroes and heroines, predictable themes, and conventional polarities. People were on quests or had lost their way or were fighting long odds or were carrying forward the banner of (and modeling) civilization or were mired in the slough of despond or were resisting all the claims of civilized society and behavior or were pursuing love interests. Deceitfulness, selfishness, and greed opposed honor, high-mindedness, and honesty against the backdrop of the South's development from the earliest days of Spanish exploration to the westward movement in Simms's own youth.

It was only gradually that Simms married the psychological acuity of some of his portraits of the interior struggles of his gothic characters and fiction to the historical romance. Helping him think through how to do so were the biographies he wrote in the mid-1840s, but also the incidents on which he focused particular fictions, such as the murder in *Beauchampe; or, The Kentucky Tragedy* (1842). However incomplete the blending of realism and romanticism or of stereotypical and socially individuated renderings through the 1840s, by the 1850s Simms fundamentally had made the transition to social realism in such works as *Woodcraft* and *The Cassique of Kiawah*. Indeed some scholars have considered *Woodcraft* the first realistic novel in America (Bakker; Wimsatt, "Realism").

In some sense disguising the transition is the fact that Simms also increasingly wrote as a humorist and, in so doing, often rendered his late narratives fabulistically, when not writing social comedy or stories of manners. This dimension of Simms's work was largely hidden, however, until the 1974 publication of *Stories and Tales*, volume 5 in the Centennial Simms edition. There, for the first time, readers had access in print to "Bald-Head Bill Bauldy." There, too, for the first time one could read together that story, "Legend of the Hunter's Camp," and "How Sharp Snaffles Got His Capital and Wife," which was published posthumously in *Harper's Magazine* in October 1870. These and other stories and tales made it clear that Simms was a fecund contributor to southern and American humor.

Humor let Simms take up issues that he could not otherwise address in print and still expect to be well received. He did so both during and after the war. The war also pushed Simms past the emerging fashion of social realism. Having destroyed the familiar, the preoccupation of much realistic fiction, the war made the liminal central (Shillingsburg, "Cub"). While his romances and tales had often explored life on the edge or in extreme circumstances, whether in war or on the frontier or on the verge of madness or in fanciful realms, it had done so against a backdrop of, and with the goal of affirming, social norms and development. In the war's wake that goal seemed absurd. Mythologized memories of a healthy past might nurture a sense of the beautiful but could not help one deal with the present. Thus Simms's conclusion, in a March 1869 letter to Paul Hamilton Hayne: "Let us bury the Past lest it buries us!" (*Letters* 5:214). Fifteen months later he lay dead in the 13 Society Street, Charleston, home of his oldest daughter, with the shell holes in the walls of the bedroom he had shared with several children.

Posthumous Reputation

The twenty years after Simms's death saw him often respectfully treated, first in obituaries, later in memoirs and columns, and also in literary dictionaries and encyclopedias. Yet Charles Richardson's 1887 *American Literature: 1607–1885* proved a harbinger of a shift: Simms, Richardson observed, was "more respected than read," having "won considerable note because he was so sectional" and then having "lost it because he was not sectional enough," although he showed "silly contempt for his Northern betters" (qtd. in Butterworth and Kibler 130). Five years later Trent's biography of Simms appeared. It was the first full-length, scholarly treatment. Its central thesis was that Simms's environment frustrated his abilities: the South was inimical to art and the life of the mind, and Charleston high society's hauteur marginalized Simms despite his talent and character. Trent's second thesis was that Simms's commitment to the romance and his romanticism meant that his works had become largely unreadable in an age of literary realism. Although Vernon Parrington and later scholars recognized Simms's impulses to realism, the two theses long shaped Simms criticism and, indeed, also helped frame study of antebellum southern literature and intellectual life (Parrington 119–30).

A Virginian born in 1862, Trent was a progressive who wanted a New South radically different from the old. He saw his pioneering study of Simms as an opportunity to criticize what the Civil War had made untenable. From his perspective the Old South was not the expanding and rapidly developing environment, with a deep history, that Simms portrayed, but a place where slavery stultified and stunted the growth and progress displayed by the North. Southern—especially South Carolinian—writers occasionally challenged Trent's agenda and conclusions, but those critiques had little impact. Not until after publication of the Simms letters in the 1950s did scholars begin to consider the author in the historical and contemporary contexts that he had rendered in his poetry and fiction. And not until after the centennial of his death did a growing number of scholars, having concluded that southern intellectual history was

not an oxymoron, begin to study in detail the culture in which Simms partici-
pated and to which he contributed so voluminously and variously.

Some of these scholars also have had agendas: they have wanted to see
Simms included in the American literary canon, for instance, or they have
wanted to defend the heritage that in their view Trent, and so many others,
inappropriately belittled or ignorantly dismissed. More fruitfully, other scholars have begun to reframe the understanding of nineteenth-century American
intellectual life by stripping away preconceptions that characterized earlier
evaluations of Simms and his contemporaries. They are closely examining the
historical record and transatlantic and other contemporary contexts and developments in the process. Although the pursuit of canonical status in a post-
canonical age seems quixotic at this point, the explosion of the canon is leading
to more varied fare being offered and may, therefore, mean that Simms, once
his work is widely available, will be more often anthologized as well as studied. Defensiveness about Simms and the antebellum South may warm the
hearts of like-minded people, just as critics of the Old South have been encouraged by shared presuppositions and disdain. Yet dueling cultural ideologies do
not advance comity and may only reinforce mutual incomprehensions. Continued, deep research in original sources and the theoretical reframing that
Atlantic history, the history of the book, and other perspectives offer—these
approaches promise most for further study of Simms, his works, and his world.

Works Cited

For amplified readings by and on Simms and on his world, go to http://simms.library
.sc.edu/bibliography.php.

Bakker, Jan. "Simms on the Literary Frontier; or, So Long Miss Ravenel and Hello Cap-
  tain Porgy: *Woodcraft* Is the First 'Realistic' Novel in America." In *William Gilmore
  Simms and the American Frontier*, edited by John Caldwell Guilds and Caroline Collins,
  64–78. Athens: University of Georgia Press, 1997.
Butterworth, Keen, and James E. Kibler Jr. *William Gilmore Simms: A Definitive Guide.*
  Boston: G. K. Hall, 1980.
Faust, Drew Gilpin. *A Sacred Circle: The Dilemma of the Intellectual in the Old South, 1840–
  1860.* Baltimore: Johns Hopkins University Press, 1977.
Guilds, John C. *Simms: A Literary Life.* Fayetteville: University of Arkansas Press, 1992.
Hayne, Paul Hamilton. "Ante-Bellum Charleston." *Southern Bivouac* 1 (October 1885):
  257–68.
Kibler, James E. "The First Simms Letters: 'Letters from the West' (1826)." *Southern Liter-
  ary Journal* 19 (Spring 1987): 81–91.
———. *The Poetry of William Gilmore Simms: An Introduction and Bibliography.* Columbia:
  Southern Studies Program, University of South Carolina, 1979.

McHaney, Thomas L. "An Early 19th-Century Literary Agent: James Lawson of New York." *Publications of the Bibliographical Society of America* 64 (Spring 1970): 177–92.

Moltke-Hansen, David. "The Expansion of Intellectual Life: A Prospectus." In *Intellectual Life in Antebellum Charleston*, edited by Michael O'Brien and David Moltke-Hansen, 3–44. Knoxville: University of Tennessee Press, 1986.

———. "Southern Literary Horizons in Young America: Imaginative Development of a Regional Geography." *Studies in the Literary Imagination* 42, no. 1 (2009): 1–31.

Nakamura, Masahiro. *Visions of Order in William Gilmore Simms: Southern Conservatism and the Other American Romance*. Columbia: University of South Carolina Press, 2009.

Parrington, Vernon L. *The Romantic Revolution in America, 1800–1860*. Vol. 2 of *Main Currents in American Thought*. New York: Harcourt, Brace and Company, 1927.

Rogers, George C., Jr. *Charleston in the Age of the Pinckneys*. Columbia: University South Carolina Press, 1980.

Shillingsburg, Miriam J. "The Cub of the Panther: A New Frontier." In *William Gilmore Simms and the American Frontier*, edited by John Caldwell Guilds and Caroline Collins, 221–36. Athens: University of Georgia Press, 1997.

———. "Literary Grist: Simms's Trips to Mississippi." *Southern Quarterly* 41, no. 2 (2003): 119–34.

Simms, William Gilmore. *Atalantis: A Story of the Sea: In Three Parts*. New York: J. & J. Harper, 1832.

———. *Beauchampe; or, The Kentucky Tragedy*. 2 vols. Philadelphia: Lea and Blanchard, 1842.

———. *The Cassique of Kiawah: A Colonial Romance*. New York: Redfield, 1859.

———. *Confession; or, The Blind Heart. A Domestic Story*. 2 vols. Philadelphia: Lea and Blanchard, 1841.

———. "Ellet's 'Women of the Revolution.'" *Southern Quarterly Review*, n.s. 1 (July 1850): 314–54.

———. "Guizot's Democracy in France." *Southern Quarterly Review* 15, no.29 (1849): 114–65.

———. *Guy Rivers: A Tale of Georgia*. 2 vols. New York: Harper & Brothers, 1834.

———. *The Letters of William Gilmore Simms*. Edited by Mary C. Simms Oliphant, Alfred Taylor Odell, and T. C. Duncan. 6 vols. Columbia: University of South Carolina Press, 1952–82.

———. *The Life of Francis Marion*. New York: Henry G. Langley, 1844.

———. *Martin Faber, the Story of a Criminal; and Other Tales*. 2 vols. New York: Harper & Brothers, 1837.

———. *Poetry and the Practical*. Edited by James E. Kibler. Fayetteville: University of Arkansas Press, 1996.

———. *The Sense of the Beautiful: An Address . . . before the Charleston County Agricultural and Horticultural Association, May 3, 1870*. Charleston: Charleston County Agricultural and Horticultural Association, 1870.

————. *The Social Principle: The Source of National Permanence. An Oration, Delivered before the Erosophic Society of the University of Alabama . . . December 13, 1842*. Tuscaloosa: Erosophic Society, University of Alabama, 1843.

————. *Stories and Tales*. Vol. 5 of *The Writings of William Gilmore Simms*. Centennial edition; introductions, explanatory notes, and texts established by John Caldwell Guilds. Columbia: University of South Carolina Press, 1974.

————. *Views and Reviews in American Literature, History and Fiction*. 2 vols. New York: Wiley and Putnam, 1845 (1846).

————. *The Wigwam and the Cabin*. 2 vols. New York: Wiley and Putnam, 1845–46.

————. *Woodcraft, or Hawks about the Dovecote: A Story of the South, at the Close of the Revolution*. New York: Redfield, 1854.

Trent, William Peterfield. *William Gilmore Simms*. Boston: Houghton, Mifflin, 1892.

Wakelyn, Jon L. *The Politics of a Literary Man: William Gilmore Simms*. Westport, Conn.: Greenwood Press, 1973.

Watson, Charles S. *From Nationalism to Secessionism: The Changing Fiction of William Gilmore Simms*. Westport, Conn.: Greenwood Press, 1993.

White, William B., Jr. *The Ross-Chesnut-Sutton Family of South Carolina*. Franklin, N.C.: Privately printed, 2002.

Wimsatt, Mary Ann. "Realism and Romance in Simms's Midcentury Fiction." *Southern Literary Journal* 12, no. 2 (1980): 29–48.

Critical Introduction

CARL WERNER

Sam Lackey

By the time *Carl Werner, An Imaginative Story; With other Tales of Imagination* was published in New York City at the end of 1838, William Gilmore Simms had established himself as a major figure in the world of American letters. However, as the 1830s marched on, new troubles mounted. He broke with his New York publishers, the Harper brothers, his wife was debilitated while pregnant, and he began to feel the effects of changes in the publishing industry and book marketplace that would soon contribute to an extended hiatus from his novel writing. And in October of 1838, shortly after the release of *Richard Hurdis*, he and his wife Chevillette lost their first child, Virginia Singleton. *Carl Werner* was borne out of this dark period, and its sales and reception did little to brighten the dreariness. Though it received a smattering of positive reviews, the work did not circulate widely and failed to make a significant impact on the literary scene. It was Simms's second short story collection and, like his first, 1837's *Tales and Sketches*, which comprised the second volume of *Martin Faber and Other Tales*, it bore a strong imprint of German influence (or "Teutonic extravagance" as Simms called it). There is also an intense focus on the interiority of the protagonists, as Simms takes great interest in probing their mental states and exploring "the origins of sin" and "social pathological complexes" (Thomas, "German Literature" 9). This focus also shows up in both volumes of *Martin Faber* and later works such as *Marie de Berniere* and *Southward Ho!*, and it seems often to accompany stories infused with the irrational and supernatural elements that Simms associated with German legends and literature.

 Carl Werner consists of two volumes. In the first are the title story "Carl Werner. An Imaginative Story," "Ipsistos," "The Star-Brethren," and "Onea and Anyta," all novellas between sixty-five and ninety pages long. In the second volume is the novella "Conrade Weickhoff," along with the short stories "Jocassée," "Logoochie; or, the Branch of Sweet Water. A Legend of Georgia," and "The Cherokee Embassage." Aside from differences in length between the five novellas and the three short stories, a clear line divides this collection into two groups. The first three stories of Volume One and "Conrade Weickhoff" in Volume Two are set in European locales and heavily influenced by a loose collection of German literary motifs and mythology; "Onea and Anyta" and the second, third, and fourth tales of Volume Two feature Native American characters and indigenous communities. Though separated by setting and content, the tales all function as prime examples of the "moral imagination," a protean idea that guided much of Simms's fiction thematically and continues to affect the ways in which scholars classify and discuss his expansive canon.

John Caldwell Guilds has shown that Simms believed all forms of fiction share certain purposes, such as achieving truthfulness and presenting a moral. For Simms, "truthfulness is never without its moral" and it requires "the treatment of vice as well as virtue, of low and vulgar characters as well as noble and generous ones" (Guilds, *Writings* xvii). As a romancer, he believed in dialectic narratives and symbolic structures that created character doubling in which moral opposites battled one another (Wimsatt 39). As Mary Ann Wimsatt explains, Simms favored "the central romance procedure" of weighing the dialectic in favor of the side representing right conduct," which seems to be another way of saying that he delivers a moral lesson or example to his audiences (39).

He may have pursued this goal in all of his fiction, but his "moral imaginative" tales place special emphasis on the "strifes between the moral principles of good and evil." The strife is usually carried out in mysterious realms and the narratives are clearly influenced by legends and myths emanating from medieval Europe and indigenous North America. He conceived these stories to be more fantastical, sublime, and purely imaginative than his historical romances, evidenced by his letter to Rufus Griswold in which he described *Carl Werner* as "marked chiefly by the passion & imagination − by the free use in some cases of diablerie and all the machinery of superstition, & by a prevailing presence of vehement individuality of tone & temper" (*Letters* 2: 224). Guilds points out that short fiction provided Simms with the latitude in subject matter necessary to indulge his "love of the marvelous" and his long-standing admiration of German romantic literature. And as J. Wesley Thomas has deftly demonstrated, "Simms's understanding of the German romantic tradition was inexorably tied to bizarre and irrational elements" ("German Sources" 129). This association of imagination with superstition, supernatural occurrences, and "vehement passions" is somewhat limited in scope but undoubtedly important for the study of Simms. To him, the moral imagination was the use of creative faculties defined in the above terms and utilized to deliver moral instruction and examples of proper conduct.

The Charlestonian often divided his work into two large groups: the "domestic tales," or "tales of the South," and the "moral imaginative," encompassing "stories under the influence of German (and Spanish or other European) romanticism, usually with exotic settings and heavy philosophical or psychological undertones" (Guilds, *Writings* xxi). Half of *Carl Werner* clearly falls under this category, but Simms viewed all of the stories in the two-volume collection as works of the moral imagination, and to be sure the four Native-American-themed tales contain many of the same components and lessons that animate the stories staged in Europe. The versatility of a tale like "Jocassée" was later indicated by its presence in 1845's *The Wigwam and the Cabin*, a collection that Simms classified under the headings of both domestic and imaginative. In all of his stories of the moral imagination, he seems to connect the wild flights of fancy involving ghosts and ancient legends with a well-defined moral allegory depicting the triumph of good over evil.

Edmund Burke is often credited with coining the idea of the moral imagination in *Reflections on the Revolution in France* when he described the crimes against civilization perpetrated by the revolutionaries: "All the decent drapery of life is to be rudely torn off. All the superadded ideas, furnished from the wardrobe of a moral imagination, which the heart owns, and the understanding ratifies, as necessary to cover the defects of our naked shivering nature, and to raise it to dignity in our estimation, are to be exploded as a ridiculous, absurd, and antiquated fashion" (qtd. in Kirk 36). In his own treatise on the moral imagination, Russell Kirk sees Burke as referring to "that power of ethical perception which strides beyond the barriers of private experience and momentary events" (38). This power is best expressed through art, and was the "gift and obsession" of figures such as Plato, Virgil, and Dante. Kirk goes on to declare that the moral imagination, maintained by men of letters acting as standard-bearers of tradition, helps to elevate us above the apes and manifests itself as "right order in the soul and right order in the commonwealth" (Kirk 39). Though he never made explicit reference to Burke's concept of the moral imagination, Simms deployed the idea in much the same fashion as his predecessor.

Simms's inclusion of moral lessons in his fiction corresponds with Burke's desire to maintain the "civilizing manners" supposedly targeted by the revolutionaries in France. For both men, these manners appear to consist of respect for women and nobility, taste, elegance, and the principles founded on Christianity. Such touchstones of civilizing morality certainly permeate the lessons found in *Carl Werner*. Simms concurs with the general notion that artists are the most well-equipped to maintain moral standards through his belief that wild and often mystical flights of fancy are best-suited for the conveyance of clear-cut moral instruction. Even if he was not intimately familiar with Burke's writings on the French Revolution, Simms was undoubtedly tuned into many of the same conservative wavelengths and equally invested in maintaining moral standards that hearken back to older traditions of European chivalry and valor.

As a phrase, the moral imagination has been put to work in a number of ways and applied to a number of different fields, from political science to theology to literature. Sociologist John Paul Lederach recently found three recurring threads linking the diverse contexts of the term: the ability to "perceive things beyond and at a deeper level than what initially meets the eye," the necessity of the imaginative act, and the quality of transcendence (26-27). Writing in 2005, Lederach approaches the term from the arena of conflict-resolution, a specialization completely different from that of Simms. Yet they share an interest in the powers of ethical perception and creative ingenuity while also subscribing to the belief that the moral imagination can transcend its surroundings and transport people to a higher plane of existence.

Simms endorsed the moral imagination's capacity to reach these lofty heights, and he regarded *Carl Werner* as one of the best examples of the concept's application and narrative expression. In the aforementioned letter to Griswold, he groups it alongside *Martin Faber, Castle Dismal,* and *Confession* as the moral imaginative tales constituting "the best specimens of my powers of creating and combining" (*Letters* 2: 224). Released on the heels of his successful early novels, the collection was dedicated to Prosper M. Wetmore, a minor New York writer and friend of Simms. An association such as this one reveals the South Carolinian's participation in an expansive literary network and speaks to his growing cosmopolitanism and burgeoning reputation. While Simms seemed to be operating under the assumption that *Carl Werner* would continue his ascendency in American letters, the wider reading public did not share his enthusiasm. As Guilds notes, Simms was not satisfied with the circulation or reception of the story collection. Years after it faded from memory, he continued to "feel that *Carl Werner* never received its due, either in criticism or in sales" (Guilds, *Literary Life* 91). Having recently split with the Harper Brothers, Simms worked with a new publisher in New York, George Adlard, whom he branded incompetent and guilty of overpricing the book. Simms also blamed the unfortunate timing of the release: the collection appeared in the midst of the so-called "money pressure" — a probable reference to the Panic of 1837 — and at a point in which "the great revolution in cheap literature" meant that "books of Tales at $2" were simply "not to be thought of" (91).

Wimsatt has demonstrated that the effects of the panic and the economic collapse that followed lasted well into the 1840s and damaged many antebellum writers' careers, including Simms (136). With cheap paperbacks readily available and newspapers often pirating popular British texts, there was little market left by the end of the 1830s for lengthy romances from the likes of Simms, Cooper, and Bird. After his income from long fiction began to drop precipitously, Simms turned to the rapid production of history, biography, geography, essays, and tales for magazines. According to Wimsatt, this development harmed his long-term reputation, as he was pushed out of his major field into "varied, occasionally trivial projects that gave the corpus of his writing a distinctly miscellaneous cast" (144).

Despite the author's frustration and the financial trouble he saw on the horizon, *Carl Werner* was received rather favorably by critics upon its release (Guilds, *Literary Life* 90). The *New York Mirror* cited the "power and brilliancy" of the imagination on display, while the *New York Review* considered it "a production of no common order in the class of works in which it belongs" ("Literary Notices" 207; qtd. in Guilds, *Literary Life* 90). Similarly, the *New Yorker* declared that the volume would help "elevate the American Romance to new heights," and the *New York Gazette* claimed that the collected tales were "equal in many of their parts to the best things [Simms] has yet presented to the public" (qtd. in Guilds, *Literary Life* 90). *The Boston Traveler* struck a slightly different, but still positive, note in stating that the tales do not exhibit traces of Simms's previous works, and thereby demonstrate his unique "versatility of talent" (3). The review from the *Traveler* also picked up on the influence of the "German school," though it maintained that Simms's treatment of the subject was still "wholly original." Conversely, the German influence was viewed less favorably in the *Boston Quarterly* and the *Knickerbocker*. Most of these appraisals date from December 1838 or January 1839, and subsequent months saw few additional ones. Notwithstanding the positive reviews, the book was beset by poor sales and limited circulation and thus did not make a lasting impression. Simms made several attempts to reissue the collection and proposed various new editions featuring "Carl Werner," "Conrade Weickhoff," and "The Star Brethren," either singly or together, but the only members of the collection destined for republication in his lifetime were "Jocassée" in *The Wigwam and the Cabin* and "Carl Werner" in book form under the title *Matilda* in 1846. Despite its undistinguished history and persistent obscurity, the collection, perhaps more than any other entry in the Simms catalogue, truly exemplifies the author's commitment to the moral imagination and his employment of unique narrative methods to convey it.

As the title story and the finest example of the goals and techniques that run through the collection as a whole, "Carl Werner" demands to be examined first. The tale begins with a frame story: the narrator and his companion walking through the dark recesses of a German forest discussing superstition and belief in the supernatural. Because they are in Germany, a land renowned for its "wild fancies" and "marvelous imaginations," the narrator's friend deems it appropriate to tell the story of the eponymous Carl Werner and his friend Herman Ottfried. Herman is described as a "good natured, laughing, and mischievous creature ... ready always for fun and frolic" but who lacks faith and has slight regard for a ghost or a sermon. Carl, on the other hand, is "superstitious to the last degree," with a memory "perfectly crowded with legends the most extravagant" and a "feverish and perpetual desire" to increase his knowledge of the bizarre, irrational, and supernatural (1: 10-11). This desire is stoked to a dangerous extent when, on the eve of Herman's departure from their native village, the two young men make a pact that should death come suddenly to either, the departed spirit must return to the still-living friend. As soon as the pact is sealed, a "hollow laugh resound[s] from the dismembered vault of the aged abbot" where they sit, signifying the blasphemy of their pledge (1: 29).

Throughout the story, the narrator takes pains to portray the long-ago German setting as a shadowy, spirit-filled realm. Before beginning the narrative in earnest, the narrator describes how the German mind has been affected by the land's ghosts, its ancient lore, and its landscape of "sinking valleys," "dense forests," "wild wastes," and "deserted ruins" (1: 9). Such a setting is prime terrain for a tale of diablerie (sorcery and the representation of devils), which is exactly what the tale becomes following the friends' pact. Herman does indeed return after suffering a sudden demise, but in the form of a demon whose features are "hell-stamped" (1: 56). The demon forces Carl to confront the terrifying fact that he prayed for Herman's death in order to learn the secrets of the afterlife, and the young dreamer, who earlier found himself literally covered with Herman's blood, must acknowledge his transgression and repair his damaged morality. But first he must fight an unstoppable compulsion to visit the ruined abbey and learn the demon's intelligence. Just before Carl falls victim to his dark impulses, an old man with strange clothes and a long white beard helps set him back on the right path. Carl confesses his sin to his wife Matilda, the sister of Herman, and together with the old man they bravely face the fiend. The moral object in this story is transparent; Thomas called it a "Faustian story dealing with the strife between the principles of hate and love for a man's soul" ("German Sources" 132). The demon obviously represents hate, and the old man symbolizes the forces of love that eventually lead Carl back to his wife and domestic felicity. The old man's mystical and almost holy benevolence also cures the title character of his susceptibility to melancholy musings and the longing for forbidden knowledge. Carl's weakness leads him to the brink, but love and duty ultimately restore him to the good graces of home and society.

Thomas confirms that the tale imitates the "German manner" in terms of mood and style, but states that it does not closely resemble any specific German story ("German Sources" 132). Those supposed characteristics of German romanticism of which Simms was so fond — superstition, supernaturalism, irrationality, and vehement passions, along with a wild landscape and desolate ruins — function here in the service of Carl's supernatural adventures and the story's overriding emphasis on the importance of humility, temperance, and love. While many nineteenth-century critics responded positively to Simms's approximation of this German manner, others claimed that Simms's depictions of German scenes and personages were a bit short on substance. The review in the *Knickerbocker* says as much when it states that Simms lacks "the proper study of the language," an appreciation of the literature, and "the knowledge of the superstitions of the people," all important prerequisites for understanding the "character and peculiarities of the Germans" (qtd. in Guilds, *Literary Life* 90). The review acknowledges that the external style is present and even cites a well-done passage, but ultimately asserts that style is not enough.

The interest in personal guilt and social responsibility that characterizes some of Simms's more psychologically-inclined fiction like *Martin Faber* also figures prominently in "Carl Werner," and it may prove to be a more substantive influence than the diablerie and superstition that Simms assigns rather generally to all things Germanic. Indeed, the most compelling moments of the story involve depictions of Carl's interior state: the "irresistible spell" and "unholy curiosity" that temporarily take control of him and the "guilty fear" he experiences when confronted by the demonic Herman. His agonized feelings and mental afflictions are probed to dramatic effect, and the characterizations in the tale remain strong, albeit occasionally overwrought. The setting is conventional but appropriately eerie. And the weakness most likely to be identified by modern audiences — the convenient happy ending and the *deus ex machina* represented by the old man — can be explained by an understanding of Simms's moral purpose. In order to affirm the triumph of civilization and man, Carl must return to the proper track after a hair-raising adventure, and the heavy-handed symbolism is a symptom of the unapologetically allegorical nature of the text. Many modern readers may reject such obvious moralizing, but in this tale, unlike others in the collection, the outdated technique does not obscure the aesthetically-pleasing qualities of a story well-told.

Having the protagonist learn proper conduct and values is necessary for the type of moral instruction Simms was looking to provide. The flights of fancy, the supernatural, and the fascination with dark impulses may serve more as accoutrements than the primary focus, but they remain indispensable in many of Simms's moral imaginative tales. By establishing a peculiar mood and presenting the threat of terror and destruction, these elements of the German style increase narrative tension and create an unmistakable contrast between the forces of light and darkness. This dynamic is equally visible in "Ipsistos" and

"The Star Brethren," the second and third stories in Volume One. In the case of the former, the German influence is direct and unmistakable. Thomas claims that the tale is "little more than a prose version of Goethe's poem 'Zueignung'" in which the eponymous protagonist rejects the worship of the false deity who rules over his ancient society (the setting is far less specific here than in "Werner") and instead pursues the ideal of truth represented by the beautiful goddess who appears to him in a vision ("German Sources" 133). The irrational and exotic is again utilized to strike fear and animate unsanctified superstition: examples include a burning mirror, serpents, gigantic figures of black marble in the magician Bermahdi's chambers, and of course an avaricious goddess with her "voluptuous involutions" and "eyes issuing streams of fire" (Simms, *Carl Werner* 1: 99-112). The overall effect, however, is hardly more than insipid. There is no forward momentum to the plot or life to the portrayals on display — just a recycled fable rendered vaguely, set in an undistinguished locale and peopled with flat characters.

Like "Carl Werner," "Ispsistos" supplies clear symbols and a conclusion that affirms the triumph of goodness and truth. "The Star Brethren" performs the same task but does so through a bleaker lesson. Originally published as the "The Spirit Bridegroom" in 1837's *Tales and Sketches*, this novella centers on the doomed love of Albert and Anastasia. After Albert is killed at the hands of an evil rival, a fallen angel inhabits his body and resumes his relationship with Anastasia. The two young lovers then seem destined for happiness. But Albert's perpetual sadness and midnight rambles spark a powerful curiosity in Anastasia; she yearns for the ability to share his sorrows and understand his condition. The angel in the form of Albert tells her not to seek his secret and warns: "Thou wilt lose what thou hast, in grasping at what thou has not, and the very hope which tells thee of a blessing to come, steals a blessing from thee while it does so" (1: 183). Eventually, Anastasia's pursuit of knowledge destroys her union with Albert and forces her to seek a new companion in the form of a mortal who does not repine or desire change, the exact condition the spirit was seeking in her. A clever ending partially atones for the tale's underdeveloped characters and derivative subject matter, as Simms once again follows Goethe's lead and liberally borrows plot points and themes from *Faust* and Burger's "Lenore" (Thomas, "German Sources" 130-31). Anastasia falls victim to the same quest for unlawful knowledge that plagues Carl, and, much like he did in his longer fictions, Simms suggests that moral wrongdoing is often due to folly, not innate perversion (Thomas, "German Literature" 9). Both Carl and Anastasia are merely guilty of misplaced priorities and over-exuberant imaginations, but unlike her male counterpart, Anastasia's higher moral perception and attempts at atonement come too late.

The final story in *Carl Werner* that wholeheartedly adopts the so-called German manner is "Conrade Weickhoff," the opening novella of Volume Two. Unlike its aforementioned kindred stories, this *Tale of the Imagination* offers a relentless portrayal of evil and horror with no redemption, hope, or respite of any kind. There is still a moral at work, but it is not presented through the demonstration of right conduct; rather, it comes solely through the depiction of moral depravity and despair. The setting is cloaked in grotesquely gothic gloom and the mood is slow-burning dread and discomfort. Nowhere else in this collection is the diablerie Simms associates with German fiction quite as evident, and he boldly presents scenes and ideas that remain disquieting even for modern readers. It should come as no surprise that this tale was also inspired by German antecedents; Thomas points to one scene especially redolent of Foque's *Undine* ("German Literature" 8). Nevertheless, the story comes across as a mostly original creation, and if the lead characters are relatively conventional and the German manner quite familiar, Simms at least supplies a memorable villain, an atmosphere of legitimate menace, and a plot that is far darker than it initially appears.

Simms returns once again to a Faustian bargain: impoverished nobleman Rodolphe Steinmeyer, on the brink of suicide after failing to win the hand of fair Bertha, makes a deal with his friend Conrade Weickhoff, who has strangely reappeared in their native district after a long absence and a rumored death at sea. In exchange for the fortune needed to marry his beloved, Rodolphe must pledge to commit suicide if his name is drawn in an annual ceremony held in honor of a perverse and dissolute count named Oberfeldt. It soon becomes clear that Conrade is actually a demon or some agent of the devil who strives to possess Rodolphe's soul through their awful suicide pact, and Rodolphe suffers great mental anguish as he attempts to start a life and family with his wife. The tale is marked by the familiar supernatural style of the other Germanic stories — dreary forests, disembodied laughs, and supernatural visitations — but the emphasis here is squarely on the grotesque and profoundly perverse. For example, in chapter twelve the narrator describes the terrible aftermath of the first ceremony in Oberfeldt's castle: "the body of the suicide lay in state in the centre of the apartment, which was illuminated with an intense glare, shooting out from strangely large torches, borne up by sable figures standing in its many niches and embrasures." The corpse's head "had been nearly severed from the shoulders," the eyes were open, and the lifeless hand still grasped the bloody knife (2: 28).

More horrifying still is the calmly malevolent Weickhoff, a portrait of subtle evil. As the narrative progresses, Rodolphe increasingly notices his friend's bright, cold glance, his ironical yet conciliating smile, and his "strange, taunting laugh" which "goes like a cold wind" into Rodolphe's bones. The beautiful Bertha, who much like Matilda of "Carl Werner" is a patient vessel of suffering, also observes Conrade's loss of human sensibilities and his "staring sort of contempt," which puts her, "for all the world, in mind of the Mephistopheles" (2: 38-43). Here, Simms creates a villain whose scornful attitude, poise, and cold formality throughout the story are just as frightening as his supernatural machinations at the end. The author also manages to include a denouement featuring tragedy and unmitigated misery on a scale rarely seen in nineteenth-century American popular fiction. While the moral lesson is clear, Simms amplifies the portrait of vice and evil required by the moral imaginative and allows it to overwhelm the forces of good and love, thereby creating a genuinely frightening reading experience.

It is fair to grant that Simms's German-inflected tales were grounded in more than just an idle interest or curiosity. Wimsatt has shown that Simms was immersed in German literature from the 1820s onward: he learned the language during his brief time at the College of Charleston, studied the literature with a group of friends under the tutelage of a German professor, and printed essays and reviews of works by Goethe and other German writers in the *Southern Literary Gazette* and the *Southern Quarterly Review* (229). The knowledge he acquired surely informed his German manner, but in the four stories above there persists a level of generality and haziness that sometimes renders many of the settings and characters hackneyed or indistinct. The American-themed stories in *Carl Werner*, however, evince more particularity of place and more nuanced characterizations, and because of their novel subject matter, they avoid the derivation that pervades the European-set texts. In the case of tales like "Jocassée" and "Logoochie," the exoticism Simms associated with the moral imagination is found in America, and the familiar moralizing and romanticized symbolic structures serve new modes of American regionalism.

In terms of enduring appeal, "Jocassée" is the most successful of the tales found in the collection. Guilds and Peter Murphy have noted that it demonstrates Simms's desire to depict a native setting in all of its natural beauty and wonder while also melding familiar romantic ideas to Native American materials. Murphy, in particular, has demonstrated how this tale of inter-tribal strife set among the Cherokee Indians in the South Carolina mountains can be read as both a prose romance typical of the American Romantic period and a myth rooted in native tradition (40-41). He goes on to say that the plot and theme of the text "relate closely not only to the morphology and nature of Cherokee myth and legend, but also their religion and cosmology" (45). The basic outlines of the myth — a pure-hearted young girl remaining eternally true to her noble lover — are common and appear in many permutations in the traditions of many different tribes. Simms may have been inspired by an Ojibwa legend that he picked up from reading Henry Rowe Schoolcraft's work, but he is known for occasionally confusing the tribal legends he learned from Schoolcraft, or in some cases simply making them up himself as approximations of the real thing (Mielke 63). Nevertheless, he still allows for the inclusion of genuine Cherokee spiritual beliefs and oral traditions, such as the feminine Sun-spirit, the purifying qualities of water, and the importance of naming and signifying physical objects (Murphy 44-46). Perhaps most importantly, "Simms lets a Native American legend stand on its own merit, providing a story that all can appreciate" and breaking the mold of typical Indian Romances of the period in which native characters are almost always viewed in relation to white characters (47).

Indeed, there is a noticeable absence of white characters in this text, aside from the narrator who relates the story and his host who takes him on a tour of the Cherokees' old haunts. There is also very little mediation or influence from the white world. Jocaseé, the brave warrior Nagoochie, and the girl's impetuous brother Cherochee dominate the narrative and fully inhabit the diegesis. Therefore, they are allowed to develop as fully-formed personages, or at least as fully-formed as most of Simms's romance characters, and are not forced to pose as points of comparison to similar or superior whites. As Murphy puts it, the characters and their culture must "be dealt with entirely on their own terms" (74). Thus Simms imagines the region as an entirely Indian space, inhabited by supernatural figures and governed by Indian religion and cosmology. And though virtue and faith, here personified by the lovely maiden, are again rewarded while the forces of hate that infect Cherochee are shown to be destructive, this time the moral lesson is not necessarily Simms's own. He borrows it from an amalgamation of native myths and legends and does his best to recreate it faithfully. His reverence for Cherokee traditions and interest in native terrain reveal his well-documented attempts to fashion a distinctly American mythology grounded in the land's own ancient past. But there is more going on here. He also historicizes the warring bands of Cherokees in "Jocassée" by grounding their story in a specific physical space consisting of real landmarks like Jocassée Lake, Keowee River, and Whitewater Falls. By mythologizing Cherokee history and representing a physical location that is distinctly native and unmediated by white influence, Simms achieves a level of innovation that is markedly absent from forgettable efforts such as "Ipsistos" and "The Star Brethren" and even from better tales like "Carl Werner" and "Conrade Weickhoff." He reimagines the old American frontier and grants his native characters a degree of narrative autonomy and humanity that is exceedingly rare in Indian-related nineteenth-century romantic literature.

Similarly, "Onea and Anyta" takes place in a distinctly native space, but the story begins after the domains of the proud Yemassee tribe have been overrun by white settlers. A valiant chief named Echotee and the few remaining survivors strike off into the "deeper western forests" where "the shadows of evening soon sank behind them like a wall, separating them forever from their native homes" (1: 220). The narrative then shifts to two young Creek warriors who discover a broad lake with a verdant island in the middle. On this island they find two beautiful maidens and instantly fall in love. The main narrative thrust is comprised of the young brave Onea's attempts to marry Anyta despite her native tribe's wish that she wed another, and it eventually becomes apparent that the maiden belongs to the lost Yemassees, who have taken up residence on the secluded island and with whom Onea must battle if he hopes to win her hand. The tale features some striking descriptive passages and an exciting wedding abduction, but Simms would have been better-served devoting more time to Echotee and his wandering flock as opposed to focusing almost exclusively, until the very end, on the rather ordinary love story. Echotee's identity as Anyta's scorned suitor is barely mentioned and Simms misses an opportunity to plumb the pathos of a potentially more interesting character than Onea, who functions much like a standard romance protagonist. Still, the natives display a range of emotions and personalities, from the courage of the young braves, to the strength of Anyta's convictions, to the treachery of her friend Henamarsa. As is the case in "Jocassée," Simms attempts to fashion native people who are recognizably human and more than simply stereotypes of the noble savage. Onea's bravery and Anyta's dutiful purity may be rewarded at the conclusion of this uneven tale, but the most compelling, though maddeningly underdeveloped, thread is the elegiac portrayal of the lost Yemassee.

In "Logoochie; or, the Branch of Sweet Water. A Legend of Georgia," Simms's native setting is a more heterogeneous site of the cultural confrontations that typify much of his frontier fiction. Like the previous text, this is a story of displacement. Following the encroachment of white settlers along the banks of St. Mary's River in south Georgia, the Creek Indians depart for the safety of more remote swamps and rivers, leaving the trickster deity Logoochie behind. Unable to part with his beloved Branch of Sweet Water and the "old woods and waters to which he had been so long accustomed," Logoochie stays put and soon grows attached to the white settlers, particularly the family of fair Mary Jones, and decides to serve them "just as he had served the red men before him" (2: 95). This service entails preventing Mary's young lover Ned Johnson from setting sail with the nefarious Yankee steamboat Captain Nicodemus Dolittle (Old Nick).

Although Mary and Ned assume narrative primacy as the tale proceeds, it is Loogochie who remains "the presiding genius of the place" and his mystical influence secures the youths' happiness. The deity represents truth and virtue in the text; if nothing else, he stands in stark contrast to many of the white settlers, who Simms often refers to as "squatters" and are said to wreak much desolation with the "sharp edge of the biting steel" (2: 70). Logoochie's desire to serve Mary may seem dubious, but it is based on the likeness he perceives between her family and his former Creeks. He is drawn to Mary due to their shared principles and conceptions of moral responsibility, and after she helps him out of a bind, he resolves to return the favor (2: 81). He must first deem Mary and Ned worthy of the land and his friendship before he rights the moral path of Ned, a kind soul who almost succumbs to the temptations of Yankee avarice and materialism plainly represented by the steamboat captain. Because Simms bestows such moral authority on a native character and seems to align reader sympathy with Logoochie rather than the whites, Peter Murphy sees the tale challenging the necessity and humanity of Andrew Jackson's 1830 Indian Removal Policy. Whether or not this is an actual preoccupation of the tale, there is no question that Simms delivers his moral lesson and deploys supernatural, legendary elements in an aesthetically-pleasing, well-wrought fashion. He also constructs a compelling account of an American region and pays homage to the native culture. The likably "uncouth god" may eventually leave the Sweet Water Branch to rejoin his countrymen, but he forgets to remove the spell he placed on the waters, ensuring that the river and its surroundings will continue to be associated with and sanctioned by the Indians who originally called them home.

If in "Logoochie" Simms hints at a certain degree of subversiveness through his sympathy with the Indian deity and his distrust of the obtrusive white woodsman, "The Cherokee Embassage," the final story in the collection, sounds the loudest cry over the iniquities of the white man's dealings with the natives. This tale is differentiated from its brethren by a relative lack of the supernatural elements that Simms usually favored in his works of the moral imagination. More than the rest of *Carl Werner*, this tale is grounded in a real historical event: in 1730, a delegation of seven Cherokee chiefs sailed to England for a meeting with King George. The narrative begins with Sir Alexander Cumming [sic] and his military retinue traveling through "a wilderness, seldom, if ever before, trodden by European footsteps" en route to the Cherokee town of Keowee, where they meet with the seven chiefs and convince them to make the journey across the Atlantic (2: 178). Much of the action takes place at sea as the chiefs encounter several new experiences: seasickness, alcohol, and a sportive monkey named Jacko. Simms also details the "bustle and exhibition" that greet their arrival in London, but the real narrative focus is on the unfortunate agreement signed by the chiefs at the urging of their "brother George" (a probable reference to the real-life Whitehall Treaty of 1730).

The narrator tells us that the treaty is a "precious specimen" of an "unfair relationship between parties originally contracting on an equal footing of advantage" (2: 197). The "cunning" Englishmen are clearly shown to deceive the Cherokee nation, and at one point the whites are referred to as "selfish traders." Worse yet, the return voyage proves disastrous for the stately Cherokees. The frank description of the unjust treaty and the unmistakably mournful tone of the narrative's latter stages distinguish the story and lend it lasting power. The characters are mere sketches and many fascinating scenes in London are glossed over, but the two sequences at sea are noteworthy: the trip to England for comedic value and the voyage back home for its harrowing depiction of loss. Furthermore, the moral lesson of the story supplies a subtle critique of European colonialism that continues to resonate today.

Whether it was due to the Panic of 1837, the uneven quality of work, or Simms's habit of churning out texts faster than audiences and critics could consume them, *Carl Werner, an Imaginative Story; with Other Tales of Imagination* was not particularly successful upon its release. It is not a central component of Simms's canon, but it is a collection that deserves more consideration than it has hitherto received. Not only does it provide an excellent example of Simms's German manner, it also features a unique brand of romantic, often supernatural regional short fiction centered on Native American communities and characters. Though the former suffers from some triteness, the latter mode has recently begun to garner more critical attention and promises to remain a popular subject for scholarship in the years to come. Though not all the stories have aged exceedingly well, the collection still stands as a testament to Simms's conception of the moral imagination, an idea that for him was both a genre of romance and the articulation of the fiction writer's higher calling. Ultimately, the collection needs to be read for two reasons: the insight it offers into Simms's techniques, goals, and innovations, and the fact that much of it is quite enjoyable.

Works Cited

Guilds, John Caldwell. Introduction. *The Writings of William Gilmore Simms: Stories and Tales.* Ed. John Caldwell Guilds. Centennial Edition. Columbia: U of South Carolina P, 1974. xi-xxiv.

——. *Simms: A Literary Life.* Fayetteville: U of Arkansas P, 1992.

Kirk, Russell. "The Moral Imagination." *Literature and Belief* 1 (1981): 137-49.

Lederach, John Paul. *The Moral Imagination: The Art and Soul of Building Peace*. New York: Oxford UP, 2005.

"Literary Notices: Book Table." *New York Mirror* 16.26 (22 Dec. 1838): 207.

Mielke, Laura. *Moving Encounters: Sympathy and the Indian question in Antebellum Literature*. Amherst: U of Massachusetts P, 2008.

Murphy, Peter. "Virtues of Romanticism in Simms's 'Jocaseé. A Cherokee Legend.'" *South Carolina Review* 35.1 (Fall 2002): 40-52.

Rev. of "Carl Werner, and Other Tales." *Boston Traveler* (4 Jan. 1839), 3.

Simms, William Gilmore. *Carl Werner, An Imaginative Story; With other Tales of Imagination*. 2 vols. New York: George Adlard, 1838.

——. *The Letters of William Gilmore Simms*. Ed. Mary C. Simms Oliphant *et al*. 6 vols. Columbia: U of South Carolina P, 1952-2012.

Thomas, J. Wesley. "German Literature in the Old South." *The American-German Review* 19 (1952): 8-30.

——. "The German Sources of William Gilmore Simms." *Anglo-German and American-German Crosscurrents*. Vol. I. Chapel Hill: U of North Carolina P, 1957.

Wimsatt, Mary Ann. *The Major Fiction of William Gilmore Simms: Cultural Traditions and Literary Form*. Baton Rouge: Louisiana State UP, 1989.

CARL WERNER,

AN IMAGINATIVE STORY;

WITH OTHER

TALES OF IMAGINATION.

BY THE AUTHOR OF
"THE YEMASSEE," "GUY RIVERS,"
"MELLICHAMPE," &c.

IN TWO VOLUMES.
VOL. I.

NEW YORK:
GEORGE ADLARD, 46 BROADWAY.

1838.

CRAIGHEAD & ALLEN, PRINTERS,
112 Fulton Street.

ADVERTISEMENT.

THE first story in this collection is founded upon a passage from an ancient monkish legend, which the lover of antiquarian lore will most probably remember. The treatment of the subject is, however, entirely my own; and the circumstance in the history of the two young men, upon which the catastrophe depends, is too frequent among the thoughtless of every nation to make it the peculiar property of any. The strifes between the rival moral principles of good and evil, have also been a subject of frequent celebration in the form of allegory; though, I believe, that, in this respect, my claim to originality will also be undisputed. In the character of the venerable guest of Matilda, it will be seen that I have ventured upon a faint delineation of one of the apostles, and that I have moreover presumed to suggest a notion of their continued toils on earth in the cause of heaven. Such a theory does not, it appears to me, seem altogether incompatible with the history of the strifes of good and evil, as afforded by the sacred volume; and, indeed, must somewhat help us in the hope which we entertain, according to the holy promise, of the final and complete triumph of the former. I trust, in what I have done, I will not be found to have trespassed beyond the limits of propriety. The other tales, with, perhaps, a single exception, belong to the same moral imaginative class with the first. They have been written at various periods in my brief career of authorship. Two of them, it may be well to state, were published with other titles than they bear in this collection. The change was made in consequence of my discovering subsequently that similar titles had been employed by other writers, which might, to the casual reader, suggest an idea of identity between them, which exists neither in the subject, nor the mode of treatment. They are only republished in this collection as they belong properly to the classification which distinguishes the work.

CONTENTS OF VOLUME I.

CARL WERNER.

CARL WERNER.

AN IMAGINATIVE STORY.

I.

" WITH what a sober and saintly sweetness do these evening lights stream around us. What a spiritual atmosphere is here! Do you not feel it?"

My friend did not immediately answer my question, and when he did, his reply was rather to the mood of mind in which I had spoken, than to the words which I had uttered. We were walking, towards the close of day, in one of the deepest parts of a German forest, through which the sunlight penetrated only with imperfect and broken rays. The vista, which was limited by the dusk, was covered with flitting shadows, and wild aspects, that won us farther at each succeeding moment in their pursuit. The cathedral picturesqueness of the scene warmed us both, and when my friend replied to me, I felt that our fancies were the same.

"You have no faith, I believe, in popular superstitions—you never yield yourself up to your dreams?"

Something of a feeling of self-esteem kept me from answering sincerely to this question. I felt, at that instant, a guilty consciousness of a growing respect for the legends of the wonderloving land in which I wandered. My answer was evasive.

"What mean you—your question is a wide one?"

"Elsewhere it might be,—but here—here in Germany—it would seem specific enough. Briefly—you have no faith in ghosts—you do not believe in the thousand and one stories which imagination hourly weaves for the ear and the apprehensions of credulity."

"To speak truly, I have not often thought of this matter until now. The *genius loci* has somewhat provoked my fancy, and triumphed over my indifference—if indifference it be. Ghost stories, though frequent enough, are, as frequently, subjects of common ridicule; and the hearer, if he does believe, finds it prudent to keep his faith secret, if it be only to escape the laughter of his companions. This may have been the case with me, and from seeking to deceive my neighbors on this head, it is not improbable that I have fully succeeded in at last deceiving myself; and have come to doubt sincerely. But of this I will not be certain. I am not sure that I should not partake of the sensibilities of any timid urchin, at the sudden appearance of any suspicious object in any suspicious place."

"Ha! ha! I see you are no sceptic. You are for the ghosts — you certainly believe in them."

"Not so!" I replied, somewhat hastily; "I cannot be said to believe or disbelieve. I have no facts — no opinions — on the subject, and therefore cannot be supposed to have arrived at any conviction respecting it. I have scarcely given it a thought, and my impressions are rather those of the temperament and memory than the mind. Warm blood makes me jump frequently to conclusions upon which I never think; and the stories of boyhood, in this respect, will, long after the boy has become a man, stagger his strength with the images produced on his imagination by a grand-dame's narratives at that susceptible period. My notions of the marvellous arise almost entirely from my feelings—feelings kindled by such stories, and, it may be, rendered vivid by a natural tinct of superstition, which few of us seem to be free from, and which may, perhaps, be considered the best of arguments in defence of such a faith."

My friend made no immediate answer — a pause ensued in our speech, but not in our movement. We walked on, and the shadows became more thick around us.   The scattered lights of evening grew fainter and fewer, and I perceived that the mood of my companion, like my own, had undergone a corresponding change.   Sad thoughts mingled with strange thoughts in our minds, and when he again spoke, it was evident that he felt the night. He resumed the subject.

"I have not been willing to believe, but I feel, and feeling brings the faith.   I have reason to suspect myself of a leaning to these superstitions, and discover myself inclining to conviction the more I indulge in solitude.   Solitude is one of the parents of superstition.   The constant wakefulness and warring strifes of selfish interests, which prevail in the city and among the crowd, drive away such thoughts, and, indeed, all thoughts which incline to reverence ; and it is only when I get into the country — among these solemn shades and deep recesses — that I find my superstitions coming back to me with a thousand other sensibilities.   It is then that my memory goes over the old grounds of my childhood; and that the fancies of an early romance become invigorated within me :—it is then that I give credence to the unaccountable story that we sometimes hear from the lips of more credulous or more experienced companions. Their earnestness and faith strengthen and awaken ours—the fancy grows into form, and the form, at length, from frequent contemplation, becomes almost sensible to the touch. We continue to contemplate until we believe; and there is not a faculty or sense that we have, which does not at last become satisfied, along with our fancies, of the rich reality which the latter have but dreamed."

"I am not so sure that they dream only," was my serious reply. "Why, if the doctrine of the soul's immortality be true — why should it not return to the spot which kindred affections have made holy —, why may it not do a service to the living ?—prevent a wrong ?—reveal a secret, or by some ministry, which could not have been performed so well by any but itself, do that which may help the surviving to some withheld rights, to some suppressed truth — or to some unlooked for n eans of safety from tyranny and injustice ?"

"True — that might have been an argument at one period in the history of the world; but the

world has grown wiser, if not better, in later days!
—a thousand modes are now in our possession for
discovering the truth, to one at that time when
spirits were allowed to return to earth. The days
of miracle are gone by. The ' spirits from the
vasty deep' do not come to us, however loudly we
may call for them."

"Who shall say that ?" was my reply. " Who
shall answer for the necessity. It may occur now
as it has occurred before, nor is it an argument
against the belief, that man has grown wise enough
to find out the truth for himself, after judicial forms,
without the need of any such revisitings of the
moon. If wisdom has grown mighty to find out the
truth, crime has also grown proportionably cunning
to conceal it ; and virtue suffers the injustice, and
vice escapes, even now, from a just punishment,
quite too frequently, when it were to be desired that
some honest ghost could be evoked from the
grave, to set the erring judgment of man aright.
Coleridge considers it a conclusive argument
against the notion, that the ghost of a man's
breeches should appear with him. This may be
a good joke, but it is a poor argument. If it be
once admitted, that for wise and beneficial purposes the just Providence shall permit the departed spirit to return to the earth, where it once abode,

it will be necessary that it should put on that garb
and appearance which shall make it more readily
known by those whom it seeks; since its purpose,
in its return to earth, might only be effected by its
appearance in proper person. I can conceive of
no difficulty in this; since it must be obvious that
as the appearance of the spectre is the work of
God, himself, with Him the toil is equally easy
of giving the spirit its guise of flesh and fashion,
and of preparing the mind of the spectator so that
his eye shall behold the object, whether it appear
in reality or not."

" The subject is one," said my friend, " which
invariably forces itself upon me when I am in solitude. We are now in a place singularly accom-
modated to thoughts and things of this nature.
There is a venerable gloom and gravity about
these old trees. You see that none of them are
young, yet the grounds have neither been cleared
nor grubbed, to my recollection, for many years.
The aged branches have stretched out innumera-
ble arms, and bend, with their accumulated weight
of years upon them, even to the ground. They
have the air of a group of sainted Druids, such as
the Romans annihilated. Black and frowning,
yonder mountain overhangs the wood, protecting,
yet threatening. It has the look of a blasted

thing, and it must be a haunted one. The ruins
which you behold at a little distance to the left,
admirably consort with the rest of the picture. A
gray mist seems to hang over and to hallow them,
until even the beautiful knoll of green which rises
in front of them seems offensively garish from the
exceeding depth of its contrast. Those are the
ruins of an ancient monastery, which the superstitious fancies of the neighborhood have long since
peopled with a fraternity of immaterials, sufficiently numerous and wild to consecrate to their
peculiar purposes a situation of the kind. They
are not often intruded upon, except by myself;
and as I have a story to tell which properly belongs to them, it will not be out of place if I tell it
to you there. Some of the old monuments will
give us a pleasant seat, and among the dead only,
as we then shall be, we shall be in no danger of
suffering interruption or disturbance from the idle
footstep of the obtrusive living."

II.

" We are in Germany," continued my companion;—" of course I do not tell you this with any
other object, than simply to remind you, that you

are in a land, of all others, one of the most renowned for its superstitions, its wild fancies, its
marvellous imaginations. The minds of its people
have become spiritualized by the popular faith; and
thought takes the shape of poetry at its birth, and
fancy is busy every where. Their rivers and their
rocks, their green knolls and sinking valleys, their
dense forests, wild wastes, and deserted ruins, like
these around us, are all haunted and venerable.
The dell and dingle have their different spirits, the
wood and rivulet theirs; and the gentle-hearted
peasants who inhabit them are, in some instances,
almost as rigidly tenacious of the privileges of the
genius loci, as they are of their own rights and religion. A tale of *diablerie* will not, therefore, seem
out of place, in a region so abundantly supplied
with this material; and the story which I am
about to relate to you, though differing materially
from those which we are accustomed to hear, is
yet as native to this neighborhood as any of the
rest. The parties who figure in it, were born in
the little hamlet of ———, not a mile distant, and
you will hear the story from any of the villagers
to whom you may refer for confirmation of it.

"It is now about fifty years since the events
which I am about to relate to you are said to
have occurred. The village of ——— stood then

pretty much as it does now, except that there were then two families in it, of which there are no descendants or surviving relics now. The family of Herman Ottfried was one of the most respectable in it; nor was that of Carl Werner less so. The former consisted only of Herman, and the fair Matilda, his sister; while that of Carl Werner existed in himself alone. He was an only child, whose mother had been long since dead, and whose father had died just before the time when my narrative begins. Herman was about twenty-five years of age, Carl Werner not more than twenty-one — yet they were inseparable friends. Matilda, the sister of Herman, was but seventeen; and it is more than probable, that the great intimacy between Carl and Herman, and the strong regard which the former professed for the latter, arose from the yet stronger feeling which he entertained for the sister. But of this anon. Herman was a good natured, laughing, and mischievous creature, ready always for fun and frolic, not easily apprehensive of danger, nor always scrupulous about proprieties in his pranks. He had good sense enough to keep him from any extravagant folly, or extreme rashness; and good feeling enough to restrain him from any excess which might inflict pain upon the deserving and the good. He was of graceful person, manly and strong, brave, generous, and well-principled.   The favorite of the village, he was yet wanting in one of those traits of character in which all beside him were abundantly provided — he had no more faith in a ghost than he had in a sermon; and though not deficient in proper veneration, he had but slight regard for either.

" In this respect, as in several others, he differed greatly from his more youthful friend and companion, Carl Werner.   Carl was superstitious to the last degree; his memory was perfectly crowded with legends the most extravagant, and he had a feverish and perpetual desire, continually, to increase his collection.   He was, in very truth, a dreamer — one of those gifted men, who see strange sights and hear uncommon sounds, which are denied to the vulgar faculty; and his senses were accordingly employed always in scenting out and searching after the supernatural.   But let me not be understood to say that Carl was a simpleton. Far from it.   He was, in reality, as I have phrased it already, a highly gifted man.   He was a poet — a man of quick and daring imagination — one whose verses were full of fire, and acknowledged to be of more than ordinary merit, — but he was rather too much of a mystic.   Deeply impregna-

ted with the traditionary lore of 'The Teuton,' and
irritably alive to all its exciting influences, the fancy which was in him, the active and subtle spirit
of his thoughts, gathered from all objects and associations food and stimulant for its own continued exercise.   His very existence, so deeply had
he drank of the witch beverage and been led away
into the haunted forests of his fancy, had become
rather metaphysical than real.   His life was passed in dreams; and even his love for Matilda, so
far from humanizing his mind and binding it to
earth, seemed to have the effect of elevating it the
more, and of making it hourly more and more spiritual; until, at length, he appeared to regard the
maiden rather as a creation of his thought — a
dream of heaven — than an object for the contemplation and the enjoyment of his senses.   His life
was thus diseased by his imagination, while yet in
the green, in the blossom, and the bud.

III.

"Between Herman and his sister, the soul and
person of Carl Werner were pretty evenly divided.   When not with one, he was with the other;
and when not separately with either, he was sure

to be with both. Though the tastes and tempers
of the two young men seemed greatly to differ to
the common eye, their sympathies ran strangely
together. Their sports and studies, though not
alike, seemed nevertheless to bring them together
always. Their habits were equally wandering,
and while the poetry of Carl made him musing,
meditative, and abstracted in his habits, it led him
the more to delight in those practical tendencies
in the mind of his companion, which suggested a
character directly the reverse. Herman, too, was
pleased with the fellowship of a thinking being,
and one who could furnish names and definitions
for all his own occasional and half-digested imaginings and thoughts. They had neither of them
much system in their pursuits, and far less in their
studies. Books they read, not by selection, but as
they happened to fall into their hands; or, rather,
Carl would read them, and describe their character
and unfold their contents to his companion, who,
in his own experience, could most generally remember adventures to correspond with and match
those which Carl related to him. In this manner
they became mutual dependants, and hence, some
of the secret of their intimacy. They would follow—each—without much, or at best with a
momentary opposition--the moods and prompt-

ings of the other — the momentary impulse being
the sufficient governor, — and to that they most
generally left the direction of studies and amusements alike.   The feeling which prompted the
one, if not exactly like that which filled the bosom
of the other, was seldom offensive to it : and we
need not wonder, thus situated and circumstanced,
if they grew together, to the almost complete exclusion of all the village beside — the fair and gentle
Matilda alone being excepted.

IV.

" Let not my preliminaries fatigue you.   I cannot get on so well without them.   My narrative
has a comprehensive ground-work, and I must
bring the several more striking features of the lo-
cality, in due order, and, not precipitately, before
your eye.   Having prepared you, I will now proceed :—

"Living, as they did, in the neighboring village,
and possessed of tastes equally wandering, and, in
the case of Carl, so mingled with romance, it will
not be thought surprising if they spent a great
deal of their leisure time among these old ruins.
They were ruins then, and no obtrusive utilitarian

has presumed, as you may see, to take from their gray loveliness by making them more useful. The charm of the spot is the same now as then — if possible, indeed, the beauty of the ruins is even greater, for the walls have suffered from subsequent tempests, and desolation has made more complete her broken temple. Time is the ally of romance, and decay takes nothing from her honors! The source and secret of their beauty have been steadily increasing; and the domain, loved by the German youth of whom we speak, is, perhaps, scarcely less attractive now to us. Touched, as these dismembered and massive fragments at this moment are, by the mellow hues of the fleeting and flickering sunlight, they are, in my eyes, immeasurably beautiful; and seem to me as they did to Carl Werner, a fitting abode for the sleepless and sad spirit — doomed to its midnight vigil of a thousand years.

" The imagination of Carl Werner had peopled these ruins with a countless host of inmates, with wild traditions, with the most pitiable and strange narratives. It was the theatre where his invention became most active, and where he continually exercised it, as much for his own, as for the pleasure which it gave to Matilda and Herman. He had explored the many cells which abound among the ruins—he had groped through the ancient chambers, until he had, from conjectures frequently exercised, come to the belief that he could actually assign the various uses to which they were put: —and, in some cases, through the aid of local tradition and domestic history, he even ventured so far as to say who were their occupants. Though superstitious to the last degree, and most wilfully credulous, Carl Werner had no idle fears. The abbey was his favorite resort even at midnight, and with Herman, who was something of a dare-devil, along with him, a ramble through the old chambers at night, when the rising moon began to peep through the cracks and fissures, was a favorite mode with Carl Werner of passing those pleasant hours. It is true, that, at such times, Matilda never ventured along with the two; but the warm and spirited fancy of Carl enabled him to embody for her ears, when they met, the sweet, strange thoughts of his mind, which, at such periods, formed the topic of conversation between him and his companion. These were themes upon which Carl never failed to be eloquent, and Matilda always loved to hear. At other times, the three would wander while the day lasted, in a sort of mental and dreamy unconsciousness, among the broken walls, turning thoughtlessly over the mar-

ble stones, laboring now and then to decipher the
inscriptions, and toiling through the ancient
grounds and over the green grave knolls about
the edifice ; until, as the sun began to wane, Matilda, with a growing and beautiful timidity — always becoming in a young and lovely woman —
would hurry them homeward, leaving the unfinished story of Carl to find its conclusion at the
evening fireside, which generally brought them
all together like one family. They were soon to
become one, it may as well be said, for, seizing a
favorable moment, the gentle and fond Carl had
whispered to the maiden that he loved her, and she
did not hesitate long to promise that she would be
his. The time was designated for the nuptials, and
the two were quite as happy as mutual love, and
so pleasant a hope, could possibly make them.

V.

"One afternoon, a few weeks prior to the time
appointed for the marriage, Carl and Matilda went
forth upon their usual rambles.   Herman went not
with them.   He had gone away from the village
on some alleged business, though, it is more than
probable, that he had simply excused himself, with

2*

a delicate sense of propriety, from adding to a party which under existing circumstances could do very well without him. The fond Carl had more than once been indebted in this manner to the kind consideration of his friend. Thus, left to themselves, the lovers wandered off in the usual direction, and were soon embosomed in the haunted shades of the ancient abbey. They seated themselves among the monuments, and discoursed of the old time stories; and, with each remembered legend, the timid Matilda, with a most natural fear, would creep closer to her lover, and the fond Carl, with a most natural protection, at length encircled her waist with his arms; and the ghosts of ancient years were forgotten by the happy pair, in the delicious realities of their present situation.

" But a sudden step, as of one approaching, disturbed their dream of felicity. It was Herman. He came, with an air of impatient pleasure and slow regret, mingled up in his manner. As he drew nigh, he handed a letter to Carl, and bade him read it.

" ' It is from my uncle, old Ulrich Ottfried of Amsterdam, and he writes for me to come to him immediately. The place he promised me is at length vacant, and I must lose no time to secure it—I must leave you.'

" ' Leave us, dear brother !' exclaimed Matilda.

" ' Leave us, Herman !' said Carl.

" ' Ay, leave you !' replied the brother, ' leave you, to be sure. Would you have me sit here, purring like a tame cat all my life, when there I have a chance to be somebody, and see the great city.'

" ' And will you leave us, Herman ?' said the girl reproachfully, and the tears stood in her eyes.

" ' Pshaw, 'Tilda ! no tears now, I beg you. They're not true—they're not natural. You know you won't miss me, and there's no reason why you should. You have Carl there, and he'll be more to you than ever I can be. He suits you better ; and I know him too well to be afraid to leave you to his hands.'

" ' Dear Herman !' said Carl, ' but you will not go soon—you will stay to the wedding.'

" ' I can't—the letter, you see, urges my instant departure ; and I'm too anxious to get the place to risk the loss of it by any idle delay. It's true, I'm sorry to part with you ; but, as I said, I leave you both in good hands. You love 'Tilda, and she loves you, and I believe you will be quite as happy with each other, as if I looked on myself, and saw all your happiness.'

" The hand of Carl pressed that of Matilda, and

her's returned the pressure, at these words. Carl
then demanded of Herman when he proposed to
set forth. His prompt answer surprised and pained his hearers.

" ' To-morrow,' said he, ' at early dawn, I
travel.'

" ' To-morrow !' exclaimed Matilda, ' dear brother, you cannot mean it !'

" ' So soon, Herman !' said Carl.

" ' Ay, to-morrow — so soon !' was the reply.
' It's hard. I find it harder than I thought, to
leave you — you, dear 'Tilda — for you have been
a dear, sweet sister to me always ; and you Carl,
who have been a brother after my heart's wish : I
find it very hard to leave you, but I can't help
it ; nor, indeed, if I could, would I. The place
is every thing to me, and I can make my fortune
in it. My uncle, if I please him, promises to take
me with him into business. Read the letter, Carl
— see how fairly the good old fellow speaks. He
is a good old fellow — he always loved me. I was
his favorite, 'Tilda — he never thought much of
you. But, never you mind — there's no good
fortune that comes to Herman that you shall not
share — both of you. So, it matters not much
which of us the old man loved — it's the same

thing; but go I must, and, as I've told you already,
I go to-morrow.'

" This seemed a settled matter in the mind of
Herman, and it produced a melancholy feeling in
that of Carl. It seemed to impress Matilda even
more gloomily, as well it might; for Herman was
an only brother, and having neither mother nor
father, the privation, she well knew, must be se-
verely felt. She had no longer spirit to remain
abroad, and closely attended by the young men,
she returned, in sorrowful temper, to her cottage.

VI.

" You may be sure that was a gloomy evening in
the house of Matilda; and not even the well-satis-
fied love of the betrothed, could make it otherwise
to either of them. Herman was quite too dear to
his sister and his friend, to suffer them, at such a
moment, to feel their own felicity as perfect, just
when they were about to be deprived of him, perhaps for ever. The maiden felt so unhappy, that
she retired at an early hour, and the two young
men wandered forth to talk over their several projects, and the various, and we may add, the sorrowful thoughts, with which their approaching

separation had filled them both.   They had been
so long as one — so perfectly inseparable, hitherto
— that it is not to be wondered at, if they were almost unmanned by it.   Carl, indeed, suffered far
more than Herman.   The latter had the excite-
ments of a new world in promise before him — the
prospects of bettering his fortunes, and, besides
this, he was of a more elastic and lively temper
than his friend.   He could very well bestow con
solation, where other wanderers would have needed
it.   Carl had been always a dependant upon Herman, whose excellent spirits and generous mood
had frequently neutralized the excessive mor-
bidness of his imagination ; and when the former
thought of this, and of his weakness in many
respects, he exaggerated to his own mind the
greatness of the privation which he was about to
undergo.   Herman tried his best to console him,
and in the earnestness of their mutual thoughts,
they gave no heed to their wanderings.   In the
first moment of external consciousness, Carl looked
up, and the ruins of the ancient abbey were before
them.   It was a fitting place for their last interview and private conference.   The silence and the
gloom of the spot accorded meetly with the sadness in their bosoms, and they at once entered the
sanctuary.   They seated themselves upon one of

the broken monuments, and sat for some moments in a moody silence. At length, Carl spoke as follows:

"'I feel cold all over, Herman, as if a breath from that old vault had breathed upon me. Your contemplated journey affects me strangely. I know not how I shall bear it. I shall not often ramble among these ruins — I may have the disposition to do so — I know I will — but I shall not have the courage.'

"'Pshaw!' exclaimed the bolder Herman — 'how you talk. I know you better than you do yourself, and venture to predict that when I am gone you will be here oftener than ever. You love these ruins.'

"'I do — I confess it! — they are to me sacred, if only for their recollections,' said Carl.

"'And ghosts!' continued Herman with a gentle laugh. 'You love their ghosts, I think, even more than their recollections.'

"'Ay, could I see them,' said the other. 'But they are shy ghosts, and — did you not hear a breathing?'

"Carl turned and looked in the direction of the old vault, as he spoke these words, but Herman only laughed at him. Carl laughed too, a mo-

ment after, when he perceived that his weakness
had been observed by his friend.

"'You have nearly roused them, Carl,' said
Herman, after his quiet chuckle had subsided.
'But for my laugh they would have been about
you. You would have conjured the reverend abbot from that shattered vault, and a pretty story
you would have of it.'

"'Perhaps'—said Carl; 'and you would have
listened to the story, Herman, without a single
interruption. Why is that? Why is it that you
can enjoy a ghost story without believing in the
ghost?'

"'Why do we enjoy a puzzle which we know
can be undone?—a mystery—when a moment's
reflection teaches us that it is no mystery? It
is because the human mind finds a pleasure in that
which is ingenious—in any thing which shows
intellectual power. A fairy tale has a spell for
all senses, not because we believe in its magic—
in its subtlety—in its strange devices and wild
conceits; but, that these subtleties, spells, and devices, appeal to natural desires and attributes of
the mind of man. They are beautiful, and as the
appreciation of which is beautiful, forms the legitimate object in the exercise of taste, they com-
mend themselves to every intellect or imagination

that possesses even common activity. You, perhaps, are less fortunate than myself, since you believe in the ghost; and a natural sense of apprehension, which your faith necessarily excites in your mind, while the story is telling, subtracts from the perfect satisfaction with which—were you as incredulous as myself—you would hear or tell it. You tremble while you narrate, and your eyes are forever looking round to see the object which your fancy conjures up.'

"'True, but I do not cease to tell the story. I go on—I would go on, though I beheld the ghost.'

"'I doubt you!' boldly said the other. 'I believe you might try to do so, for I know the extent of your moral courage; but your imagination is too powerful for your control; and this I sometimes fear. I sometimes fear that you may suffer greatly, when I am gone, in the conflict between your imaginative faculty, and your good sense. While I was with you, I had no fear; for when you looked round for the ghost, I laid it with a laugh. It will rise and haunt you when I am gone.'

"'How can you speak thus, or fear this, when, in the same breath, you deny its existence?' demanded Carl.

" 'Oh, I do not deny its existence *to you*,' said Herman — 'we can always have the ghost we call for, for imagination is a god. It is the only creator under heaven. Yours is of this sort, and the worlds you people are sometimes too extensive for your sway. They will rebel against you.'

" 'I fear them not !' said Carl. 'It is my joy to create, and I sometimes pray that with my bodily eyes I may behold the dim but glorious visions of my mind. Yon old abbot, sleeping in the dust and sanctity of a thousand years,—could he rise before me now and answer a few questions, I should be most happy.'

" 'Do not trouble yourself to call upon him — he will not trouble himself to come.'

" 'Yet, I am sure,' responded the reverent Carl, turning an anxious look upon the vault, as if soliciting the buried saint to give the lie to his comrade, 'yet, I am sure, that it is not because he cannot.'

" 'What other reason !' said Herman. 'He cannot, my dear Carl, and if he could, he would not. He sees — if the dead may see aught — all around him that he hath ever known or loved in life ; and for us, whom in life he never knew, he hath too little sympathy, to come at our bidding.

There might be some motive for those lately dead to reappear at the requisition of those who still have human and earthly affections struggling with the cares and woes of earth ; and I would that it were possible we could evoke them. I, too, should be a summoner, Carl—I, too, should pray that my bodily eyes might behold—not the objects of my mind, but the creatures of my heart! I would give worlds, if I had them, once more to behold my dear mother.'

" ' Could she know your wish, Herman, would she not appear, think you ?' demanded Carl.

"'The suggestion makes against your argument, Carl,' replied the other—' immortal as she is, she must know, she must hear my wish; yet she does not appear ! wherefore does she not ?—she cannot — it is written — she cannot ; and it is, perhaps, wise and well that she cannot. It might alter my plans — it might affect my purposes — it might disturb the existing condition of things without making them better.'

" ' Herman,— could I believe with you, I should be unhappy ; but I cannot. I feel assured that the spirit may return, and make itself known. I do not say visibly to the eye, but in some way or other, to one or more of the senses. Do you re-

member the story of Dame Ulrica, and the silks
that rustled in the tiring chamber ?'

"'Ah, no more of that, Carl; and as you are
now getting fairly on the track of the hobgoblins,
we may as well stop our confabulation, else shall
we not go to bed to-night. Of one thing be sure,
if I can revisit you after death, I will————'

"'Will you promise me *that*, Herman ?' demanded the other eagerly.

"'Ay, that will I, though I shall try to do it in
such a manner as not to scare you. I shall sneak
in like a gentle ghost, and shall speak to you in
the softest language. Will you really be glad to
see me ?'

"'Glad!—you will make me happy. It will
be a prayer realized. Promise me, dear Herman !
—we are about to separate, we know not with
what destiny before us. The means of communi-
cation are few between us, and our anxiety to know
of each other will sometimes shoot far ahead of
our capacity to receive or yield intelligence.
Promise me — though heaven grant that you may
live long years after me — that should any thing
befal you, and the power be with you, you will
come to me — you will tell me of your own condition, and guide me aright in mine ; for my sake,
and for the sake of your dear sister, who will so

soon be a part of my life. Will you do this —
will you promise this, dear Herman.'

" ' I will — to be sure, I will, Carl,' was the reply.

" ' Seriously — solemnly ?' demanded Carl.

" 'Seriously — solemnly !' said the other; 'but,'
he continued — ' if I am to take all this trouble,
and expose myself to all risks of wind and weather
merely to oblige you, you must do me a similar
favor; for, though I do not believe in any such
power on the part of the spirit once gone from
earth, nor am I particularly curious on the subject;
yet, while agreeing to satisfy you, Carl, I may
just as well exact a similar promise from yourself.
Dead or alive, Carl, it will always give me pleasure to see you. I have loved you as a brother,
in life — I have no fear to behold you after death.'

" ' It is a pledge — a promise, Herman !' was
the ready answer; and with the utterance of the
pledge, a hollow laugh resounded from the dismembered vault of the aged abbot.

VII.

They sprang at once to their feet. Herman
laughed back in return, but he remained where he

3*

was. Carl trembled like a leaf, but he leapt over the stone on which he had been sitting, and made his way fearlessly towards the vault. Herman followed him. The marble of which the vault had been built was fractured in several places, so that the interior was clearly visible from without. Carl would have entered it, but Herman opposed his doing so.

"' Why should you go in — we can see the venerable dust where we stand,' and the eyes of the two peered into the now silent chamber with a scrutinizing gaze that promised to suffer nothing to escape them.

"' Look!' said Carl; ' look, Herman! dost thou not see!' and he pointed to a corner of the vault while speaking.

" The eyes of Herman saw nothing, however, or he was not willing to acknowledge that they did; but Carl was more ready to believe, and consequently more able to see, for, even while he pointed out the object of his sight to Herman, he watched it as it glided away through an aperture of the vault—a pale bluish flame—a fragment, as it were, of light—that seemed first to crawl along the walls of the chamber, and then suddenly to disappear through one of its many fissures.

" ' What is it that you see ? I see nothing,' said Herman.

" ' A light like that of a taper—a small, creeping light, that passed out of the corner to the east.'

" ' Some slimy worm,' said Herman, ' though I did not see it at all.'

" ' Strange !' exclaimed Carl ; ' but you heard the laugh, Herman ?'

" ' Yes,' said the other, ' but whether it came from the vault, or from the opposite wall, I will not pretend to say. Some urchin may think to frighten us from the other side. We will look in that quarter.'

" Carl now followed his companion, but he followed him unwillingly. Like all true romancers, he had got just enough of the mystery. He was unwilling to press the matter farther, lest he should discover that which might jeopard his prize— which might enable him, indeed, to ' point the moral,' but which would spoil, rather than ' adorn, the tale.' This, however, was the desire of Herman. He would have given as much to discover that the source of the laugh was human, as Carl would have bestowed to prevent such a discovery. The hopes of the latter prevailed. They searched behind the suspected walls, but found nothing ;

and the benefit of the laugh was clearly with the superstitious Carl. After this they left the ruins. The hour was getting late, and as they had still a great deal to say of sublunary concerns, it did not need that they should take the haunted abbey for this purpose. The next morning Herman took his departure. Carl saw him a little way upon the road; and when they were about to separate, one of the last words of Carl was to remind him about his promise. Herman laughed, but freely renewed it. Was it a fancy of Carl, or did he hear the laugh faintly repeated among the rocks behind them, several seconds after his companion had disappeared. It might be an echo merely, but the circumstance troubled the mind of Carl, who could not avoid thinking of it for weeks after.

VIII.

" At length the dreams of the dreamer gave way to more urgent realities. He became a married man; and his bosom was too much filled with the thoughts of Matilda, and his eyes were too much occupied with gazing upon her, to permit of the intrusion of any busy ghost or wandering vision upon either thought or sight. Marriage has a

wonderful tendency towards making men practical.
The tendency, indeed, is sometimes too direct and
rapid to be altogether pleasant. Not that this was
the case with Carl. Far from it. He was impro-
ved in more respects than one in the change of his
condition. His mind needed some qualifying and
subduing influence to change its direction — to turn
it from the too constant contemplation of those
baseless fabrics which had heretofore but too much
occupied its regards; and to bring it back to human necessities, and, through their medium, to the
just appreciation of merely human joys. It is no
less true than strange, that for the first three weeks
after marriage, Carl did not dream at all, as had
been, for as many years before, his nightly, and,
to speak truth, his daily custom. For three whole
weeks he lived a common man — had earthly notions of things — addressed himself to earthly labors — and did not once, in all that time, pay a
single visit to the ancient abbey. But when the
three weeks were over, he began again to dream,
and to wander. The old abbey again received
him as a constant visitor, and the presence of Matilda with him did not greatly lessen his devotion
to the sanctity and superstitions of the spot.

" Perhaps, indeed, it was Matilda that somewhat
contributed to the superstitions of her husband.

She was a religious being — deeply impressed with the spirit of faith and worship, even if she lacked the divine intelligence which might have enabled her to discriminate between the holy things of the sanctuary, and those meretricious symbols, and mocking shadows, which the arts of one class, and the fears of another, have decreed for worship, and declared no less holy than the true. The *spirituelle* held a large place in her composition ; and if her imagination lacked the activity of Carl's, her yielding weakness rendered her susceptible to the full influence of his. This weakness increased the activity of a faculty to which it was constantly appealing ; and though the terrible forms and fancies to which the mind of Carl frequently gave birth and performance, only drove the timorous wife more earnestly to her prayerful devotions, she did not seek to discourage him in a practice which had so beneficial an effect. Unconsciously he practised upon her fears, moving her to devoutness through an unseemly influence ; and with equal unconsciousness on her part, her fears stimulated his superstitious tendencies even to error, by giving continual employment to an imagination which daily became more and more morbidly active, and consequently dangerous.

"Herman had now been gone for some months. At first he wrote to them freely and frequently, but after a while his letters grew fewer and less satisfactory, and at length months went by without bringing them any intelligence of their neglectful brother. Matilda sometimes complained of this, and thought unkindly of Herman; but Carl, like a true friend, always found some excuse for his neglect, in the pressure of business, and the accumulation of other duties and friends.

"'Besides, he need not write, Matilda, when he has nothing particular to say. No news is good news commonly; and when a letter comes, Matilda, you know you always dread to open it, for fear of hearing evil. Herman will not forget us, be sure.'

"'But he may be sick, Carl.'

"That was always a suggestion which silenced her husband, and he felt doubly unhappy on such occasions, as, in addition to the fear with which such a suggestion seemed to inspire Matilda, there was an unpleasant consciousness in his own mind which dreadfully troubled him. At such times, strive as he might, he could not help thinking upon the promise which Herman had given him, and he felt that, however he might regret the death of his brother-in-law, such an event would be lessened of much of its evil, if that promise could be kept. Such thoughts he felt were criminal, and to do Carl all justice, we should add, that he strove manfully to resist them. But he could not resist them, and they grew upon him. After a little while, he thought of nothing else. He did not need the gently-uttered fears of Matilda, who continually spoke of her absent brother, to remind him of his promise and of his mortality; and in his dreams the image of that well known friend, stretched out pale, and motionless, in the embrace of death, came but too frequently to his mind, not to lose, in time, many of its terrors.

IX.

"One pleasant afternoon, the two, Carl and Matilda, rambled forth, according to their usual custom, towards the ancient abbey. The sun was just about setting, and he made a glorious descent. His rays streamed through the broken walls by which they walked, and they paused to contemplate the picturesque effect of their scattered beams, gliding among tombs, in which the dust that once was life, and strength, and ambition, could no longer feel their warmth. While they looked,

a cloud suddenly arose in the heavens, obscuring
and shutting out the bright glories which had won
their gaze, from the shattered walls which they had
made golden but a moment before. The sudden
clouding of the sky brought an instinctive gloom
to their mutual minds, and without seeming to
notice the absence of any connexion between the
phenomenon upon which they looked, and the object in her thoughts, Matilda quickly remarked:

" ' I hope, Carl, that nothing is the matter with
Herman.'

" Strange to say, the thought that something
was the matter with her brother, was even then
the busy thought in the mind of Carl. He replied
after a moment's pause—

" ' Indeed, Matilda, I hope not.'

" A slight laugh rose from the ruins, and the
conscious soul of Carl was smitten within him.

" ' Had he been sincere in the utterance of that
hope ?' was the question which he asked himself
when he heard the laugh ; but it was a question
which he dared not answer. Matilda did not seem
to have heard the sound which had touched him
so deeply; and he was sufficiently collected to
conceal his agitation from her. But while they
spoke together, though but a few moments had
elapsed, the cloud had veered round, and now

hung in the sky directly before them. Somehow, this appearance affected Carl seriously. He coupled the cloud with his own thoughts, and his imagination grew busy in its contemplation. It did not seem a common cloud to his eyes; and its progress, from a speck in the pathway of the sun, to a mantle, in whose pitchy bosom the dying but glorious orb was to find his splendors utterly subdued, was a marvel to a mind so subtle as his. His fancies grew firm and strengthened when he saw that Matilda observed the wonder also.

" ' That is a strange looking cloud, Carl!' she exclaimed — ' see how it rolls — over and over — onward and onward — and yet there is no wind. It is coming towards us.'

" The flight of the cloud seemed to have increased in velocity. It neared them rapidly, and was evidently descending. When above them, it seemed to open and to expand, and from its bosom Carl felt the warm drops upon his face.

" ' It rains !' he said, ' let us go into the abbey.'

" ' I feel none,' said Matilda.

" ' Indeed! it is full on my cheek !'

" The eyes of Matilda turned from the floating mass that had now passed over them, but when her glance met the face of her husband, she screamed in terror.

" 'Father of heaven!' she exclaimed, ' be with us! Carl, my husband, your face is covered with blood!'

" 'Say not so!' he cried, ' what can it mean?' He wiped his face with his handkerchief, and the stains were visible to his own eyes; and when he looked down upon his garments, they, too, were covered with the same sanguinary color. The wonder was greater still, when they looked in vain to find a drop upon the person of Matilda. Yet her arm had been fast locked within his, and the very hand which had sustained her's was sprinkled plentifully with the stains.

X.

" They hurried home in consternation. The thought of Matilda was upon her brother; and she regarded the events of the evening as ominous of his fate. But why did the blood stains fall only upon her husband? Why were her garments untouched? This was a mystery to her; but not to Carl. He thought he could explain it, but he forbore to speak. He dared not. His thoughts and feelings were not what they should have been. He was guilty, in his secret soul, of improper feel-

ings, if not of improper wishes, and he knew it.
Supper was soon served, and, like a good wife,
regardful only of her husband, Matilda urged Carl
to eat, for she beheld his abstractedness. He ate
without knowing that he did so. She, however,
could eat nothing, and as soon as the repast was
over, she retired for the night. But Carl felt that
there was no sleep for him; and a feverish mood,
for which he could not account, prompted him to
sally forth. He would have gone to his wife's
chamber—he tried to do so—for he knew what
were her apprehensions, and he wished to soothe
them—but he could not. Something impelled
his footsteps abroad—a spirit beyond his own
drove him forward; and with a desperate mind
he rapidly hastened to the abbey, as if there, and
there only, he should find a solution of the marvel which had distressed him. His heart seemed
to grow strong in proportion as his thoughts grew
wilful; and without any of those tremors which
had ever before possessed him when he rambled,
with a purely mental and not a personal feeling,
among the ruins, he boldly plunged into their recesses.

" The night was a clear, but not a bright one.
The stars were not numerous, but they were un-
clouded. The air was still, and was only now

and then apparent in a slight breathing, as it came through some little crevices in the wall. The silence of the place was complete — was its solitude complete also? Carl asked of himself the question, as he walked beneath the massive archway of the fabric — still solid and strong, though broken and impending; for, the masons of old, wrought, not less to make their works live than to live themselves. They live, like all good workmen, in their labors. The roof, broken in many places, let in the scattered starlight, and sufficiently, though imperfectly, revealed to him the place. He went forward, full of sad and truant thoughts. He took his seat upon one end of a dilapidated stone which had often sustained him before. His elbows rested upon his knees, and his hands supported his head. It was in this posture that he mused with feelings which sometimes brought him back to impulses and a course of reflection not unworthy of his better nature. They reproached him with the heartlessness of his curiosity, as if it were not the tendency of mind always — great mind, which overlooks the time, and lives for God, and for the species — to disregard nice affections, and the tender blossoms which decay.

"'Herman, Herman!' he exclaimed, 'I have been unworthy of thee. Thou hast loved me with the love of a brother, while I have thought

4*

of thee even as the ancient augur of the victim, which he slaughtered for unholy wisdom ! I have prayed in my secret soul — I have prayed for thy death — that I might have improper knowledge.'

"Again did a slight laugh come to his ears. He looked up with a shudder. A small blue light crawled along upon the opposite wall, like some slimy reptile, and while Carl watched its progress with solemn interest, the laugh was repeated almost beside him. He started, and almost at the same moment he felt one side of him grow chill. A breath of ice seemed to penetrate him from the east. He turned his eyes in that quarter, and the spectacle that then met his gaze paralyzed every faculty of his body. The form of Herman Ottfried was there, sitting beside him on the other end of the grave stone. He could not speak — he could not move. His eyes were riveted upon the spectre, and the glare which was sent back from those of the unearthly visitant, was that of hell. A scornful leer was in it — a giggling hate — a venomous but laughing malice.

"'Her — Her — Herman!' Carl tried to speak, but a monosyllable was all that he could utter.

"'Ha, ha, ha!' The vaulted abbey rang with the echoes of that infernal laugh.

"'Mercy! mercy!' screamed the unhappy Carl, as he lifted his hands and strove to close his eyes against the dreadful presence. But the elbows refused to bend — he could not raise them. His knees in the mean time gave way, and he sank senselessly upon the damp ground of the abbey.

XI.

" When he unclosed his eyes, which he did in the fullest consciousness of his situation, and consequently in the extremest terror, he was rejoiced to find himself alone. The grave stone, at the foot of which he lay, was untenanted. The abbey was silent, and though he dreaded, at every step which he took while making his way out, to hear the dreadful laugh, and to behold the hellish visage, he yet suffered no farther interruption while in the abbey. When he had left it, however, and was about to enter the main street of the village, he was encountered by a drunken man.

" ' Hallo, friend !' exclaimed the bacchanal, ' whither so fast ? Stop and hear a song — stop and be merry.'

" And, in the voice of one satisfied with himself and all the world, the drinker carolled with tolerable skill, one of those famous dithyrambics in which the German muse has frequently excel-

led. The eye of the unhappy Carl was turned, half
in hope, and half in despair, upon the man. He
had heard of the soporific effects of wine—of its
ability to drown care, and produce a sweet forgetfulness of his sorrow, and he felt inclined to the
temptation ; but a sudden thought of Matilda shot
through his brain, at that lucky instant, like an
arrow. He knew not the lateness of the hour, and
was ignorant how long he had been from her.
He knew that he had swooned away, and knew
not how long he had remained in his stupor. It
might be near daylight, and what, — if such were
the case, — what must be her fears? Domestic
love came to his succor, and he rejected the over-
tures of the bacchanalian, who nevertheless continued to pursue him. He followed the unhappy
Carl to his very door, now persuading, and now
striving to provoke him by every manner of taunt
and sarcasm, to partake of the intoxicating cup
which he proffered. But the sufferer was firm,
though more than once it came to his thought that
wine was good against sorrow. He was not yet
so deficient, however, in other resources, as to fly
to this doubtful succedaneum.

XII.

"It was not so late as Carl had fancied it, and his wife was still awake. He had not been away much longer than was his wont, when he went forth on his usual evening rambles ; and though she had suffered from his absence, yet it was not through any apprehensions for his safety. Still she had no complaints, and the pleasure in her eyes when he did return, was, probably, one of the best arguments against his wandering forth again. She was still melancholy and apprehensive, and when she observed the anguish, not to say the agony, which was apparent in every feature of his face, her apprehensions underwent a corresponding increase.

"'What is the matter, Carl ? What has troubled you ?' she demanded of him in agitated accents.

"'Nothing, nothing!' with an effort, he made out to reply.

"'It is something—something terrible, dearest husband—your cheeks are haggard, your eyes are wild—you tremble all over. Tell me, tell me, my husband, what is it that troubles you.'

" ' Nothing,' he again replied — ' return to your bed,' (she had risen when she beheld his face,) ' return to your bed and heed me not. I will be better soon.'

"He quieted, if he did not satisfy her. She returned to the couch as he bade her; and he prepared to follow her. But there was one duty which he omitted that night, which, from his childhood, he had never neglected to perform before. He did not pray. He strove to do so, but his mind could not be brought to address itself in supplication. He forgot the words; and others, foreign to his object, took their places. He gave up the effort in despair. He could think of nothing but the terrible laugh, and the demoniac visage which had met him in the abbey. All the next day he was like one whose senses wandered. His wife strove to soothe his mood, which was fitful — and to attract his attention, which strayed continually; but he smiled upon her kindly, with a sickly smile, and gave no farther acknowledgment. As night approached he grew visibly agitated, and as he became conscious that his efforts at concealment were unavailing, he sought his chamber, to hide in its dimness what he might not otherwise conceal. But his agony seemed to increase with his solitude. Dreadful images were about him in his

chamber, and a chuckle, like that he had heard in
the abbey, was uttered, at intervals, even over his
shoulder. He descended to the apartment in
which he had left Matilda, preferring that she
should see the agony that he could not endure
alone. But her presence gave him no consolation, and her solicitude became an annoyance.

" ' Trouble me no more !' he exclaimed, in tones
which she had never heard from his lips before,
replying to one of her fond appeals to know the
cause of his sufferings. ' Trouble me no more —
it is nothing — nothing which I may tell you.'

" She turned from him in sorrow not less deep,
though less acute than his, and the tears filled
her eyes. His heart reproached him as he beheld
her action, and readily conceived her pain ; but
there was a wilful impulse in his bosom, which refused to permit of his making the usual atonement. Sullen and sad, he glowered about the
apartment 'till night came on, and supper was announced, when Matilda saw that his agitation was
visibly increasing. With the meek and blessing
spirit of an angel, forgetting the harsh rebuff
which he had given her, she approached him —
threw her fond arms about his neck, and implored
him to smile again upon her. He tried to do so
but the effort produced only a ghastly grin, no

less shocking to her eyes than the effort had been irksome to his mind. He went to the supper table, and, unobserved by him, her glance watched him while he strove to eat. He left the table in horror, for the face of Herman stared at him from the plate. There was no hope of escape from the pursuing fiend, and the unhappy Carl rushed out of the house. Where should he go?

"'To the abbey! to the abbey! I will speak —I will demand its meaning. I will know and hear all. If it be Herman, in truth—my brother and my friend—'

"'Ha! ha! ha!'

"The infernal laugh was at his elbow. He turned in desperation to behold—not the gorgon stare which had so terrified him in the abbey, but a face rather good natured than otherwise— the face of the bacchanalian who had encountered him on the preceding night. A mischievous grin was upon the features of the stranger, whose broad mouth and little twinkling eyes, with the fat, hanging cheek, and the red and pimpled nose, seemed the very personification of fun and frolic. Not a feature in his face appeared of demoniac origin. The subtle malignity of the satanic attributes were entirely wanting, and in place of them, reckless mirth, indifferent to all matters but good cheer, was the prevailing expression. But the laugh! That, certainly, had been very like the laugh he had heard in the abbey. No two sounds could have seemed more alike to the ears of Carl. A new thought entered his mind with this conviction. This drunken fellow might have been the proprietor of the former laugh, as he certainly was of that which he had just heard. To him might be ascribed the design to frighten himself and Herman. When he looked into the cunning, merry, blubber-face of the reveller, conjecture became conviction. 'It must be so!' said Carl, half aloud.

" ' To be sure it must,' exclaimed the other. ' We will have a glass together now, though you did refuse to be a good fellow last night. Come. Here's old Dietrich hard by. I can answer for his liquors, though I cannot for his conscience. I believe in the one, and — damn the other. Come, my friend, let's try him.'

" Carl was half disposed to be civil with the stranger. The notion which had suddenly possessed him that he and the ghost of the abbey were one and the same person, brought a singular relief to his mind; and he was half persuaded to forgive him the impertinence of the fright which he had received, in consideration of the solution of the mystery which the conjecture brought. The stranger pressed him, expatiating upon the sweets of wine, and the luxury of good company.

" ' Wine,' says he — ' wine, Carl——— '

" ' How the devil does he know my name !' thought Carl to himself, but he did not say it.

" ' Damn my instinct,' said the other — ' I find it the hardest thing in the world not to know, what, indeed, it is not necessary that I should know.'

" ' What do you mean ?' said Carl.

" ' Oh, nothing — I was only regretting that my passion for wine — I had almost thought it an instinct — should sometimes make me indifferent to the sort of company I fall in with. Here, I've been on the eve of eulogizing the rich Hochheimer to you, who are a judge, doubtless, of the noble beverage, simply because, in my intercourse with mankind, I meet hourly with so many to whom the eulogy is a sort of key to their tastes, that it is now almost habitual with me to dwell upon it. To you, however, any idle talk upon the merits and effects of good wine would be only an impertinence.'

" ' I am no judge — I drink little,' said Carl, to whom the seduction of appearing more than he was, or of knowing more than he did, had always been a very small one.

" ' You belie yourself,' said the stranger — ' I know that you are a judge — I see it in your face. Come with me — you shall give me your opinion of the wine of Dietrich.'

" ' Nay, you must excuse me,' said Carl.

" ' Can't — never excuse a man from his wine,' said the other, bluntly. ' Excuse a milk-sop, of course — but never a man.' And as he finished a sarcasm which has led thousands of goodly young men to their ruin, he familiarly took the arm of Carl to lead him forward to the tavern. But Carl was not vain of being esteemed manly in this respect. His philosophy was that of an English poet, whom he never read :

> ' Who drinks more wine than others can,
> I count a hogshead, not a man —'

and he gently, but firmly refused.

" ' Why, man,' said the other, ' Am I then mistaken in you. I thought you a good fellow, who loved good company, good wine, and a good story —'

" ' Good story !' exclaimed Carl, touched in the right place.

" ' Ay, a good story — a tale of the mountains — of the miners, and the red demons of the mines — the gnomes and the salamanders.'

" ' Have you, indeed, such stories ?' inquired Carl, now rather curious.

" ' Ay, that have I; and, nearer home, of the old abbey here. I can tell you a ghost story of those ruins, that 'll make every hair of your head stand on end.'

" Carl hesitated and lingered, and his companion laughed at his hesitation. That laugh chilled him — it reminded him of what he had been willing to forget. It reminded him of the face of Herman — the ghastly grin upon his lips, and the dreadful laugh — so like to that of the stranger, which he had then heard. He broke away from the arm which held him.

" ' Not now,' said he, ' you must excuse me. I have business to attend to.' And with these words, amid the curses and the derision of his companion, he hurried forward to the abbey.

XIII.

" A spell, whose power seemed to be irresistible, prompted him in the direction which he took. A will, superior to his own, yet compassing and controlling it entirely, drove him onward to the abbey. What proper motive had he there? None.

His duties were all elsewhere — with his wife —
in his own home. What could he gain to see
once more the dreadful spectre which had affright-
ed him? An unholy curiosity stimulated the answer to this question. Knowledge — Knowledge.
To know that which is forbidden — to win the secrets of two worlds — was the hope of Carl, as it
has been the unwise hope of thousands. He did
not remember, while he indulged this vain desire,
that the 'tree of knowledge, is not that of life;'
still less can it be said to be that of happiness.
Thought is not often happiness; and where thought
takes the wings of the imagination, and strives
ever after the ideal, it is too apt to be torture and
strife, as it must finally be death. Death, indeed
— death and time are the grand illuminators. To
wait is to be wise. Alas! for Carl — he had not
only to wait but to endure.

  " 'I must pluck up courage!' he mentally exclaimed. 'I demanded to see him; I must not
shrink from the encounter. Let him speak to me —
let him say he is happy — and I will ask no more.'

  " What right had he to ask so much? Were
it his right, would it not be revealed? Would the
just God withhold from him a right? He did not
ask himself these questions, for Carl, like all of
his species, was but too apt to contemplate, through

     5*

the medium of a shallow vanity, the deity in his
own heart, as if the dwelling-place of fears and
feebleness, of vain caprices and false-founded passions, could ever be the home of divinity.

"He entered the abbey walls—he trod among
the crumbling ruins, but his heart shook within
him. Again he sat upon the tomb-stone — again
did the sudden and sinuous light crawl before him
upon the walls. He felt the chill enter and curdle
the blood within his bosom, and he knew that the
spectre was sitting at his side. He dared not look
round upon him. He almost sank upon the
ground; but the resolve of his mind sustained him,
and he tried to compose himself.

" 'Why should I fear?' he said in his thoughts.
'If it be Herman, he will not harm me — if it be
not Herman, what other has claim upon me!'

"As if the spectre had seen his heart, and in
this manner commented upon its fears and weakness, the dreadful laugh which had so shocked him
before, was again repeated. The blood ran cold
in the bosom of the mortal, but his firmness had
not departed. The resolve was still in his mind,
and after a brief pause, in which he struggled successfully with his terrors, he turned his eye boldly
to behold the spectre. The same dreadful presence
met his glance as on the preceding night. But the

novelty had passed away, and with it some of the
terrors. He felt that he could now survey it, distinctly, resolutely, if not calmly. He did survey
it — and what a spectacle! The face was that of
his friend, that of Herman Ottfried, indeed; but,
oh! how different. It was the face of his brother
and his friend, but in place of the gentleness and
good nature that made its prevailing expression
heretofore, the features were all hell-stamped — the
skin was all hell-dyed and darkened. Carl nearly
fainted — his heart seemed to wither within him as
he gazed. But he continued to gaze. His resolve,
built upon high, but erring, moral purpose — was
not now to be shaken. Nor, indeed, could he do
otherwise than gaze. The eyes of the spectre,
like those of the fabled basilisk, rivetted his own.
The glare which shot from them, like a yellow va-
por, seemed to exercise upon him the power of a
spell. He gazed till he was infatuated; yet he
writhed all the while beneath the scornful malignity of the spectre's glance.

" ' What would you with me?' he screamed,
rather than spoke. He could easier scream than
speak; and the words were scarcely intelligible to
his own ears. He was once more answered by
that infernal laugh. He shivered as he heard it,
but it did not increase his terrors. It rather made
him indignant.

" ' Who are you ?' he cried, in tones more temperate, and with a spirit even more resolved than before. ' Who are you ?—what are you ? I know you not.'

" ' Herman — thy friend—he for whose death thou pray'dst, that thou might'st possess his secret. Would'st thou not hear it ?'

" Such was the terrifying response of the spectre whom he had summoned.

" ' Thou liest !' cried Carl, boldly. ' I uttered no such prayer.'

" ' Thou did'st,' was the prompt reply, ' in thy heart thou did'st, and thy prayer is granted. Herman Ottfried is no more — he is beside thee.'

" ' I believe thee not !' was the courageous reply. ' My friend still lives ; and if he did not, I would not believe that such as thou seemest, and art, should be his representative. He is good, and thou —'

" ' Art damned ! — thou would'st say !' and the spectre concluded his sentence — ' And thou say'st truly, Carl Werner. I am as thou say'st. Yet, look once more upon these features, and, blasted and blackened as they appear to thee, say if they are not those of him who was thy friend—of him who was Herman Ottfried.'

" ' I believe thee not !' cried Carl, trembling all over.

" ' Thou shalt—thou dost believe me, Carl Werner,' replied the spectre. ' Thou know'st that I am he. Did I not pledge myself to meet thee — to tell thee all — to give thee intelligence — to ease thy curiosity ? I am come. I am ready. Art thou willing — art thou prepared to hear ?'

" ' Not from thee — not from thee !' cried Carl, in agony. ' Away! leave me—trouble me not with thy falsehoods. My friend is living — Herman Ottfried, I know, still lives ; and if he did not, thou never couldst have been the spirit which filled his frame, and gave impulse to his actions. He had no malice such as glares from thine eyes — he had no foul passions such as hang about thy lips.'

" ' Thou reasonest like a child, Carl Werner. Hear me and believe. The first truth is death — the second judgment. Mortality is a state of dreams and shows—presentments which impose only on mortal senses. We throw off all disguises for the first time, when we arrive at the first truth, which we never know until death. We acquire all truth when we reach the higher form of judgment. In death, we know for the first time what we are and have been — in judgment, we know what we shall be.'

" ' Then thou canst tell me nothing,' said Carl, fearlessly — yet trembling all the while.

" ' Yes—I can tell thee what I am !' exclaimed the spectre in reply ; but it needed no words to unfold that which was but too clearly discernible in the blasted and blasting expression of his countenance as he thus replied. Carl saw this expression, and the shudder that shook his frame sufficiently apprized the spectre that it was unnecessary for him to relate that which the quick imagination of Carl so readily conceived. He grinned fearfully as he witnessed the tremblings of his mortal companion, and the malicious and hateful expression re-aroused the courage of the youth.

" ' Yet, though I cannot but see that thou art one of the damned and blasted of heaven—one of the thrice blasted perchance ———.'

" ' Thou art right !' exclaimed the spectre, while lurid fires of a hellish agony seemed to kindle in, and to dart forth from his eye—' thou art right ; I am indeed, one of the thrice—ay, one of the seventy times seventy times damned of the Eternal ; and I defy him amid all his fires.'

" He paused as he spoke these words, and his clenched hands were lifted in air, and thrust upwards, as if he would do battle even at that moment with the deity. Carl shuddered and shrunk from the fearful presence ; but his soul grew strengthened within him in due proportion to the revoltings which he felt at such foul blasphemy.

"I believe thee!' he exclaimed, and his own clasped hands were raised in prayer while he continued—'I believe thee; but I believe not that thou art Herman Ottfried—it is impossible—I believe not that he is dead.'

"'Thou shalt have confirmation to-morrow. His blood was upon thee yesterday—his shadow is before thee now. Dost thou not believe me—wilt not thou hear some of the secrets which thou didst once so desire to know. Where is thy curiosity—where is thy thirst, Carl, after knowledge? Has thy marriage changed thy nature, and art thou willing to be the mere cur of the household, and forego that noble ambition which made thee seek after wisdom, as if it were life—as if it were more than life to thee—as if it were happiness? Is it happiness to thee no longer? Is thy sense dulled for its enjoyment? Go to, Carl, I had not thought this of thee. Go to thy wife—get from her the needle and the net-work, and find in her example thy fitting employment. Thou hast not the soul for my secret—thou wouldst fear to hear it.'

"'Fiend—foul fiend, and bitter devil!' cried the fierce Carl, provoked by the taunting of the spectre beside him — ' I fear thee not, though I would not have thy secret. I hold thee to be a cheat, and thou but slanderest the noble spirit of my friend. Have at thy throat, monster, in the name of heaven and its blessed ministers. Have at thy throat! and let the great God of the heavens and the earth determine between us.'

' " Ha, ha, ha !' was the only response of the spectre as Carl uttered these words. The replication of the crumbling walls to the infernal laugh was tremendous ; but it did not shake the desperate courage of Carl Werner. He sprang upon his glowering and grinning enemy, with outstretched arms and fingers, and he aimed to clutch the fearful image — not a whit alarmed at the increasing fiendishness of its aspect — by the throat; but the object melted in his embrace, at the moment when it seemed most secure. His arms grasped his own body ; and, stunned with confused thoughts and defeated passion, the unhappy Carl gazed around him in a stupor, which was not at all diminished as he found himself alone.

XIV.

" To a certain extent, this stupor brought with it a desirable insensibility. He trembled no longer.

He was almost reckless. A reaction in his mind
had taken place, and from having been one whom
every thing before, however slight, could startle,
he was now one whom nothing could affect or
move. He rushed through the abbey. He thrust
his fearless head into all its recesses—into tombs
and niches, cells, and ruinous and long untrodden
apartments, with most admirable indiscretion. He
summoned his tormentor from the places in which
he had hidden himself, and defied the presence
which he invoked. But all was silent; and, exhausted with fatigue, and chafed with his disappointment, Carl at length departed from the abbey
in hopeless despondency. The next day, even as
the spectre had predicted, he received the fatal intelligence of the death of Herman. This news
was but too confirmatory of what he had seen and
felt. It gave life and body to his fears. The
grief of Matilda was great, but it would be vain
to undertake to describe that of her husband. To
her, his agony—dearly, as she well knew, he loved
her brother—seemed strange and unaccountable.
She little dreamed of the nightly revelations which
were made to his senses. With a praiseworthy
sense of propriety and a manly tenderness, he had
carefully withheld from her, though still longing

to reveal, the fearful secret which he possessed. But how could he say to her that he had seen her brother, or seen him as he was — a thing upon whom the curse of God had fallen, and who had been delivered over by his judgment to the awful ministers of eternal wrath. He felt that he must keep his secret, and bear with its horrible burden as best he might. But, as evening drew nigh, the horrors of his heart grew less and less supportable. He felt that he must again perform his vigil. He must again repair to the place of his trial and his torture ; and this, by a secret conviction of his mind, he felt must be done, until he had courage to hear, and was willing to believe, all the horrible intelligence which the spectre might think proper to convey. He had bound himself solemnly to the meeting, and he could not shrink from the terms of his pledge. Yet, where and when was it to end ? This was the dreadful question which his soul answered in utter hopelessness.

" ' In my death. Yet it will end soon, for I cannot stand this strife much longer.'

" Such were his thoughts and words ; and their truth would readily be believed by those who were conscious of the sudden and singular change which had taken place in his person. All the villagers remarked it. He was haggard and listless — he

saw and heeded nobody — he moved through the
streets like a ghost, and Matilda — the beloved
wife of his affections — no longer filled his heart,
and commanded the devotion of his eye. She
strove to find out the secret of his sorrows, and to
soothe them. But vainly would the physician seek
to heal, while he remains ignorant of the cause of
the distemper. We must lay bare the wound to
extract the poison; and in the purity of her soul
she did not even imagine the horrible nature of
that secret which was preying upon his. Her efforts were in vain. Night came on, and though
she strove to keep him at home, the spell was too
powerful to permit her to succeed.

"'Where is it you go, dearest Carl? Why,
night after night, will you go forth in so much sorrow, and with features so wild, so full of apprehension; and when you return — so full of horror —
so haggard — so dreadful? Tell me, dear husband, whither it is you go, and why it is you suffer in this manner.'

"'Nay, do not heed me, dearest,' said the unhappy man, with a gentleness of manner which
made his sorrows only the more touching — 'do not
trouble yourself about me. I have busy and vexing thoughts, and shall not look well until they are

digested into form.   When I resolve them, then
will I remain with you, and be at peace.'

" ' What thoughts are they ?' she demanded;
but he smiled, and answered her evasively.

" ' Ask me not — not now,' he replied, and resisting her solicitations to be allowed to go forth
with him, he rushed out of the house.   She followed him to the door, and looked after him in the
street ; and her own apprehensions were greatly
increased as she beheld the erratic impulse of his
movement, and the feebleness of his step — the one
betokening the disorder of his mind, the other the
debility of his body.   While she looked and trembled, with the big tear gathering slowly in her eye
and stealing silently to her cheek, the accents of a
mild but strange voice met her ears at a small distance, and, turning, she beheld an old man standing before her.   He was a stranger to her, and
evidently a stranger in the place, since his air and
costume were very different from any that she had
ever before seen.   His beard was long and white
like silver, and hung down neatly smooth and
clean upon his bosom ; his hair, equally long, and
not less white, streamed with similar smoothness
down his back and shoulders.   It was evident that
he was a person of very great age, yet his skin
was clear, of a pure white and red, and unmarked

by a single wrinkle. His mouth was small, and
wore a sweet expression, and his eyes were full of
benevolence. He carried a little staff, and a bundle
which probably contained a single change of raiment — it certainly could not have held more; and
he seemed like some venerable traveller, who had
an unconquerable desire for travel, and had learned
to narrow his wants to the smallest possible limits,
consistent with the superior claims of an intellectual nature.

"'Daughter,' he said, 'Peace be with you.
Can you give me shelter and food for the night?
I am a stranger, and would abide with you.'

"The heart of Matilda, like that of Carl, was
open as day, and the stranger most probably had
seen in her countenance that he would not be refused; for, even as he spoke, he prepared to enter.
He was not deceived in the person he addressed.
With a sweet voice, full of respect — for his venerable white hairs had impressed Matilda with a
proper and gentle awe — she bade him welcome,
and having closed the door — after giving a long
lingering look to the form of her husband, who
was rapidly passing from her sight — she led the
way for her aged guest, into an inner apartment.
There she spread before him the simple repast
from which the unhappy Carl had fled. The old
6*

man blessed the bread ere he broke it, and blessed the giver. He then ate heartily, and at intervals conversed with Matilda, who sat with him at the table, though she ate nothing. Her heart was too full of doubt and sorrow to suffer her to eat, and while her guest spoke, the tears gathered unbidden, and without her consciousness, to her eyes. He saw them.

"'Daughter, you weep—you are unhappy. Why is it—what is your sorrow.'

"'Alas! father, are we not born to sorrows. Is there one who escapes?'

"'True, my child—sorrow is human, and to grieve is the attribute of man, and perhaps his blessing. They are blest who can weep. God loveth those whom he chasteneth; for it is through trial only that we gain virtue, and through virtue only that we gain heaven. The untried are the unblessed, for then is the work harder for them, and the prospect of virtue more remote. Such, my daughter, is not your case. The fire even now is purifying you, and if you grieve, you do not murmur. Sorrow, like a goodly medicine that is to work for our healing, must be submitted to without murmuring. Whence come your sorrows, my daughter—let me know them. I have travelled much among men, and I know many of the arts of healing. I have some skill which I may boast, in curing those hurts of the mind which come from our indiscretions, and are to be healed by our humility. Let me know what grieves you, and hear to my counsel."

" 'I grieve not for myself, my father, so much as for one that I love — my husband.'

" 'You are married then ?'

" 'I am, and to one of the best of men ; but he is thoughtful even to sadness, and I fear that his thoughts are sometimes too vexing for his mind, which they very much disorder. Something troubles him very greatly even now, and before you came he went forth in deep anxiety, which it was painful to me to behold. He will be away until near midnight, or even after ; and when he returns, it will seem that some dreadful strife hath shaken him — his face will be pale as if with sudden fright — his eyes wild, staring, almost starting from their sockets, and his whole appearance that of a man almost distraught.'

" 'And how long hath he been troubled in this wise, my daughter ?' demanded the aged stranger.

" 'But a few days,' Matilda readily replied ; for there was something so encouraging in the appearance of the old man, that, although a woman rather disposed to reserve in her manners, she felt that she could have freely told him every secret of her bosom.

" ' But a few days—and before this time, he hath shown none of these habits?'

" ' None, father—none of this wildness and affliction. He hath been thoughtful ever, and fond of sad thoughts,—but he hath never been wild and stern as he is now, and never did he go abroad in this fashion after the night.'

" ' You tell me of one,' said the stranger, after a brief pause given to thought—' You tell me of one who hath done a sudden wrong, and whom a just conscience is smiting sorely; or, one, perchance, who is fond of his error, or, from a false and unseemly pride, who persisteth in it.'

" ' Oh, no, father—I cannot think it. Carl would never wrong human being. He is the most just and honorable of our village—that everybody says of him.'

" ' That may be, my daughter, but is there no wronging of God and of one's self—which is also a wronging of God, as it perverts the service of the creature from the place and power to which it is due. Can you tell me that Carl Werner has not done this.'

" Matilda tried to think, before she answered, whether she had mentioned her husband's name.

She did not recollect having done so, and yet the old man had pronounced it. Before she could resolve this thought or reply, the stranger continued :

" ' It is always a bad sign to see one, on a sudden, depart from a good habit, my daughter. You say that your husband seldom or never went forth at night, but always preferred to remain at home, until now.'

" ' Yes, father, — but it is with evident reluctance that he now leaves me. It is like tearing himself away that he rushes out of the house, soon after nightfall, and goes off I know not where.'

" ' To return miserable,' said the old man. ' To bring him back to an old habit, my daughter, is probably to give him the peace of mind which you say he seems to lack. Have you striven to keep him at home, my daughter, since you have seen the evil of this habit ?'

" ' I have, my father, but without success,' was the reply.

" ' You must do it,' said the old man with vehemence — ' you must do it. A good wife, who loves her husband, and is beloved by him, has a thousand sweet arts of persuasion which will not fail to procure from him her wishes. Your husband loves you.'

" ' Of a truth, I think it.'

" ' Then, my daughter, if you love him, you shall not fail to persuade him, if you seek to do it. You must keep him at home. He must not go abroad. These nightly wanderings make his infirmity. They prove that he is subject to some evil influence, which thus exacts his obedience, and imposes upon him this form of service. You, and you alone, can save him ; for, as the evil influence strives through the powers of hate, it can only be safely contended with by the powers of love. This is the war which is ever going on between the two great principles by which the world is divided. You must prove that the principle of love in your bosom is stronger than that of hate in the enemy of your husband. Can you prove this, my daughter ; for, unless you can, Carl Werner is lost to you forever, as he certainly will soon be lost to himself.'

" ' I can—I will !' cried the devoted wife, with terror and love both equally mingled in her countenance ; for the words of the venerable old man had deeply impressed her, and a something in his air and manner assured her that he was worthy of all confidence.

" ' I can—I will, my father—only tell me what I shall do—how work—what say.'

" ' Love needs no counsellor, my daughter, for

it is God's nature, and is by instinct wise. True love, I speak of; and not the idle fancies which the profligate and vain have misnamed love. If you love Carl Werner with a true wife's love, you will seek that he should be always with you — you will seek to make him happy. These are your present tasks. You must begin by keeping him from this wandering habit. He must not go forth again at night — for he flies from the principle of love, to pay homage to the principle of hate. Withdraw him from that foul worship, and he is safe, and you are both happy.'

" It would be needless to dwell upon, or to detail, the farther dialogue which then took place between the young wife and her venerable guest. It is sufficient to say that the longer she listened to to his counsel, the more she became impressed with its force, and with the necessity for its adoption. While she heard him she had no wish for sleep, and hours seemed to pass away like minutes until the clock struck the midnight hour, and she then grew more than ever alarmed at the absence of her husband. She was desirous of putting into use and exercise the advice which the old man had given her, and would have sallied forth, even then, to look after him, when the stranger dissuaded her from it.

"'Do you remain,' he said, 'while I go forth and seek him.'

"'You!'—she said—'no, father, you are too old and feeble, and your limbs are weary with the long day's travel.'

"He rose, as she spoke these words, and as he moved over the floor, she was answered. Where had those aged limbs acquired that strength and elasticity which they now exhibited?

"'But you know not where to seek him, my father.'

"He smiled; and she did not doubt, when she beheld that smile, that the aged man knew better where to find her husband than she did herself. He paused as he crossed the threshold, and bidding her be of good cheer, he blessed the house and departed.

XV.

"Meanwhile, what of Carl Werner? With a fearful instinct he proceeded, upon leaving his dwelling, to the place of meeting with the spectre. Vainly did he strive against the fascination which impelled him to seek the abbey. Why should he so wilfully seek that which was so full of torture?

He had now no wish to hear the revelations of the
dead — he had no thought, certainly, to profit by
them, when brought by one whose very presence
was so terrific; still less did he desire to owe his
knowledge to a source so foul and fearful. These
were his thoughts, nor his thoughts merely.
These were his frequent resolves throughout the
day. ' I will not go to-night,' his lips muttered
at all hours; yet, with the coming of evening, his
good resolutions failed him. A power which he
strove vainly to resist, drove him onward; and like
the criminal, reluctant yet compelled, he appeared
regularly at the appointed hour at the summons of
his tyrant. Carl felt that there was a judgment in
all this. He felt that it was a decree of heaven
against him for the unholy feelings and desires of
his heart. Yet, where, and when, and how, was
this to end? He dared not think! His knees
trembled beneath him as he put this question to
himself, and felt, with the increasing weakness
and misery of every moment, that it could end
only in his death.

" This conviction was despair. Despair has its
strength, but it is the strength accorded by a demon at a fearful price. The price was hope and
peace — the penalty was the loss of two lives —
the life of the present, and the life to come. Carl

felt that they were already gone, and all his
thoughts were now given to the demon. The
principle of hate grew active in his fears, and the
principle of love grew feebler and feebler, in the
continual decay of his hopes. The strife was not
only against Carl Warner, but it was against the
sweet young wife of his bosom. He felt it to be
so, himself, as he found himself continually laboring not to think of her.

" We need not say, that in the abbey that night,
the same hour of torture was passed by Carl, in
company with the demon, as before. The belief
that his friend was the victim and the slave of hell,
sent forth by the infernal monarch to perform a
duty which he dared not disobey, was the racking
conviction to Carl. Vainly he demanded of the
spectre to disavow the features he had assumed.
His prayer was idle. Would the principle of
hate yield up his chief vantage ground? As well
might he implore indulgence from that power,
whose only office is punishment. He raved to the
demon—defied his malice, and vainly flattered
himself that the passion which he showed to his
tormentor, was, in reality, a re-assertion of his virtue. Thus do men hourly chain themselves with
their own sophisms. The very tumult in his soul,
and the violence of his lips, as they sprang from a

feeling of hostility, were, in truth, only so many
tributes to the principle of hate. The fearless
calm, the gentle earnestness of love, were not in
his heart. It was rather a place of fears and strife;
and every moment of his paroxysm, increased the
number of avenues through which sin might enter
and perpetuate its sway. The conflict nearly destroyed the mortal. Almost exhausted, Carl
rushed from the ruins; and, this time, he left the
demon squat upon the tomb-stone, where he had
sat all the time of their conference, glowing and
grinning at the agony, and yelling forth his dreadful laughter, as he beheld the flight of the victim.

XVI.

"Carl was not permitted to reach his home in
peace. A group of revellers stood in his path
as he was about to enter the village. They
danced and sang at his approach, and soon gathered around him with tumultuous cries. They
sang in his ears the praises of revelry, and invited
him to join them.

" 'Be not churlish, brother,' was the cry —
' why cherish care? why mate with sorrow? why
deny thyself to live? The wine, the wine, boys,

and here's health and a fresh heart to our new companion.'

"Carl envied them their felicity; and their language, for the first time in his life, seemed sweet in his ears. Hitherto, he had led the life of an abstemious and wholly studious youth, rejecting utterly those noisy and spendthrift pleasures which are so apt to lead astray the young. He began to think that he had erred in his practice, and had been guilty of injustice to a class of persons who were a great deal wiser than himself. The torments which he had just undergone, prepared him for this way of thinking. He hesitated, murmured, looked vacantly around him, and they took him gently by the arm, and renewed their solicitations. Among the foremost of these, he now recognized the bacchanalian who had before assailed him. But he was not intoxicated on this occasion; and while he spoke with the words and warmth of a boon companion, his language was carefully chosen and gently insinuating. Carl began to yield; his eyes were already turned in longing upon the tavern—his feet were at the guidance of the individual we have just spoken of—in his thought, the indulgence of wine began to assume the appearance of a leading and necessary object: and in another moment the powers of evil would have made large strides towards the possession of their victim, when another hand pressed the arm of Carl Werner, and a gentle, but strange voice, in his ears pronounced the name of his wife.

" ' Matilda—she waits you, Carl—she suffers at your long absence. Will you not go to her ?'

" The old man whom we have seen setting forth from the house of the wife in search of the husband, stood at his elbow. He had come in time. His words operated like magic, and Carl broke away from his conductors.

" ' Matilda—my wife—my poor wife !' he exclaimed—' Yes—let me go to her.'

If the words of the aged man were so quick and powerful to move Carl Werner, his presence seemed to have no less an effect upon those who sought to lead the youth astray. They shrank away from the stranger with hisses, and though reviling him, they still fled. Carl was surprised at this, and the more surprised and horror stricken when he distinguished among the howls and hisses of the flying crew, the horrible laugh which had so much haunted him before. The old man took no heed of their clamor, but composedly conversed with Carl while they proceeded to the lodgings of the latter, with all the calmness and

7*

ease of one whom a confidence of superiority keeps
from anger towards an inferior, as certainly as it
protects from harm.

XVII.

"Carl felt better and happier in the embraces of
his wife when he reached home, than he had felt
for some days before. The principle of love was
reviving within him. The conversation of their
aged guest contributed largely to this improvement. They could not but acknowledge the influence which they could not but feel. Yet he
could scarcely be said to converse. His words
seemed so many laws settling doubts and silenc-
ing controversy. He spoke from authority — from
an authority, seemingly, even beyond that of strong
common sense and great experience. Carl was
surprised and pleased to find himself able to listen
to his words; and though the terrible strifes which
he had recently undergone were still busy in his
mind, he yet found pleasure in his new companion. Much of the old man's conversation seemed,
indeed, to be intended for his particular case. He
spoke of the 'various encounters to which mor-
tals were subject. The necessity of confidence in

heaven's justice — the willingness to wait — the readiness to endure. He then spoke of the principle of love as he had spoken to Matilda. He insisted upon it as sufficiently strong to withstand the opposite principle of hate, and to trample over it in the end. The conflict, he said, would be long and perilous, and it would be continued through nations and individuals to the end of time ; — patience, he said, and perseverance, prompted by the spirit of love, which is eternal, would be certain to achieve the victory. In the meantime, it would be necessary that the labors of love should be increased and strengthened. We should strive to love one another, as the best policy, and the noblest moral economy. Every falling off in our affections from each other, was a gain to the rebelling principle of hate, and kept back humanity from its hope of heaven. Every increase in the amount of human love, was a succor to the sovereign principle ; as much so, as, in the warfare among men, would be the accession of new numbers. To love one another is to conquer evil, for as evil toils through the principle of hate, it can only be successful over us, by engendering in our bosoms hostility to our fellows, and a general faithlessness of each other, which must produce hostility. To confide, should be the first lesson, as it is always the first and noblest proof of love!'

"This counsel strengthened Carl Werner and his wife, and made them both think. Carl felt calmer as he thought, and retired to his chamber with new and better resolutions. The old man prayed with the two before they retired; but though Carl knelt with the rest, he yet found it impossible to pray. He could only think, and his thoughts were confused, apprehensive, and not given, as he felt himself, to the sovereign principle of love. When he retired to his chamber, he resolved to pray alone; but he could not. He knelt by the bedside in vain. His tongue seemed to cleave to the roof of his mouth. His brain seemed to glow like fire, and he longed once more for the presence and the conversation of the aged man. He slept but little during the night, and when Matilda awakened at intervals, she heard nothing but his groans.

"The next day the old man sought an opportunity of conversation with Matilda in secret.

"'My daughter,' he said, 'your husband must not go forth to-night. You must exert all your strength—all the strength of your love; spare no prayers, no solicitations, but you must keep him at home. He goes to pay homage to the principle of hate. He must break his bondage. He must withhold his homage ; and he must prove that he renounces the hateful worship, ere the principle of love will come certainly to his aid. He will not find relief — he cannot be happy — till then ; and he must do this himself. We can do nothing towards it, save by our prayers, and these will be of little avail, until, of his own resolve, he breaks to you the secret of his sorrow. When he freely and voluntarily declares to you the trouble of his mind, he will find relief. To confide our wo to a beloved one, is to find healing. He must acknowledge this truth, ere he can hope for healing ; and it is a truth that he must teach himself. I warn you, therefore, unfold nothing that I have said to you, which shall move him to this determination, else it will be of no avail. We may tremble, but we must be silent; and if our fears become stronger than our hopes, we must then only resort to our prayers.'

" That day the old man gave Carl himself a lesson which had its effect in promoting the wishes of all, though, to the passing thought, it would seem to have no necessary connexion with the misfortunes of the latter. He saw him in a condition of stupor, sitting upon the threshold, and evidently unconscious of all things around him.

" ' My son,' he said, ' we do not all our duties when we have said our prayers. Indeed, we may be said to do none of them, if we do but this. Our prayers are offered that we may have strength and judgment to perform our duties rightly and thoroughly. The first of these is industry. The decree of God — one of the first — is one of the elements of religion. " Thou shalt earn thy bread in the sweat of thy face." He who prays merely, and toils none, is a hypocrite, and though he may deceive himself and his fellow men, he cannot deceive God by his professions.'

" ' Alas! my father — I would work,' said the unhappy Carl, ' but I cannot — I am sick — I am sad — too sad — too sick to work.'

" ' Hast thou tried, my son.'

" ' Of what use to try, my father. I feel that I should do nothing.'

" ' The will is the service, my son. God tasks not your service, but he receives the free tribute of your heart, and if the will is free to serve him, the amount of your body's service is of little regard. Try — let the will govern the limbs, and they will do much. Certainly, thy labor will lessen the troubles of thy mind, which, in most cases, spring from the tyrannous imbecility of the frame.

Try, my son — thy labors will avail thee much
more in thy sadness than all thy prayers.'

" Carl obeyed, and strove diligently to labor,
and though he did but little, yet he felt better from
what he did.   The old man conversed with him
while he toiled, and he gathered goodly counsel,
and pleasant consolation, from his words.   But as
the day waned, the agonizing apprehensions of
Carl were renewed.   The fascinating spells of the
demon began to work upon his mind, and his increasing disquiet became visible to his household.
At supper he was unconscious of the meats before
him, until the words of the aged guest aroused his
consideration, while he prayed for a blessing upon
the repast.   Carl gradually grew fixed in mute
attention as he listened to the terms of this prayer,
which was, in some respects, peculiar.   The old
man prayed that ' the fond husband might ever be
heedful of the affections with which he had been
endowed by the confiding wife — that he might
heed the meaning of her pale cheek, her tearful
eye, and laboring bosom — that he might never
estrange himself from one who looked so much, so
entirely to him, for countenance and comfort — and
that the ways of error into which frail mortality
was ever but too prone to fall, might never seduce

the regards of the comforter, from the weak but confiding heart to which they were entirely due.'

"Much more after this fashion was said by the old man, but these words had their effect. Carl looked upon his wife with eyes of closer inquiry than he had fixed upon her for many days. He saw, for the first time, that her cheek was pale — as if death had set his hand upon it — that her eye was full of tears — and that her bosom heaved with an anguish which her lips had never spoken. Her eye caught the glance of his own while he gazed, and she burst into a flood of tears — rose from the table — rushed to the spot where her husband sat, and threw herself at his feet. How dreadfully was he shocked by this movement! How bitterly did he reproach himself! He felt that he had been selfish — that, heedful of his own sufferings only, he had given neither eye nor thought to hers. He sank down upon the floor beside her; and he muttered broken words, imploring forgiveness. The venerable guest saw that the moment was come, when love was to obtain the mastery or forever fail; and without being seen by the two, he left the apartment. But his words had been deeply impressed upon the mind of Matilda, and she needed not his presence to prompt her in the performance of her task. She poured out her full heart to her husband, told him of her fears during his absence, of her sufferings as she beheld the sapping and overcoming character of his, and implored him, for the love which he had once vowed her, as earnestly as if she had lost it. Long and trying was their conference, and more than once the wife despaired of her object. But though she trembled, she yet implored, and the principle of love prevailed. The heart of Carl was touched — the seal removed from the fountain — and he poured forth, in her astounded but unshrinking senses, the whole strange and dreadful secret.

XVIII.

" He had scarcely done so, when he heard a tap on the window, as of one claiming admission. He started, he trembled—a guilty fear rose in his throat and choked him.

" ' It is he — the demon — the spectre !' he exclaimed, gaspingly.

" ' Bid him enter,' cried the old man, who had returned to the apartment without their perceiving either his departure or his entrance, and who seemed perfectly conversant with the whole narrative —

"'Bid him enter, Carl.'

"But Carl hesitated and trembled. He moved not; and Matilda rose to her feet.

"'I fear nothing!' she exclaimed — 'I will throw open the window. If it be the spirit of Herman Ottfried, he will not harm me. If it be other than his, it cannot. God be with me — for I will do it!'

"The voice of the old man arrested her, as she was about to do what she had said.

"'Daughter!'

"She turned, and saw that his eye rested anxiously upon Carl, and she then understood that the office belonged to her husband. She did not need to look upon him twice. He had been praying while she spoke, and he now rose.

"'No, Matilda — the task should be mine. I have looked upon the fiend before — I do not fear to look upon him again. Still less do I fear — having your eyes upon, and your prayers for, me.'

"A horrible yell of laughter reached his ears from the outside, and half unmanned him. He shivered all over; but just then the aged guest repeated these words, as if for himself.

"'The Lord is my strength, and my redeemer.

He is with me, and I fear not the evil one. Be of good cheer, oh, my soul, for in this is thy strength. Thou shalt prevail in the strife with thy enemy, even as love prevaileth over hate, and the spirit of God over the spirit of the devil.'

"With a single blow of his fist, Carl threw wide the shutter, and though his voice trembled while he spoke, yet the words which he uttered were distinct —

" ' Enter — if it be God's will — enter!'

XIX.

"The mocking spectre was once more before him — and the grin of malice and imagined victory was again visible upon his countenance, until he beheld the form of the venerable guest, still kneeling upon the floor, with eyes and hands uplifted to heaven, and seeming as if he beheld him not. Then his whole aspect was altered. His grin became a bitter scorn, and, though he still wore the exact features of Herman Ottfried, yet the whole expression was so changed to that of a hellish hate, that, even to the eyes of Carl, the likeness seemed almost gone.

" 'Thou here!' exclaimed the spectre, addressing the aged man.

" ' Thou seest!' was the reply.

" ' I see — but thou art here in vain — thy
prayers will avail him nothing — he hath bound
himself to me. My power is upon his pledge.
He cannot escape — he must meet me where I
will ; and when he forbears to come — when,
urged by such as thee, he presumes to disobey, I
will seek him with redoubled tortures, where he
hides, and tear him from thy very altars. Carl
Werner — I command thee. Come !'

" Carl trembled all over, and he felt an irresistible power dragging him forward. At this moment the old man spoke —

" ' His pledge shall be fulfilled — but not to
thee. Look, Satan! — God hath heard the prayers of love — and his messenger comes to release
the thrall of hate. Look ! — the pledge is re-
deemed ?'

" As he spoke, he pointed to the opposite corner
of the apartment, upon which his eyes had been
earnestly fixed, even while the demon was addressing him. There, visible to all, stood another
spectre, having the precise features of Herman
Ottfried, and the very expression which he was
wont to wear in life. The contrast between the

one and the other spectre, both having the same features, was prodigious! They represented different principles. The one had borne the features of punishment — the other came with the mild attributes of mercy. Alike in every feature, they were yet as utterly unlike as night and day.

" The demon put on a look of agony, mingled with hate and disappointment, as, with a howl and hiss, he fled from the presence of the spectre whose features he had worn for the purposes of hate, but whose glance of benignity and love he could not withstand. Howling with hate, he fled ; while the gentle spirit advanced into the apartment.

" ' Oh, brother, dearest Herman !' cried the sister, with a joyful accent, as she rushed towards him. She sunk down upon the spot where she would have embraced him, and her eyes beheld his shadowy form melting away, even like the last gleam of a lovely sunset into the distant shadows.

" ' Look to your wife, my son,' said the aged man — ' she swoons — give her help.'

" Carl raised his wife, and in a little while she recovered — but the aged man had disappeared. They never saw him again.

8*

'IPSISTOS.'

"With this—
I mix more lowly matter; with the thing
Contemplated, describe the mind of man,
Contemplating; and who, and what he was,
The transitory being that beheld
This vision,—when, and where, and how he lived."

Wordsworth.

'IPSISTOS.'

I.

WITH the first tokens of the gray dawning, and while yet the thin gray mists lay like a gauzy veil above the half-canopied mountains, the gates of the great city were thrown open, and the people thereof began to pour forth in mighty crowds. Like a swollen torrent, that forces its way over the barrier and broken rocks, they came roaring and rushing, less with the innate feeling of power than of enjoyment. A universal spirit of intoxication seemed to possess the multitude, and by tens, by twenties, and by hundreds, with wild and dissonant cries of mingling yet discordant voices, they pressed their way through the narrow gateway, and came forth clamoring upon the plain. The aged and the yet green in youth—wise, venerable men—devout matrons,—trembling and hopeful maidens,—and sportive childhood, that laughs and leaps, were mingling together, until, even ere the sun had yet risen, the vast esplanade in front of the city was covered with their forms. One mighty will seemed to move in every heart, and to unite all voices in a universal song, as if for some great deliverance. An hundred thousand tongues mingled in the strain, and the hills that surrounded them gave back the melody with a seven-fold echo.

"Lofty and beautiful is the temple that stands above the hill!" Such was the song of the multitude.—"Lofty is the temple on the high hill, and lovely is the goddess who sits in power therein. Let us to the temple, oh! ye people. Let us bow down before the goddess thereof, and bury our faces in the sacred dust that lies at her footstool. Let us put her feet upon our necks, and grow great by reason of our abasement. Let us carry the fatted lamb and the bleating kid, for sweet is the savor of the burnt offering in her nostrils, and she smiles when the flamen smites the heavy ox in the forehead, and his dying blood besprinkles her garments. To the temple on the hill, oh! ye people,—to the lovely goddess who dwells therein. Let us fly to her worship,—let us bring our offerings,—the fatted lamb and the calf, and the bleating kid,—let us twine about their necks the flowers that are in season, and hang their brows with clusters of the bleeding grape, that so we may show our love for the goddess and the priests, and our reverence for the white temple that stands lofty upon the hill."

And when these words were ended, the shouting of the far-stretching multitude grew great again, like the clamor of meeting winds and waters; and they ran towards the white temple that rose proudly on the high hill in the rosy light of the morning — the swift leading the way, and the strong rushing after, giving no heed to the cries and the groans of the feeble and the young, whom they overthrew and trampled in the fury of their flight. Well did they know that the goddess whom they sought would freely forgive the evil which happened only from the overflowing of their zeal in her worship. And many were the priests that did homage for that people around the altars of the goddess. And they prayed before her presence, that she would come forth and lend grace to her worshippers by the smile of her benignant countenance. And the multitude brought great store of gold and jewels, and with gifts of value rewarded those who served them in this wise. They brought bracelets for the arms of solid gold, and bright drops of amber and of pearl —

of jewels from the mine, and pale blue water-gems
rom the deep — to hang around the necks, and
fasten in the ears, of that sacred priesthood.　And
the holy men prayed steadfastly before the goddess for the multitude, and the goddess vouchsafed
to hear and to smile upon their prayers.　And the
golden gates of the temple were thrown wide, and
the multitude shouted anew by reason of their exceeding joy; and, in the madness of their devotion, many of them rushed towards the golden entrance, ere the priest had yet veiled the glory
shining from within; but were driven back and
blinded by the streams of excessive light which
encountered them as they came.　But soon the
gong sounded, which was the signal for the goddess to appear — and the guards that waited upon
the priests, with their golden lances, drove back
the impatient multitude from the path of the procession, which was to move towards the great city,
that it might be blessed with the presence of the
goddess.　Then, as the crowd gave way, came
forth the car of the sun, borne by the sacred ox,
whose horns, covered with gold, had each a glorious emerald shining thereon.　And the rays of
that golden orb dazzled the eyes of those who too
confidently beheld it, and they threw themselves
upon the sands as it came, and the sacred ox

pressed with heavy feet upon their necks. Then, perched upon a crystal bough, and borne by a lovely boy, whose long yellow hair floated in trained luxuriance down his back, came forth the milk-white pigeon, which bore the words of the goddess to her distant worshippers; and the boy that carried the pigeon was blind from his birth, and it was the eyes of the sacred bird that guided him in his progress; and sometimes, as he went, the pigeon would fly off from the bough to bear the words of the goddess to the priesthood, and at such moments the boy stood still. Next came one whose arms were bound to his side, and he was clothed in yellow garments, and he bore upon his head a crystal globe, which was the sign of eternity, and within might be seen a butterfly with folded wing, and this was the sign of immortality. He was followed by an hundred others, bound and attired like himself, and their bonds were a token that they opposed not the will of the goddess; and they bore the globe and butterfly by turns. As they advanced from the temple, the mighty and mixed multitude, which had fallen into sudden silence when the golden sun came forth, now, as suddenly, rose into clamorous rejoicing — the hills shook in their shouting; and, from the vast circle of the plain, the continued voices bore to the city

the glad tidings of the coming of the goddess.
Next came the slaves—an hundred ebon-dyed
slaves from Ethiopia—and they bore heavy cen-
sers of crystal; and ever and anon they scattered
sweet incense among the people. A girdle of silver cloth was wrapped about their loins, and they
wore a collar of silver, and a chain about the neck,
of silver also. A chosen band followed these, of
the youth dedicated to the priesthood; and they
wore no badges, and their garments were of the
coarsest woollen. After these came the sages, the
wisest and the most venerable among those who
had given themselves to the service of the goddess from their childhood. They wore long white
beards, and they were greatly reverenced among
the people by reason of their close neighborhood
to the goddess, and as they were the first to know
and to declare her irrevocable decrees. In their
secret abodes they had traced the history and duties of the heavenly bodies—had locked up the
niggard sciences in narrow cells, making them
servants, and denying them to that world which
they were intended to inform; but which, in its
inferior ignorance, might only have abused their
offices. To these succeeded the artificers, the
painters, the builders, the workers in fire, and the
secret properties of subtle minerals. Then came

the high priest, an experienced magician, than whom the great city knew none more wise and more in favor with the goddess. He stood upon the platform, which was of solid brass, upon which the throne of the goddess was raised. His robes were of sable, but under them might be seen a belt of purple and living fire. A serpent twined itself about his arm, and sometimes lifted its green head above the shoulder of the priest, whose hand grasped it by the middle. As he advanced, his presence announced that of the Deity, and was acknowledged by an astounding shout from the anxious multitude. The car of the goddess, itself a temple, now rolled heavily through the brazen entrance. It was drawn by the ponderous behemoth, whose hoofs were coated with silver, and whose forward step shook the solid earth over which he came. Around the car, a troop of lovely priestesses danced on feet that spurned the air, and their forms, flexible as light, melted and sunk away into continual and changing shapes of grace and luxuriance ; and tears of light gathered in the eyes of the young men of the multitude, as they looked upon their voluptuous involutions. These closed the procession, and as they passed from the brazen door of the temple, it shut, of itself, with a startling and tremendous sound.

II.

But there was one of all that mighty and mixed multitude, that felt not with the rest — that saw not with their eyes, nor measured the things he saw by their understandings. He came with them from the city, for he dared not remain behind, in that time of general jubilee; but his voice joined not with the rest in swelling the clamor of rejoicing. With slow steps and a sick spirit, he followed far behind, and his heart grew cold in his bosom, as he beheld their wild impatience, and witnessed the headlong fury of their devotion. Their cries stunned and troubled him, and the big tears gathered upon his eye-lashes.

" Beautiful, indeed," murmured Ipsistos to his own heart, — " beautiful, indeed, is the goddess, — lovely beyond the loveliness of woman, whom the keen eye of the builder beheld, where she lay buried in the bosom of the solid rock, whence his nice hand and searching instrument of steel, gave her release. With the fine touch of endowing art he removed the rude dints of the heavy masses which had lain so long upon her visage, and brought back the light into her features, and the

life which belongs only to expression, which had
been banished from them so long. In her temple
have the people raised her, and they behold in her
countenance nothing but perfection. In her they
see the embodied form of the universal and diffu-
sive truth, and they claim for her the possession of
a perfect beauty. But to me all the sweet conviction, which makes the heart confident in its hope,
and brings it peace, seems utterly denied. To
me she does not seem the true; neither, though she
is beautiful, can I esteem her the perfect beauty
which so immutable a goddess should be. She
wins not my heart when I behold her, — her charms
gather only upon mine eyes. With reluctant
hand I lay the first fruits upon her altars even as
I am bidden, but she knows that it is only as I am
bidden that I bring them, and though she smiles
upon others, she, methinks, hath a frown only and
ever for me. I pray to her for the blessing, and
she withholds it; yet wherefore should she withhold it when I pray only to be wise. Alas! I
inquire of these things in vain. The mists gather
more thickly around me, and when my brethren
cry loudest in rejoicing for the light which as-
cendeth, then, upon my sight, the darkness falls
more heavily than ever. My soul is sorrowful
within me. The prayer that I make returns upon

9*

me with the bitterness of rejection. Wherefore
should this be so? Wherefore, of all this multitude, should I, alone, be joyless and voiceless?
My brothers—they come back from the temple,
having the song still upon their lips, and the smile
still in their hearts. My sisters enter with laughter the dwelling of my father, though poverty sits
upon the hearth, and weeps because of the cold.
The smile of the goddess hath blessed them, until
they forget the withered and wrinkled grandsire
whom they leave famishing at home. Alas! for
me, when I see the burnt offerings and the fruits
upon the altars of the goddess, I think not upon
her worship, but upon his want. Wherefore
should the goddess need as a testimony of our
homage the waste of her own fruits, which had
else cheered the heart and strengthened the limbs
of age and poverty. Wherefore — ah!"

A terrible voice sounded in the ears of the
youth :

"Ipsistos!"

He shivered with terror as he looked up. The
car of the goddess was rolling onwards, and her
eye was fixed upon him with a glance that seemed
to search and freeze his soul. The voice of the
chief priest, a second time, reached his ears in low
accents, unheard by any but the youth.

"Ipsistos! The eye of the goddess is upon thee. She looks into thy heart. She beholds thy discontent. Beware!"

The youth sank upon his knees, and clasping his hands above his head, he bowed his face to the dust while the car passed onwards.

"Alas!" moaned the stricken youth as the crowd rolled between him and the priest, "I am doomed!"

And there he lay prostrate and desponding, while the elated crowd, forgetting all wretchedness of their brother, felt only the triumph of that power which permitted them to kneel!

III.

"Ipsistos!" said the sacred messenger of the temple, touching the melancholy youth with the spiral rod of his office, — "thou art called."

"Whither?" demanded the youth.

"To the temple!" was the answer of authority.

"I obey! — I follow thee!" said the youth, with fear and trembling.

"It is well. Bermahdi awaits thee."

And Ipsistos prepared to follow as he was commanded, and his heart was full of fears; for had he

not heard from Bermahdi that the goddess was a
jealous goddess – quick to see the falling off of
the worshipper at her altars, and terrible in her
punishments for every departure from the law as
it is written.

"Fare thee well, my father," cried the youth,
—"I am commanded to leave thee for a while."

"Who commands thee, my son?" said the venerable man.

"Bermahdi."

"Ha!—Thou hast sinned, my son. Thou
hast sinned against the goddess."

"I fear me."

And the old man trembled, and fell upon his
face, as the favorite of his eyes departed.

IV.

Ipsistos stood in the presence of Bermahdi, the
white-bearded, and his heart sank within him.
Wondrous was the chamber in which he stood,—
strange were all the objects and aspects around
him. The roof of that chamber was vaulted like
the sky, and studded with a thousand stars. Clouds
hung aloft, now rising and now receding, and
from them, at moments, Ipsistos could see the keen

and cold eye of the goddess looking down upon
him. The vault was upborne by gigantic figures
of black marble, that moved around him in a constant circle ; and, ever and anon, a heavy instrument of sounding metal told the progress of the
never stopping hours. A burning mirror stood
upright against the wall, and Ipsistos beheld within it the constant progress of things as they concerned the people of the goddess. And he saw
himself within it, even he, Ipsistos, but the figure
paused not, but disappeared at the waving of the
hand of Bermahdi. The chief priest sat before a
table of red porphyry, on which the characters and
signs of the seasons were inscribed. Instruments
of strange form, and to him, unknown uses, lay
upon the table. Bermahdi was a magician of
unbounded wisdom, and his studies were as various as the faces of the stars of heaven. He seemed,
even then, to be toiling in the divine arts of astro-
logy ; and when Ipsistos regarded his stern but
venerable aspect, and saw the strange instruments
around him, and beheld the books in languages
unknown, gathered with great pains and at wondrous cost from the remotest nations,—his awe,
mingling with the apprehensions which his soul
felt at the summons of the sacred messenger, be-

came a sort of terror, and he trembled in the presence of the holy man.

"Ipsistos!" said Bermahdi, "approach!"

And as the youth drew nigh to the table an hundred serpents sprang forward, with hissing fury and open jaws, ready to devour the intruder; but, at the word of Bermahdi, they crawled back to the slimy baskets where they had lain coiled in sleep, and offered no farther interruption to his approach.

"Ipsistos! thou had'st been doomed but for thy youth. Thou art poor and feeble, else thou had'st perished. Had'st thou been high among the people, — high of birth and fortune, — this night thou had'st fed the sacred serpents of the goddess, whom, in thy secret thoughts, thou hast contemned. Wherefore is this madness, Ipsistos? Thy brothers are devout worshippers, — they come with glad hearts and full hands to the temple, — they bend with reverence before the altar, — they heed the words of the goddess, and question not her laws. But thou dost not, Ipsistos. In thy vain soul thou hast asked — 'why is this?' With thy shallow understanding, thou wouldst judge the decrees which are written for the world. Why dost thou not believe, and trust, and do homage like thy brothers?"

"Alas! father! wherefore? It is from thee

that I would have the answer. Thou art the favored of the goddess, — I pray thee implore her that she tell me, why I am other in spirit than my brothers?"

The holy man frowned gloomily as he listened to these words of the unhappy youth.

"What, boy! — wouldst thou demand of the goddess, why is this, and wherefore is that. I tell thee that thy presumption prays a sudden judgment upon thee. Thy vain thoughts are working out thy doom."

"Be merciful, father. I would not offend with my presumption. I would school my heart unto humility. It is to know the right only that I ask to know at all. My prayer is for wisdom only."

"Thy prayer is insolent, boy. What! shall we be all Magi. Shall wisdom be a thing to cast in equal lots, — shall we demand of the goddess to be other than we are. Foolish and audacious boy. Thou must learn to obey, ere thou art wise — to trust those who are the born counsellors of the land, — who have authority for judgment from the goddess. Hast thou lived so long, and art thou still ignorant of her power? Hast thou seen nothing to shew to thee the might which she has, beyond that of thee and all thy people, and which she puts forth daily through the hands of those who tend upon her altars? Hast thou not listened to her oracles? Does she not foretell the plague which kills, the tempest which desolates, the ruler of the city who shall best serve its interests, the coming of the enemy whom ye fear? Does not her power dissipate the enemy, stay the plague, repair the city, provide the ruler? Is thy people prosperous or not?"

"Alas! father, poverty sits upon the hearth of my sire, and the flesh is shrivelled upon his aged limbs. The city is prosperous, but my father lacks bread for his hunger, and he hath no raiment against the cold."

"And what of this, idle boy. What is the pleasure or the life of one, or even of a thousand, in consideration of this great argument. Thy life is but a span at best, and something must end it. The goddess that gives thee life, hath surely a right to prescribe its laws, its limits, and its vicissitudes. Believe this, and thy father suffers little ; but even this pretence shall be denied thee for complaint. Thou shalt carry from the temple this night the food which shall make him strong, and the garments which shall bring the blood back into his aged limbs. Will that content thee?"

"I will bless thee for it, father."

"And be true and joyful in thy worship of the goddess?"

" I will strive — with all my soul and with all my strength, I will strive," replied Ipsistos.

" Thou shalt, or it shall be worse for thee. Lo! — Here shalt thou see the power of the goddess. Thou shalt behold sights never yet vouchsafed to thy people. Look! What seest thou?"

And, as he spake, the magician uttered a word of power, and the brooding cloud rolled away from overhead, and the sun hung his broad and burning shield above the eyes of Ipsistos, though, it was then the mid hour of the night, so that they were confounded and darkened by the blaze. And when he looked again, the cold pale moon was shining in its place.

" Thou hast seen the mansions of the sun and moon, — they are ever present to the goddess, and visible at her command. Some of her power she will now confer, even upon thee, that thou may'st no longer doubt of her worship. Grasp me that wand of ebony which thou seest upon the edge of yon fountain."

The youth did so, and of a sudden it became a serpent in his grasp. He flung it to the ground, and it once more became a wand of ebony.

" Thou seest; but that is not all. Thou shalt cross unharmed upon those fiery bars over which it is written that every devotee should go. But

first put off thy sandals, and put on these sacred
shoes which have been hallowed upon the altar of
the goddess."

The youth put on the shoes as he was directed,
and at the same instant a part of the wall opened
before him, and he beheld a bridge of fire-bars
which spanned a cavernous hollow of vast extent,
in which he could see nothing, but from which
there came a continual roaring like the evening
anthem of the sea. The youth shrank back from
the trial, but Bermahdi encouraged him.

"Fear nothing!" he said, — "For thou wearest
sandals which have been hallowed by the goddess." A voice, soft but clear, sad but melodious,
reached his ears an instant after, which repeated
the words of encouragement.

"Fear nothing, Ipsistos. There is nought to
harm thee!"

"What voice is that!" cried Bermahdi, with
looks of unfeigned astonishment.

"Was it not the voice of the goddess?" said
Ipsistos, — "methought it was she who spoke."

"Ay, it was, — it must have been!" cried
Bermahdi, — "it must have been the goddess.
Thou seest, my son, that she loves thee. Fear
nothing."

" Fear nothing, Ipsistos," said the gentle voice once more.

And the heart of Ipsistos was full of joy as he heard it, but the countenance of Bermahdi was troubled. The youth felt tears of pleasure steal out upon his cheek, for the tones of that sweet speaker sunk like music and peace into his heart. He feared no longer, Boldly he advanced upon the blazing bars, which, to his great wonder, gave out no heat. And when he had passed over the bridge to the opposite side of the cavern, he stood in the presence of the goddess. But her looks were lovely no longer. Anger blazed in her eyes, and her lips were distorted by reason of the passion within her breast.

" This is strange," said Bermahdi, — " strange that she should frown upon thee, Ipsistos, when thou hast passed through the first trial of the noviciate. Thou wilt become a noviciate, my son."

" Wherefore, father ?"

" See'st thou not that she frowns upon thee ?"

The youth was silent.

" Ha! dost thou refuse ?" cried Bermahdi.

" No, no — I refuse not — but suffer me to think upon it, my father. I am not yet worthy — I would meditate upon the wonders I have seen."

" Thou shalt! Go now in safety. The path

is clear. Nothing shall harm thee on thy way.
But see that thou hast early thought upon this, my
son. Thou hast thought, already, too much or too
little, and thy error must be amended. Remember ! the eyes of the goddess are upon thee."

Again the gentle voice whispered in his ears.

"Fear nothing, Ipsistos;" and when he looked
upon the statue of the goddess, her features were
convulsed with anger. A stream of fire seemed
to issue from her eyes, and with a shivering fear
that ran through all his veins like a sudden ague,
the youth fled from her terrific presence.

V.

He fled, but the gentle voice still lingered in his
ears, and as he left the portals of the temple, its
tones of encouragement were repeated.

"Fear nothing, Ipsistos. I am she whom in thy
secret soul thou lovest ; and I am powerful to pro-
tect thee. Let the tyrant rage ; he shall not prevail against thy thought, nor against the true worship which is already living in thy spirit. He may
cast thee into a dungeon — he may load thee with
chains — in his brute anger he may buffet thee,
and with his keen thong he may cover thee with

stripes ; but of a surety shalt thou live through all, and glorious shall be thy triumph in the end. Fear nothing, Ipsistos — for, so long as thou keepest my voice in thy ears, so long shalt thou live, and so sure shall be thy great victory over thy enemy. Thou shalt tread upon his neck, Ipsistos."

And the youth grew bold to speak to the voice as he hearkened to these grateful words, and he said —

"And how, oh, sweetest whisper of the night — thou that stealest upon mine ear like a music from heaven, and sinkest, blessing, into my heart like a balmy food thereof ; — how am I to keep thee forever nigh to me ? Tell me, that I may not lose thee."

" By keeping me ever in thy heart, as thou dost now. By seeking me as thou hast ever done !"

"How ! blessed voice — have I ever sought thee before, when, until this hour, mine ears remember not to have heard thee."

" Thine ear hath not heard me, Ipsistos, but day and night, even from the hour of thy birth, have I spoken to thy heart. Thou hast truly called me a music from heaven, and a balmy food thereof. I am both — for I am that principle without which

10*

no music could be such in the ears of the good, and no food could give nourishment."

"What art thou!" demanded the trembling youth.

"Truth! Doth not thy own heart teach thee?" was the answer.

"Alas — but it did not!" replied Ipsistos.

"Of a surety it did, Ipsistos, from the first moment when thou felt'st that thou could'st not love the creature which thy people worship with a wild and headlong idolatry. Thou could'st not think her beautiful, because, in thy own heart, thou beheld'st a yet lovelier image."

"And shall I see thee with mine eyes, oh, thou, whom my soul worships," cried the youth, sinking on his knees, and lifting his hands together, as if the object of his adoration stood even then unveiled before him.

"Yea, thou mayst if thou so wishest it; but I warn thee, Ipsistos, in the hour that thou regardest me with thy human eyes — in that hour shalt thou surely die. Art thou ready?"

Prostrate in the dim night, the youth sunk down in silence. But in silence he remained not long.

"Give me to behold thee," he cried aloud to the voice — "Give me to look upon the blessed and beautiful features of that divine being who is in my lifted heart, and death shall be welcome. Gladly will I embrace it, for thy sake, sweetest and loveliest of the dreams that have won me from sleep, and made life, itself, a dream."

"Thou art bold, now, Ipsistos ; but when death looks upon thee with his grim aspect, and claims thee for his own — "

"Even then will I be bold !" cried the undaunted youth.

"When thou feel'st his steely grasp upon thy shoulder !"

"I will laugh upon him — I will defy him with a song in thy praise."

"When he drags thee to the roaring blaze, and the burning fagots crackle and hiss around thee ! — "

"Ha ! — must it, then, be so !" cried the youth, shuddering, and covering his face with his hands.

"Perhaps !" said the voice. "Wilt thou not then shrink from thy faith ? Wilt thou not then forswear me ? Wilt thou not deny that thou hast seen my face, and hearkened to my counsel, as thou dost now ? Death is terrible, Ipsistos !"

"I will not ! Though death be terrible, I will not shrink from the danger — I will not deny thee, nor forget the faith which I have pledged thee, and which I pledge thee here."

" And yet 'twere pity, Ipsistos, that thy youth should perish thus.   Think of thy old grandsire."

" Ah !"

" Thy brothers and thy sisters."

" Alas! they need me not.   Did they love me, and need me more, I were less bold, perchance, in this encounter.   My grandsire hath not many days of life, and even were I gone from him, but little were his loss therein.   The promise which thou makest me, moves me more than these fears and losses which thou describest unto me.   Give me to look upon thy divine presence, and see the beauties which are there, and I am ready for the stake, and for the cruel executioner.   Tell me, shall I not behold thee now ?"

" Not yet !" cried the voice.   " Thou could'st not see me now, even if thou would'st, and I were willing to suffer thee.   There are scales upon thine eyes, which must first fall off.   There is yet a fetter upon thy thought which must be broken ; and thou hast learned lessons in thy mind, which must be unlearned, ere thou can'st behold me.   Yet shall I not be utterly unseen of thee.   Even now, if thou lookest keenly, thou may'st behold a faint shadow of my person beside thee, and, as thou strivest to behold me and hearkenest to my voice, my features shall grow clear unto thine eyes, — thy flesh to my touch,—thy soul shall be filled with my spirit. But I warn thee, in that time thou diest. Thy danger begins with thy knowledge, and in the moment of thy greatest victory, shalt thou perish."

And the youth gazed as he was bidden, and a shadowy form passed beside him, and the stars yielded in their places, and all things swam before his sense. When he looked again, the shadow and the voice were gone.

VI.

"I bring thee food, my father," said Ipsistos; and he placed before the aged man the viands which had been given him by the high priest of the temple.

"Ha! my son,—be thou blessed among the sons of men, as thou art blest and beloved by thy sire. Whence got'st thou these meats—this bread, and the luscious grapes which thou puttest before me."

"From Bermahdi."

"From Bermahdi!—Blessed be Bermahdi—blessed be the holy temple—forever honored the goddess therein."

And the aged man kneeled as he said these
words, and the young women and the sons kneeled
also, all but Ipsistos.

"How, my son, — wherefore kneelest thou not
with us ? — would'st thou withhold thy blessings
and thy thanks ?"

"My thanks have been already given, my father.   I have spoken with Bermahdi in the temple."

"In the temple ! — Ha !   have I been so blessed in my old age as to behold a son of mine who
hath had admittance to the temple of the goddess.
Let me look upon thee, — let me kneel to thee, my
son, for of a truth the goddess hath greatly favored thee."

"Kneel not to me, — look not upon me, father,
but eat of the meats sent thee by Bermahdi.   I
am blind, and weak, and not worthy of thy regard."

"But thou saw'st the wondrous things of the
temple, my son, — the giants which are there fet-
tered beneath the feet of the goddess, — the sacred serpent that speaks at her bidding, — the holy
owl of counsel, and the ape, the ox, the emer-
alds —"

"I saw many things, my father, of which I
took little heed."

"Little heed, my son, — little heed !   What

meanest thou? Thou took'st little heed of what
thou saw'st in the temple! What! thou wast
frightened; the wonders overcame thee? Thou
wert blinded and astonished by the blaze. It was
enough, my son, to confound thee. It is my
wonder how thou saw'st any thing, — how thou
cam'st alive from that glorious presence. But the
goddess strengthens whom she loves, and by these
tokens, Ipsistos, thou art beloved of the goddess.
Grant it be so, — grant it be, — then would my
gray hairs go down to the grave in peace."

But far other was the prayer in the heart of Ipsistos, and he turned away in silence from the ad-
miring gaze which the doting old man fixed upon
him. And the brothers and sisters murmured
among themselves, and marvelled much at the
favor of the goddess towards Ipsistos. And they
said, " Wherefore is this favor of Bermahdi?
Have we not been the first ever to bring our offerings to the temple? Though they were mean, yet
we brought of the best in our store; and our prayers and songs were the loudest in the presence of
the goddess. And was not Ipsistos a loiterer by
the way-side, and when did he raise voice or song
in honor of the temple? The goddess hath surely
meant, for one of us, the favor which Bermahdi
hath so blindly bestowed on him."

"And what said Bermahdi to thee, my son?" demanded the grandsire.

"He would have me in the service of the goddess," replied Ipsistos.

"Ha! thou dost not say it!" cried the rejoicing father.

"He! a servant in the temple!" cried the eldest of the brothers. — "Ha! ha! ha! This is a folly, if not worse. Thou speak'st idly, Ipsistos, — I trust thou dost not wilfully declare thy falsehood."

"I speak the truth only, my brother," meekly replied Ipsistos.

"I will not believe it," cried the rest. — "Wherefore should they make thee a servant in the temple. What hast thou, — what art thou? Thou art mad, Ipsistos. Thou art poor, and what is thy father? Made he not bricks for the city, even for those who are now living and can declare his craft; and what is thy craft, but the same, Ipsistos, which thou art only too idle to follow."

"True, true, Ipsistos, — thou must surely err in this," cried the old man, sorrowfully. — "Wherefore should Bermahdi choose thee to serve in the temple. Thy brothers speak but reason; — and yet, my children, Ipsistos hath never yet told me other than the truth."

" And it is the truth only which I tell thee now, my father. Bermahdi hath commanded me to serve in the temple, in season to become a priest."

" A priest!" cried the elder brother in amazement.

" A priest!" cried they all, in wonder at the apparent madness or gross presumption of the youth.

"Thou a priest!" said the elder brother. — " What should make thee a priest, when thy awkward hands let fall the garlands ere they reach the altar."

"Thou a priest!" exclaimed the eldest sister. — " How would thy long arms look in the holy garments? — they would drag about thy heels like a great mill-sack."

" Only to think," said the younger sister, the favorite of Ipsistos, " only to think of making thee a priest, Ipsistos, when I have ridden upon thy shoulders a thousand times."

" Nay, flout not thy brother, my children — ye make me sad as I behold his sorrows. Flout him not, though, in truth, my son, thy story is most strange."

" Yet true, my father. Do not these fruits speak for me? They are from the altar of the temple."

This could not be denied. The brothers and

sisters of the youth had seen them carried to the temple. And the old man marvelled much upon the mystery; he could not yet be satisfied of his son's truth, for when had the son of a maker of brick, been called to such sacred office. Meanwhile, a grievous suspicion of Ipsistos grew in the hearts of his brethren. And they whispered among themselves, and their evil thought came to the ears of the father.

"He hath stolen these things from the altar of the goddess. Of a truth he hath committed sacrilege."

And with these words the aged man dashed from his lips the untasted viands, and his jaws were distended with the horror of the thought.

"What hast thou done, Ipsistos? My son, my best beloved, wherefore hast thou done this thing?"

"They wrong me, my father, for, of a truth, I am not guilty of this base crime. The fruits were given to me, for thee, by the hands of Bermahdi."

"Swear it, by the temple and the goddess! and I will believe thee," said the father.

"It will not then be a greater truth than it is now, my father. Believe me, as I tell thee, but I will not swear ;" and he rushed from the dwelling as he spoke these words.

" He is guilty !" cried the brothers with joy, but the old man hung his head in shame.

" Alas !" he cried, " wherefore was I born to this dishonor."

And the sons hurried away to the chief priest, to declare the theft and to restore the consecrated fruits ; but the old man lay upon his face at the door of his habitation, and would not be comforted.

VII.

" And ye say," said Bermahdi, to the brethren of Ipsistos, " ye say that your brother is no true servant of the goddess — that he bows not in reverence at her altars — that he gives not his soul with the fruits which he offers — that he loves not her high places, nor the holy priesthood that minister before her ?"

" Of a truth, we say it," replied the envious brethren.

" Ye are wrong," answered to them the high priest, " ye know not the heart of your brother.

What though he worship in another fashion from ye, still is he a devout worshipper. I have seen into his soul, my children ; it is no less pure than yours. The goddess hath chosen him for her altars, and ye are no less honored in her choice than is he. Hence was her gift to him, for thy grandsire, of the fruits and meats which he carried home to your habitation. Do him no injustice, therefore, by your ungentle thoughts, for truly do I believe him honest. Yet, I would not, that ye should hold me unnoteful of your zeal. Ye shall give it employment. See that Ipsistos lacks not, nor falls short, in his flow of service. If ye deem him laggard — if ye notice any falling off in his outward devotions, though it may import no loss of love within — yet bring me true report of his backslidings, that I may counsel him providently, and tutor him unto the good work which is ready for his hands. And, as ye have so fully shown your zeal for the altars of the goddess, ye shall have like share with your brother of the fruits therefrom. Take ye, and eat, and bear ye home to your grandsire, of the fruits which remain unconsumed. And let this be a sign unto ye, that ye are all the care of the goddess, and your house henceforward shall be the abiding place of blessing and abundance. Go ye now — remember well what I have

spoken in your ears touching the devotion of Ipsistos, and come to me and reveal in secret what
ye may misdeem of his thoughts and misdoing ;
for though I believe not that your brother is erring, yet the best of us falter in our walks of duty,
and the strongest sink at times under a weakness
of sinew which should make them sorrowful and
ashamed. Go now, and the blessing of the goddess be upon ye."

And the brethren of Ipsistos went away, with
hearts of rejoicing and with hands of plenty ; and
they rejoiced not more because of the favor of the
goddess than of the charge which had been given
them to be watchful of the doings of their brother.
And in their hearts they abused the counsels of
the holy Bermahdi, for, whereas, he had given it
in charge to them to report on the backslidings of
Ipsistos that he might be providently led back into
the fold of the temple, and they took his words as
a direction to find evil in his wanderings, and to
prove the flaws in all his performances. And
those that Bermahdi had named as zealous for the
goddess, grew to be zealous spies upon the failings
of their brother ; and in their hearts they said —

" Bermahdi will punish Ipsistos if he goes aside
from the path leading to the temple. He means
11*

not to counsel but to condemn, for is not the goddess a jealous goddess, and does not her breath
destroy the offender, though it be a sin of his ignorance only, and his first sin. Of a surety will
she destroy this brother, whose pride of heart lifts
him above us, and who, in a vain conceit of soul,
thinks to be wiser than his father. Well—he
shall not be missed when Bermahdi calls for the
victim."

Thus communing, they returned to the dwelling
of their father, and their hearts were filled with
wrath when they found that their grandsire now
loved Ipsistos more than before, and took but little heed of the abundance of fruits which they had
brought with them from the temple. And he called
upon them to rejoice with him, and to implore blessings upon their brother, saying—

" Verily, Ipsistos, my son, thou art my best beloved, and the favorite of the goddess. Join with
me, my children, and give praise to your brother;
for he hath cheered our hearth with the blessings
of heaven, and hath smoothed my passage to the
tomb. Blessed of the goddess, Ipsistos, be thou
also the blessed of thy father and thy brethren."

And the brothers murmured among themselves,
and, more than ever, they hated him by reason of
the exceeding love of their father. All hated him

but the young maiden, his **sister**, the youngest of
all, whose name was Damaina ; and she flung herself upon the neck of Ipsistos, and called him her
dear brother, and shed tears of joy and reverence
upon his neck.   And the brothers turned from beholding her, and they spake together apart, and
they asked of each other how best they should obey
the commands of Bermahdi, and seek out the backslidings of Ipsistos.

VIII.

But the youth heeded not their doings, nor imagined the feelings in their hearts.   In his own a
sweet sadness prevailed, a shadow from his searching thought, that moved over strangest places,
and wandered into worlds far beyond his arm.
His life strayed afar from the accustomed paths of
his boyhood; for the voice was ever in his ears,
— the voice whose tones were a perfect melody
which he might not resist, — and they led him
away from the crowded places, and they tempted
him to fields which had ever been forbid.   In the
presence of his brethren he had little comfort, and
his mood found no fellowship among those who
had once given him most sweet society.   With

sad eyes, but without complaint, did his grandsire
behold the shadow that was upon the youth, and
the friends of his boyhood, and his young sister
Damaina, the best beloved of all, reproached him
loudly for his desertion.   But Ipsistos only sighed
to them in return ; and he walked apart to hide
the tears which were in his eyes, though his heart
was softened only with a becoming joy.

" They chafe with me now," he said to himself
in musing, " but will they chafe with me when I
bring them to a sight of her whom my soul loveth ;
when they look upon the divine light of her eyes,
and feel the blessed tones of her voice sink like a
balm from heaven into their hearts."

And a holy pride filled his bosom as he thought
that he should bring those who loved him to such
superior enjoyment.   And he followed the voice ;
and came to a mighty wood which was dusky with
gigantic forms, each having a double shadow.
And he wandered away among the shadows 'till
they grew like a bannered army around him, and
he laid himself down at their feet, and they hung
above him, and he thought unutterable things.
But the thoughts gave him pain at length, for they
came like pictures that pass rapidly in the uncertain light before the eye.   And he failed to know

them or perceive their offices. Vainly did he strive to fix them with his revolving mind; but they fled from him, looking behind them as they fled, and showing him glimpses of their beguiling features. Through the dim mazes of his mind he struggled to trace their flight, but others came between, and so he was confounded ; and he prayed for counsel and help from the voice, and even as he prayed he slept.

IX.

And the sleep of the youth was troubled, and strange visions prevailed in his slumbers. A thousand streaming lights, that seemed half girt with a drapery of cloud, danced around him in the closing void. Then, as they departed, mighty shadows rose even from the earth at his feet, and they floated away from before his sight, only to give place to other and mightier shadows yet. These came in sable and timed array, — a gorgeous company of trooping forms, having strange shapes that yielded to the light; and they bore solemn banners that went trailing through the sky. Then, a mightier form than all the rest, — a shadowless form, full of light that yet gave none forth, —

came following after, and Ipsistos saw that it wore
a crown upon its head, and yet the face beneath
it was hidden from his straining gaze.   From the
midst of the crown rose a broad tongue of flame,
that waved to and fro among the clouds by reason
of the rapid motion of the shadow.   And the
shadow stood still when it hung above the spot
where the youth was sleeping, and the tongue of
fire which was upon the crown ceased to move in
the wind.   And, even as he looked, Ipsistos beheld a sheet of flame pass out from the tongue,
and it fell from cloud to cloud, and it parted them
all, and it rested upon his own forehead.   And at
the same moment the mighty shadows which had
hung around him, with brows of dusk and threatening, took to flight with a rushing noise, and the
youth could hear them scream while they flew, as
if pursued by a mighty terror.   And a bright
light, like the bursting of a meteor, fell around
him, and he heard a voice like that which had
counselled him before, louder and more piercing
but not less musical, that stopt his ascending spirit, and riveted his wandering thought.

"Arise, Ipsistos, thou art called unto thy office.
Thy sleep is over.   The light is around thee,—
the promise of the day.   Tarry not, but come."

And a shivering fell upon the sleeper as he heard these warning accents, and marvelled at the increased power of the voice: and his heart sunk within him, not as he felt unwillingness to serve as he was bidden, but because he despaired of doing his service fitly, by reason of his inability. And he said to himself as he awakened, —

"Now, wherefore should I be chosen for this mighty work? Am I not the son of the brick-maker, — is not my extraction mean, and, of a certainty, I have not been taught in the mysteries of the college, nor in the divine languages of past ages? I am but mocked with this sweet delusion, — I do but cheat myself with the vanities of mine own heart."

And the voice came to his ears again from among the pale groves, that lay behind him in the silence of their birth-hour. And the voice was sweeter in his ears than ever, and it was strong also. And it cheered him with words of encouragement.

"Wherefore should'st thou doubt of thy own fitness for the work of her whom thou lovest? I tell thee, Ipsistos, that the servant is honored by the service, and the work of truth takes no honor from the proudest and the wealthiest, — nay, not even from the wisest in the land. Thy humility

is becoming in thee, and is the best wisdom thou
canst bring to my service.   But thou must be bold
too, and confident, — humble, because thou well
knowest how little is thy knowledge in respect to
truth, — bold, as it is thy purpose to have knowledge of the truth only.   Come to me in this valley of shadow, — build here thy altars ; and hither bring the constant offering of thy heart, not of
thy hands.   Come."

And the voice melted away in his ears, and the
youth heard nothing but the murmuring of the
wind as it streamed upon its way among the
branches of the bending lindens.   But he rose as
he was bidden, and went forward to the silent
dwelling of the shade from whence the sounds had
arisen.   And, as his feet faltered, by reason of his
uncertainty, the voice whispered him on his true
path, and strengthened him to come.

X.

And Ipsistos sought the pale groves where the
voice dwelt, and he entered them with fear and
trembling.   A mystery hung over them like that
which hangs above the mansion in the dreams
and darkness of the night.   And a sound, like

that of a complaining water, that keeps a cease-
less travel through all hours, and murmurs as it
has no rest, filled the groves ; and he heard no
other sound. And he prayed that he might heark-
en to the voice again ; and it fell upon his ears
like a string smitten by the winds at a far distance ;
and the youth lay upon his face and trembled, for
the words of the voice had no meaning to his ears.
But while he lay upon the earth, and moaned in
his grief, he felt the breathing of a warm air
around him ; and when he looked up, lo ! a bright
eye was gazing down upon him from the leaves of
the tree above his head. And he saw nothing but
the eye ; but he straightway knew it for the eye of
the voice whose blessed sounds had sunk so deeply
into his heart ; and he murmured a fond prayer of
thanksgiving for the blessing which had been
vouchsafed him, even according to the promise of
the voice in his behalf. " Thou shalt not see me,
— thou canst not see me, even if thou wouldst and
I were willing, — until the scales have fallen from
thine eyes, and until thou hast unlearned much
which stands in the way of thy knowledge now ;
but" — and with glad heart, did he remember the
promise of the voice — " when thou givest up thy
whole soul in my service, then shall my features
come out before thee." And the youth prayed

fervently for the consummation of the blessed promise, for his heart was full of the beauty of the
eye which looked down upon him from the cloud,
and with the sweetness of that melodious voice
which had cheered him and led him on his right-
ful path.   And, even where he stood, did he build
an altar to the voice and the eye, and morning and
evening did he steal away from the press of the
city to offer up his homage to the divine spirit
which he so much loved.   And the more bright
did the eye appear unto his eyes, and the more
musical the voice to his heart, so, in the like degree, did the countenance of the goddess worshipped by his people, put on frowns.   And he now
saw what he had not seen before, that in her face
were the shadows of many passions of evil which
belonged to men.   Was not her eye fixed upon
him with hate, and did she not smile upon those
whom he well knew to be base and unworthy, as
they brought her rich offerings which the hand of
violence had despoiled from the weak, and the arts
of the cunning had inveigled and taken from the
confiding.   "And can the goddess be true?" asked Ipsistos of himself, "whose judgments tally not
with justice. Shall she smile upon the wrong doer,
and share of the spoil which comes of the wrong.
Is mere power, which the wild colt hath in his

madness,—a power to destroy,—the sign of the
perfect goddess ?   Shall my heart receive her
laws for truth, and grow fond of her smile, when
it approves of violence, and the sin that spoils and
strikes ?"   And the voice in his heart answered
" No ;"—and with free footsteps he hurried away
at evening to his lonely worship in the forest ; and
while he prayed, a halo of light gathered about
his brow, and, looking upward, he beheld the perfect face of the benign and blessing spirit which
he sought.

XI.

He saw the perfect face, and never did the vision of his dreams, or the imaginings of his hopes,
seem half so divine or beautiful.   The face looked
forth from a cloud, the edges of which were transparent with a golden light ; and as the lips opened
to speak, the words came forth in visible rays,
and the sounds fell upon his heart in melody, and
the air blossomed with odor.   And the light from
her lips fell upon his own, and his soul was lifted
into the highest hope, when he heard the tones of
his own voice, and felt that they were like hers.
And he gave praises aloud to the divine spirit that

looked down upon him, and he spake in song, even in the holy song of the prophets who had perished for the truth. And the voice told him that his song was sweet in her ears, and worthy of her altars. Till the night cloud settled down upon the pale groves where he worshipped, did Ipsistos linger in the place which became so holy to his heart; and wings lifted his feet that night when he returned to the humble dwelling of his father.

Wings lifted his feet, for he had a divine purpose in his heart.

XII.

" What !" he exclaimed, " shall my eyes only look upon this gracious presence ? Shall this blessing come to me only ? Is there none worthy to share with me this joy, — to partake with me of this glorious truth, — to live with me in the triumph which is promised me, and which must be mine !"

And he mused thus by the hearth of his aged grandsire, and he saw not that the old man slept in his seat. Then came to him Damaina, the best beloved of all his sisters, and she threw herself around his neck, and she said to him, —

"See, our grandsire sleepeth, Ipsistos,—he will fall from his chair,—help me to bear him to his couch."

And in his heart an instant voice cried,—

"Thou art she who shall share with me this blessing,—even thou, my gentlest Damaina; for thy heart is pure, and thy soul loveth the truth, and thou hast reverence for the aged, and clamorest not in the high places with the presumption of ignorance. Thou art worthy of this joy, Damaina. It shall be thine."

And he lifted his sleeping grandsire to his couch of straw, and that night he said nothing to the young maiden. But when the gray dawn had risen to his summits in the east, then did Ipsistos come to the chamber of the maiden, and he cried to her with a persuasive voice, and these were his words,—

"Come forth, Damaina, my beloved. I would have thee go with me. Now, while the day is young, and the hours are blessed with the vigor of a night's repose, go forth with me into the forest. I will show thee some precious flowers, and thine eyes shall behold a loveliness which thou hast never seen before!"

And the maiden came forth with the step that

12*

dances to the music of a gentle heart, and a youthful but pure fancy.

"Whither dost thou lead me, my brother? But I care not whither. I know thy walks must be the loveliest, for well I know how much thou seekest the things which are so. Lead me, then, my brother, —I will joy in the flowers which give thee joy; and my heart shall drink of the same sweets with thine."

And Ipsistos rejoiced greatly because of the fondness of the maiden.

"If she will love the things which I love," he mused to his own soul, "she will soon see the glories which delight mine eye."

And he led her to the pale groves where he worshipped; and he shewed her the simple temple which his hands had built. And he bowed himself before the temple, and he called upon the maiden to do likewise.

"Wherefore, my brother?" asked Damaina.

"It is the temple of the true goddess, my sister. I have beheld her divine presence even among these trees. She will be with me anon."

But the maiden trembled, and forebore to kneel with her brother, by whose words her soul was confounded.

"What altar is this for the goddess, — what

true goddess is this of whom thou speakest, Ipsistos?"

"She who is truth, — whom the truth alone makes beautiful, — makes strong, — makes immortal."

"Ha! my brother, — but these words of thine are strange to mine ears. Have we not long worshipped this goddess? Stands not her white temple upon the high hill that looks down upon the city of our fathers."

"No! her temple is in the white heart! It is with you and with me, my sister, if we blind not ourselves wilfully, and refuse not to yield our hearts to the truth. Stay, — hear you not her voice?"

"I hear nothing, my brother, but a faint murmur as of a wind that sighs among the decaying trees."

"It is her voice! Kneel with me, dearest sister, and the melody shall sink into your heart."

But Damaina did not then kneel by reason of her great surprise. But Ipsistos knelt, and he prayed with a passionate plea that the sweet voice should fill the ears of the sister whom he loved. And when the maiden heard his prayer, her heart strove within her; and she mused to herself, and said, —

"Surely this brother loves me, — surely he is wise and good;"—and even while he prayed she sank down on the turf beside him, and her prayers were joined with his. And the sound, which was but a murmur in her ears before, now took a shape of music, — faint at first as the first plainings of the harp troubled by the rising wind, but gathering into fulness at last, and swelling into expression that will not be restrained. The heart of the maiden trembled within her, but it was with a new-born joy, and not with any fear, that it trembled; and she began to love the voice with a love like that of Ipsistos, though, to this time, she had no knowledge of the blessed spirit which he had seen, save by the gentle tones with which she had spoken to her ears. Yet, all the while that she prayed beside her brother, the face was looking down upon them both, though the maiden beheld it not. And the eyes of Ipsistos were opened, and he beheld the form of the true goddess, even as she had promised that he should behold her. And she smiled upon him, so that he felt the wings growing upon his shoulders, but her words were grave in his ears.

"Thy prayer is granted thee, Ipsistos, — thou hast seen me according to the desire of thy heart.

But thy hour is at hand, my son, — thou hast but little time to live."

And the youth bowed his face to the earth, and his heart spoke in prayer.

"Art thou ready, Ipsistos? The death-angel will demand thee soon."

And the youth replied sadly, but without faltering, —

"Joy of divine love, I am ready."

And the lovely image faded away in a sweet smile from his sight, and the music died away among the pale groves; and the two, Ipsistos and Damaina, rose from the place where they had worshipped; and their souls were lifted into thought, so that neither spoke as they took their way, with slow feet, back to the habitation of their father. Yet the words of the voice to Ipsistos came not to the ears of Damaina, neither did his lips reveal to her the doom which awaited him.

XIII.

And towards evening the two went again to the place of their secret worship. But this time they went not in secret. Eyes were upon them that regarded not the object of their devotion, and hearts were busy to find evil in the things which their hearts desired. The brethren to whom Bermahdi had given it in charge to heed the backslidings of Ipsistos, followed with cautious footsteps upon his path, and beheld the place where he worshipped. And they took heed that he bent himself down before the altar which his own hands had raised, and that he prayed to other than the goddess of the temple. And they hurried to the chief priest with the tidings, and he gave them a rich bounty and much praise for their zeal in his behalf. And he bade them keep secret what they had seen, and seek out more knowledge yet of the doings of Ipsistos. And they were spies set upon their brother, who told the chief priest of his outgoings, and followed him from place to place. But nothing did they say of Damaina, the sweet maiden, who bowed with her brother before the strange altar of his worship. And nothing did Ipsistos know of the doings of his brothers; and he gave little heed to his fears, that counselled him to be cautious in what he did. For the spirit of truth which he worshipped, worked within him, and a fire lighted up his tongue. So that when the elders, and the chiefs, and the rulers of the people, were gathered together in the high places, he could not be kept from speech, and he came to where they were assembled; and he penetrated into the high places, even among the mighty men of the city, the famous in arts and arms, the sages and the law-givers. And he cried to them with a loud voice, and all fear had utterly gone out of his heart. And he told them of the wonders which his eyes had seen, and his ears had heard, even of the wonders of that new goddess which had vouchsafed to smile upon one so lowly. And he prayed that they might give heed to his counsels, that they might be blessed also by her countenance. And he would have led them to his place of worship, even to the pale groves where he had raised his altar; but they mocked at his madness, and marvelled at the fondness of the youth.

And they were astounded, and said, one to another —

" Who is he that speaks to us with so bold a voice — is he not one of the dust-carriers ? — wears he not of the blue which is the cloth of the laborer ? — is he not of the suburbs — the son of the brick-maker ?"

And they drave him out from among them, and they shut the door against his face.

XIV.

Then, Ipsistos, with a heart sore for his people, went into the market-place, where were gathered together many of his own condition, and to these he cried aloud, and he prayed that they might give ear to his tidings, and he promised to show them strange things. And they were angered when they beheld him on the eminence, and hearkened to the words of his exhortations. And one said—

"Is not this Ipsistos, the son of the brick-maker — and shall one of our own sort claim to be wiser than we?"

And another cried—

"The mortar is even now upon his jacket, yet would he talk for the magi."

"Where should he get this impudence," cried a third, "to speak to us in words of counsel? Were we not boys together—have we not often played together on the same hill-side?"

"I know him well; he liveth in our street — he is a fool that dreams — let us stop his mouth."

Then came one from Bermahdi, the high priest, who whispered in the ear of a huge man whose anger was greater than the rest, and these were the words of his speech —

" Thrust him down, brother, he is insolent ; — doth he pretend to be wiser than us ? — thrust him down, I tell you ; — it shall be good if we do so."

Then said another who came from Bermahdi —

" He hath reviled the goddess, whose white temple is upon the hill — thrust him down — let the grass grow in his mouth !"

" Stone him !" cried a third.

And the huge man, whose name was Brassid, lifted a rock and flung it at Ipsistos, and the rock smote the youth upon the ear and sorely wounded him. And Ipsistos fled from the wrath of the multitude ; and he fled, not from fear but from sorrow, as he beheld many among the multitude with whom he had played even when a boy. And he had a purpose in his flight, and he fled towards the pale groves where he had raised the altar. And the multitude pursued him, and they reviled him and stoned him as he fled. But when the youth reached the groves he paused in his flight, and he turned full upon the multitude — and his eye was lifted, and he beheld the goddess whom he worshipped, looking down upon him from the cloud. And the sweet voice spoke in his ears —

" Ipsistos — thy hour is come !"

" Let the hour be blessed by thee, oh! image
of divinest joy, and thy servant hath no fears. He
is ready."

And he laid his hands upon the horns of the altar, and he looked out upon the multitude. And
he began a song of thanksgiving and of praise,
though their voices were bitter with revilings. And
they rushed upon him where he stood, and they
tore him from the horns of the altar. With a
blind fury they set upon him, and the strong men
seized each of them a limb.   And Brassid was the
man who bade them do violence upon him.   And
they dragged the youth to and fro, and they rent
his limbs apart, and scattered them asunder even
while the life struggled in his bosom.   And when
they had done the deed, they were confounded,
and knew not what they had done.   But Brassid,
the strong, who was of a mean craft, he laughed
to scorn the confusion of the multitude.   And
with loud cries he rushed upon the altar which Ipsistos had raised with his own hands, and he would
have torn the altar from its place, but a sudden fear
seized upon him.   For a bright eye looked out
upon him from the cloud, with a look of exceeding sorrow; and the sounds of a sad voice came
upon his ears like a passing wind ; and these were
the words of the voice —

" What! ye have slain your master — he who hath wrought for you; and now would you destroy his work? Go! — but come to me at evening."

And none saw the eye, or heard the voice, but Brassid, and, for a brief time, he was too greatly astonished to speak. And the people would have rushed upon the altar even as he had done, but he stayed their fury:

"Enough! Wherefore should we pull down this pile which is but of wood, and the work of him whom we have destroyed. Let it stand, in token of his folly."

And he led the multitude back to the city, but the voice went with him.

XV.

And the aged man, the grandsire of Ipsistos, died that night by reason of his exceeding grief; and the house of the brethren was the house of mourning. But Damaina, the young sister of Ipsistos, she stayed not to join with them in the song of lamentation. Her heart was with Ipsistos, by the lonely altar, among the pale groves of the forest. And though it was a fear of the wrath of the multitude that kept the brethren away from seeking his mangled remains to give them burial, yet no such fear stayed the footsteps of Damaina. And she went forth from the dwelling when no one beheld her, and with a sorrow that was beyond any dread of what the vengeance of man could do, and she sought out the place of worship in the forest, even among the dusky shadows of the night. And lo! when she came to the spot, a bright halo was shining above the altar. And wherever a limb of Ipsistos had fallen, there also hung a silver light ; and by this token the maiden well knew that the lovely goddess smiled upon the purpose which was in her heart. And the maiden gathered up the scattered remains, and she looked about for a place to lay them ; and even while she looked, the earth opened before her at the foot of the altar, and a flame, like a flame from heaven, came down and hung above the place. Then did Damaina see the meaning of the goddess whom her brother had loved, and she laid his bleeding limbs therein. And the earth closed over them when she had done, and she prayed with a fond heart above the grave. And her prayer was accepted, and she saw the bright face looking down upon her, even as it had looked down upon Ipsistos ; and by this sign did the maiden know that the blessing of truth was growing perfected in her heart. And while she kneeled before the altar she heard the footsteps of one approaching, and she would have risen in fear, and fled from the place, because of the night. But the voice of the goddess commanded her to stay and fear nothing.

" He who cometh," said the voice, " is a worshipper like thyself. He will do thee no manner of harm."

And it was Brassid that came; he who led the multitude against Ipsistos ; and the maiden trembled when she beheld him in spite of the promise of the goddess. But Brassid approached the altar with a trembling greater than her own. And the strong man humbled himself with his face in the dust ere he drew nigh unto the altar. He had no strength in his limbs because of the guilt in his heart, and he prayed like one who repenteth and is full of sorrow for his misdeeds. Then Damaina, the maiden, had pity of his sufferings, even though he smote her brother, and she prayed to the goddess in his behalf. And he cried, —

" Who art thou that pleadest for a wretch like me. Know'st thou not that blood is on my hands, — even the blood of the good and the innocent ?"

Then the maiden answered him, saying, —

" I am the maiden Damaina, even she, the best beloved sister of Ipsistos, whom thy hand hath

13*

slain; but if thou weepest for that deed, shall I not forgive thee, with a heart as tender of mercy as thine own? Bear witness, oh, beautiful goddess whom my brother loved, bear witness that I forgive this unhappy man, — even from my inmost heart do I forgive him."

While thus she prayed before the altar, the pale groves were lighted up with a sudden glory; and the two beheld the bright face, and the lovely features of the goddess, and her words came to them in authority. And she bade the man, even Brassid who slew Ipsistos, draw nigh to the altar, and when he came as he was commanded, and bowed by the side of Damaina, lo! it was the form of Ipsistos that stood between them, — and the image of the youth smiled sweetly upon him, even upon Brassid his murderer, and his words were these in his ears:

"Thou hast driven me from the work which was assigned me, — it is commanded that thou labor to the fulfilment thereof. Go, therefore, and the smile of the goddess be with thee; — in my blood shalt thou find a cement which shall build a stronger and a higher temple than the white temple upon the hill."

And Ipsistos spake nothing to Damaina, but

he looked upon her with a smile of blessing and
love, and so passed from her sight.

XVI.

And from that hour a power seemed given unto
Brassid to work great things. And he went
among the people of his craft in the market place,
and he taught them, so that they hearkened with
reverence to his voice. And the people came to
hear him from all quarters of the city, and after
hearing him they went away sad and thoughtful.
Day by day, and night by night, without weariness and without fear, did Brassid teach along the
highways, of the wonders which he had seen, and
the greater wonders which he had heard, and a
power was given to him of the goddess, so that
whoso came to hear, though it were in scorn only,
remained to do homage to the wondrous truths
which he brought, and followed him, by reason of
this homage, whithersoever he went. And the
numbers increased daily of those who followed him.
Then did the chief men of the city hold counsel
with the priests of the temple upon the hill, how
best to overcome this preacher of strange doc-
trines. And they sent persons against them with

authority to seize and punish. But the multitude
rose up in defence of Brassid, even as they had
risen against Ipsistos at his summons, and they
pelted the servants of the temple with stones, and
they ran furiously upon the temple. And they
dragged the goddess from her throne, and they
drove forth the priests from within it. And Brassid bade them smite the head from the false goddess, and drag her carcass in the dust. And they
tore the white temple asunder, so that one stone
stood not up against another. And when this had
been done, then did Brassid bid them bring the
white marble of the temple to the pale groves
where Ipsistos had built his altar, and they raised
a temple loftier than that upon the hill, and they
raised it even over the grave of Ipsistos whom they
had slain. And in the temple over against the altar there descended a divine form from heaven,
but over the face thereof hung a bright and shining veil; and on the veil was written these
words :

"To those, only, who, like Ipsistos, love me ere
yet they have known me, my veil shall be uplifted."

And the people built a high monument to the
memory of Ipsistos with the huge stones with
which they had slain him; and Brassid wrote the

inscription upon the monument, which was as follows :

"IPSISTOS !
we, who hated the truth, slew him
because he loved it :
May the truth teach us better knowledge
of our friends, so that we cut not off our own
heads !"

But Damaina, the sister of Ipsistos, beheld nothing of these things. They saw her not after that hour when the goddess had given it in charge to Brassid to complete the labor of Ipsistos. And they raised for her a tomb beside that of her brother, but left open the door thereof, as thinking she might yet come. But to this day she came not.

THE STAR BRETHREN.

THE STAR BRETHREN.

I.

"I will come to thee, at midnight, dear Anastasia — with life only will I fail thee."

These were the parting words of the enamored boy; and the tones of his voice, not less than the language which he used, spoke for his deep devotion.

"At midnight, dear Albert," was the reply.

"I live not till then!" said the youth, passionately; "and, if thou meet me not, Anastasia — if thou fail me — "

"Fear me not!" was the low but emphatic interruption of the maiden. "In life or death, dear Albert, I am only thine. I will not fail thee."

The leaves of the grove parted, and by the pale glimmer of evening the two might be seen taking their farewell and fond embrace. She, a tall and slender maiden, lovely as the light, and softer than the new born zephyr ; and he, manly and strong, yet young — having a frame of the most perfect symmetry, and a face full of beauty and expression. A fond, sweet kiss, a parting word and sigh, an earnest and longing glance of rapture — and the lovers separated.

They had not, however, been unseen. The eyes of jealousy were upon them, and the gloomy and fierce Wallenberg — a suitor for the hand of the damsel — had watched them throughout the interview.

"At midnight !" he muttered, as he saw the youth depart. "It is well — I will be there also." And he shook his hand after the departing form of Albert, and his brow was covered with a cloudy anger, which sufficiently denoted the terrible thoughts of his mind, and the malignant feelings which were working in his heart. Yet Wallenberg was a nobleman of high birth, and renowned for deed of valor and great achievement. He was not less so, for his great family estate and wide possessions. These had commended him to the family of Anastasia D'Arlemont, with which he was connected. They all knew him for a coarse, rude, rough-handed nobleman ; yet, as the terrors of his claws were calmed in gold, he was thought

no unfitting match for the gentle and shrinking
Anastasia. But she trembled at his approach, and
it was with a pang like death that she learned how
far his suit had met with the approbation of her
parents. Her attachment to Albert was unknown
to them, and to have made it known, would, she
well knew, avail her nothing. The passionate
persuasions of her sanguine lover relieved her
from the difficulty before her. He had persuaded
her that her only hope was in flight — in flight
with him. There was nothing so terrible in that.
Would she not have died for him ? Could she live
without him ; and what was life, with such a bear
as Count Wallenberg. Albert found but little
difficulty in convincing her reason, through the
medium of her heart — the medium through which
young damsels are most usually convinced. At
midnight, then, she was to fly with him. Such
were the resolves of the lovers; but Wallenberg
resolved otherwise.

Albert of Holstein was even then a student in
one of the German universities of the time, the
name of which is unnecessary to this narrative.
He was, at the period of which we write, just entering his eighteenth year. Until his sixteenth, he
had been under the guardianship of a good, but
weak and misjudging mother. While yet an in

fant, he had lost his father, who had fallen in a domestic feud with some rival baron, occasioned by
a difference of opinion on some matter of great
importance or of no importance at all, which had
suggested itself to them for discussion, while over
their cups. The son—Albert—but for a mind
and temper naturally excellent, would have been
utterly ruined by the various and misconceived indulgences of his surviving parent. Nature, however, who is not often strong enough for so trying
a toil, resisted the mother long enough to save the
son from utter ruination; and, when sixteen years
of age, he was ready to go to college. After the
usual preparation, he was admitted into one of the
leading universities, where he soon had occasion to
test for himself the propriety of that course to
which he had so imprudently been subjected. It
is not our object, however, to analyze or dwell
upon the impressions of his mind under the new
changes of his condition — affecting, as they must
have done, the whole structure of his early habits,
and pruning and converting, as it were, the dead
branches of excess into a new and fresh capacity
of life. It is enough to say that he rapidly threw
aside the follies of habit and of thought which the
error of his mother had engendered. The resources of his own mind — a case not very common—

.enabled him to contend with, successfully, and finally to counteract, the thousand mistakes of a foolishly fond parent, and a cringing crowd of domestic parasites.

II.

The night came — a sweet night of many and bright stars — a night for secret, and sacred, and stolen love. But it was not a night for love only. It was a night for hate, also, — for jealousy and murder. There was one who watched for the coming of Albert as anxiously as did the gentle Anastasia ; but it was with not such sweet and fond regard as that which filled her devoted bosom. With the darkness he stole into the silent groves which had been assigned for the meeting, and there waited for the hour and the victim. He had no scruples at any crime — his hand had been often imbrued in blood, which was not always shed in battle — and he was resolved, at every hazard, to remove his rival. He had seen enough in the brief interview which he had witnessed, to feel that, however secure he might be of the preference of the family, he was very far from the hope of a like

14*

preference in the estimation of the maiden, while
Albert lived.   It was the natural error of a wretch
so coarse as Wallenberg, to imagine that he would
be more successful when he should have slain the
youth.   The poor maiden despised him ; though, as
he was favored by her parents, she dared not give
open expression to her disapprobation and scorn.
She was compelled to submit in silence which
seemed satisfied.   Perhaps, she would not have
so readily consented to fly with Albert, but for the
tyranny of the union they were about to force
upon her.   The necessity of the case would seem
to justify her fatal resolution.   The suit of Albert
had been denied, and the language of denial by
her parents had been also that of contumely and
reproach.   There was no hope for her but in flight ;
and the preparations of the lovers were secret to
all but Wallenberg.   As we have seen, his jealous
eyes had watched them — his keen ears noted their
arrangements, and now, his keener knife was ready
to prevent them.   This sort of remedy was characteristic of the time.   The strong arm carried out
the strong word, and justice, which is now a matter of calculation and cunning, was then a thing of
muscle and brutality.   The murderer lurked in
the shadow of the groves, and the lover, impatient
for his prize, stole hurriedly through their reces-

ses. His heart was elate with its hope, and his footstep was that of joy. He had almost reached the place assigned for the meeting—a close bower of sweet shrubs in the centre of the garden. But the foe and fate lay in his path, and he was not permitted to reach it. He heard the rustling of the bushes.

"Dearest,—I am here," he murmured at the sound.

"And I am here!" was the fierce word of Wallenberg, as he plunged the cruel weapon into the bosom of the youth;—"this, boy, for thy presumption."

The only word uttered by the unhappy lover, was the name of his mistress; and he lay in the sleep of death at the feet of his murderer. Wallenberg stole away in silence when his felon deed was done; satisfied that his own hope grew strong in the annihilation of that of his rival. He knew not the heart of Anastasia.

III.

How slowly passed the hours to the maiden, while she waited for the coming of the youth. From the lattice, long and anxiously had she looked forth, listening for the dear accents of his whispering voice ; and when the clock tolled forth the full hour of midnight, impatient to behold him, she stole hurriedly down into the garden, treading its flowery mazes, but seeking him every where in vain. Her heart already began to fill with those thousand mysterious fears, and apprehensive forebodings, which are natural enough to a German maiden, when she fancied she heard a sigh. She followed the sound, and something seemed to float in the air before her. A gentle breath moved the leaves overhead, though elsewhere a universal stillness prevailed. The sigh was repeated — the breathing zephyr still guided her from above, and when it ceased to move, the lifeless body of her lover lay at her feet. With a single shriek, scarcely less lifeless than himself, she sank down beside him, and was only aroused to the consciousness of a greater misery by a terrible voice which sounded in her ears.

" Away with her !" cried the furious father, — " take her home — remove her from my sight."

She clung to the inanimate form, which could no longer return her fond caresses.

" You shall not — no ! no ! I will not leave him. I will cling to him to the last."

But what could her strength avail against that

of the brutal retainers, assisted by the bloody Wallenberg. They tore her from the corpse with unmeasured violence.

" He is yet warm !" shrieked the maiden—"he is not dead—I may yet save him—he will hear my voice. Oh! leave me—leave me with him, I implore you."

" Home with her, I say," were the words of the implacable father, which silenced her entreaties. She shuddered to behold the malignant and savage exultation which were impressed upon his features as he spoke. With the sight, a fearful fancy gathered in her brain. She suspected him—her own father—of the cruel crime, and this suspicion increased her misery. The true assassin, looking on the while, remained unknown. Inquiry in a little time, having labored without success to find the criminal, forbore its task ; and if, at any moment, public suspicion rested any where in particular, the object was one quite too high for the arm of public justice.

IV.

Meanwhile, the corpse of Albert was removed to his former lodgings, and from thence to the

family vault in the country. But a strange report
—none knew whence—came to the ears of Anastasia. It was whispered that Albert of Holstein
was still alive. The story went that a skilful physician and careful hands had kept the spark of
life in his bosom, and that hopes were entertained
of his final recovery. But these hopes, though
they inspired new ones in the heart of Anastasia,
were for a long time illusive, and, perhaps, injuri-
ous. They kept her mind in a state of feverish
inquietude, and prolonged, if they did not increase,
the sickness at her heart.

But little time was allowed her, however, for
idle meditation upon fancies such as these. Count
Wallenberg pressed his suit, and would not be denied. In vain did the maiden plead for time —
for a brief indulgence to her sorrows. At that
early period in the history of civilization, parents
did not often trouble themselves to give ear to the
tastes and desires of their daughters. They did
not, in the present instance; but with the most cruel
disregard to her complaints and prayers, they decreed her to the great bear, her wealthy lover.
They doomed her to the sacrifice, and the day was
appointed for placing the victim before the altar.
We may not speak of the anguish of Anastasia on
being instructed to prepare for the nuptials with

Wallenberg. She felt that it would be far easier to die. But, hopeless of any aid from without, and having no succor or show of mercy from within, she prepared to resign herself without struggling to the fate which now seemed inevitable.

It was only a few weeks after the death of her lover, when this scarcely less cruel doom was uttered in her hearing. She fled to her chamber, desperate and desolate. She knew not where to turn for consolation or counsel. It was midnight. She threw herself down before her window, and wished and prayed for death. The very associations of memory, so full of pleasure and joy as the reality had been, now brought her infinite pain. They told her what she had enjoyed, but they also told her what she had lost, and lost for ever. She felt that it would be sweet then to lapse away into forgetfulness, and, fleeing from the pressure and the care of life, rejoin her departed lover in the dwellings of the blessed.

Musing thus, and hopeless of all things and thoughts, she starts and trembles. A sudden terror is upon her. Her blood freezes in her veins — her very heart grows cold. What is it that she hears — what is it that rises up before her sight?

Well may she start and tremble. The faint and exquisite tones of music which now seek her ears are such as she had long been accustomed to hear from the lips of Albert. The words are those of a familiar song, and the tones cannot be mistaken. They breathe of the same sweet passion — they speak the same blessed language. It is Albert's voice and music, and Albert must be at hand. Breathlessly, and half fainting, she lingered and listened to the strains. She did not dare to move — indeed she could not — while she heard them. But soon they melted away in distance, and the winds only remained sighing mournfully through the lattice. Her frame seemed fastened — frozen to the ground; and her terror, becoming insupportable at length, with a shriek she rushed to the innermost recesses of her chamber, and burying her head in the thick drapery of the couch, strove, in this way, to fly and hide from those strange and terrible surmises which were fast gathering in her soul.

But the strange and startling minstrelsy pursued her even there, and its fascinations proved too powerful for her mind to resist. She braved all the terrors of her imagination, in the hope again to hear it. With the approach of the next midnight she again sought the lattice, and listened impatiently for the returning strains. They came at last, obedient to her senses. The same sweet, mysterious air, rose swelling upon the night wind, and was borne, as it were, directly to the window where she sat. The tones were full of the warmest melancholy — faint, but full — strange, but sweet — mysterious and vague, but as familiar as if they had all been learned in childhood. She was no longer terrified; and, obeying an impulse which she now found irresistible, and having no fears, she gently undid the lattice, and looked out with far-searching eyes among the trees of the garden. Nor did she look in vain. She beheld a form retreating away among the thick crowding trees, so nearly resembling that of her departed lover, that she involuntarily uttered his name. She was answered by a sigh — so mournful, so deep, that it seemed to reproach her for the indifference of her grief — for her consenting to the bridal sacrifice which had been decreed by her father. Her sorrows burst forth afresh with this thought, and she was convulsed by her emotions. She lost all guidance of her reason at that moment, and called upon Albert deliriously.

Had her voice indeed so much power? Had the deity spoken from her lips, and was it in truth her lover who now stood before her? Fair and

manly as when at first she had beheld him, she
beheld him now.   He looked even lovelier and
nobler than ever.   No trace of his hurts was perceptible.   He was alive, and utterly uninjured.
She grew faint as she surveyed him.   She trembled with a feeling of awe, lest, at that moment, she
should be standing in the presence of a spectre.
His eyes, though clear and intelligent as ever,
were sad, and full of a solemn expression.   They
looked the divinity of wo — such an expression as
might well belong to a fallen and defeated deity. A
mingled feeling of love and adoration, which she
stove vainly to restrain, filled and inflamed her
heart. How gentle were all his tones — how soothing his words — how tender their utterance. How
sweetly did he assure her of his existence — of his
continued love for her, even while that existence
was doubtful.   He had been in deep extremity
from his wounds — on the verge of dissolution,
from which he had been saved only by the marvellous skill of his physician.   The moment of his
recovery brought him once more to the feet of her
without whom the skill which had saved him would
have been rejected.   He had risked all danger
once more to see her — to hear from her lips that
she was not lost to him yet — that she would be
none other than his.   How easy to give that assu-

rance, — how sweet to receive it.   Long did they linger in the sacred and silent garden, in fond communion, with no watcher but the stars, and no thought but of that true and blessing love which they seemed to smile upon and sanction.

But the difficulty of escape from the approaching bridal with Wallenberg distracted the maiden, in the midst of all her new-born hopes and pleasures.   She had poured into her lover's bosom all the sorrows which had troubled hers.   His composure satisfied and reassured her.

" Fear nothing," he said, " I shall not lose you. I will save you from this hated bridal.   You shall be mine, Anastasia — mine only, believe me."

" I do — I do," she repeated, fervently.

" Be ready, then, as I shall counsel you, and fear nothing."

He gave her directions for meeting him, made his own preparations for flight, and with mutual impatience they waited the approaching and appointed evening.

It came — the hour which had been designated for the marriage of Wallenberg.   The chapel of D'Arlemont Castle was pompously illuminated — the company were already assembling in crowds, and every thing was gay comparison, amusing scandal, and good-humored clamor.   There were aunts and uncles, cousins and friends — the whole world of various and motley elements which such an occasion so commonly brings together. At the head of a long train of connexions and dependants came the bridegroom, as full of his own consequence as of impatience for the ceremony. The hour was dawing nigh for the sacrifice — but a voice, under the lattice of Anastasia, said to her in a whisper, which, though soft, yet reached her ears —

"Come — come to me, beloved — I await thee, Anastasia!"

A mournful but a sweet voice was his — a voice of melody and love, — and she answered it in like language — "I come."

She stole away by a private passage into the garden. She joined her lover, and they fled from the boundaries of her father's domain, long before the assembled company had dreamed of her absence.

V.

"WHERE is she? — where is Anastasia, my bride? — why comes she not?" was the demand of Wallenberg.

Where was she, indeed? The hour had elapsed
—the moment was past — why came she not, in
glittering robes, heading, in kindred gladness, the
garlanded group of damsels that had gathered to
wait upon her? The castle was soon in commotion, and a strange anxiety filled every countenance. The bridal chamber was empty — the
maiden was not to be found. The castle was
searched from turret-top to donjon, but in vain.
They were compelled to seek her elsewhere. They
hunted through grounds and gardens, dispersing
every-where, but without success. They next
sought the forests. As they penetrated the thick
woods, the sky suddenly became dark and overcast — vivid flashes of lightning added to, while
illuminating and making perceptible, the gloom.
A storm of frightful energy passed over the wood,
prostrating every thing before it, and subsiding
with equal suddenness. The sky became instantly clear, and the moon shone forth in purity, unconscious of a cloud. The firmament had not a
speck. The bewildered groups proceeded in their
search. A soft and gentle strain of melody seemed to imbody itself with the winds. They followed the sounds into a dark and gloomy enclosure
of high overarching trees, thickly fenced in with
knotted vines and brushwood. The thunderbolt

15*

had been there, and it was scorched and blackened. They advanced — the music still leading them onward — until, in a small recess, they found indubitable tokens of the maiden, in the half-consumed remnants of her hat and shawl. They now beheld her destiny. They saw that she had been spirited away by the fiend. She had become the victim of the demon. He had triumphed in the garb of the early and lost lover — and she had fallen a victim, in a moment of sad credulity, to the arts of a designing and an evil angel. They continued the pursuit no longer. She was lost to them for ever — but still not lost. Amid the horrors of the tempest she pursued her way with her lover.

" Oh, save me, Albert —what a dreadful storm !" was her pleading and terrified address, as they hurried on through the devious paths of the forest. The violence of the storm filled her heart with apprehensions. She knew not the fearful extent of her security.

" I will—fear not, dearest — there is no danger."

" It pursues us," she cried, with increasing terror.

" It will not harm us — it will soon be over," was his assurance.

A stream of ground lightning, like a wave of

the sea, rushed up the hill at that moment, and followed close upon their footsteps. The maiden darted forward in desperation — Albert seized her in his arms, and throwing aside her hat and shawl, which encumbered him, he bore her away like an infant. He bore her to the edge of the forest, and laid her down upon the greensward in safety.

VI.

WHEN she recovered from the faintness which had overcome her, the storm had passed away — the night was beautifully clear. The moon had risen, and the gray forests looked sweet and hallowed in her light. A gentle strain of music rose upon the distant breeze, and still more contributed to the soft loveliness and languor of the scene.

The bright eyes of Albert looked down into the dewy orbs of Anastasia, and she thought she never before had seen them look so beautiful. His arm supported her, and she fancied its pressure had never been so fond before. She was blest in that embrace — and fear, and sorrow, and fatigue, departed in the consciousness that she then felt of having all that she lived for, and all that before had been denied her love.

" We must proceed, my Anastasia — our dwelling is not far — we can reach it by the dawn. Our steeds are now in waiting."

While the moon was yet shining, they stood upon the rocky cliffs which overhung a beautiful river. A proud and lonely castle stood in sight upon the highest crag. The stream glided below it with a pleasant freshness, and rippling away among the shelving rocks, in the placid moonlight, it seemed to the eyes of the happy Anastasia a home of faëry — a very heaven for the heart of truest love.

VII.

THE bird sings falsely who sings only of sunshine. The song must sometimes speak of clouds. Happy were the two — happy in the last degree — in their mutual loves and constant intercourse. Albert was all that Anastasia could desire in a lover — he was fond — he was gentle. His language was kind, always — and his very whispers were musical. But he was melancholy — he was always sad — even when he was most happy. He seemed never to forget the mutability of happiness. Yet his sadness was never gloom, nor did he at any time complain. Still, the very fact that he asked for no sympathy, and that she knew not how to address herself for his relief — these still made her unhappy. There was yet another cause of disquiet to the fond Anastasia. Their dwelling was so lonesome. True, Albert seldom left her, and there were a thousand pleasant amusements which he had provided; but her heart was too human for such a solitude; and the very winds that mourned in music through the rocky crevices, and the gentle river that rippled sweetly at the castle's base, and the sweet birds that carolled in the groves, and the stars that sang together harmoniously in their courses, all seemed to tell her of the many bright eyes, and cheerful hearts and voices, with which she had been accustomed to mingle. These thoughts gave her some occasional annoyances, but a sweet word from Albert consoled her.

"For a time, dearest, we must keep in solitude, to avoid the search which your father will doubtlessly institute after you. We must keep in secret — we must avoid all exposure — and here they will not be very apt to seek us."

She was satisfied — she seemed to be satisfied, at least — and that was something.

VIII.

One night they walked along the edge of the precipice, and looked abroad upon the night and river. The stars were shining in profusion, and not a breath murmured but harmoniously.

" Tell me," he said to her, in a sad but gentle tone, " tell me, Anastasia — do you not tire of our love, and the solitude to which it dooms you ?"

" Not of our love, oh, no ! dearest Albert, but sometimes I feel so lonesome."

" Yet are you not alone — am I not with you always ? With you, dearest, I have no such feeling. You are all to me, Anastasia, and I feel no want when you are absent. Ah ! feel like me, I implore you, my beloved. When you repine about your solitude, I mourn — I am unhappy."

" Be not unhappy, Albert — I will repine no longer. I feel that you are all to me, and wherefore should I repine for any change that may lose me all ?"

" Wherefore !" he replied — seizing her wrist with a strong gripe as he pronounced the word after her, with a singular energy. " Wherefore !

indeed? Repine not, dearest, or you may indeed lose all!"

"What mean you, Albert?" she demanded, with some apprehension.

"Look!" he exclaimed; and she beheld, even as he pointed, where a bright star shot away from its sphere in erratic flight, bearing along with it a momentary train of glory, which, as it belonged to, and came from, the sphere alone, was soon extinguished upon leaving it.

"Look," he cried, "look at that star! Be not weary of thy place of watch and quiet, lest thou become extinguished also. Thy sphere and temple are in one heart — thou canst not inhabit many."

He paused, and his eye seemed to trace afar upon its flight the pathway of the vanished star. She looked at him with anxious apprehension. His eye seemed rapt in sorrowful contemplation, and though he shed no tear, the expression was that of a sublime and subdued sadness. She threw her arm tenderly around his neck, and she felt that a thrilling shudder went all through his frame.

"It grows cold — let us return, my beloved," she said to him, fondly.

" Leave me for a while, Anastasia—I will come
to thee soon.   Leave me now."

His words were gently spoken, but she felt that
they were rather a command than a solicitation.
She left him at his bidding ; but ere she went, she
threw her arms again about his neck, and sweet
and pure was the kiss given by their mingling lips.
She went towards the castle ; but, looking backward as she went, it seemed to her that she saw a
bright and beautiful star moving across the river
to the crag whereon he stood.   At length she beheld it remain stationary beside him, and the distinct outline of his person was developed by its
rays.   She turned away with a strange terror —
she dared not look again ; but hurried onward
with trembling steps to her chamber in the castle.

IX.

It was late that night before Albert came to the
chamber, and yet she had not slept.   A strange,
sweet strain of music, wild, yet fine, came to her
ears at midnight, and soon after she heard it, he
appeared.

His looks were sad as when she left him—and
he did not seem pleased to find her watchful.

" Thou hast not slept, Anastasia ?"

" No — I waited for thee, Albert. I can hope for no sleep when thou art absent."

" But sometimes I would have thee sleep, simply because I am absent. Ah, my beloved, would that I might sleep, and sleep for ever, when I can no longer be with thee."

" That music — that sweet music, Albert — whence did it come ?"

" Wilt thou not sleep now, my beloved ? — I am with thee," was the evasive reply ; and Anastasia understood the gentle form of chiding which he had adopted. She obeyed the suggestion — she tried to sleep, and did sleep, but her slumbers were greatly broken — she knew not why; and whenever she awakened it was to hear whispering voices and sudden gusts of music, that seemed to be passing around the apartment with a rush of wings.

X.

It was yet early morning when Anastasia awakened and beheld Albert just about to leave the chamber. She called to him, but he only smiled, shook his head, waved his hand gently, and hurried from her sight. She rose quickly from the couch, and moved to the window, from which she beheld him hastening down the rocks. He looked back and caught her eye, and his finger was raised as if in warning. The thought of the shooting star came that moment to her mind, and she hurried back to her couch.

He returned about mid-day, and seemed unhappy. He started frequently, and looked around him, as if in anxious expectation of the approach of some desired person.

"You are troubled, Albert," said Anastasia. "Can I do any thing for you?"

"Yes!" was the sudden and almost stern reply. "See not that I am troubled. When thou canst serve or sooth me, I will seek thee;—when I do not seek thee, Anastasia, believe me, thou canst not serve me. Seem then not to see that I suffer."

"And thou dost suffer, Albert?"

"I live!" was the terrible response; and oh! the immortal grief that looked forth in that moment from his eyes.

"Would that I could die for thee, Albert!" was her exclamation, as she flung herself upon his bosom. He folded her fondly in his embrace, while he replied to her as follows:

"Thou canst better serve me than by dying for

me, Anastasia—and far better serve thyself. Live for me."

" Do I not, dear Albert ?"

" No — not yet — thou dost not live for thyself."

She looked up wonderingly at the speaker—he proceeded, and his voice was full of solemnity, and there was an intense earnestness in his face which she did not dare a second time to look upon.

" Love thy condition for itself. Seek not to see, and ask not to partake of, mine. Is there any thing unknown to thee ?—it is better for thee that thou shouldst not know it. Has it come to thee in a dream that a joy was in the valley await-ing thee, beyond any ever known to thee before ? Turn thy footsteps with a fond solicitude from the path which leads to the valley. The dream was a lying one, sent for thy ensnaring. Thou wilt lose what thou hast, in grasping at what thou hast not ; and the very hope which tells thee of a blessing to come, steals a blessing from thee while it does so. Beware, Anastasia, that thy head misleads not thy heart, and thy fancy consumes not thy feelings. Do we not love each other, Anastasia ? Couldst thou have a fonder or a truer love than mine ? Let it suffice thee —joy in what thou hast ;—pray to thy God, Anastasia ; pray that, if thou dost not

yet, thou mayest soon learn to love thy condition
as thyself — it is more than thyself to thee."

He kissed her, and left her with these mysterious lessons, over which she pondered in doubt and
sadness.

XI.

The advice of Albert was good, but how unreasonable.   How is it possible for man, unless denied to hope, to be content with his condition?
How much less possible for woman !   To be content with existing things is to desire no change —
to hope for nothing better — to live without a
thought of heaven.   The requisition of Albert
sank deep into the mind of Anastasia, but not to
produce the effect which he desired.   It came to
her as a restraint, and not a direction — as a con-
troller, and not a guide.   Was he to suffer, and
was she to be denied to share with him in his
griefs, to console him under his torments?   Love
itself rose in rebellion against such a requisition.
And when she beheld his sadness visibly increase
with each successive hour, her fond heart — her
sleepless affections — could no longer remain paci-
fied and silent.

" Albert, dear Albert, you do me injustice. I am strong to share with you — ay, to endure all your afflictions. I feel that I love you too well not to rejoice in pain when I know that every added sting to my heart takes from that which is preying upon yours. Unfold to me your griefs — say what afflicts you. Let me hear the worst, and you will see how I can smile to place my hand with yours in the flame, and, looking into your eyes of love the while, feel and fear none of its searching fires."

It was thus she implored him for his secret — her arms twining about his neck in the fondest embrace — her dark, sweet eyes, looking with the warmest devotion at the same instant into his own.

" You know not what you ask," was his reply. " You ask for wo — for eternal wo — for a doom for which you were never destined. Why, oh! why will you be dissatisfied? Have you not my love — all my love — my heart, truly and entirely yours? The love of the unselfish and unexacting man — of one who is above meanness or its reproach — is the richest possession ever yet given to the woman heart. Wherefore would you seek for more?"

16*

"You do not give me your heart—you will not give me its sorrows. It is for these I ask."

"You have them, Anastasia—it is only the name you desire to know. You have them already."

"How?"

"Your present care—your anxiety to know them—is your sorrow now. You see that I am grieved—and you grieve to see it. That is enough for me, and should be enough for you. You give me your sympathy when you grieve at my suffering. You prove to me your love for me when you wish to see me glad. I am satisfied with thus much in the way of proof—be you satisfied, dearest Anastasia, with the degree of confidence I have already shown you. Seek not to hear more. I, who know how much you can console, and how greatly you ought of right to suffer with me, deny you any farther knowledge of my griefs than this. I would not have you even see so much. But, at least, I desire that you should seek to know no more."

XII.

Compelled to be silent, she yet remained unsatisfied. A feverish curiosity was gnawing at her

heart. What could be the matter with Albert?
Were they not secure in their retreat?—was he
impatient so soon of the pleasant fetters which
love and her fond arms had woven around him?
She conjectured, vainly, of a thousand causes for
his suffering, dismissing, as idle, each suggestion
of her mind, as soon as it presented itself. Her
thoughts were sleepless, and they kept her so.
That night she heard strange noises in her chamber — strange though slight. She had resolved
to keep awake, and yet, even while she strove, it
seemed as if a blessed breeze came about her, in a
murmuring whisper, that glided into song at length,
and filled the air with a slumberous power. She
felt the sleep wrapping her still resisting limbs as
with a garment of melody, and though she strove
to burst its fetters, and her eyes persisted occasionally in looking forth, they were at length compelled to yield the struggle. Yet, ere they
closed entirely, it appeared as if a red and lovely
light, pointed and raying out like a golden star,
wavered and flickered around the couch where
she slept, fondly clasped in the arms of Albert. It
was not quite dawn when she awakened from
that sleep, and then it seemed as if she had been
awakened by a cold and sudden wind, which passed over her face while yet in a state of dim and

doubtful consciousness; she felt the form of Albert, which before had lain quietly beside her, suddenly convulsed as if with spasms; and when she turned to him and met the glance of his eyes, they were wild beyond description. They glanced sadly, and almost with an expression of gloom upon her, and she felt as if he had repulsed her. But when, under the agony of that thought, she threw her arms around his neck, he returned her embrace with a fondness that answered fully, if it did not exceed, her own.

XIII.

All that day he was absent among the neighboring rocks and woods. She had asked to go forth with him, but he had resolutely, though gently, denied her. Her thoughts, during his absence, were all given, in spite of her will, to the one absorbing subject — the mystery of his sorrows. By a strange instinct, her mind continually reverted to the image of that star, that seemed to cross the river, and station itself close beside him where he stood. A next and natural transition of her thought reviewed the singular sensations which she had experienced just when sinking into slum-her, and when awakening the previous night and morning; and she now remembered, among other circumstances which had attended her sleep, that it had followed soon after the kind kiss which Albert had impressed upon her eyes. The more she meditated this matter, the more perfectly was she convinced that the kiss of Albert had produced that obliviousness which she was so very desirous to avoid; and, as she was resolute, in spite of all his counsels, to discover what she could of the occasion of his sorrows, she determined, if possible, to escape the repetition of that kiss upon her eyelids when, at a future time, she desired that her eyes might be kept open. It is not difficult for a woman to effect her object when she aims to do wrong; and it will be seen that Anastasia was only too successful in repressing sleep when her husband desired to impose it on her.

That very night she determined to try her experiments; and accordingly, as a first step, she aimed to set Albert's mind perfectly at rest as to the degree of quiet which was in hers. When he returned to the castle, which he did at early evening, she received him with the fondest and most satisfying smiles. Her good-humor and cheerfulness, easy but not obtrusive, delighted him, and she now saw the truth of what he had told her.

He was happy as he saw her happy, and his sadness passed away, leaving not the trace of a cloud upon his brow, as, to his eye, she appeared content with her condition. Joyfully — ay, with an intoxication of joy — he clasped her to his bosom, and his words were never fonder, and his kisses never half so sweet. She half resolved, if the appearance of contentment on her part could produce such a vast improvement on his, to make it her study to obey him. Alas! why have we not always the strength to obey good impulses only!

"Be ever thus, my Anastasia — be ever thus, and we are most happy. You will then see no sorrow on my brow, and I will secure you against all that might otherwise assail your heart."

"I will pray Heaven to be as you wish me, Albert. I have little else to pray for."

She retired for the night, and he promised to follow her very soon. When she had gone, he clasped his hands, and his eyes looked up in hope to the blessed starlight that came shining through the grated window of the castle. He spoke in low tones of soliloquy as he looked up to the wheeling and flickering fires.

"Let her but continue thus, and I am safe. There will then be no more wanderings — no more flight — no more incertitude. I shall resume my

station — I shall ever more burn with the fixed
fires that the winds move not — that the capricious
seasons check not — beyond the control of the
mortal, beyond the power and caprice of the immortal. Yes, dearest Anastasia, in thy constancy
— in thy content — in thy love of thy condition,
clamouring for no change-begetting knowledge, I
shall be secure, and we shall both be happy."

It was not long after this that he retired to the
chamber of his bride.

XIV.

She had played her part to admiration — she
had completely deceived her husband. She little
dreamed of the evils which spring from all decep-
tion — even where the end seems to be most innocent, and where a superficial thought esteems it
praiseworthy. She wished to know his griefs —
she persuaded herself because she could then the
better administer to and heal them. This was
her duty; and so regarding it, she entirely forgot
that obedience, in the inferior mind, is a duty also.
Albert was perfectly convinced that Anastasia
was dissatisfied no longer. That conviction
brought back his cheerfulness. His was a pecu-

liar destiny ; and to be thought happy by her, and
to make her satisfied with his lot, by perfect happiness in hers, was, according to the terms of that
destiny, the condition of his own happiness. Believing and confiding, with renewed and increased
fondness, he leaned over her, as she seemed to
sleep, and sweet and long was the fond kiss which
he pressed upon her parted lips.

She did not sleep — she was watchful.   With a
pertinacity that did not suffer fatigue or pause, she
kept resolutely awake until midnight.   Remembering the kiss upon her eyelids which her husband had usually given her, and to which she at-
tributed the deep slumber which always seemed
to have followed it, she contrived so to dispose her
arms as to throw one of them effectually over her
eyes, and thus to prevent the possibility of his lips
pressing upon them.   She found the position an
unpleasant and tiresome one after a little while ;
but, bent upon her design, she determined to suffer
the annoyance rather than forego her purpose.
When a woman once sets her mind upon any thing,
it is no small matter which is to divert her from it.

Midnight came at last, to her great satisfaction.
She heard the clock of the castle toll forth the
hour with a solemn emphasis, and she could scarcely restrain the deep sigh of her heart from forcing

its way to a corresponding sound to her lips.
But she did restrain herself, and in a moment after
she distinctly felt a cold wind rush through the
apartment. At that moment Albert half rose in
the couch, and bent over her. She felt his breathing distinctly lift the lighter curls of her hair, and
with a keen ear he listened to her respirations. He
tried with a gentle finger to detach her arm from
its close place over her eyes ; but the arm seemed
all at once to have become most obstinately rigid,
and he failed in his efforts, in which he did not
persevere for fear of awaking her. As if satisfied
that she slept, he seemed to turn away ; and the
arm, so obstinately immoveable before, was now
slightly lifted, without being removed from her
eyes, and only sufficiently to enable her to give a
single glance around the apartment. As she had
seen before, she now distinctly beheld a shadowy
outline at the foot of the couch, in whose massive
brow a bright pale star shone fixedly and soft. A
moment more had elapsed when the form of Albert became suddenly convulsed, and she could
scarcely forbear the fond impulse which prompted
her to forget every precaution, and clasp him in
her arms ; but the secret stirred in her mind at that
moment, and she maintained her position and silence, though several convulsions, each successive

one more severe than the preceding, shook his form
as with so many dreadful spasms.   They were
scarcely over when a cold breath of air seemed
to pass above her neck, and she distinctly felt the
body of Albert sink down helplessly beside her.
Her heart beat impetuously — she could scarce
suppress her breathing, and nothing but the most
resolute determination enabled her to forbear
shrieking aloud.   She did forbear, however ; and
once more venturing to look forth, she now distinctly beheld two shadowy forms glide through
the apartment, with each a red and similar star
shining brightly upon his forehead.

XV.

Anastasia could bear this no longer, particularly when, turning to the side of the couch where
Albert lay, his body was cold, corpse-like, and immoveable.   Conviction forced itself upon her—
the secret was discovered, and the burden was insupportable.   She shrieked aloud in her agony ;
she clasped the lifeless body in her arms, while her
eyes, addressing the star-fronted shadows that stood
at the foot of the bed, seemed to appeal to them
once more for the restoration of the inanimate form

beside her. With the first accents of that wild and fearful shriek, indicating, as it did, the sudden and startling intelligence which her mind had received, a visible effect was produced upon the strange aspects before her. While she looked, she beheld one of the stars rise slowly, and sail away without obstruction through the spacious windows, while the other wavered and flickered about as if in the gusts of an uprising storm. A storm, indeed, seemed to rage through the apartment. The shadowy figure appeared to expand into a rolling and tossing cloud, in the midst of which, as if it were the centre of its action, the bright star now grew more bright, and of a deeper red, and shot forth the most angry fires on every side. Nothing could exceed the terrors of Anastasia. The star seemed now to approach her, and gust after gust, like the rushing of so many heavy wings, passed and repassed over the couch where she lay, lifting and rending its silken drapery. She cried aloud once more in her apprehension.

"Forgive, forgive me, dearest Albert — forgive me that I have offended. Come to me — be as thou wert — I will obey thee — I will never offend thee more."

"Too late — too late," cried a voice of sorrow rather than of anger from the bosom of the cloud, which now hung, like a dense wreath of vapour, just above the couch where she lay.

"It is too late, dearest Anastasia — I can return to thee no more."

"Wherefore — wherefore?" was the interrogation of the terrified woman.

"It is the doom!" was the hollow answer from the cloud; and the star that still shone from the vague form before her seemed to shed drops of blood, that fell even upon the garments of her couch, as the mournful voice thus responded to her inquiry.

"Alas! alas! wherefore is this doom!" she cried once more to the shadow and the star.

"Thou hast already asked too much. I warned thee, my Anastasia. Was it not enough to know that thou wert happy? Why wast thou not satisfied with thy condition? Thou hast destroyed the hope and the happiness of both by thy impatient thirst after the why and the wherefore."

"Alas! and for this are we to be disunited, my Albert — for so slight a cause as this are we to lose the blessing we have lived for?"

He replied to her in an allegory.

"Does the flower please thee? — wherefore destroy it to know whence come the scent and the beauty? The odor flies when thou dost so — and the beauty fades. This is life — this, always, the happiness of the mortal. But thou art mortal no longer, my Anastasia — thou art now destined to share, even as thou desiredst it, the terrible doom which is mine!"

"What meanest thou, Albert?" she inquired, tremblingly, as these fearful words reached her ears.

"Albert no longer," cried the star. "Thy lover was a god!"

She sank from the couch where she had lain as she heard these words, and she now lay extended along the floor.

"Rise, Anastasia, still beloved, though mine no longer — rise," said the star, "and I will tell thee what is given to thee to know."

She rose — she stood tremblingly in the presence of that fiery eye that looked down upon her, while the cloud in which it was imbedded hung over her like a protecting and mighty shield. How glorious, how fearful, were the words which followed.

XVI.

"When I bade thee regard the flight from heaven of a lovely star but a few nights ago,
17*

Anastasia, I called thee to witness my own fate. That star was a kindred light with mine, seduced by me, as I had been seduced, from the sweet and beautiful abode where it shone, happy and adored, on high. I had my abode beside it, and was the worshipped deity of a mighty nation. No eye brighter then mine looked forth from the eastern summits — no more pure or peaceful planet gave light to the returning shepherds. Like the star whose flight I pointed out to thy regard, I fell from my place of glory, and the secret of my fall was in the commission of thy error. I was discontented with my condition."

The spirit-lover paused, and the hapless Anastasia wrung her hands in hopeless misery. He proceeded —

" For ages, before the birth of time, had that lovely abiding-place been the assigned station from which I shone. Millions of lovely spirits shone and revolved around me, with a light partly borrowed from mine ; but oh! how unapproachably inferior to me. I was beloved — I was worshipped; but, like thee, Anastasia, I knew not to be content in my place, and incurred, in a hapless moment, a doom not unlike, but far more terrible than thine."

The maiden moaned upon the floor of the apartment, but without the utterance of a single word. At that moment a pale star sailed along by the window, and from the dim cloud, of which it was the centre, she heard a voice crying mournfully —

"Come !"

Albert replied with a promise of compliance, and the spectre-glory floated away in the distance from her sight. He proceeded in his narration :

"One night — one fatal night — looking down from my place of watch, I beheld, in undisturbed quiet and loveliness, the various and the wondrous worlds around me. A pale form passed hurriedly along upon one planet, the earth, and it waved its hands, and it shrieked in agony, and its cries of sorrow came to my ears, even afar off as was my dwelling. Thine was that form, Anastasia — thou wert the mourner."

"Alas ! alas !" cried the hapless woman — but she could exclaim nothing farther.

"Thine was the form, and such was the agony of thy piercing shriek, that inly I mourned for thee — I deemed it a cruel injustice that such as thou shouldst suffer. Thou wert so lovely and so sorrowful, and the sweetest loves in the thoughts of the blessed, are those which are most allied to sadness."

With these words the spirit paused in his narra-

tion, and the cloud in which the eye hung and
shone now veered away and approached one of the
windows of the apartment. At the same time,
many stars, floating in like forms, came before the
window, and strange words passed between Albert
and the rest, in tones of the most sweet but subdued
and melancholy music. In a few moments they
floated away like the last, and her companion again
approached and hung above her in the apartment. He continued his narration:—

"With the thought and the desire which came
to me as I surveyed thee, Anastasia, a dim and
giant form came rushing towards me, from the
piled clouds that lay like so many rocks and tow-
ers in the northern horizon. His speed was like
that of the lightning; and he made his way among
the stars around me, obscuring their lustre, and
scorning their obstruction, with the rapid rush of
a mighty tempest. When he approached me, he
lay suspended on his outstretched wings, the cur-
tain of which clouded the earth and concealed it
that moment from my sight, and he gazed upon me
with an air of sorrowful pride, mixed with the most
mortifying expression of contempt. 'I have heard
thy wish,' he cried — 'thou canst dare to regret,
but not to repair. Thou canst see, but thou hast
not the courage to share the suffering which thou

seest. Truly, thou art a generous spirit — noble in the estimation of the highest, and worthy of the fixed place which thou holdest.' Such were his words of scorn, and they touched my pride. 'And what better fortune is thine, dark spirit?' I replied to the intruder. 'What hast thou to boast beyond me — in what is thy better portion?' He answered readily, and his voice went through me with a strange and mighty power, so that I trembled in the sphere in which I had never before been shaken.

" 'I am free,' was his fierce and proud reply. 'I am free.'

" I heard his words with a throbbing and speechless admiration, and began to feel a fond desire that I too might be free. I little knew then the nature of the blessing which I sought. I little thought that, to be free, I should for ever after be alone !

" But I was not yet free, and I replied to him still as the appointed servant of my master: 'My state is glorious — my home is one of lights, and love, and perpetual flowers; and my duty is only to watch for the Mighty One.' He replied in greater scorn —

" ' Thy home is one of lights — true — but they are spies which are set upon thee to report

when thou errest — the love which is given thee
is not given for thyself, but for thy service — and
the flowers of which thou art mad to boast — look,
fool, they are woven into chains. Thou art a
slave but to spy upon others — thou art spied
upon thyself, and held worthy of love only as thou
dost the appointed task of the menial.'

"He had spoken to me a dreadful truth — so I
deemed it at the time, and in my thoughts I wished myself free — free as the fierce and mighty
form that lay prone like a fearless giant, proud
and scornful in his might, before my eyes. I wished for freedom, and with the wish I felt the golden
link melt away that secured me in my station —
the bands of flowers, which like a chain had held
me with a spell which no foreign power or agency
could have broken, now, at my single wish, were
relaxed from about me, and a mighty and clear
voice from a world a thousand worlds above me,
came to me like the sudden sound of a trumpet —

" ' Thou art free!'

XVII.

"Dreadful freedom ! That instant I felt myself
alone. I was detached from the sphere in which

I had borne so small a labour, and enjoyed such a high and worshipped glory, and I floated away into a thousand regions, and journeyed with the mighty spectre which had seduced me to his sorrows and my own shame. But ere I had utterly left the sphere in which I had dwelt so happily and so long, I heard the sad lament of my companion stars, stronger, yet more humble in station than myself, whom I had left behind me. It was a strain which told me my destiny, and shaped out my only future hope, as it detailed my own duty to myself and to the mighty master.

"CHORUS OF THE STAR BRETHREN.*

I.

"' Wo to us and to thee,
Star most beloved —
Thy world and ours
Tumbles, and falls abroad —
Thou, in thy weakness,
Brother, most erring —
Thou, in thy loneliness,
Thou hast destroy'd it !

II.

"' They bear away —
They the dark spirits

* Imitated from a chorus of spirits in the " Faust" of Goethe

Whose pleasure is ruin !—
They bear away
The hope and the harmony
Wreck'd into nothingness!
While we weep over
The beauty that's lost !

III.

"' Mighty among the stars,
Bright one, rebuild it!
In thy own bosom
Rebuild it again !
Begin a new being
With spirit unshaken,
Then shall new music
Unite the now sunder'd !'

"Such was the mournful anthem which my brethren sang in sorrow at my departure and fall, and whose strains followed me afar, and still follow me. I hear them now ; and thou too, dearest Anastasia, with whom I had commenced that new being, and through whose beloved agency I had hoped for my restoration, with thee beside me, partaking my immortality and glory in that high place — thou too mayst hear them now."

And she did hear, for a gust of the breeze, that seemed full of perfume, floated that moment by the window, and her ears distinctly noted the last words of the melancholy and imploring anthem : —

" Mighty among the stars,
 Bright one rebuild it!
 In thy own bosom
 Rebuild it again !
 Begin a new being
 With spirit unshaken,
 Then shall new music
 Unite the now sunder'd !"

" I had commenced that new being with thee, my Anastasia, and hoped to have succeeded in my labours ; but the very danger which I feared, and against which I strove to counsel thee, has wrecked the fond hope within my bosom, and now drives me forth once more, alone, to commence my toils anew.   Thou wast not content with thy condition or with mine — thou hast committed mine own error."

" And is there no forgiveness, Albert ? — let me but be tried once more, my beloved — "

" Thou shalt be tried, Anastasia — this is thy doom, no less than mine.   Thou hast striven to know — it is now thy destiny — thou art now doomed to partake of mine."

" Ah ! happy — happy shall I be, Albert, if so permitted."

" Alas ! Anastasia, thou knowest not what it is — thou canst not dream of its terrors," was the mournful answer of the spirit to the fond assuran-

ces of the devoted woman. " Thou deemest that,
to share my destiny, thou wilt still remain with
me."

" And will it not be so, my Albert ?"

" Alas! no !" was the sad reply. " It is my
doom of loneliness which thou art to share — my
doom of isolation. Thou wilt not go with me,
nor I with thee, yet we must both go forth. Thou
hast to seek, as well as myself, for that condition
among the mortal which is borne without repining,
and with no desire of change. Make thyself
kindred to such a spirit, and thou livest with me
when I rejoin the stars."

She lay shrieking at the foot of the cloud, which
now slowly descended, and seemed to encircle her.

" Come !" exclaimed a sober and sad, yet soft
accent, at the window ; and there, in her sight,
floated once more the kindred star which had followed her lover ; she felt herself lifted from the
ground, and enveloped in a fold of the softest and
the sweetest air, while the bright eye of Albert,
starlike and pure, came close to her forehead.

" What wouldst thou ?" demanded Anastasia,
in her bewilderment.

" Impress upon thee my immortality with my
doom," was the answer ; and that moment she
felt the star pressing like ice upon her forehead.

It seemed to sink, cold and chilling, into her very brain, and she shrieked with the momentary agony of that feeling. In another instant she was released from his embrace, and, whirling round with a motion not her own, she now found herself wrapped in an airy mantle like that of her companion, and she was conscious, while floating away —away into the fathomless abysses of the air— that she shone from the centre of a cloud like the star which had personified her lover. Her next feeling was that of utter isolation. She beheld the beautiful star, which she had loved as a mortal, sailing along, with a slow and steady light, above the rocks and the river, and she strove to follow and rejoin it. But a power restrained her movements and checked her will, and she now felt herself borne unresistingly in an opposite direction. Then, for the first time, did she feel the horrible nature of that destiny which she had so passionately desired to share with him. The fearful truth which he had uttered came like a knell of agony to her suffering soul, as she felt and feared, in that desolate moment, that she was destined for ever after to remain alone!

ONEA AND ANYTA.

ONEA AND ANYTA.

I.

THE Yemassee was no longer the great nation. They had set their fortunes upon a cast, and the throw was fatal. Civilization triumphed. The Carolinians, in spite of the sudden massacres under which they had suffered at the beginning of the war, were at length successful; and at Coosa-whatchie, or the "town of refuge," the Yemas-sees lost their best leaders. With these, they lost all spirit, and their surviving warriors were unequal to the task of restoring their fortunes. Scattered and without counsel, they yet fled, as if by a common instinct, to their sacred town of Pocota-ligo, where, in the presence of their priests and the protection of their gods, they had faint hopes yet of effecting by prayers and superstitious ceremonies, what, hitherto, their own fearless valor had utterly failed to accomplish. Their resources were now nearly exhausted — their villages in flames; and relying as they had done, upon the hope of obtaining possession of the chief city and provisions of the whites, their fields had, in the greater number of cases, been left without cultivation. Their Spanish allies, always deceitful, after stimulating them to war, had left them to contend with it single handed. On hearing of the defeat and slaughter of the Yemassees, such of them as had been sent from St. Augustine to their succor, returned to the shelter of its walls, under the influence of a sudden panic. The neighboring Indian tribes followed the base example, and either returned to their forests, or made concessions, and bound themselves by treaty to the conquerors, giving hostages for their future good behavior. Not so with the unhappy Yemassees. They were still too proud to beg for that peace, which they yet needed more than all, and which alone could save them from extermination. They were too brave to desire peace when their slain brothers remained unavenged. They resolved, therefore, to carry on the struggle to the last; and, crowding into the holy town of Pocota-ligo, they proceeded to strengthen themselves in their position, as well as they might, there to await the approach of the Carolinians.

They fortified the town, somewhat after the fashion of the European settlers, with the trunks of trees and the larger branches, rudely bedded together. This done, divided between hopes and fears, they passed the brief time which elapsed between their preparations and the assault. They had not long to wait. Their defences, which, manned by Europeans, and against savages, might have proved adequate to their purposes, proved no barrier against the pursuer. The impetuous onset of their sanguine assailants could not be withstood by those, made already apprehensive by previous experience, of the result; and their frail bulwarks were stormed, and Pocota-ligo in flames, in the same fearful hour of assault. The scene was terrible; but, though despairing, the Indians did not think of flight. The men fell, and the women filled their places. A dreadful massacre ensued: naked and howling, but tearing and rending as they ran, men, women, and children, darted to and from the blazing dwellings, shrieking for that revenge which they could obtain in part only. They neither gave nor asked for quarter; and in the darkness of night and the confusion of the scene, they were enabled to protract the conflict with the success which must always follow courage, and the valor of men fighting fearlessly for their homes. Through the night the

battle lasted, but as soon as the day broke upon
them, the struggle was over.   The first glimpses
of the morning found the bayonet at the heart of
the few surviving warriors, who still lived, but only
at the mercy of those to whom in all their successes
they had shown no mercy.   But few of them es-
caped.   Before sunrise, the fight was ended, and
the great nation of the Yemassees was stricken from
existence.

II.

On the eastern banks of the Isundiga, or Savannah river, there is a lofty tumulus, which the
insidious waters of the stream have long since begun to undermine.   On the summit of this tumulus, the morning after the termination of this fatal
combat, stood a Yemassee warrior.   The blood
upon his visage—his torn garments and broken
instruments of war, sufficiently testified to the re-
cent strifes in which he had been engaged.   It
was Echotee, a valiant chief, who stood upon the
tumulus.   His limbs were weary with toil and
flight—his eye was dim, and the melancholy sadness of the Indian mouth was heightened into hate
and anguish.   He busied himself in fitting new

sinews to his bow, and sharp flint heads to his arrows. The hunting shirt which he wore—a finely
dressed buckskin of the brightest yellow, fantasti-
cally inwrought with shells and beads—such decorations as the tasteful woman, Hiwassee, his wife,
had fondly chosen for the purpose—was torn in
many places, and spots of the darkest red were
contrasted with the bright yellow of the garment.
Wounded, lone, and sorrowing, yet Echotee did
not despair. His eye had exile in it, but not fear;
neither did he despond. Firmness and manly
resolution shared with sorrow the habitations of
his soul. Anxiously, at moments, he looked towards the forests behind him, as if in expectation;
but their dark intricacies uttered no sound or
voice, and he turned his eyes away in disappointment. Then, after a brief pause, taking his way
down from the tumulus, he moved to a little streamlet that trickled at the foot of the mound, and passing partially through it, at length made its way to the
bosom of the Isundiga. Stooping to the stream,
he drank freely of its waters; then, returning hastily to the mound, he proceeded, with a slender
shingle, with which he had provided himself, to dig
an opening in the hillock, as if contemplating a
place of sepulture. While he dug, he sang in a

low but unsubdued tone, a chant, in which he la-
mented the fortunes of his fellows : —

"They are gone, and the night covers them.
My feet have no companion in the chase — the
hollow woods speak to me with the voices of
shadows — there is no life in their sounds. Where
art thou, Washattee — where speedest thou, whom
none yet has overtaken. On the far hills that rise
blue at the evening I see thee — thou hast found the
valley of joy, and the plum-groves that are ever in
bloom. But who, brother, shall gather thy bones —
who take care of thy spirit — where shall the
children look, when they seek for thy grave. Thou
art all untended in the green valleys, and the ghosts
of the slain bend over thee with many frowns.
Comes she, the maid of thy bosom, to dress the
board of the hunter ? Brings she at evening thy
venison ? When the night is dark, and the brown
vulture stoops on thy path, and snuffs up blood of
thy spilling, I fear for thee, my brother. Thou
canst not sit in the green valley, for the warrior
lives who has slain thee, and mine arrow may reach
him not. Yet will I sing for thee, Washattee — I
will sing for thee thy death-song, and tell the ghosts
who frown, of thy many victories ; thou wert mighty
in the chase — the high hills did not overcome
thee. Thy boyhood was like the manhood of

other men — thou didst not creep in thy childhood.
From the first, thy feet were strong to walk, and
what speed of the warrior was like unto thine?
Well did they call thee the young panther — the eye
and the might of the young panther's mother was
thine. The strong tide, when thou swammest,
bore thee not back — thou didst put it by like an
infant. In the chase, thou wert an arrow which
laughs at the bird's wing — in the battle, thou wert
a keen tooth that goes deep in the heart. Thus
said the Muscoghee, when his eyes swam in the
cloud as he lay under thy knee — thus said the
Catawba, when thy hand struck through the long
willows by the lake of Sarattay. The ghosts of
the Muscoghee and the Catawba shall wait for thy
coming, and meet thee to serve, when thine eye
opens upon the green valley, and thy shadow darts
forward on the silent chase. But thou, oh Yemassee — thou of the broad arrow and the big wing
— it is sad for thee when none but Echotee may
stand up for thy people. Thy wing is down
among the reeds that lie beside the river — thy
broad arrow is broken on the plain. Thy shadow
grows small upon thy tumulus, and I speak thy
name in a whisper. Opitchi-manneyto looks on
thee in wrath. He joyed in the last cry of Sa-
nutee — he joyed when the death-song came thick

from the lips of Chigilli — he joyed when the pale
faces cut the sinews in thy thousand arms. Who
shall sing thy greatness, Yemassee — what warrior
to come after? What woman with long hair shall
creep through the forest, looking in the evening
for thy scattered bones? Who shall scare the
wolf from thy carcass, as he tears thy flesh beneath
the moon. The fox burrows under the hearth of
the hunter, and there is no fire to drive him away.
Silence lives lonely in thy dwelling. Thou art
gone. Spirit of many ages! thy voice is sunk
into a whisper; and thy name, it is an echo on the
hill tops. Thy glories are the graves of many
enemies, but thy own grave is unknown."

The death-chant of the warrior was broken. A
sudden cry of sorrow reached his ears from the
neighboring woods, and was immediately succeeded by the appearance of about thirty other
Indians, of both sexes, emerging from the shadowy
umbrage. These were all that were left of his
nation. Echotee looked on them for an instant
with sudden interest, but his eyes were again as instantly dropped upon the ground, and his hands
continued to labor upon the grave which he had
begun. Meanwhile the Indians advanced, bearing
along with them, from the woods, the dead body
of a warrior. This was Washattee, the warrior

whose death-song had been just sung by his brother. Beside this, Echotee gave no other sign of
sorrow. No trace of that grief which might be
supposed natural to his uttered lamentations, was
visible in his action or face. His words seemed
to fall from lips of marble. His was the majesty
of wo, without its weakness.

Washattee had fled with the few survivors from
the fatal field of Pocota-ligo; but his wounds were
fatal, and he only fled from a quick to a protracted
form of death. He perished in the forests when
no longer in danger from the pursuing foe. They
were now to bury him. The ceremonies of burial
among the savages are usually simple. The warriors, as they assisted to deposite their comrade in
the grave, chanted over him a song, not unlike
that which has already been recited. They enu-
merated his victories over the Catawba, the Muscoghee, and other nations — his particular successes
in the chase; and their only and common regret
was, that his death had not been avenged in the
blood of the victor. While they sang, Echotee,
who remained silent all the while, placed beside
him, in the grave, his bow, his arrows, knife, pipe,
and a plentiful supply of flint arrow-heads, to meet
the emergencies of the chase in the shady vallies,
to which, according to their faith, his steps were

already bending. This done, and the soft mould heaped upon him, after a brief consultation, they stepped one by one into the order of march known as the Indian file, making but one footstep for the eyes of the pursuer, and followed, at equal distances, the guidance of the brave Echotee. By the side of the latter, came, in tears, the young and beautiful Hiwassee, the maiden who, but a little time before, had broken with him the wand of marriage — the sacred wand of Checkamoysee. To the deeper western forests they bent their way, and the shadows of evening soon sank behind them like a wall, separating them forever from their native homes.

III.

Many years had now elapsed, and men ceased to remember the once noble nation of the Yemassees — once the most terrible and accomplished people of the southern forests. They had even gone out of the memories of their ancient enemies, the Creeks ; and the Carolinians, while in the full enjoyment of the fertile lands which had been their heritage, had almost entirely forgotten the hard toils and fearful perils by which they had been acquired. It was in the morning of a bright day in October, that a small Indian canoe might have been seen ascending the river St. Mary, up to its source in the Okeefanokee swamp, a dismal region, which lies between the Ockmulgee and Flint rivers, in the state of Georgia.

There were but two persons in the canoe, both Indian hunters of the Creek nation ; a gallant race, well known for high courage among the tribes, and distinguished not less by their wild magnanimity and adventure, than by their daring ferocity. The warriors were both young, and were numbered, and with strict justice, among the *élite* of their people. At peace, for the first time for many seasons, with all around them, they gave themselves up to the pleasures of the chase, and sought, in the hardy trials of the hunt for the bear and the buffalo, to relieve the inglorious and unwelcome ease which this novel condition of things had imposed upon them. Our two adventurers, forsaking the beaten track, and with a spirit tending something more than customary to that which distinguishes civilization, had undertaken an exploring expedition into the recesses of this vast lake and marsh, which, occupying a space of nearly three hundred miles in extent, and in very rainy seasons almost completely inundated, presented,

19*

amidst the thousand islands which its bosom con-
ceals, fruitful and inviting materials for inquiry
and adventure. Girt in with interminable forests,
the space of which was completely filled up with
umbrageous vines and a thick underwood, the trial
was one of no little peril, and called for the exercise of stout heart, strong hand, and a world of
fortitude and patience. It was also the abiding-
place of the wild boar and the panther—the
southern crocodile howled nightly in its recesses —
and the coiled snake, ever and anon, thrust out its
venomous fangs from the verdant bush. With
words of cheer and mutual encouragement, the
young hunters made their way. They were well
armed and prepared for all chances; and fondly
did they anticipate the delight which they would
entertain, on relating their numerous adventures
and achievements, by field and flood, to the assembled nation, on the return of the ensuing spring.
They took with them no unnecessary incumbran-
ces. The well tempered bow, the chosen and
barbed arrows, the curved knife, suited to a transition the most abrupt, from the scalping of the enemy to the carving of the repast, and the hatchet,
fitted to the adroit hand of the hunter, and ready
at his back for all emergencies, were the principal
accoutrements of the warriors. They troubled

themselves not much about provisions. A little parched corn supplied all wants, and the dried venison in their pouches was a luxury, taken on occasion only. They knew that, for an Indian, the woods had always a pregnant store; and they did not doubt that their own address, in such matters, would at all times enable them to come at it.

Dreary, indeed, was their progress. An European would have despaired entirely, and given up what must have appeared, not merely a visionary and hopeless, but a desperate and dangerous pursuit. But the determination of an Indian, once made, is unchangeable. His mind clothes itself in a seemingly habitual stubbornness, and he is inflexible and unyielding. Though young, scarcely arrived at manhood, our warriors were too well taught in the national philosophy, to have done any thing half so womanlike as to turn their backs upon an adventure, devised coolly, and commenced with all due preparation. They resolutely pursued their way, unfearing, unswerving, unshrinking. The river narrowed at length into hundreds of diverging rivulets, and, after having run their canoe upon the sands, they were compelled to desert it, and pursue their farther way on foot. They did not pause, but entered at once upon the new labor; and now climbing from tree to bank — now wading

along the haunts of the plunging alligator, through
pond and mire — now hewing with their hatchets
a pathway through the thickest branches, they
found enough to retard, but nothing to deter them.
For days did they pursue this species of toil, passing from island to island — alternately wading and
swimming—until at length, all unexpectedly, the
prospect opened in strange brightness and beauty
before them. They came to a broad and lovely lake, surrounded on all sides by the forest,
through a portion of which they had passed with
so much difficulty, and to which the storms never
came. It lay sleeping before them with the calm
of an infant, and sheltered by the wood, the wild
vine, and a thousand flowers. In the centre rose
a beautiful island, whose shores were crowned with
trees bearing all species of fruit, and emitting a
most grateful fragrance. The land was elevated
and inviting, and, as they looked, the young warriors conceived it the most blissful and lovely spot
of earth. Afar in the distance, they beheld the
white habitations of the people of the strange land,
but in vain did they endeavor to reach them.
They did not seek to adventure into the broad and
otherwise inviting waters; for occasionally they
could behold the crocodiles, of the largest and
fiercest class, rising to the surface, and seeming to

threaten them with their unclasped jaws, thickly
studded with their white sharp teeth. While in
this difficulty, they beheld a young maiden waving
them on the opposite bank ; and Onea, the youngest of the two hunters, attracted by the incompa-
rable beauty of her person, would have leapt without scruple into the lake, and swam to the side on
which she stood, but that his more grave and cautious companion, Hillaby, restrained him. They
observed her motions, and perceived that she directed their attention to some object in the distance.
Following her direction, they found a small canoe
tied to a tree, and sheltered in a little bay. Into this
they entered fearlessly, and putting out their pad-
dles, passed in a short time to the opposite shore,
the beauty of which, now that they had reached
it, was even more surpassingly great than when
seen afar off. Nor did the young Indian maiden,
in the eye of the brave Onea, lose any of those
charms, the influence of which had already penetrated his inmost spirit. But now she stood not
alone. A bright young maiden like herself appeared beside her, and, taking the warriors by the
hand, they sung sweet songs of pleasure in their
ears, and brought them the milk of the cocoa to
refresh them, and plucked for them many of the
rich and delightful fruits which hung over their

heads. There were oranges and dates, and cakes made of corn and sugar, baked with their own hands, which they cordially set before them. Many were the sweet glances and precious sentences which they gave to the young warriors, and soon did the gallant Creeks understand, and gladly did they respond to their kindness. Long would they have lingered with these maidens, but, when their repast had ended, they enjoined them to begone — to fly as quickly as possible, for that their people were cruel to strangers, and the men of their nation would certainly destroy them with savage tortures, were they to return from the distant chase upon which they had gone, and find the intruders. "But will they not give you," said the fearless Onea, "to be the bride of a brave warrior? I shame not to speak the name of my nation. They are men, and they beg not for life. I, myself, am a man among my people, who are all men. They will give you to fill my wigwam. I will do battle for you, Anyta, with the knife and the bow; I will win you by the strong arm, if the strange warriors stand in the path." "Alas," said the young girl, "you know not my people. They are tall like the pine trees, which rise above other trees; they look down upon your tribe as the prairie grass that the buffalo tramples down, and the

flames wither. The sun is their father — the earth
their mother — and we are called the daughters of
the sun. They would dash you into the flames, if
you told them of a lodge in the Creek wigwam
for a maiden of our tribe."

" The Creek is a warrior and a chief, Anyta,
and he will not die like a woman. He can pluck
out the heart of his foe while he begs upon the
ground. I fear not for your people's anger, but I
love the young maid of the bright eye and sunny
face, and would take her as a singing-bird into the
lodge of a great warrior. I will stay in your cabin
till the warriors come back from the hunt. I am
no fox to burrow in the hill side."

" You will stay to see me perish, then, Onea,"
said the girl — a gleam of melancholy shining
from her large dark eyes — " for my people will
not let me live, when I speak for your life."

" See you not my bow and arrows, Anyta? Is
not the tomahawk at my shoulder? Look, my
knife is keen — the sapling may speak."

" Your arm is strong, and your heart true, you
would say to Anyta; but what is one arm, and what
are thy weapons, to a thousand? You must not
linger, Onea; we will put forth in the little canoe.
I will steer to a quiet hollow, and when thou art

in safety I will leave thee, and return to thee
again."

IV.

It was with difficulty the hot-headed Onea was
persuaded to comply with the suggestions of pru-
dence, and nothing but a consideration for the
safety of the maiden had power to restrain his im-
petuosity. But, assured that, in the unequal contest of which she spoke, his own individual zeal
and valor would prove unavailing, he submitted,
though with evident ill grace, to her directions.
A like scene had, in the meanwhile, taken place
between Hillaby and Henamarsa, Anyta's lovely
companion, which was attended with pretty nearly
the same results. A mutual understanding had the
effect of providing for the two warriors in the same
manner. Entering once more the canoe in company with, and under the guidance of their mis-
tresses, they took their way down the lake, until
they lost sight of the island on which they had
first met. They kept on, until, far away from the
main route to the habitations of the tribe, they
came to a beautiful knoll of green, thickly covered
with shrubbery and trees, and so wrapt from the

passing glance of the wayfarer, by the circuitous
bendings of the stream, as to afford them the safety and secrecy they desired. The maidens informed them that they alone were in possession of
the fact of its existence, having been cast upon it
by a summer tempest, while wandering over the
rippling waters in their birchen canoe. They
found it a pleasant dwelling-place. The wild
fruits and scented flowers seemed to have purposely embellished it for the habitation of content and
love, and the singing birds were perpetually car-
roling from the branches. The vines, thickly in-
terwoven above their heads, and covered with
leaves, afforded them the desired shelter; and
gladly did they appropriate, and sweetly did they
enjoy, its pleasures and its privacies. But the day
began to wane, and the approaching evening indicated the return of the fierce warriors from the
chase. With many vows, and a tender and sweet
sorrow, the maidens took their departure for the
dwellings of their people, leaving the young
chiefs to contemplate their new ties, and the novel
situation in which they had placed themselves.
Nor did the maidens forget their pledges, or prove
false to their vows. Day after day did they take
their way in the birchen bark, and linger till
evening in the society of their beloved. The

hours passed fleetly in such enjoyments, and happy months of felicity only taught them the beauty of flowers and their scents, and the delights of an attachment before utterly unknown. But the wing of the halcyon ceased to rest on the blessed island. Impatient of inactivity, the warrior Hillaby came one day to the vine-covered cabin of Onea; his looks were sullen, and his language desponding. He spoke thus:

"It is not meet, Onea, that the hawk should be clipped of his wings, and the young panther be caged like a deer; let us go home to our people. I am growing an old woman. I have no strength in my sinews — my knees are weak."

"I would go home to my people," replied Onea, "but cannot leave the young fawn who has taken shelter under my protection. And will Hillaby depart from Henamarsa?"

"Hillaby will depart from Henamarsa, but Hillaby has the cunning of the serpent, and can burrow like the hill-fox. He will no longer take the dove to his heart, dreading an enemy. He will go home to his people — he will gather the young men of the nation, and do battle for Henamarsa. Onea is a brave warrior — will he not fight for Anyta?"

"Onea would die for Anyta, but he would not

that Anyta should perish too. Onea would not destroy the people of his wife."

"Would they not destroy Onea? They would hang his scalp in the smoke of their wigwams—they would shout and dance about the stake when his death-song is singing. If Onea will not depart with Hillaby, he will go alone. He will bring the young warriors ; and the dogs who would keep Henamarsa from his wigwam—they shall perish by his knife, and the wild boar shall grow fat upon their carcasses."

Thus spoke the elder of the two warriors, and vain were the entreaties and arguments employed by Onea to dissuade him from his purpose. The Indian habit was too strong for love, and his sense of national, not less than individual pride, together with the supineness of his present life, contrasted with that restless activity to which he had been brought up and habituated, rendered all persuasion fruitless, and destroyed the force of all arguments. Deep, seemingly, was the anguish of Henamarsa, when she learned the departure of her lover. A settled fear, however, took possession of the bosom of the gentle Anyta, and she sobbed upon the breast of the brave Onea. She felt that their happiness was at an end—that the hope of her people was insecure—that the home

of her fathers was about to suffer violation.   She
saw at once all the danger, and did not hesitate
to whisper it in the ear of Onea.   All her hope
rested in the belief, that Hillaby would never succeed in tracing his way back through the intricacies of the swamp to his own people ; or if he did,
that he would not succeed in guiding them to the
precise point in its recesses, in which her tribe had
found its abode.   But Onea knew better the capa-
cities of a warrior among his people.   He seized
his bow and equipments, and would have taken
the path after Hillaby, determined to quiet the
fears of his beloved, even by the death of his late
friend and companion ; but the maiden restrained
him.   She uttered a prayer to the great spirit, for
the safety of herself and people, and gave herself
up to the wonted happiness of that society for
which she was willing to sacrifice every thing.

V.

A new trial awaited Onea.   One day Anyta
came not.   The canoe was paddled by Henamarsa alone.   She sought him in his wigwam.
She sought to take the place of his beloved in his
affections, and would have loaded him with caresses.

" Where is Anyta ?" asked the young warrior.

" She is no longer the bride of Onea," was the reply. " She has gone into the wigwam of a warrior of her tribe — Henamarsa will love Onea, in the place of Anyta."

" Onea will love none but Anyta," was the reply.

" But she is now the wife of Echotee, the young chief. She can no longer be yours. You will never see her more."

" I will tear her from the cabin of the dog — I will drive my hatchet into his skull," — said the infuriated warrior. He rejected all the blandishments of Henamarsa, and taunted her with her infidelity to Hillaby. She departed in anger from his presence, and he lay troubled with his meditations as to the course he should pursue with regard to Anyta. His determination was adopted, and at midnight, in a birchen canoe prepared through the day, he took his way over the broad lake to the island. It lay, but not in quiet, stretched out beautifully under the twinkling stars that shone down sweetly upon it. These, however, were not its only lights. Countless blazes illuminated the shores in every direction — and the sound of lively music came upon his ear, with an influence that chafed still more fiercely the raging spirit in his

20*

heart. There were shouts and songs of merriment — and the whirling tread of the impetuous dancers bespoke a feast and a frolic, such as are due, among the Indians, to occasions only of the highest festivity.

Drawing his bark quietly upon the shore, without interruption, he went among the revellers. No one seemed to observe — no one questioned him. Dressed in habiliments the most fantastic and irregular, his warlike semblance did not strike the minds of the spectators as at all inconsistent with the sports they were pursuing, and he passed without impediment or check to the great hall, from whence the sounds of most extravagant merriment proceeded. He entered with the throng, in time to witness a solemn ceremonial. There came, at one side, a gallant chief, youthful, handsome, and gracefully erect. He came at the head of a chosen band of youth of his own age, attired in rich furs taken from native animals. Each of them bore a white wand, the symbol of marriage.

On the other side came a like party of maidens, dressed in robes of the whitest cotton, and bearing wands like the men. What bright creature is it that leads this beautiful array? Why does the young Muscoghee start — wherefore the

red spot on the brow of Onea? The maiden who
leads the procession, is his own, the gentle Anyta.
Grief was in her face; her eyes were dewy and
sad, and her limbs so trembled that those around
gathered to her support. The first impulse of
Onea was to rush forward and challenge the array
— to seize upon the maiden in the presence of the
assembly; and, by the strength of his arm, and
the sharp stroke of his hatchet, to assert his claims
to the bride in the teeth of every competitor. But
the warrior was not less wise than daring. He
saw that the maiden was sick at heart, and a fond
hope sprung into his own. He determined to witness the progress of the ceremony, trusting something to events. They dragged her forward to
the rite, passive rather than unresisting. The
white wands of the two processions, males and fe-
males, were linked above the heads of Echotee and
Anyta— the bridal dance was performed around
them in circles, and, agreeable to the ritual of the
tribe to which they belonged, the marriage was
declared complete. And now came on the ban-
queting. The repast, fruitful of animation, proceeded, and the warriors gathered around the
board, disposed alternately among the maidens,
Echotee and Anyta presiding. Onea stood apart.

"Who is he who despises our festival — why

does the young man stand away from the board? The brave man may fight and rejoice—he wears not always the war paint—he cries not for ever the war-whoop—he will come where the singing birds gather, and join in the merriment of the feast."

Thus cried a strong voice from the company, and all eyes were turned upon Onea. The youth did not shrink from reply—

"The warrior says what is true. It is not for the brave man to scorn the festival—he rejoices at the feast. But the stranger comes of a far tribe, and she who carries the wand must bid him welcome, or he sits not at the board with the warriors."

Anyta slowly rose to perform the duty imposed upon her. She had already recognised the form of her lover, and her step was tremulous and her advances slow. She waved the wand which she held in her hands, and he approached, unhesitatingly, to her side. The Indians manifested little curiosity—such a feature of character being inconsistent, in their notion, with the manliness indispensable to the warrior. Still there was something marked in the habit worn by Onea, which taught them to believe him a stranger. At such a time, however, the young men, intriguing with their dus-

ky loves, rendered disguises and deceptions so frequent, less notice ensued than might otherwise have
been the case, and the repast proceeded without farther interruption. Then followed the bridal procession to the future dwelling of the couple. The
whole assembly sallied forth, to the sound of discordant music, each with a flaming torch within
his hand. They frolicked with wild halloos in the
train of the bridal pair, waving their flaming
torches in every direction. A small stream, consecrated by a thousand such occurrences, rippled
along their pathway, upon approaching which,
they hurled the lights into its hissing waters, leaving the entire procession in darkness. This was
one part of the wonted and well known frolic.
The transition from unaccustomed light to solemn
darkness, producing the profoundest confusion,
the merriment grew immense. One party stumbled over the other, and all were playing at con-
traries and cross purposes. Shouts of laughter in
every direction, broke the gloom which occasioned
it, and proved the perfect success of the jest.

But, on a sudden, a cry arose that the bride was
missing. This, perhaps, contributed more than
any thing beside to the good humor of all but the
one immediately concerned, and the complaint and
clamor of the poor bridegroom met with no sym-

pathy. His appeals were unheeded—his asseve-
rations received with laughter and shouts of the
most deafening description. All mirth, however,
must have its end ; and the joke grew serious.
The bride was really missing, and every thing
was in earnest and unmitigated confusion. Vainly did the warriors search — vainly did the
maidens call upon the name of Anyta. She
was far beyond the reach of their voices, hurrying down the quiet lake with Onea, to the green
island of their early loves and unqualified affections.

There was one who readily guessed the mystery
of Anyta's abduction. The heart of Henamarsa
had long yearned for that of Onea. The rejection of her suit by the scrupulous warrior had
changed its temper into bitterness ; and a more
vindictive feeling took possession of her breast.
She determined to be revenged.

The warrior lay at sunset in the quiet bower,
and he slept with sweet visions in his eyes. But
why shrieks the young maiden, and wherefore is the
strong hand upon him? Who are they that bind
with thongs the free limbs of the warrior? Vainly
does he struggle for his release. Many are the
foes around him, and deadly the vengeance which
they threaten. He looks about for Anyta—she

too is bound with thongs. Above him stood the form of Henamarsa, and he well knew who had betrayed him, yet he uttered no reproach. She looked upon him with an eye of mingled love and triumph, but he gave her no look in return. He knew her not.

They took him back to the island, and added to his bonds. They taunted him with words of scorn, and inflicted ignominious blows upon his limbs. They brought him food and bade him eat for the sacrifice ; for that, at the close of the moon, just begun, he should be subjected, with the gentle Anyta, to the torture of fire and the stake. " A Creek warrior will teach you how to die," said Onea. " You are yet children ; you know nothing," — and he shook his chains in their faces, and spat on them with contempt.

VI.

That night a voice came to him in his dungeon. Though he saw not the person, yet he knew that Henamarsa was beside him.

" Live," said the false one — " live, Onea, and I will unloose the cords about thy limbs. I will make thee free of thy keepers — I will carry thee to a quiet forest, where my people shall find thee never." The warrior spake not, but turned his face from the tempter to the wall of his prison. Vainly did she entreat him, nor forego her prayers, until the first glimmerings of the day light urged her departure. Rising, then, with redoubled fury from his side, where she had thrown herself, she drew a knife before his eyes. The blade gleamed in his sight, but he shrunk not.

" What," said she, " if I strike thee to the heart, thou that art sterner than the she-wolf, and colder than the stone house of the adder ? What if I strike thee for thy scorn, and slay thee like a fox even in his hole ?"

" Is there a mountain between us, woman, and canst thou not strike ?" said the warrior. " Why speakest thou to me ? Do thy will, and hiss no more like a snake in my ears. Thou hast lost thy sting — I should not feel the blow from thy knife."

" Thou art a brave warrior," said the intruder, " and I love thee too well to slay thee. I will seek thee again in thy captivity, and look for thee to listen."

The last night of the moon had arrived, and the noon of the ensuing day was fixed for the execution of Onea and Anyta. Henamarsa came again to the prison of the chief, and love had full possession of her soul. She strove to win him to his freedom upon her own conditions. She then proffered him the same boon upon his own terms; but he disdained and denied her. Deep was her affliction, and she now deplored her agency in the captivity of the chief. She had thought him less inflexible in his faith; and, judging of his, by the yielding susceptibilities of her own heart, had falsely believed that the service she offered would have sanctioned his adoption of any conditions which she might propose. She now beheld him ready for death, but not for dishonor. She saw him prepared for the last trial, and she sunk down in despair.

The hour was at hand, and the two were bound to the stake. The torches were blazing around them — the crowd assembled — the warrior singing his song of death, and of many triumphs. But they were not so to perish. Relief and rescue were at hand; and looking forth upon the lake, which his eyes took in at a glance, Onea beheld a thousand birchen canoes upon its surface, and flying to the scene of execution. He knew the warriors who approached. He discerned the war paint of his nation; he counted the brave men, as they urged forward their vessels, and called them by their names. The warriors who surrounded him

rushed, in a panic, for their arms— but how could
they contend with the choice men of the Creeks—
the masters of a hundred nations? The conflict
was brief, though hotly contended. The people of
Onea were triumphant, and the chief and the beautiful Anyta rescued from their perilous situation.
The people whom they had conquered were bound
with thongs, and the council deliberated upon their
destiny. Shall they go free? shall they die?
were the questions — somewhat novel, it is true,
in the history of the Indians, whose course of
triumph was usually marked with indiscriminate
massacre. The voice of Onea determined the
question, and their lives were spared.

"Will you be of us and of our nation?" asked
the conquerors of the conquered.

"We are the children of the sun," was the proud
reply — "and can mingle with no blood but our
own."

"Our young men will not yield the fair lake,
and the beautiful island, and the choice fruits."

"They are worthy of women and children only,
and to these we leave them. We will seek elsewhere for the habitations of our people — we will
go into other lands. It is nothing new to our fortunes that we should do so now. The spoiler has
twice been among us, and the places that knew us

shall know us no more. Are we free to depart?
Let not your young men follow to spy out our new
habitations. Let them take what is ours now, but
let them leave us in quiet hereafter."

"You are free to go," was the response, "and
our young men shall not follow you."

The old chiefs led the way, and the young followed, singing a song of exile, to which they
claimed to be familiar, and calling themselves the
Seminole — a name, which, in their language, is
supposed to signify, the outcast. All departed,
save Anyta, and she dwelt for long years after in
the cabin of Onea.

END OF VOLUME I.

CARL WERNER,

AN IMAGINATIVE STORY;

WITH OTHER

TALES OF IMAGINATION.

BY THE AUTHOR OF
"THE YEMASSEE," "GUY RIVERS,"
"MELLICHAMPE," &c.

IN TWO VOLUMES.
VOL. II.

NEW YORK:
GEORGE ADLARD, 46 BROADWAY.

1838.

CRAIGHEAD & ALLEN, PRINTERS,
112 Fulton Street.

CONTENTS OF VOLUME II.

CONRADE WEICKHOFF.

CONRADE WEICKHOFF.

I.

IT was the easiest thing in the world for Rodolph Steinmyer to become enamored of the fair Bertha, the only daughter of the Baron Staremberg. It was not so easy a matter to obtain the approval of the proud old baron. Rodolph was noble, of excellent family; but what is nobility without money? This was the question with the baron — the leading question in every reference which he made to the pretensions of Rodolph to his daughter's hand. Would nobility, merely, keep a castle, find retainers, man the walls against the enemy, or even — not to descend too hurriedly — furnish the table and provide the daily cheer? Manifestly, it could not; and so the noble lineage of Rodolph Steinmyer did not go far toward commending him in the sight of the sturdy father of his sweetheart. It

rather made against him ; as it called for that consideration in society, and rendered necessary those
shows of place and pretension, which could never
be expected of one not of high birth ; and which,
in the event of Rodolph becoming his son-in-law,
would only have the effect of adding an encumbrance of great amount to his own already encumbered establishment. The baron was quite as
poor as he was proud ; and this probably was, in
all respects, a very proper consideration. It was
necessary that Bertha should re-establish the old
house. The castle wanted repairs ; and Bertha's
eyes were looked to, whenever it became a question how money should be raised for the purpose.
The castle wanted furniture ; and Bertha's lips, it
was thought, might do much toward fitting it up.
Bertha's beauties, in short, were the only treasures
to which the old baron could possibly refer, whenever he contemplated any of the many difficult,
but absolutely necessary, expenditures of his household. To throw them away upon a beggar — to
give Bertha to Rodolph, was, therefore, a matter
entirely out of the question. It is true, the baron
knew well enough how fondly the two loved each
other ; but what of that ? Is the love of a young
girl to be considered, even for a moment, in oppo-

sition to the cupidity or caprice of her relations?
It would be exceedingly foolish to suppose so.

II.

Bertha thought otherwise. She loved Rodolph
very much; quite as much, indeed, as he loved
her. They seemed formed entirely for each other;
and never were two young, thoughtless hearts, so
mutually devoted. Day after day did their eyes
meet, and their thoughts mingle; and day after
day increased their mutual dependence with their
passion. It is true, Rodolph was poor, but Bertha
never thought of that. His garments were none
of the best, but they were worn by Rodolph. His
castle was old, unfurnished, untenanted, and he
had no cattle. But then, she never felt any wants
when with Rodolph, and she never thought of any
want but himself, when he was absent. It was
well for her, perhaps, that she had a papa who was
more thoughtful. The baron's consideration amply atoned for the daughter's thoughtlessness. If
she thought only of Rodolph — he thought nothing of Rodolph. If she thought nothing of the
possessions of her lover — the old baron consi-

dered nothing else. Between the two, therefore, the subject, on all sides, was amply investigated.

III.

It was not the good fortune of Bertha to know any thing of her father's concern in this matter, until long after he had gravely considered it. But one day there came a new wooer to the castle of Staremberg. This was a bachelor baron, whom Bertha had never seen before, and who dwelt in a noble palace at some little distance. She, poor girl, never dreamed of the object of his visit; but Rodolph was a little more suspicious. He no sooner heard of it than he set off, post haste, for Staremberg castle. He came in a desperate hurry, determined to put his *affaire du cœur* to a final issue. His manner indicated no little excitement. He thrust aside, one after another, the sluggish retainers, in a most unaccustomed and most unbecoming manner; and even the bachelor baron, himself, Baron Brickelewacksikow, — whose name the reader will please remember in future, without requiring us to write it — happening to stand bolt upright in the very passage through which the youth was pushing his headlong way, was tumbled

incontinently against the wall, much to the detri-
ment of his knees and shoulders, and the discom-
fiture of his spirit. Rodolph was evidently in a
hurry.

IV.

In the presence of the Baron and Baroness Staremberg, Bertha very judiciously being absent,
the youthful Rodolph found himself much sooner
than he expected. He certainly felt, as he looked
upon their distinct faces, that he need not have
been in such an exceeding hurry. The old baron
looked quite as grim as the Saracen that his grandfather slew in the fifth crusade, the reeking head
of whom was painted in gigantic lines upon the
trembling tapestry before them; the baroness, if
possible, more outrageously grim, and not a whit
less unhandsome than her liege lord, sat like a
stone fortress of exceeding strength and dimen-
sions, upright in his way. She looked impene-
trable as a dozen dungeons. Rodolph was no
longer in a hurry. He really began to wonder
what he had come for; he certainly had not the
gift of languages at that moment, and would — if
he had known any thing about that burning and

shining light, at this early period — have given
the world for only half an hour's preliminary conversation with the Reverend Edward Irving.

V.

The conference was sooner ended than began.
It was a desperate necessity ; and, with a violent
effort, Rodolph contrived to find his parts of speech,
though he still stammered and stuttered most an-
noyingly.   But when he had said his say, and the
obtuse senses of his two arbiters had at length ap-
preciated his object, there was a joint burst of astonishment, almost amounting to horror, from
their several lips, at the atrocious insolence of his
demand :

"What! do you, Rodolph Steinmyer, dare to
ask of me in marriage the hand of lady Bertha of
Staremberg ?" exclaimed the baron.

"*My* daughter !" shrieked the baroness, in a
fit of holy horror.

"Presumption !" exclaimed the baron.

"Blasphemy !" groaned the baroness.   And
they looked to one another, and they looked to
the confounded youth, and they looked to the
heavens and to the earth, and then they turned

simultaneously again upon the pleader, and demanded to know if they had heard him rightly. They were willing to believe that they might have misunderstood him.

VI.

But the youth had plucked up courage during the brief and sudden progress of their indignation. With an air of greater resolution than before, he repeated his demand; and was just about to give sundry good reasons why he should be considered the properest person in the world to take charge of a maiden so young and interesting as Bertha of Staremberg, when the baron, with more coolness and composure — perhaps, too, with something more of condescension in his manner — proceeded to interrupt him :

" Say no more, Rodolph; say no more. You are a good youth, and I knew your father. He was my most intimate friend, and I loved him very much — very much, Rodolph. I love you too, Rodolph; you are a good youth, but you cannot have Bertha."

" No; you cannot have *my* daughter," cried the old lady.

"No; you cannot have our daughter," said the baron.

"I am shocked," said the baroness, "that you ever thought that you could have *my* daughter."

"It is, indeed, very surprising, Rodolph, that you should have fallen into such an error," said the baron; "but now that I have explained it, I trust that you will give up such a foolish, such an extravagant idea."

"Such an audacious — such an impious idea — *my* daughter!" exclaimed Lady Staremberg, with an echo to her husband like that of Killarney.

"Never!" exclaimed the youth, with a voice of thunder. "Never! Give up Bertha? Better tell me to give up life."

"Ay, and that might be advisable, when there's no money. Life, without money, is but a baggage wagon, on a long march, without stores or provisions," very coolly responded the baron; "Bertha you can never have, unless your castle is manned, and repaired, and furnished, and you can show me wealth like that of baron — the baron with the big name — to whom, if he is pleased to accept her, I propose to give her hand. Produce proofs of wealth like his, Rodolph, and, as I loved your father and love you, I shall give you a decided preference."

The youth, muttering curses, hurried away in despair, bent upon carrying up his appeal to a gentler, if not a higher court.

VII.

Rodolph flew instantly to Bertha, with a degree of impatience that might have seemed less than respectful, but that it was duly mixed up with a sufficient share of tenderness; he unfolded his cause of difficulty, related his love at length, recounted the scene with her parents, and resolutely declared that he neither would nor could live without her. The poor girl was sufficiently overwhelmed with the novel character of her situation. She had never deliberated much upon the condition of her heart, which, like a gipsey's child, had been allowed all along to do just what it pleased; and the sudden and unaccustomed contraction of all its liberties, just now threatened it, had an effect not less paralyzing on her than it was maddening to him. She knew not how to consider her affliction, or in which way to turn first. It was now, for the first time, that Rodolph had declared himself; the words were strangely new to her ears, but somehow they came naturally enough, and as

a thing of course, to her heart.   That heart fully
responded to them; and, certainly, she loved the
youth quite as much as it was possible for her, and
p roper for a young maiden of seventeen, to love.
The strength of her attachment to the youth became fully evident to herself, when she understood
the intention of her parents to give her to the baron with a long name.   She confessed how much
she loved him ; shed a world of tears ; showed by
look, word, and action, that she was miserable at
the thought of marrying another; and when the
youth, flattered with these manifestations, was bold
enough to propose that she should avail herself of
the present opportunity to change the air of her
father's castle for that of his own, which he assured
her was far more likely to be beneficial to her
health, to his great surprise, she flatly refused him.
Bertha was a good child ; and the holy law which
teaches us to love father and mother, in order that
our days may be long in the land, was not less a
feeling and an instinct in her heart, than a principle in her mind.   Her soul was too pure, too secure in its natural whiteness, to permit even love
to obtain a triumph over its sense of duty.

VIII.

Rodolph was in despair. Never was lover more eloquent and impassioned.

" And you will not, Bertha ?"

" I dare not, Rodolph."

" What ! you will consent to this sacrifice. You will let them bind you to that old dotard, whom you hate. You will let them tear you from the arms of the man you profess to love —"

" Whom I do love, Rodolph," was the gentle chiding.

" Oh ! Bertha, how can you consent to this ? How can you submit to be made a thing of barter ; of a mercenary love of wealth ? Think, my beloved, of the long years before us both — years of bliss or years of blight, simply as you shall decree at this moment. Can you hesitate if you love ? Can you hesitate if you think ? It cannot be very long before father and mother will both depart ; and then, — dear Bertha, — where then will be your consolation ? Nowhere, but in the bosom of a kindred love. You cannot hesitate. You owe it to me, to yourself, to all ; to your promises and pledges of the past ; to your hopes of the future ;

to love, to truth; for how can you promise love
to him, having a love for me? how can he believe
it, even should you falsely declare it? It is a
higher duty which you owe to heaven — infinitely
beyond that due to your parents — to speak the
truth always, and more particularly where the affections, our most valuable wealth, are so deeply
interested. Say to me, then, that you will be
mine. Fly with me now. In another hour the
opportunity may be lost, and never return to us
again. In another hour, dearest Bertha, tyranny,
which is the foe to love, may sacrifice us both on
the altar of worldly interest. We shall be torn
apart, and separated for ever."

Rodolph was eloquent, but the maiden was
most firm. To the young mind, taught properly,
there is no consideration so revolting as the diso-
bedience of a child; and it must have been the
worst of all parental oppression, that of actual violence, which could have made Bertha of Staremberg take any step in opposition to the will of her
father. She sighed and sorrowed unaffectedly;
repeated her vows of love to Rodolph, and promised him eternal faith; but the youth was not to
be satisfied after this fashion. He renewed his solicitations; and it was only when he had exhausted all his arguments, entreaties, and breath toge-

ther, that he tore himself away from her restrain-
ing arms, and rushing forth from the castle of
Staremberg in a fit of despair, hastened furiously
to a neighboring wood, in a paroxysm which
seemed to promise the most desperate results.

IX.

Rodolph sought the wood of the Black Forest
in no enviable temper. He buried himself in its
deepest recesses; for his thoughts were dark like
its own glooms, and horrible, like the numerous
spectral images by which tradition had tenanted
them. He was of a quick and irritable disposition; and he had not been sufficiently tempered
by the vicissitudes of life to bear meekly and quietly with any contradiction. The opposition of
Bertha's parents was bad enough; but he had
never anticipated any from herself. That she
should refuse at first was to be expected; but that
she should continue to deny to the last, was no
less unreasonable than unmaidenlike; and with
half a resolution to do what he was about to do,
in her despite, as well as in his own despair, he
drew the long keen hunter's knife from his girdle,
elevated its blade sufficiently in air to make the

descending blow fatal, and in another instant it would have found its sheath in his heart, when, just in the nick of time, his arm was arrested by a grasp from behind. He turned fiercely upon the unwelcome intruder, and shrank back in horror from the glance that met his own. Whom did he see? What did he see? Was it real, or was it only the spectre of his old comrade, the gallant Conrade Weickhoff, who was reported to have perished at sea full three years before?

"Conrade Weickhoff!" exclaimed the youth, half in horror, half in inquiry.

"Rodolph Steinmyer," was the response of the stranger, who smiled in the most natural manner in the world as he pronounced the name.

"Are you my friend Conrade?" demanded Rodolph.

"More like, than you are to Rodolph Steinmyer," was the reply.

"And living?"

"Did you not feel my grasp? Was it so *light* that you have need to ask the question?"

"Whence came you, Conrade? Where have you been? They said that you were drowned at sea; and they have mourned for you as one no longer of earth."

A wild laugh, and a bright sarcastic twinkle of

the eye, were the only answer which, for the moment, the new comer gave to the rapid inquiries of the youth. He seemed to chuckle pleasantly at the idea of being a dead man; and there was something exceedingly irreverent — so Rodolph thought — in the manner of his ancient comrade, while dwelling upon this topic. But Conrade was always a wild fellow, whom nobody could manage, and who was reported, indeed, to have given himself over to studies and practices of diabolism. So general was the opinion among his friends, that when the news came of his death by sea, the remark was frequent among them, that the devil had reason to congratulate himself upon the acquisition of a new companion, so much after the fashion of his own heart.

X.

The first surprise being over, and Rodolph being now satisfied that it was Conrade himself — a person of very substantial flesh and blood, and no ghost — that stood before him, the conversation naturally turned upon the desperate act which Rodolph had been about to commit, when his friend so opportunely interrupted him.

2*

" What could have persuaded you to this, Rodolph ? what motive for this rashness ?" was the
demand of Conrade.

The youth told his story, and Conrade chuckled so heartily that the lover grew indignant.

" Why, what the d——l do you find in it to laugh
at ?" he demanded fiercely.

" Be not rash," said the other ; " and, I pray
you, take not your neighbor's name in vain. The
devil may be much nearer to you than you imagine. If I laugh, I mean no offence, you may be
sure. I only laugh at the folly of love, which so
beguiles and misleads men of otherwise very excellent understanding. Did you hope to get the
girl by cutting your throat ?"

" Not to get her, surely ; but to live without her
would be worse than death."

" Perhaps so ; but I think not. Life is com-
fortable, always provided you have enough of it ;
and that a man may always have, if he will look
for it where it may be found. But what do you
intend now to do ? I have kept you from death
once ; when I turn my back, you will whip out
your cold steel again, and try the thing over, and
it may be, another time I shall come a moment or
two too late."

" Perhaps," said Rodolph, with some phlegm.

" Perhaps is no answer to a friend," said the other, taking his hand affectionately. " Be more like yourself; let old times begin again. Let us once more be true friends to each other ; for, believe me, Rodolph, though time has been between us, and we have been so long separated, I feel toward you as ever."

Rodolph could not reply, but he returned the gentle squeeze of his friend's hand, and the tears filled his eyes.

" You weep, Rodolph, and I am answered," said the other. " I see you have the same heart as of old. I, too, have been left unchanged in all my trials. We are again friends."

They embraced affectionately, and after a little interval given up to the renewal of former pledges, after the picturesque and sentimental manner common, even at that early period, among the German youth, they again began to discourse about the purposed deed of Rodolph, and the causes which had led to it. A few moments were passed by Conrade in silence ; then, abruptly speaking, he demanded :

" And you are required to man your castle, refit and repair it, and altogether exhibit resources such as the baron with a long name ?"

The youth sighed forth a melancholy affirmative.

"You shall do it," said the other.

Rodolph looked up angrily, as if he had been laughed at.

"You shall do it."

"How ?"

"I will help you to fortune."

"You ?"

"Yes — I — Conrade Weickhoff. It shall be the first proof which I will give you that my friendship for you is the same that it ever was. I am able to do what I promise. I am able to give you the means to go forth as proudly as your baron with a long name, and to exhibit wealth even more extensive. We shall satisfy Bertha's parents, and you shall have the maiden without delay."

Rodolph looked on his friend in silent wonderment. He thought him dreaming. He knew that Conrade's family had been quite as destitute as his own. Where could he have got his new ability to do what he promised. He must surely be mad, thought Rodolph ; but when he looked at Conrade, never did face seem more confident and earnest. The expression of his countenance was conclusive.

"Speak out," said Rodolph, impetuously ; "tell

me all; explain to me the sources of your ability, and torture me no longer with a hope so extravagant as to seem desperate and foolish. Let me hear upon what you build, that I may know whether it be worth while to live for it or not."

"It is always worth one's while to live, so long as there are maidens like Bertha Staremberg to live with. I know the maiden; she is a heaven in herself; and were it not, dear Rodolph, for my friendship, I should certainly seek her love on my own account."

"Ha!" said Rodolph, furiously.

But the other checked him in his paroxysm.

"Fear nothing, I am not your rival. I will help you to Bertha; the means are even now in your own power, and I will disclose them to you. But come apart with me to some pleasant place, where we may sit while talking. There is, or should be, an old abbey in this neighborhood, where I have often rambled. The grave stone of an armed knight shall yield us a pleasant seat, and then we can talk more freely. I hate fatigue; and standing up when one can sit, is like submitting to bondage when one can fly. The sense of restraint is, of all others, the most hateful to me; and, when I can help, I will have none of it. Come."

XI.

They went to a spot more secluded in the forest, and there they found an old abbey church, which Rodolph did not remember ever to have seen before. With every spot of it, however, his companion seemed familiar; he talked of this family burial place and of that, and began to give a long history of the knight whose crossed legs in marble they were then sitting upon, and he might have gone into details of a thousand years — for he betrayed a strange familiarity with past events — had not Rodolph, with a more selfish object, hurriedly interrupted him. Conrade laughed heartily at the impatience of his companion, and his pale features were full of a pleasantly satirical expression, and his eyes danced with a wild, strange glare, as he looked quizzingly upon the feverish restlessness of the lover; but he saw that it would not do to tax the youth's temper too far, and so he proceeded quietly to his purposed explanation.

" You have heard of the late Count Oberfeldt of Manfrein ?" he demanded.

" The *late* Count Oberfeldt ? What ! is he dead ?" responded Rodolph.

" Died last night," was the reply.

" Why, he was quite well — I saw him on the edge of the forest, riding with a stranger, only two days ago. He must have died suddenly."

" Quite — as suddenly as a sharp knife, such as that you were about to use an hour ago, could carry him off, hurriedly applied to the carotid."

" Murdered ?"

" No ; he committed suicide."

" Is it possible ? He was always a bad man !" remarked Rodolph, quite thoughtlessly and innocently.

" Ahem !" responded the other. " Bad or good, I say not. He was a wild, irregular, strange sort of person, whose pleasures and pursuits differed materially from those of the rest of the world. It is not for us to say whether he was right or wrong in their adoption. His accountability is not to us, and so far the subject is foreign to our discourse. You knew him, Rodolph ?"

The question was answered affirmatively.

" You know that his wealth was great ?"

" Yes."

" A dozen different castles — fine domains every where — well provided ; retainers in abundance ; good wines and wealth in profusion. These were his, and, strange to say, though living a profli-

gate life, he died having them all in his possession."

" Stranger still," remarked Rodolph, " that,
having them in possession, he should voluntarily
have given them up."

" Perhaps not.   Satiety is a worse death than
the knife.   It is the death of that necessary provocative, without which life must always stagnate.
Wise men pray that they should never have all
their desires satisfied.   Oberfeldt was not a wise
man.   His desires were narrowed to his animal
propensities, and he was unfortunate enough to
grasp and gain all that he desired.   They tired him
out in the end, and grew into a fatigue, so he cut
the carotid, and got rid of them."

" The d—l has him!" said Rodolph, coolly.

" That 's none of our business," said the other,
warmly ; " and let me advise you, that to speak
of persons with whom our own acquaintance is
imperfect, is not always to do them justice.   You
may discover that truth for yourself in time ; for
the present, let us talk of your own affairs, and
then of Oberfeldt's, so far as they may concern
you."

" But how can the affairs of Oberfeldt concern
me?   I see not that," said Rodolph, impatiently.

" But you shall see, when you have heard.   The

great wealth of Oberfeldt is to be divided, and you are, if you desire it, one of his legatees."

"If I desire it!" exclaimed Rodolph, hastily; "speak out, my friend. Wealth to me is every thing at this moment; and though I see not why Oberfeldt should have left me any of his, I am not unwilling to avail myself of his bequest. I should not reject one from the d——l himself."

"You are only too accommodating," said the other, gravely. "But hear. You are one of his heirs, if you desire it. He was a singular creature, and has made a singular disposition of his property. He has left it subject to division, among any dozen men who will pledge themselves to follow his example ——"

"What! cut their throats?"

"Even so; but after a peculiar plan. He does not desire them to cut their throats on the instant, or together. He requires only one amateur at a time. Once a year, the anniversary of his own suicide, is to be celebrated by a selection from among his followers — his college, as he calls them —— and the martyr is to be chosen by lot."

"Monstrous idea!" said Rodolph.

"Very!" responded the other.

"And what then?" said Rodolph.

"Why, only this," was the reply; "I have de-

termined to avail myself of all the advantages of
Oberfeldt's will. I will become one of his devi-
sees. I will get one of his fine castles. I will
get his manors and retainers, his stock and his
treasure. I will take all that the bequest bestows.
I am fond of money, for its power and its purposes. I have none of my own. It matters not to
me whether I die by my own hand, the hand of
my enemy, or the worst of all hands, that of star-
vation. Life is not life, unless for what it yields
us. I do not deprive myself of life, if I lose nothing when I perish; and at present I have nothing to lose. I go to-night, with others, to Man-
frien castle. I swear to the performance of all the
conditions exacted by the will; I jump into my
new possessions, and hasten to their enjoyment.
I will begin to live from that hour; heretofore I
have not lived — it is high time that I should. I
counsel you to do likewise. Go with me to-
night; swear with me to the conditions; avail
yourself of the wealth they give you, and be happy
while you may."

"Great heaven!" exclaimed the other : "How
can you advise me thus, Conrade? how can you
determine thus yourself? What! pledge myself
to commit suicide?"

"What were you but just now about to do,"
demanded the other, with a sneer, "when I came

up so happily, and held back your hand? Is the present plan worse? Is it not better; far better, in all respects? You get something now for the commission of the act, when, before, you could have derived no advantage from it. You get the very wealth you wanted; you get the woman you love, who else would be lost to you for ever. Can you hesitate?"

Rodolph bent down his head. It sank on his bosom despondingly. The thick drops of perspiration stood upon his brow, for a great mental strife was going on within.

"Think," said the tempter, "think what you will gain — wealth, Bertha. Think what you will lose — Bertha, wealth — all that would be worth living for."

Rodolph was silent; the other continued:

"And she will be the victim, not less than yourself; the old baron with the long name will bear her off in triumph. She will be immured in his castle; her arms will enfold him in their embraces; his coarse lips will riot upon the sweet innocence of hers; he —"

"No more — no more," exclaimed the desperate youth, tossing his hands toward heaven; "I will go with you to-night; I will swear to the conditions. Bertha shall be mine, and mine only.

I cannot live without her; I cannot bear that she should be the bride of another."

XII.

That night the ceremonial was an awful one in the great hall of Oberfeldt's castle. The body of the suicide lay in state in the centre of the apartment, which was illuminated with an intense glare, shooting out from strangely large torches, borne up by sable figures standing in its many niches and embrasures. The corpse presented a sight horrid from its wounds, and hellish from it expression. The head had been nearly severed from the shoulders, by the desperate stroke which the deceased had given himself. The eyes were unclosed; the lids seemed to have been drawn in under the brows, and the whites gleamed out with a meteoric lustre, through the filmy humidity with which death had wrapped them. The testamentary document lay upon the breast of the deceased. His hand, still grasping the fatal knife, with all the bloody traces of the deed yet upon it, rested upon the paper. Around him stood the persons who were prepared to avail themselves of the dreadful advantages of the will before them. Their

number was completed upon the entrance of Rodolph and his friend. The lover looked upon
the scene with horror; but he had nerved himself
to the deed. He gazed vacantly upon his associates; and his passing scrutiny did not serve to
reconcile him in any great degree to the step
which he was about to take. With the exception
of his friend Weickhoff, he saw none among the
assembled college before him who had any claim
to gentility. They were either debauchees, or
gamblers, spendthrifts, and wretches who fasten
themselves as a disease upon society, and contribute to the corruption of that body upon which
they are engrafted. But he had no time for reflection. Weickhoff led the way, and by his audacity evidently controlled the rest. He drew the
document from the grasp of the suicide, and without the pause of a second, dashed down his signature in bloody characters at the foot of the con-
ditional pledge which followed the testament, and
to which its reference was special, and done after
the most approved legal requisitions of those ages.
The example was soon followed by the rest; and
signature after signature appeared upon the fatal
sheet, until Rodolph was the only one left who
had yet to sign. He lingered, and a light touch
of a finger pressed upon his wrist. It went like

3*

a cold wind into the artery beneath. He looked
up in a tremor, and his eyes met those of Weickhoff. What a glance did they encounter! So
bright, so cold; so ironical, yet so conciliating;
such a sneer, yet such a smile. There was a mad
prompter in the heart of the youth at that moment,
and he rushed forward to the body of the dead
man; he clutched the pen in his fingers, and began
writing the letters of his name after the rest. As
he wrote, to his great horror and suprise, the same
letters, as he severally wrote than, appeared one
after the other in a blank space in the body of the
instrument above. A sickness seized upon his
heart; but he desperately proceeded. The deed
was done — the name written — the contract was
completed; and, in the next moment, he felt himself clasped in the arms of Weickhoff.

"Now, indeed, Rodolph, my friend, you are
mine," was the exclamation of his comrade. What
a strength seemed in the nerves of Weickhoff!
The embrace nearly stifled him; and yet Weickhoff was slender in the extreme; pale, even to
wanness; and with a general air of feebleness,
which looked rather like disease than stength or
life. Had Rodolph been asked the question before, he would have unhesitatingly said that his
own were infinitely greater than the physical pow-

ers of Weickhoff; yet now he seemed but an infant in his grasp. But Weickhoff had been a traveller, and Rodolph naturally enough concluded that he had acquired hardihood by trial and adventure.

XIII.

Revelry of all sorts, indulgences the most wild, excesses the most licentious, followed the conclusion of the dreadful ceremonial in the castle of Oberfeldt. A luxurious banquet was prepared, and every temptation of gross and festering debauch, common to that era, was provided and partaken of by that melancholy circle of uncongenial confederates. The terms of the will were read to them by Conrade, who took a leading part in their festivities. But, though of appalling and curious nature, there was but one of all the college that heeded its conditions. That was Rodolph. He listened in a vague sort of consciousness. His feelings and thoughts were too various and crowded to suffer him to think correctly ; and the emotions with which he felt himself seized, were rather those of a young, unsophisticated heart, finding itself, for the first time, in a novel and

strange situation, than of a thinking mind engaged in analyzing it.   Conrade discovered this, and
plied all his arts, which were neither mean nor
few, in order to dissipate the lover's melancholy.
He succeeded in part.   He dwelt with ridicule
upon the passages of the will which seemed most
to have impressed the youth ; then adroitly paint-
ing the happiness which must follow the possession
of the fortune, in giving Bertha to his arms, he
had the satisfaction to discover that, by degrees,
the moody apprehensions of the youth wore rapidly away.   But still Rodolph could not relish
the associates around him, and with whom he found
himself, by his own act, associated in so strange a
brotherhood.   Men he would have been ashamed
to know before, he now found himself connected
with in life and death.   That death, too, now that
he was in the possession of the means of life,
seemed to have acquired terrors which it had not
some few hours ago.   He had never asked himself the difference of situation and mind between
the desperately hopeless man, and him to whom
the world is full of hope and promise.   He was
yet to learn this difference.   The glozing lips of
the tempter had persuaded him too readily to believe that suicide at one moment and at another
was the same thing to the same person, and he had

admitted too readily a proposition so false, as one
entirely true. There are times when it is not difficult to part with life — alas! how often is it the
case that we would rather give up heaven itself
than lose it!

XIV.

At a late hour the college separated. The sitting was broken up, and the several members prepared to retire to the spoils and possessions which
the will of Oberfeldt had assigned them. The
dangers and conditions of that will; the pledges
of terror which they had made — filled as they
were with wine and frolic, and gloating on the vast
wealth placed within their enjoyment — gave them
but little concern. Their next celebration was
required to be held at the same place, on the same
night of the ensuing year. A year was secured
to them of licentious and unrestrained enjoyment;
and to most of them a new world of happiness
was opened upon them by this heretofore unknown
privilege. They gave themselves but little concern about the one of their number who must be
chosen for the next year's sacrifice. It was enough
that they had a bond of fate for that period of time.

Reckless in their lives before, they were not less so in reference to the hour of their death. They could lose but little, as life had never fairly been possessed by any among them.

The thoughts of Rodolph troubled him more greatly on this subject; but the presence of Conrade, who clung to his friend, and employed his mind and fancy by a continual reference to Bertha Staremberg, served to keep them down and to restrain them. They did not separate as did the rest.

"I will attend you," said Conrade; "you must instantly seek Bertha, or you may be too late. Your baron with the long name may be in a hurry, and Staremberg has shown you that he does not hold you of sufficient importance, though he loved your father so very much, to wait any very long time for his son. Your retainers, I see, are ready; and Oberfeldt, like a hospitable man, has provided handsomely for his friends. These dresses are very rich. Follow my example."

In an instant Conrade Weickhoff arrayed himself in a splendid suit, that lay on the table before him, which was covered with the richest dresses of every pattern and size. Without pause for reflection, Rodolph did the same, and they were soon equipped. In the court below fine horses were caparisoned; and Weickhoff did not scruple to single out a noble barb for himself, while designating another for his friend. They were soon mounted, and the morning sun found them scouring over the space which separated the two castles of Oberfeldt and Staremberg.

XV.

You should have seen Rodolph Steinmyer and his friend Conrade Weickhoff, on their fine black chargers, come prancing into the courtyard of Staremberg. You should have seen the consternation of all the spectators. The baron with the long name stood aghast; but a moment before he had been certain of his prey, of which he now felt exceedingly doubtful. Staremberg looked wild, but not dissatisfied; while his lady, dazzled by the guady trappings of the horses and their riders, could only lift up her skinny hands, and exclaim:

"My eyes! my eyes!"

To make a long story short, the presence of Rodolph became very agreeable to the father and mother, no less than to the daughter. They were delighted with him, and his horses, and his friends, and his retainers, and every thing that was his.

There were now no objections to his suit. The baron always had loved Rodolph as he had loved his
father.   It was only a strange obliquity of understanding on the youth's part that kept him from
making the discovery. The old lady had all
along desired that Rodolph should be the choice
of her daughter; it was only a proper feeling of
maternal pride that had prompted her to say the
contrary. It was strange how naturally and well
all old difficulties were smoothed and explained
away; and Rodolph, good youth! only wondered at his own dullness, at not having seen things
in their proper light before.

"My son," exclaimed the dear old baroness, in
a fit of enthusiastic fondness, " the desire of my
heart is now realized; I can go down to the
grave in peace, since *you* are to be the husband of
my daughter."

Conrade Weickhoff chuckled irreverently and
loud. The baron with the long name expostu-
lated; but Staremberg told him bluntly that he
had never loved his father as he had loved the
father of Rodolph; a speech which the bachelor
knight took in high dudgeon, but without receiving any redress for it.   That night a wild, practical joke which Conrade Weickhoff played off
upon him, sent him away half dead with affright,

half naked, and at midnight. The wooing went
on smoothly after this; no difficulties stood in the
way, all parties were satisfied, and the marriage
followed as soon as circumstances would permit.
In the arms of the lovely Bertha, Rodolph almost
forgot the dreadful ceremonial which he had witnessed, and of which he had partaken, at the castle
of Oberfeldt.

XVI.

But he was not allowed to forget so readily.
His friend Conrade Weickhoff, like a true friend,
kept him in memory of his honorable engagements. During the honeymoon, however, Conrade most strangely kept aloof from the dwelling
of the lovers; and, for that brief period, it may
safely be affirmed that never was dwelling more
favored by the sunshine of happiness. The two,
thus united, seemed only to live for one another;
and such was the warmth and strength of their
mutual attachment, that the most casual or close
observer must have seen that their future joy, if it
depended only upon themselves, must be un-
alloyed and permanent. Alas ! it did not depend ·entirely upon themselves. The alloy was

at hand, and the friend of Rodolph, strange to say, was the first to administer it. A month had passed, or more, when Conrade suddenly made his appearance. Will it be believed, that Rodolph was pained to see him? So it was. The presence of his friend brought with it the recollection of the dreadful engagement which he had made, and to which he had seduced him. He sickened at his sight, and turned away. But his aversion was not seen by Conrade; at least, the latter did not seem to see it. He resolutely approached, and took the hand of Rodolph in his own, and addressed him in the soothing and sweet language of friendship. But even the tones of his voice, so soft and pleasant to his ear, and the words of good faith which Conrade uttered, were all neutralized by a strange, taunting laugh, a suppressed chuckle, which his friend of late had most unaccountably adopted.

"D—n that strange laugh which you have," said Rodolph, abruptly; "I do not like it; it goes like a cold wind into my bones. Where the d——l did you pick it up?"

"You do not like it, then?" said the other, and he laughed again, more unpleasantly than ever.

"Like it, Conrade! How should I? It is the strangest, most annoying chuckle I ever heard in my life. Drop it, for my sake, I pray you, and take up some better habit."

Conrade was obliging enough.

" I will try to rid myself of it," said he, " since it annoys you, though the effort will be a hard one. It is so natural to me."

"Natural to you!" exclaimed Rodolph; " why, I do not remember to have ever heard it before you went to sea ?"

" Perhaps not ; it is a foreign acquisition, no doubt, and not the less natural for being so. The journey through life is chiefly taken that we may pick up our nature as we go along. Our nature is not born with us, as foolish people imagine. We choose it from a variety, as we choose our dresses ; and our happiness depends very much upon the sort of stuff and color we make choice of. Perhaps, if you observe closely, you will see that the most fickle people are those who have a variety — the most fortunate those who have but one. It is my error to have chosen some that do not sit graciously ; that laugh, for example, which you do not like. My smile pleases you better, I doubt not ?"

And Conrade, as he spoke, turned his glance upon the face of Rodolph, with an expression which was even more annoying to the youth than the chuckle of which he had complained. He was about to say so to his companion, but the fear of being thought querulous, and his own increasing consciousness of a state of nervous excitability, determined him to say nothing.

"I am feverish, I think, this evening, Conrade," he said to his friend; "do you not think so?"

He extended his hand as he spoke; but when the fingers of Conrade pressed the wrist, it seemed to him that he was chilled as by an ague. He withdrew his arm instantly, and looked with astonishment upon his comrade, whose smile, like that of a basilisk, was fixed upon him.

"You are disordered," said Conrade, a moment after, with a show of concern in his countenance. "You should take medicine. I will ride over to Oberfeldt's castle, and get you something. He had a fine laboratory, and made his own chemicals."

"God forbid!" exclaimed Rodolph; "Nothing from that d—nable place, in heaven's name."

"We will not speak of the absent," responded the other gravely. "But let us to the castle; some wine will cheer us both, and, possibly, put you in better health and spirits."

XVII.

"Rodolph, dear Rodolph!" said Bertha one day to her husband, standing at the castle entrance, and looking forth upon the retreating figure of Conrade Weickhoff, who had just left them; "there is something about the baron Weickhoff that is very annoying to me. I do not like him, Rodolph."

"He is my friend, Bertha," responded Rodolph, with a gravity that seemed to rebuke her no less than his language.

"I know it, dear Rodolph, and I try to like him, because he is your friend; but forgive me, dear Rodolph, when I tell you that all my efforts are in vain. I cannot like him; I do not feel at ease in his presence."

The youth looked curiously upon the blooming and blushing woman of his heart, and, strange to say, he loved her the more because she could not tolerate his friend. He dared not speak out his feelings and thoughts, however, for there was between the two a manifest contradiction which he had sought, but vainly, to reconcile. In his own estimation, Conrade had ever been his friend. In

4*

boyhood they were inseparable, and, certainly,
the very possession of his wife and present happiness was owing entirely to Conrade. Should
he oppose to these substantial services the capri-
ciousness of taste which found fault with a look, a
glance, or a ridiculous chuckle? Nothing could
be more idle or unjust in the eye of reason and
good sense; yet, in his heart, that glance and
chuckle were more than enough to counterbalance
all the substantial services which his friend had
rendered him.

"And what is there, dear Bertha, in Conrade
Weickhoff that displeases you?"

"He is so cold," said she, innocently.

"Indeed!" exclaimed the other, not altogether
so well pleased with his wife, and rather more
pleased with his friend. "Indeed — cold — in
what manner, Bertha?"

"He seems to have lost all human sensibilities,"
was her reply. "When he speaks, it is only to
sneer at his neighbors. Does he hear of any virtues which they possess, he is sure to know and to
speak of their defects and foibles. He laughs,
too, at sacred things — at age and character —
and does not seem to relish the respect which
others show to them. Then that strange, horrid
laugh, which he has; and sometimes, when you

turn suddenly, you catch his eye fixed upon you with a staring sort of contempt, which puts me, for all the world, in mind of the Mephistopheles whom you remember to have seen upon the tapestry in the old hall at Staremberg, where he tempts our ancestor, the Teuton, on the brow of the Harz. He sometimes frightens me to look at him, and my blood is chilled when he speaks to me, or laughs. I cannot like him, I'm afraid."

" Nor I," thought Rodolph, but he did not say it. The words of Bertha saddened him more than ever, though he loved her the more when he found how large was the degree of sympathy between them. A common aversion is not unfrequently the occasion of a common love.

XVIII.

" Your wife does not like me, Rodolph," said Conrade to the former, one day, some time after this interview. " I am too blunt ; I speak out my mind too freely, and so offend her. She has been brought up by that old beldam, your mother-in-law of Staremberg — forgive me, Rodolph, if I cannot speak very affectionately of her — and has imbibed many of those antiquated, stiff notions, which would fetter all freedom of speech and intercourse. I am a plain man, and can't bend myself to conciliate people of his temper. You must take me as you find me, or not at all. I know I have my faults; I am neither very amiable nor very handsome. I have seen the world, and, thanks to Oberfeldt, I am quite too independent to find it necessary to play the hypocrite, and give men credit for qualities which they have not. Your wife loves not ascetics, and I am too much of one to please her. Better, therefore, that I should cease to trouble you with my visits. Now and then I may look in upon you, and I need not say how ready I am, with the old feeling, to serve you whenever you need me. In such case, all that you need do, is to visit me. I shall always rejoice to see one so dear to me."

Rodolph tried to explain for, and to excuse his wife; an error of judgment, which a wise husband will never commit.

"You mistake Bertha entirely, my dear Conrade; you do her injustice. Her reserve is natural to her, and she meets every body as she meets you."

"No, no, Rodolph, I know better. The difference is marked between her reception of me and others."

"By heaven, Conrade, but it shall not be so.

You are my friend, and my wife shall treat you as such."

Strangely contradictory were the thoughts and feelings of Rodolph on this occasion. Conscious himself of a changed temper toward his friend, he sought to hide the alteration from scrutiny by a show of proper indignation toward his innocent wife; and he fumed and foamed for ten minutes in violent speech accordingly.

"Nay, be not angry, Rodolph," said his companion, in a style of soothing which was exceedingly annoying.

"I will be angry, Conrade. I have reason to be angry. My wife do injustice to my friend! I will be angry!"

A sarcastic smile played over the lips of Conrade at this insincere ebullition. Well he knew that Rodolph's aversion was not less strong than that of Bertha's; but he took especial care to conceal his conviction on this subject. Rodolph, in the mean while, hurried to Bertha's chamber, leaving Conrade in the hall. He had worked himself into a petty sort of fury, by repeating Conrade's language to himself as he went through the passages, and he was in no small tempest when he came into her presence. The fury of his first assault astounded her, and she could not reply,

till, all on a sudden, she beheld the glaring eyes
of Conrade peeping through the opened door of
the apartment. A new emotion — a sudden
strength, which seemed supernatural — possessed
her on the instant. She darted from her seat,
threw herself before the little family altar that
stood by the bedside, and prayed aloud to heaven.
The practical rebuke was felt by her husband.
He sank down before the altar beside her, and
their mutual hands were clasped in prayer. When
she looked round to the door of the apartment,
the face of Conrade Weickhoff was no longer to
be seen.

XIX.

A month had passed before Conrade again
visited Rodolph. In that period a change had
taken place in the dwelling of the latter. Bertha
and her young husband were happier than ever.
She was " as women wish to be, who love their
lords." Her heart was light now, like that of a
bird in spring. He, too, though troubled sometimes with serious thoughts, was yet conscious
of an intenser satisfaction than his heart had
ever known before. Conrade beheld this at

a glance. His manner was more guarded than usual. His temper seemed to be subdued. He was even conciliatory, though reserved; and, in the flush of her heart's tide of joyful emotions, Bertha half forgot her old hostility. She even smiled freely upon, and talked with the ancient friend of her husband; the whole world, at that moment, seeming to her young and delighted spirits, full of associations which were all good and beautiful.

Conrade congratulated Rodolph upon the grateful prospect before him, and in a manner which was far less disagreeable than usual. He spent the day pleasantly enough with his friend; but left the castle after sunset, alleging a pressing necessity for his presence elsewhere. On leaving, however, he amply made amends to himself for his own forbearance. His last words, at parting, left a sting that rankled dreadfully in the bosom of the youth. The words were simple enough, and seemed only a passing inquiry.

"What month is this, Rodolph?" said he, as it were unconsciously, while mounting his sable steed.

"July," was the stammered reply.

"July!" Conrade seemed to muse a while; then speaking as follows, he rode away:

"I shall not see you for some time, Rodolph;
not, I think, before November.   Then I must see
you, you know."

Big drops stood upon the brow of Rodolph;
he rushed to the gloomiest chamber of his castle,
and he felt not that night the caresses of his wife.
Well did he understand the significant, yet simple
language of his friend.   The fifth of November
was the first anniversary after the self-murder of
Oberfeldt.

XX.

It came too rapidly — that dreadful month.
We need not try, we should fail utterly, to describe
the agony of Rodolph, at its approach.   It was a
madness — that subdued sort of madness in which,
while the faculties of mind all struggle in confusion, there is still a sufficient consciousness of its
own impotence and utter despair, to restrain it
from any vain and idle ebullition.   In a few days
the flesh seemed to have fallen from his bones;
his eyes were lustreless, yet full of a feverish glare,
like those of Weickhoff, and seemed shooting out
from their sockets.   His very limbs seemed pal-
sied, and refused their offices.   He was incapable

of exertion. All things contributed to this agony
of soul under which he labored. The pregnancy
of Bertha had advanced greatly. A few days,
and he might be a father; and she, as this thought
came to her mind, she clung to her husband with
all the strength of a new-born passion, and, burying her head in his bosom, dwelt fondly upon the
blessing which was at hand. How more than
sweet was life at that moment! How dreadful
the idea of death, as an appointed prospect in the
vista of time ! How much more dreadful the
strong probability of that death, so near, and so
terrible, which the coming anniversary announced!
Wonder not that he thrust the one most beloved
of all from his arms, when these awful images
assailed him. Wonder not that he rushed away
from her embrace to the deepest cell of his castle,
and threw himself in utter abandonment of soul
upon the cold and clammy pavement.

The night came — a night of exceeding beauty.
Rodolph moved through his dwelling like a blind
man. He tottered in his mental incertitude, not
less than in his body's debility. He was about to
visit his wife in her chamber, when he was conscious that some one stood suddenly beside him.
He looked round, and it was Conrade Weickhoff.

" The hour is late, Rodolph," said Conrade,

"we have little time to spare. Your horse is saddled in the court. We must keep our engagements."

"God of heaven! Conrade," exclaimed the youth, "how can you speak of this accursed business so coolly?"

"Why not? I had long since prepared my mind for it," said the other, "and so, I presume, had you."

"No — no! — The thought is dreadful!"

"Nor will it be less so by poring over it. But why should this thought be so dreadful to you now? You are only in the same situation in which I found you a year ago, even should it fall to your lot to perish. Then, only for my hand, you would have done that, the image of which now so dreadfully affrights you. I see not the substantial difference."

But there was a substantial difference, and Rodolph saw and felt it. How desolate was he then — how hopeless — how desperate in love and fortune — with how little to live for! Now — what had he not, in possession, calculated to make him in love with life — what sweet ties — what ministering affections — what hopes — what joys, what desires and delights! He reproached his friend bitterly, as he thought upon these things.

" Would that I had never seen you, Conrade,"
he exclaimed, bitterly.

" I should have been spared this language,
then," said the other, with a tone of reproach,
which had its effect upon the sensitive mind of the
hearer. Rodolph was too much of a dependant
upon his friend to quarrel with him ; and begging
his forgiveness, he inquired into some trifling particulars connected with the coming proceedings at
the castle of Oberfeldt.

" The chances are no more against you, Rodolph, than against myself and all the rest. It all
depends on fortune. Your good luck has always
been conspicuous ; it will not fail you now."

" True, true," said the other, musingly, and
with renewed hope ; but a moment after, his brow
became clouded again.

" But it must come some day or other, Conrade
— next year or the next."

" Sufficient for the day is the evil thereof.
Death itself must come some day or other, and
with this greater disadvantage, that you have no
specified time for preparation. The Oberfeldt
contract takes nobody by surprise. But the lot
may never fall to you, Rodolph."

" How ? — it must some day or other."

" No ! our college is never less. For every

man taken from us by lot, we choose another
member to fill his place, from applicants who are
always sufficiently numerous. The new comer
shares the chances with you precisely as did the
old; and as luck's all, it may be that it shall
never fall to you to perish by your own hand;
and you may die, in a ripe old age, after the
fashion of the most quiet abbot, in all the odor of
sanctity, and with all the comfortings of a full
household around you."

The gamester's hope consoled and strengthened
Rodolph.

"I will be ready in a moment," said he.

" Where are you going?"

" But for a moment — I would see Bertha."

" Better not; you will only mingle useless
tears."

"I must go!" said Rodolph, firmly; "I must
tell her that I am about to ride forth for an hour
or two, or she will be alarmed."

Conrade chuckled, but did not seek farther to
restrain his friend. The parting between Rodolph
and his wife — he suffering all the agony of his
situation, yet under the necessity of hiding it from
her; and she full of all the tenderness of a wife,
so soon to become a mother — was a trying one
to him, and a sweetly tearful one to her.

" God bless you, dear Rodolph, and return
you soon."

He hurried away, and the two friends were
soon mounted upon their fierce and coal-black
steeds. They employed neither whip nor spur,
yet they flew over the space between the two
castles, before Rodolph conceived himself to be
fairly on the road.

XXI.

They arrived late, but still in season. It was
yet half an hour to twelve, and Rodolph had
sufficient time to survey the assembly. What a
motley crew! A full year had passed since he
had seen them, and yet, on most of them, what a
change had that time brought about! Dissipa-
tion had done its work. Unaccustomed resources
had brought unaccustomed indulgence. The
wallow of the beast had swallowed up the spirit
of the man; and degradation had succeeded to
licentiousness, with the unerring rapidity of an
upward flying spark. Rodolph, who, in the arms
of a faithful and pure wife, had kept, to a certain
extent at least, the original whiteness of his soul,
turned from them in disgust. Their foul and

5*

brutal language frightened as well as disgusted
him.   Conrade, on the contrary, whose mental
and moral man was infinitely more flexible, ca-
roused and clamored with them most freely after
their own fashion. He did not seem to dislike, but
rather appeared desirous of promoting their excesses.   The wine cup was freely plied, and yet
Rodolph could see that, while filling for others,
his friend himself drank nothing.   Yet his laugh
— that strange laugh — was among the loudest,
and his words had sway over the boisterous group
of turbulents that gathered in a mass around him.

Suddenly, the heavily swinging bell, in the
tower overhead, thundered out the hour.   The
heart of Rodolph died away within him.   His
bones were chilled — his blood frozen — his knees
tottered feebly beneath the burden of his own
weight.   The eyes of Conrade were upon him —
his words were in his ears —

" Rodolph ?"

Cold sweat stood in massive drops upon the
youth's forehead, and his lips parted feebly in a
vain effort at a hurried prayer. The wild chuckle
of his friend at this moment drove away the
pleading minister at heaven's gates ; and desperately seizing his arm, Conrade led the way for the

rest into the adjoining hall of state and dreadful
ceremonial.

XXII.

Demoniac, indeed, had been the taste which fitted up that apartment. Grotesque images stood
glaring around upon them from the swaying and
swinging tapestry. Sable shafts and columns,
broken and cragged, seemed to glide about the
walls. Gloomy and dark draperies hung over
the doors and windows, fringed with flame-like
edges; and sprinkled drops of blood, like a rain
shower, as they entered the hall of doom, fell upon
their dresses. Rodolph clung to the arm of his
friend, even as an infant in a sudden terror clings
to that of a mother or a nurse. He was almost
lifeless in his accumulating fears and fancies. But
that laugh of Conrade, annoying as it was at every
other period, had now the effect of reassuring him.
It had in it a sort of scorn of all these objects of
dread — so Rodolph thought — which re-nerved
the apprehensive youth; and boldly they walked
forward together. The board of death was spread
— the board upon which Oberfeldt had slain himself. The outlines of his bloody form were printed

upon its covering; and there, in an hour more, his successor was doomed to lie. And who was that successor? That was the question which Rodolph propounded momentarily to himself: "Who? who?"

There was no long time for deliberation. Conrade led the way. There was a strange cry of assembled voices from a neighboring apartment, seemingly from cells beneath the stone floor upon which they stood. It was like laughter, and yet Rodolph distinguished now and then a shriek in the dreadful chorus which followed it. Faint notes of music — the sudden clang of a trumpet — and then the rapid rushing and the crash of closing doors, as if a sudden tempest raged without — these were the sounds and images which accompanied the act, in which the fraternity now engaged, of drawing for the fatal lot.

Blindly, madly, stupidly, and reeling like a drunken man, Rodolph, under the guidance of his friend's arm, approached the table, and the massive iron vase, from which the billet was to be taken. Desperately was his arm thrust forward into its fatal jaws. His fingers felt about its bottom, and he drew forth the card. He knew not what he had drawn; he dared not look upon it. He believed his doom to be written.

A signal announced the ceremony to be over—

the preparatory ceremony.   A bright light played around the vase, and the several members of the college advanced with the lots which they had drawn.

" Give yourselves no trouble, my friends," exclaimed one, whose voice Rodolph instantly recognised to be that of Conrade. " You need not examine your billets, since mine tells me what yours must be. I have the good fortune to be chosen successor to our great founder. It is for me to set you an example in following that of Oberfeldt. The billet of death has fallen to my lot." And, as he spoke, he displayed the fearful and blood-written scroll loftily in the sight of the rest.

XXIII.

Rodolph was speechless with varying emotions. His own safety ; the loss of his friend ; the composure with which Conrade announced his doom, and prepared himself for it ; all oppressed him with the strangest sensations. Conrade again spoke :

" I go to prepare. In the adjoining chamber, agreeable to the directions of Oberfeldt, lies the knife and the garment which are to prepare me for his doom. There also are the candidates who seek to fill my place. From one of these it is for me to choose. Fear not, my friends, that I shall choose one unworthy to associate with you. My pride is, that my successor shall be worthy of me."

With these words he left the hall. He returned in a few moments, bringing with him another, of whose face, though Rodolph knew him not, he did not seem altogether ignorant. Conrade was robed for death; and the double-edged knife, with which Oberfeldt had slain himself, smeared still with the purple blood of the preceding victim, was uplifted in his hand.

"This is my successor," exclaimed Conrade. "He is named Hans Busacher; you will swear him upon my body, as you have each of you sworn upon that of Oberfeldt."

With these words he prepared to mount the throne of death, when his eyes met those of Rodolph, which were full of irrepressible tears. He whispered in the youth's ears:

"Rodolph, the hour which takes me from life, gives a double life to you. Busacher tells me that you are a father. Hurrying by your castle, the intelligence reached him from a domestic. A fine son links you now more than ever to Bertha and to life."

Without waiting for reply, the intrepid Conrade leaped upon the table. He gave but a single look and parting nod to the assembly; then, drawing the keen edge of the knife with a heavy hand over his throat, his eyes were fixed, a second after, in the dim haze and utter insensibility of death.

Silence was among the rest, but a heavy groan burst from Rodolph, drowned, however, in a burst of shrieks and yells, from the cells below, which were appalling. But there was little time allowed for speculation upon these matters. The uninitiate now advanced to the table, and each member crowded round to repeat the terms of the oath to Hans Busacher which he was required to take. He did not shrink, though he had gazed upon the awful event which had just taken place. With one hand upon the body of Conrade, the fingers of the other grasped the pen, and signed the instrument; and Rodolph saw, ever as Busacher wrote, that the name of Conrade faded from the body of the instrument above, while that of Busacher, letter by letter, rose visibly in its place. The ceremony over, he rushed from the horrible connexion, and was soon blessed with the sight of that dear pledge of love, of which Weickhoff, in the moment of death, had informed him.

XXIV.

The escape from his present danger was a new life to Rodolph. In just proportion to his former extreme apprehensions, was his feeling of security now. He did not, for the present, trouble himself with thoughts of the future. There was time enough, month after month, in the long, sweet year before him. His thoughts were all due to his wife and child; to the beautiful boy, in whose infant lineaments Bertha had already clearly traced out all the features of the father's face. The days, the weeks, flew rapidly by in the freshness of so new and pure a pleasure. Joy vainly spread forth his witcheries, to delay the feet of time. Months had now elapsed, and a cloud began to gather upon the brow of Rodolph, a cloud which even the caresses of his wife and infant failed at all times to disperse.

One day Bertha said to her husband — her child being in her arms, and she being within those of Rodolph —

"Dearest, I am sad to see you so. Wherefore is it? Why are you gloomy? And you groan, Rodolph, oh, so deeply in your sleep, as if you had some secret and dreadful sorrow. Tell it me, Rodolph. Share it with me, dear husband. If I cannot soothe, I can better assist you to endure it."

How freely, how joyfully would he have revealed to her, if he had dared, the awful secret that was harrowing up his soul. Better if he had done so; but he was not sufficiently assured of that mighty strength which is in the bosom of a woman who loves devotedly, and he doubted her ability to bear the horrible recital of what he knew and dreaded. She implored him in vain; he evaded and denied, until she grew unhappy, as she saw that he did evade.

At another time she said:

" Dear Rodolph, you do not pray with me now, as you were wont to do. When we were first wedded, it was so sweet to kneel with you, and pray together, each night before we slept, and confess to each other our mutual errors and unkindnesses. Now, dear Rodolph, I pray alone. Wherefore is it, Rodolph? Ah, husband, shall we not again pray together? Shall we not kneel tonight, and renew our former custom?"

He looked at her with the desperate fondness of a dying man — so fondly, so earnestly, so despairingly. He folded his arms around her; he pressed his lips long and lovingly to hers; and he promised her that their prayers should be once more united.

That evening, when they had sought their chamber, she proceeded to exact the fulfilment of his pledge. She led him to the altar, and they kneeled together, and the pure hearted woman began to pray aloud. Rodolph was silent, or strove vainly to utter a corresponding prayer. On a sudden, he started up with a wild shriek; he thrust his eyes in his palms, and fled from the apartment; and that night he came not again to the expecting arms of his wife. He had seen the face of Conrade Weickhoff peering from behind the altar upon him; that horrible grin upon his lips, and a glare from his eyes that seemed satanic.

XXV.

While it was yet early, he had a visit the next morning from Hans Busacher, who had recently become a neighbor, and was in possession of the domains formerly belonging to Conrade Weickhoff. Rodolph trembled and shuddered to behold him, not only as his neighborhood reminded him

of his friend, but because there was something in
the face of Busacher very much like that of Conrade. There was nothing offensive, however,
either in the person or the manners of the new visiter. He was courteous and affable, seemed to
have always moved in the best society, and, in
every respect, might have been considered a very
model of gentility. There was, perhaps, something of loftiness in his air, which some may have
regarded as stiffness, and he was essentially di-
vested of all those softer feelings which beguile
humanity with dreams. He was cold in the extreme, if not a phlegmatic. Rodolph and himself
conversed for a good while on indifferent topics,
and the youth, who, wanting in decision of character, himself needed some stronger spirit upon
whom to lean, began to be pleased with his visiter,
and was really grateful to him for having called.
When Busacher was about to go, Rodolph warmly made his acknowledgments, and grasping the
hand of the former with a strong gripe, he begged
that he might again soon see him at the castle.

"I know not," said the other, with composure,
"that I shall soon have that pleasure. This is
July. I go in a few days upon a journey to the
borders, where I have to make some arrangements

in respect to property. I shall return by November, when I shall see you again, of course."

The very language of Conrade a year before. The visiter was gone; and, during the rest of that day, unseen by wife or domestics, Rodolph tottered, like a paralytic, through a dark gallery of his dwelling.

XXVI.

Let us skip over the intervening period. Nothing need be said in all this time of the increasing mental agony of Rodolph. It will be sufficient to know that his despair and suffering were even greater than during the year before. Life had grown dearer to him; he was bound to it by new ties; and Bertha and his child grew lovelier and more necessary to his heart, with every increase of the doubt and the dread which were gathering and groping there.

The night came, and, to his surprise, Hans Busacher was again his visiter.

"I am but now returned from the borders," were his first words; "and knowing that your course lay with mine to-night, I concluded to stop in passing, and bear you company."

"What an alteration in his voice!" said Rodolph to himself. "I have certainly heard that voice frequently before."

Thus he mused as he looked upon his visiter, and he shuddered with the strangest emotions. He parted from Bertha, suppressing his grief as well as he could, but full of the most painful presentiments.

"Come back soon, dear Rodolph," she cried to him entreatingly, and he promised her, but with a choking accent.

The companions soon reached Oberfeldt castle, and, one by one, the several members of the college were soon assembled together. Let us not dwell upon the preparatory display on this occasion. We already know the rites and orgies which were initial. We have already seen the decorations of the dismal chamber, and the dreadful hall. They were now the same. Rodolph well remembered each fearful characteristic. The same scene was renewed in all its parts; and, amid crowding forms, and stimulated even into madness by similar objects, sights, and sounds, as had attended the proceedings of the previous anniversary, he, with the rest, advanced to the iron vase. They drew their billets in turn, and when Rodolph

6*

lifted his into the light, the doom of self-murder
was decreed to him in characters of blood.

XXVII.

His head swam — his heart sickened — he tottered from the fearful board, and stammering out
his intention to the rest, passed into the adjoining
apartment, where he was to choose his successor,
and prepare for the execution of his doom.

"Poor fellow!" said one, "he does not seem
to like it."

"No," said another, "but better him than us.
It will always be a year too soon when the time
comes, and so no doubt he thinks it."

"Wonder how he likes leaving his wife," said
a third; "they say he is very fond of her."

"Psha! is she fond of him? is the question.
She will have no loss; she's quite as lovely as
ever, and I will take some pains myself to console
her," said a fourth, who was one of the most
self-complacent of the group. It is in this brutal
fashion that vice presumes to speak of the superior virtue which it hates and fears. Little did
the pure minded Bertha at that moment imagine
that such as these were the associates of her hus-

band. Thus had the conversation proceeded for some time in the hall, when some one remarked upon the long absence of the victim :

" He stays long !"

" Yes ; his choice is difficult. It is to be hoped he brings us a proper man, a good fellow; not too proud to know his friends and neighbors."

" If he does," said a third, " we should rejoice in the exchange, for he will then give us a more sociable and better fellow than himself."

The delay of Rodolph to return, at length provoked anxiety. He was sought for, and was nowhere to be found. The successor was unchosen — the fatal garment unassumed — the knife of death unappropriated. The unhappy youth dared not fulfil his pledges. Life was too sweet — death too terrible — and scarcely enjoying the one, or only destined to enjoy it in horrors, he had yet fled from the utterly bereaving embraces of the other. He had availed himself of the few moments which were allotted to the victim for solitary preparation, to hurry through a neighboring passage, and regain the court-yard. There, mounting his steed, he had fled with all desperation, and a full half hour had elapsed after his departure before his flight was discovered.

XXVIII.

There was a general hubbub among the collegiates when the discovery was made. All was confusion and uproar.

"The coward!" several of them exclaimed, "thus to fly from death."

"Dishonorable!" cried others, "not to meet his engagements." Some proposed to pursue and put him to death; and this opinion was about to be carried, when Hans Busacher, who had, in all this time, preserved the profoundest silence, now interposed as follows:

"We may not do as you propose, my friends; we are bound by our contract to a different course. What says the will of Oberfeldt on this subject? and how, under his directions, are we to punish a member who flies from his honorable pledge? We are not to harm a hair of his head; we are not to shed a drop of his blood; we are not to break a limb of his body; we are not to abridge a portion of his breath; but we are to do all — we are to compel him to the performance of the deed by a will and act of his own."

"How can that be done?" was the general

exclamation. They were astounded, for none of them remembered any such requisitions in the document.

"Does the will say so?" was the inquiry of one and all.

"You shall see for yourselves," was the reply. They read, and, sure enough, there were plainly written down the fatal requisitions. They were aghast, and Hans Busacher smiled scornfully as he beheld their confusion. After a brief pause, he proceeded:

"Our task is not so difficult as you imagine. Why does Rodolph Steinmyer fly from death? Because he is in love with life! Why is he in love with life? Because there are many things in life which make it worthy of his love. What do we, then, my friends? Evidently, we are to deprive him of all those objects which make him regardless of his honor. Our work begins from this moment. Come all of you with me into the private room of council. There let us confer together, on the best plan for bringing our brother back to the consideration of his duty."

What they did, to what they pledged themselves, and what they designed in that secret conference, may not be said. They separated after a brief interval; and the shade of Oberfeldt

growled at the passage of the anniversary without
yielding him any additional companion.

XXIX.

Let us follow the flight of the devoted Rodolph.
The poor youth fled madly to his home.   In desperation, upon the bosom of his wife he poured
forth the whole dreadful narrative.   A silent horror seized upon her.   She was dumb; she was
stupified with dread.   She knew of but one re-
source, and she called upon God!   She implored
her husband to kneel with her before the same
altar, and he did so; but when, like her, he strove
to call upon God, a wild yell arose from the floor
beneath him — a yell of fiendish derision — that
drowned all supplication.   At the same moment,
a fierce implacable glare shot out from two eyes
behind the altar, that seemed like dim and baleful
stars, looking forth amidst the gloomy and sudden
gusts of September.   Rodolph sank fainting upon
the floor, and Bertha, prostrating herself upon his
body, prayed fervently to heaven for the succor
and the safety of the doomed one !
The night passed — a night of horror.   The
day came and passed — a day of increasing hor-

ror, as it was one which contributed in a thousand ways to the hopelessness of Rodolph.

"Let us fly," said the devoted wife; "let us fly, my Rodolph, into other countries. We shall then be beyond the reach of these people. You can then be at peace, and happy."

He embraced her, and they determined upon flight. In secrecy he prepared money and jewels for use in a foreign land. His horses were in readiness, a faithful retainer intrusted with the secret only, and every arrangement was made for a start at midnight. It came, and stealing forth with his infant son in his arms, and his wife clinging to his side, Rodolph, when all were asleep, descended to the porch where the carriage was in waiting. They entered the vehicle, and departed; but as they drove through the portals, they heard voices calling them back, and then a chuckling laugh, which seemed like that of Conrade. They reached a deep wood, when suddenly the sky became overcast, and they could no longer find their way. A storm of lightning came up, and the horses grew frightened. Strange cries, as of men in battle, reached their ears from the distance, and as they drove forward desperately, the horses sank back in terror from some object which lay in their way. Provocations like these had aroused all the courage of Rodolph. He alighted from the carriage, and approached the object which had so alarmed the horses. The distinct outline of a man's body, which seemed lifeless, lay in the path. A groan reached his ears. He stooped to the body, to feel if life were yet in its bosom. The figure stretched up its arms, as if to embrace him. At that moment, a sharp flash of lightning showed him the face of Conrade Weickhoff, the head nearly severed from the body. He dashed down the bloody carcass; leaped again into the vehicle; while shrieks of demoniac laughter seemed to run and gather in the air, pursuing all around him. With his own hands, nerved by desperation, he drove the careering horses over the carcass, and heedless of the road, made his way forward.

"Whither so fast?" cried a strange voice, in front of him. "Would you cross the river in such a freshet, when the bridge is swept away? Turn, instantly, or you must perish."

It was a sort of instinct that prompted the next movement of Rodolph. The horses were wheeled round, and, driving without an aim, he drove till daylight. At dawn, the extensive and beautiful domains of a fine castle lay before him.

"Where am I?" he demanded of a peasant.

"At the castle of Baron Rodolph of Steinmyer," was the reply.

Rodolph was again at home.

XXX.

There was a destiny in all this. Rodolph began to perceive how desperate was the contest before him. He devoted himself to meditation upon the means of his escape, and for hours he was absorbed in thought, to the exclusion of all outward consciousness. At length he called to him a faithful adherent :

"Claus," he said, "you will take the lady Bertha and her child to Staremberg castle. You will begone instantly, and put yourself in readiness."

He then sought Bertha, and told her his intention.

"Once secure at Staremberg, Bertha, and you will not encumber my flight. You can follow me when you hear of my safety in another land. Take with you these jewels and this gold. They will serve us at a future time, and bid defiance to want."

He opened the caskets as he spoke, but, instead

of gold and jewels, there lay nothing within but a
few rocks in an envelop. That envelop was a
bloody napkin, marked " Oberfeldt," and having
on it a purple stain, which gave the idea of a
rudely impressed hand and dagger. The sight
almost blinded the horror-stricken youth. The
doom was gathering around him.

At length Bertha and the child, under the
guardianship of Claus, set forward upon the journey to her father's castle of Staremberg. Rodolph
separated from her at the gate with many tears.
When they were gone, he mounted his steed, and
rode away gloomily into the forest. It was late
in the day when he determined to return. He
had meditated his plan thoroughly, and had, at
length, devised a scheme which, he flattered himself, would enable him successfully to fly from his
persecutors. When he reached the edges of the
forest a bright blaze illuminated it, with a light
beyond that of day. He was bewildered by the
conflagration, and hurried forward. When he
had fully emerged from the obscurity of the woods,
he knew the extent of the evil. His fine palace
was in flames. He reached the gates, and found
all his retainers in consternation. The fire was a
mystery ; nobody could account for it. While
he gazed upon the blazing ruins, he saw amid the

burning masses, two bright eyes glaring upon his own. If he had not been well acquainted with the hateful glare of those eyes, he was yet not ignorant of the source of that fiendish laugh, which rose high above the rock when the tottering walls went down in a final crash. How much less difficult did it now seem to Rodolph to die! Suffering had already began to blunt sensibility.

XXXI.

Like an abandoned wretch, he rode over to Staremberg castle. He could not depart without seeing Bertha and his child. Their absence had already half reconciled him to the worst. But where were they? Neither baron nor baroness had yet seen their daughter and grandson.

"Trifle not with me, I pray you," cried Rodolph, in his agony. "Bring me to them. I am in no mood for sport; I cannot brook delay."

When assured that they had not yet made their appearance, with a mad yell he rushed away into the forest. The retainers of Staremberg followed in pursuit; and the old baron himself, who tenderly loved his daughter, did not withhold himself from the search which was instituted for her. It

was the fortune of the unhappy Rodolph to gain
the first tidings of his beloved.   Midway between
his own and Staremberg castle, the carriage lay
overturned, and almost torn to pieces.   The horses
were stiff dead, and yet there were no marks or
wounds upon them.   They seemed literally to have
been blasted.   The dead body of a man lay
stretched out before a portion of the vehicle,
wearing a dress like that of Claus, to whose cus-
tody Bertha had been intrusted; but what was
the horror of Rodolph, on approaching the body,
to discover the features of his ancient comrade,
Conrade Weickhoff, once again visibly before him.
And the horrible image unclosed its eyes, and
glared upon him, as with a lustful longing, from
beneath the sickly glaze which still overspread the
rapidly decaying orbs.

The fear of death was no longer a fear with
Rodolph Steinmyer.   The goods of life were
gone — the things which he had lived for, and
which had made life a province of delight super-
seding the desire in his mind for any other, were
all gone.   The wife and the child were torn from
him for ever — murdered, doubtlessly, by the
demon fingers of his foul associates, or the demon
agents of that awful being with whom, it was now
the fear of Rodolph, he had been commercing

but too freely. As he thought on these matters, however, he congratulated himself that, though bargaining with the demon, he had sold him nothing but his life — he had not traded away his soul! Rodolph was not so subtle a casuist as the devil! A yell of derisive laughter rose in the air around him, the moment that his lips gave utterance to the absurdity; and he distinctly beheld the long, bony, and skinless fingers of Conrade Weickhoff stretching up toward him from the carcass.

He rushed away from the dreadful place and spectacle. Madness seemed to prompt his course, and desperation gave him wings. But there was method in his madness. His mind had reached that stage of frenzy in which nothing can touch it farther. He was now insensible to hope and fear, as he was indifferent to life. One met him in his flight, whom he saw not, but the voice of Hans Busacher he knew.

"We go together," said Hans.

"We do!" was the reply.

"You are waited for!" said the former.

"Who waits?" demanded Rodolph, fiercely.

A finger rested upon his wrist, and the touch seemed to enfeeble him, while the other briefly replied —

"Oberfeldt! — Weickhoff! — Bertha!"

7*

"Ha! I am ready!" was the desperate, but shuddering response; and they entered together the gates of Oberfeldt castle, which immediately closed heavily behind them. There was now no escape for Rodolph, but he thought not of that.

XXXII.

Shouts received the fugitive — shouts of laughter, of scorn, of encouragement and cheer, rang in his senses. The members of the college were all assembled, as if they had been waiting for, and apprized of his coming. He looked round the apartment, and noted their several faces. His emotions were not such as they were when he had previously met his colleagues. He had now no fears. His limbs were firm — his muscles rigid and inflexible — his nerves unshaken. Yet the pomp of death around him was even more gloomily grand than ever. The tapestry, that seemed made up of gathering shadows, of mighty spectres, and the awfulest forms, appeared to contract momently around him. Huge torches, borne in the hands of mute images, waved with a flaring and smoky light, in dense niches of the apartment. Faint tones of music, followed by an occasional shriek of laughter, and sometimes by one of pain, came to his senses; and more than once, as if nearer at hand, the plainings of a child seemed to assail him, as if from his own murdered innocent. This fancy at once drove him forward to his purpose.

"I am ready," he exclaimed to the confederates.

"Not so," said Busacher; "you are to choose your successor. The candidates await you."

"Must I do this?" demanded Rodolph, shrinking from the task of entailing his own dreadful doom upon another.

"You must!" was the reply; and Busacher led the victim to the chamber in which his preparations were to be made. Many were the candidates who were there, claiming the privileges of eternal sorrow, in connexion with a momentary indulgence. With eyes closed, Rodolph extended his hands, determined to leave to fate that choice which he was bent not to make himself. The person he touched came forward, and Rodolph, when he looked upon him, beheld a fair youth, even younger than himself, in the man he had selected. He would have amended his choice. He would have taken one of the degraded and besotted candidates whom a long familiarity with vice in all its forms had made callous to all conditions, and utterly hopeless of the future.   But he was not allowed to do so, nor would the infatuated youth, so chosen, himself permit of any change.   Bitterly, but too late, did Rodolph deplore his error; but regrets were idle at such a moment.   He robed himself in the un-hallowed investiture of self-murder.   He clutched the bloody knife in his desperate hand.   He led his youthful successor into the hall of death.   He stood with him before its altar.   A dreadful strug-gle was going on within his bosom; for the good angel of a guardian conscience had not yet entire-ly given up its trust.   But, when he beheld the doubting and the sneering glances of those around him, and when he thought of the wife and child whom he had lost, he hesitated no longer.   Fear-lessly he leaped upon the bloody board, and the knife was uplifted.   As he gave the fatal blow, a shriek, a scream — the voice of a woman in a deep agony — reached his ears, with the rushing of feet from an adjoining chamber.   He knew the tones of that voice.   They were those of Bertha. Half conscious only, he strove to raise himself from the bloody bier, and his eyes were turned in the direction whence the sounds proceeded.   The tapestry was thrown aside, and his wife — her child

in her arms — her hair flying in the wind — her
movements those of a love bordering upon madness — rushed toward him where he lay. He
strove, in the agony of death — for the last sickness was fast overcoming the life-tide at his heart
— to extend his arms to receive her; but, at that.
moment, the form of Hans Busacher passed between them.

"Keep me not back," cried the wretched woman, "he is mine — he is my husband."

"He is mine!" cried Busacher, in a voice like
the falling of a torrent — so deep, so startling —
so sudden at the first. The dim eye of Rodolph
gazed up at the intruder, and the form of Busacher seemed changed to that of Conrade Weickhoff. There was the same scornful smile upon
his lips, and the ears of the dying man were conscious of the same horrible, chuckling laugh,
which had characterized his friend. While he yet
looked in amaze, the figure seemed to grow and
to expand, and he was now aware that the dreadful
personage before him was about to assume another
aspect. While he watched with the last lingering
consciousness of life, and while the breath flickered faintly, and was drawn unresistingly toward
the fearful presence which he watched, he beheld
the features change from those of Conrade, into a

yet more dreadful character. Then did he feel, for the first time, how completely he was the victim; since, in place of him who had been his friend, he saw, in the moment of his final agony, the triumphant and stony glare which marks the glance of the demon Mephistopheles, whose slave he had become.

LOGOOCHIE;

OR,

THE BRANCH OF SWEET WATER.

A LEGEND OF GEORGIA.

LOGOOCHIE.

I.

WITH the approach of the white settlers, along
the wild but pleasant banks of the St. Mary's
river, in the state of Georgia, the startled deities
of Indian mythology began to meditate their
departure to forests more secure. Tribe after
tribe of the aborigines had already gone, and the
uncouth gods of their idolatry presided, in num-
berless instances, only over their deserted habitations. The savages had carried with them no
guardian divinities — no hallowed household altars
— cheering them in their new places of abode, by
the acceptance of their sacrifice, and with the
promise of a moderate winter, or a successful
hunt. In depriving them of the lands descended
to them in trust from their fathers, the whites seem
also to have exiled them from the sweet and mys-

tic influences, so aptly associated with the vague
loveliness of forest life, of their many twilight
superstitions. Their new groves, as yet, had no
spells for the huntsman; and the Manneyto of
their ancient sires, failed to appreciate their tribute
offerings, intended to propitiate his regards, or to
disarm his anger. They were indeed outcasts;
and, with a due feeling for their exiled worshippers, the forest-gods themselves determined also
to depart from those long-hallowed sheltering
places in the thick swamps of the Okephanokee,
whence, from immemorial time, they had gone
forth, to cheer or to chide the tawny hunter in
his progress through life. They had served the
fathers faithfully, nor were they satisfied that the
sons should go forth unattended. They had consecrated his dwellings, they had stimulated his
courage, they had thrown the pleasant waters
along his path, when his legs failed him in the
chase, and his lips were parched with the wanderings of the long day in summer; and though
themselves overcome in the advent of superior
gods, they had, nevertheless, prompted him to the
last, in the protracted struggle which he had
maintained, for so many years, and with such
various successes, against his pale invaders. All
that could be done for the feather-crowned and

wolf-mantled warrior, had been done, by the divinities he worshipped. He was overcome, driven
away from his ancient haunts, but he still bowed
in spirit to the altars, holy still to him, though,
haplessly, without adequate power to secure him
in his possessions. They determined not to leave
him unprotected in his new abodes, and gathering,
at the bidding of Satilla, the Mercury of the
southern Indians, the thousand gods of their
worship — the wood-gods and the water-gods —
crowded to the flower-island of Okephanokee, to
hear the commands of the Great Manneyto.

II.

All came but Logoochie, and where was he?
he, the Indian mischief-maker — the Puck, the
tricksiest spirit of them all, — he, whose mind,
like his body, a creature of distortion, was yet
gentle in its wildness, and never suffered the
smallest malice to mingle in with its mischief.
The assembly was dull without him — the season
cheerless — the feast wanting in provocative.
The Great Manneyto himself, with whom Logoochie was a favourite, looked impatiently on the
approach of every new comer. In vain were all

his inquiries — where is Logoochie? who has
seen Logoochie? The question remained unan-
swered — the Great Manneyto unsatisfied. Anxious search was instituted in every direction for
the discovery of the truant. They could hear
nothing of him, and all scrutiny proved fruitless.
They knew his vagrant spirit, and felt confident
he was gone upon some mission of mischief; but
they also knew how far beyond any capacity of
theirs to detect, was his to conceal himself, and so,
after the first attempt at search, the labor was
given up in despair. They could get no tidings
of Logoochie.

III.

The conference went on without him, much to
the dissatisfaction of all parties. He was the
spice of the entertainment, the spirit of all frolic;
and though sometimes exceedingly annoying,
even to the Great Manneyto, and never less so
to the rival power of evil, the Opitchi-Manneyto,
yet, as the recognized joker on all hands, no one
found it wise to take offence at his tricks. In
council, he relieved the dull discourse of some
drowsy god, by the sly sarcasm, which, falling

innocuously upon the ears of the victim, was yet
readily comprehended and applied by all the rest.
On the journey, he kept all around him from any
sense of weariness, — and, by the perpetual practical application of his humor, always furnished
his companions, whether above or inferior to him
in dignity, with something prime, upon which to
make merry. In short, there was no god like
Logoochie, and he was as much beloved by the
deities, as he was honored by the Indian, who
implored him not to turn aside the arrow which
he sent after the bounding buck, nor to spill the
water out of his scooped leaf as he carried it from
the running rivulet up to his mouth. All these
were tricks of the playful Logoochie, and by a
thousand, such as these, was he known to the
Indians.

IV.

Where, then, was the absentee when his brother
divinities started after the outlawed tribes? Had
he not loved the Indians — had he no sympathy
with his associate gods — and wherefore went he
not upon the sad journey through the many
swamps and the long stretches of sand and forest,
that lay between the Okephanokee, and the ra-

8*

pidly-gushing waters of the Chatahoochie, wher
both the aborigines and their rude deities had
now taken up their abodes. Alas! for Logoochie! He loved the wild people, it is true, and
much he delighted in the association of those
having kindred offices with himself; but though
a mimic and a jester, fond of sportive tricks, and
perpetually practising them on all around him, he
was not unlike the memorable buffoon of Paris,
who, while ministering to the amusement of thousands, possessing them with an infinity of fun and
frolic, was yet, at the very time, craving a precious mineral from the man of science to cure him
of his confirmed hypochondria. Such was the
condition of Logoochie. The idea of leaving the
old woods and the waters to which he had been
so long accustomed, and which were associated in
his memory with a thousand instances of merriment, was too much for his most elastic spirits to
sustain; and the summons to depart filled him
with a nameless, and, to him, a hitherto unknown
form of terror. His organ of inhabitiveness had
undergone prodigious increase in the many exercises which his mind and mood had practised
upon the banks of the beautiful Branch of Sweet
Water, where his favorite home had been chosen
by a felicitous fancy. It was indeed a spot to be

loved and dwelt upon, and he who surveyed its clear and quiet waters, sweeping pleasantly onward with a gentle murmur, under the high and bending pine trees that arched over and fenced it in, would have no wonder at its effect upon a spirit so susceptible, amidst all his frolic, as that of Logoochie. The order to depart made him miserable; he could not think of doing so; and, trembling all the while, he yet made the solemn determination not to obey the command; but rather to subject himself, by his refusal, to a loss of caste, and, perhaps, even severer punishment, should he be taken, from the other powers having guardianship with himself, over the wandering red men. With the determination came the execution of his will. He secreted himself from those who sought him, and in the hollow of a log lay secure, even while the hunters uttered their conjectures and surmises under the very copse in which he was hidden. His arts to escape were manifold, and, unless the parties in search of him knew intimately his practices, he could easily elude their scrutiny by the simplest contrivances. Such, too, was the susceptibility of his figure for distortion, that even Satilla, the three eyed, the messenger of the Indian divinities, the most acute and cunning among them, was not unfrequently over-

reached and evaded by the truant Logoochie.
He too had searched for him in vain, and though
having a shrewd suspicion, as he stepped over a
pine knot lying across a path, just about dusk,
that it was something more than it seemed to be,
yet passing on without examining it, and leaving
the breathless Logoochie, for it was he, to gather
himself up, the moment his pursuer was out of
sight, and take himself off in a more secluded
direction. The back of Logoochie was, itself,
little better than a stripe of the tree bark to those
who remarked it casually. From his heel to his
head, inclusive, it looked like so many articulated
folds or scales of the pine tree, here and there
bulging out into excrescences. The back of his
head was a solid knot, for all the world like that
of the scorched pine knot, hard and resinous.
This knot ran across in front, so as to arch above
and overhang his forehead, and was crowned
with hair, that, though soft, was thick and woody
to the eye, and looked not unlike the plates of the
pine-bur when green in season. It rose into a
ridge or comb directly across the head from front
to rear, like the war tuft of a Seminole warrior.
His eyes, small and red, seemed, occasionally, to
run into one another, and twinkled so, that you
could not avoid laughing but to look upon them.

His nose was flat, and the mouth was simply an incision across his face, reaching nigh to both his ears, which lapped and hung over like those of a hound. He was short in person, thick, and strangely bow-legged; and, to complete the uncouth figure, his arms, shooting out from under a high knot, that gathered like an epaulette upon each shoulder, possessed but a single though rather long bone, and terminated in a thick, squab, burlike hand, having fingers, themselves inflexible, and but of single joints, and tipped, not with nails, but with claws, somewhat like those of the panther, and equally fearful in strife. Such was the vague general outline which, now and then, the Indian hunter, and, after him, the Georgia squatter, caught, towards evening, of the wandering Logoochie, as he stole suddenly from sight into the sheltering copse, that ran along the edges of some wide savannah.

The brother divinities of the Creek warriors had gone after their tribes, and Logoochie alone remained upon the banks of the Sweet Water Branch. He remained in spite of many reasons for departure. The white borderer came nigher and nigher, with every succeeding day. The stout log-house started up in the centre of his favorite groves, and many families, clustering

within a few miles of his favorite stream, formed
the nucleus of the flourishing little town of St.
Mary's. Still he lingered, though with a sadness
of spirit, hourly increasing, as every hour tended
more and more to circumscribe the haunts of his
playful wandering. Every day called upon him
to deplore the overthrow, by the woodman's axe,
of some well remembered tree in his neighborhood; and though he strove, by an industrious
repetition of his old tricks, to prevent much of this
desolation, yet the divinities which the white man
brought with him were too potent for Logoochie.
In vain did he gnaw by night the sharp edge of
the biting steel, with which the squatter wrought
so much desolation. Alas! the white man had
an art given him by his God, by which he
smoothed out its repeated gaps, and sharpened it
readily again, or found a new one, for the destruction of the forest. Over and over again, did Logoochie think to take the trail of his people, and
leave a spot in which a petty strife of this nature
had become, though a familiar, a painful practice;
but then, as he thought of the humiliating acknowledgment which, by so doing, he must offer to his
brother gods, his pride came to his aid, and he
determined to remain where he was. Then again,
as he rambled along the sweet waters of the

branch, and talked pleasantly with the trees, his old acquaintance, and looked down upon little groups of Indians that occasionally came to visit this or that tumulus of the buried nations, he felt a sweet pleasure in the thought, that although all were gone of the old possessors, and a new people and new gods had come to sway the lands of his outlawed race, he still should linger and watch over, with a sacred regard, the few relics, and the speechless trophies, which the forgotten time had left them. He determined to remain still, as he long had been, the presiding genius of the place.

V.

From habit, at length, it came to Logoochie to serve, with kind offices, the white settlers, just as he had served the red men before him. He soon saw that, in many respects, the people dwelling in the woods, however different their color and origin, must necessarily resemble one another. They were in some particulars equally wild and equally simple. He soon discovered, too, that however much they might profess indifference to the superstitions of the barbarous race they had superseded, they were not a whit more secure from the occa-

sional tremors which followed his own practices or
presence. More than once had he marked the
fright of the young woodman, as, looking towards
nightfall over his left shoulder, he had beheld the
funny twinkling eyes, and the long slit mouth,
receding suddenly into the bush behind him. This
assured Logoochie of the possession still, even
with a new people, of some of that power which
he had exercised upon the old ; and when he saw,
too, that the character of the white man was plain,
gentle, and unobtrusive, he came, after a brief study, to like him also ; though, certainly, in less
degree, than his Indian predecessors. From one
step of his acquaintance with the new comers to
another, Logoochie at length began to visit, at
stolen periods, and to prowl around the little cottage, of the squatter ; — sometimes playing tricks
upon his household, but more frequently employ-
ing himself in the analysis of pursuits, and of a
character, as new almost to him as to the people
whose places they had assumed. Nor will this
seeming ignorance, on the part of Logoochie,
subtract a single jot from his high pretension as an
Indian god, since true philosophy and a delibe-
rate reason, must, long since, have been aware, that
the mythological rule of every people, has been
adapted, by the superior of all, to their mental

and physical condition; and the Great Manneyto
of the savage, in his primitive state, was, doubtless, as wise a provision for him then, as, in our
time, has been the faith, which we proudly assume
to be the close correlative of the highest point of
moral liberty and social refinement.

VI.

In this way, making new discoveries daily, and
gradually becoming known himself, though vaguely, to the simple cottagers around him, he continued to pass the time with something more of satisfaction than before; though still suffering pain at
every stroke of the sharp and smiting axe, as it
called up the deploring echoes of the rapidly yielding forest. Day and night he was busy, and he
resumed, *in extenso*, many of the playful humors,
which used to annoy the savages and compel their
homage. It is true, the acknowledgment of the
white man was essentially different from that commonly made by the Indians. When their camp-
pots were broken, their hatchets blunted, their
bows and arrows warped, or they had suffered any
other such mischief at his hands, they solemnly
deprecated his wrath, and offered him tribute to

disarm his hostility. All that Logoochie could
extort from the borderer, was a sullen oath, in
which the tricksy spirit was identified with no less
a person than the devil, the Opitchi-Manneyto
of the southern tribes. This — as Logoochie
well knew the superior rank of that personage
with his people — he esteemed a compliment; and
its utterance was at all times sufficiently grateful
in his ears to neutralize his spleen at the moment.
In addition to this, the habit of smoking more frequently and freely than the Indians, so common
to the white man, contributed wonderfully to com-
mend him to the favor of Logoochie. The odor
in his nostrils was savory in the extreme, and he
consequently regarded the smoker as tendering, in
this way, the deprecatory sacrifice, precisely as
the savages had done before him. So grateful,
indeed, was the oblation to his taste, that often, of
the long summer evening, would he gather himself
into a bunch, in the thick branches of the high
tree overhanging the log-house, to inhale the reeking fumes that were sent up by the half oblivious
woodman, as he lay reposing under its grateful
shadow.

VII.

There was one of these little cottages, which, for this very reason, Logoochie found great delight in visiting. It was tenanted by a sturdy old farmer, named Jones, and situated on the skirts of the St. Mary's village, about three miles from the Branch of Sweet Water, the favorite haunt of Logoochie. Jones had a small family — consisting, besides himself, of his wife, his sister — a lady of certain age, and monstrous demure — and a daughter, Mary Jones, as sweet a May-flower as the eye of a good taste would ever wish to dwell upon. She was young — only sixteen, and had not yet learned a single one of the thousand arts, which, in making a fine coquette, spoil usually a fine woman. She thought purely, and freely said all that she thought. Her old father loved her — her mother loved her, and her aunt, she loved her too, and proved it, by doing her own, and the scolding of all the rest, whenever the light-hearted Mary said more in her eyes, or speech, than her aunt's conventional sense of propriety deemed absolutely necessary to be said. This family Logoochie rather loved, — whether it was because

farmer Jones did more smoking than any of the
neighbors, or his sister more scolding, or his wife
more sleeping, or his daughter more loving, we
say not, but such certainly was the fact. Mary
Jones had learned this latter art, if none other.
A tall and graceful lad in the settlement, named
Johnson, had found favor in her sight, and she
in his; and it was not long before they made the
mutual discovery. He was a fine youth, and quite
worthy of the maiden; but then he was of an in-
quiring, roving temper, and though not yet arrived at manhood, frequently indulged in rambles,
rather startling, even to a people whose habit in
that respect is somewhat proverbial. He had gone
in his wanderings even into the heart of the Okephanokee Swamp, and strange were the wonders,
and wild the stories, which he gave of that region
of Indian fable — a region, about which they
have as many and as beautiful traditions, as any
people can furnish from the store house of its primitive romance. This disposition on the part
of Ned Johnson, though productive of much disquiet to his friends and family, they hoped to
overcome or restrain, by the proposed union with
Mary Jones — a connexion seemingly acceptable
to all parties. Mary, like most other good young
ladies, had no doubt, indeed, of her power to con-

trol her lover in his wanderings, when once they were man and wife ; and he, like most good young gentlemen in like cases, did not scruple to swear a thousand times, that her love would be as a chain about his feet, too potent to suffer him the slightest indulgence of his rambling desires.

VIII.

So things stood, when, one day, what should appear in the Port of St. Mary's — the Pioneer of the Line — but a vessel — a schooner — a brightly painted, sharp, cunning looking craft, all the way from the eastern waters, and commanded by one of that daring tribe of Yankees, which will one day control the commercial world. Never had such a craft shown its face in those waters, and great was the excitement in consequence. The people turned out, *en masse,* — men, women, and children, — all gathered upon the sands at the point to which she was approaching, and while many stood dumb with mixed feelings of wonder and consternation, others, more bold and elastic, shouted with delight. Ned Johnson led this latter class, and almost rushed into the waters to meet the new comer, clapping his hands and screaming

9*

like mad. Logoochie himself, from the close hugging branches of a neighboring tree, looked down, and wondered and trembled as he beheld the fast rushing progress toward him of what might be a new and more potent God. Then, when her little cannon, ostentatiously large for the necessity, belched forth its thunders from her side, the joy and the terror was universal. The rude divinity of the red men leaped down headlong from his place of eminence, and bounded on without stopping, until removed from the sight and the shouting, in the thick recesses of the neighboring wood; while the children of the squatters taking to their heels, went bawling and squalling back to the village, never thinking for a moment to reach it alive. The schooner cast her anchor, and her captain came to land. Columbus looked not more imposing, leaping first to the virgin soil of the New World, than our worthy down-easter, commencing, for the first time, a successful trade in onions, potatoes, codfish, and crab-cider, with the delighted Georgians of our little village. All parties were overjoyed, and none more so than our young lover, Master Edward Johnson. He drank in with willing ears, and a still thirsting appetite, the narrative which the Yankee captain gave the villagers of his voyage. His long yarn, be sure, was stuffed with wonders. The new comer soon saw from Johnson's looks how greatly he had won the respect and consideration of the youthful wanderer, and, accordingly, addressed some of his more spirited and romantic adventures purposely to him. Poor Mary Jones beheld, with dreadful anticipations, the voracious delight which sparkled in the eyes of Ned as he listened to the marvellous narrative, and had the thing been at all possible or proper, she would have insisted, for the better control of the erratic boy, that old Parson Collins should at once do his duty, and give her legal authority to say to her lover — " obey, my dear, — stay at home, or," etc. She went back to the village in great tribulation, and Ned — he stayed behind with Captain Nicodemus Doolittle, of the " Smashing Nancy."

IX.

Now Nicodemus, or, as they familiarly called him " Old Nick," was a wonderfully 'cute personage ; and as he was rather slack of hands — was not much of a penman or grammarian, and felt that in his new trade he should need greatly the assistance of one to whom the awful school mys-

tery of fractions and the rule of three had, by a
kind fortune, been developed duly — he regarded
the impression which he had obviously made upon
the mind of Ned Johnson, as promising to neutralize, if he could secure him, some few of his
own deficiencies.   To this end, therefore, he particularly addressed himself, and, as might be suspected, under the circumstances, he was eminently
successful.   The head of the youth was soon
stuffed full of the wonders of the sea; and after a
day or two of talk, all round the subject, in which
time, by the way, the captain sold off all his " notions," he came point blank to the subject in the
little cabin of the schooner. Doolittle sat over
against him with a pile of papers before him,
some of which, to the uneducated down-easter, were
grievous mysteries, calling for a degree of arith-
metical knowledge which was rather beyond his
capacity.   His sales and profits — his accounts
with creditors and debtors — were to be registered,
and these required him to reconcile the provoking
cross currencies of the different states — the York
shilling, the   Pennsylvania levy, the Georgia
thrip, the pickayune of Louisiana, the Carolina
fourpence — and this matter was, alone, enough
to bother him.   He knew well enough how to
count the coppers on hearing them.   No man
was more expert at that. But the difficulty of

bringing them into one currency on paper, called for a more experienced accountant than our worthy captain; and the youth wondered to behold the ease with which so great a person could be bothered. Doolittle scratched his head in vain. He crossed his right leg over his left, but still he failed to prove his sum. He reversed the movement, and the left now lay problematically of the right. The product was very hard to find. He took a sup of cider, and then he thought things began to look a little clearer; but a moment after all was cloud again, and at length the figures absolutely seemed to run into one another. He could stand it no longer, and slapped his hand down, at length, with such emphasis upon the table, as to startle the poor youth, who, all the while, had been dreaming of plunging and wriggling dolphins, seen in all their gold and glitter, three feet or less in the waters below the advancing prow of the ship. The start which Johnson made, at once showed the best mode to the captain of extrication from his difficulty.

"There — there, my dear boy, — take some cider — only a little — do you good — best thing in the world — There, — and now do run up these figures, and see how we agree."

Ned was a clever led, and used to stand head

of his class. He unravelled the mystery in little time — reconciled the cross-currency of the several sovereign states, and was rewarded by his patron with a hearty slap upon the shoulder, and another cup of cider. It was not difficult after this to agree, and half fearing that all the while he was not doing right by Mary Jones, he dashed his signature, in a much worse hand than he was accustomed to write, upon a printed paper which Doolittle thrust to him across the table.

"And now, my dear boy," said the captain, "you are my secretary, and shall have best berth, and place along with myself, in the 'Smashing Nancy.'"

X.

The bargain had scarcely been struck, and the terms well adjusted with the Yankee captain, before Ned Johnson began to question the propriety of what he had done. He was not so sure that he had not been hasty, and felt that the pain his departure would inflict upon Mary Jones, would certainly be as great in degree, as the pleasure which his future adventures must bring to himself. Still, when he looked forward to those adventures, and remembered the thousand fine stories of Captain Doolittle, his dreams came back, and with them came a due forgetfulness of the hum-drum happiness of domestic life. The life in the woods, indeed — as if there was life, strictly speaking, in the eternal monotony of the pine forests, and the drowsy hum they keep up so ceaselessly. Wood-chopping, too, was his aversion, and when he reflected upon the acknowledged superiority of his own over all the minds about him, he felt that his destiny called upon him for better things, and a more elevated employment. He gradually began to think of Mary Jones, as of one of those influences which had substracted somewhat from the nature and legitimate exercises of his own genius; and whose claims, therefore, if acknowledged by him, as she required, must only be acknowledged at the expense and sacrifice of the higher pursuits and purposes for which the discriminating Providence had designed him. The youth's head was fairly turned by his ambitious yearnings, and it was strange how sublimely metaphysical his musings now made him. He began to analyze closely the question, since made a standing one among the phrenologists, as to how far particular heads were intended for particular pursuits. General principles were soon applied to special developments in his own case, and he came to the conclusion, just as he placed his feet upon the threshold of Father Jones's cottage, that he should be contending with the aim of fate, and the original design of the Deity in his own creation, if he did not go with Captain Nicodemus Doolittle, of the " Smashing Nancy."

XI.

" Ahem ! Mary — " said Ned, finding the little girl conveniently alone, half sorrowful, and turning the whizzing spinning wheel.

" Ahem, Mary — ahem — " and as he brought forth the not very intelligible introduction, his eye had in it a vague indeterminateness that looked like confusion, though, truth to speak, his head was high and confident enough.

" Well, Ned —"

" Ahem ! ah, Mary, what did you think of the beautiful vessel.　Was n't she fine, ch ?"

" Very — very fine, Ned, though she was so large, and, when the great gun was fired, my heart beat so — I was so frightened, Ned — that I was."

" Frightened — why what frightened you, Mary," exclaimed Ned proudly — " that was grand,

and as soon as we get to sea, I shall shoot it off myself."

" Get to sea — why, Ned — get to sea. Oh, dear, why — what do you mean?" and the bewildered girl, half conscious only, yet doubting her senses, now left the wheel, and came toward the contracted secretary of Captain Doolittle.

" Yes, get to sea, Mary. What! don't you know I'm going with the captain clear away to New York?"

Now, how should she know, poor girl? He knew that she was ignorant; but as he did not feel satisfied of the propriety of what he had done, his phraseology had assumed a somewhat indirect and distorted complexion.

" You going with the Yankee, Ned — you don't say."

" Yes, but I do — and what if he is a Yankee, and sells notions — I'm sure, there's no harm in that; he's a main smart fellow, Mary, and such wonderful things as he has seen, it would make your hair stand on end to hear him. I'll see them too, Mary, and then tell you."

"Oh, Ned, — you're only joking now — you don't mean it, Ned — you only say so to tease me — Isn't it so, Ned — say it is — say yes, dear Ned, only say yes."

And the poor girl caught his arm, with all the
confiding warmth of an innocent heart, and as the
tears gathered slowly, into big drops, in her eyes,
and they were turned appealingly up to his, the
heart of the wanderer smote him for the pain it
had inflicted upon one so gentle. In that moment,
he felt that he would have given the world to get
off from his bargain with the captain; but this
mood lasted not long. His active imagination,
provoking a curious thirst after the unknown; and
his pride, which suggested the weakness of a
vacillating purpose, all turned and stimulated him
to resist and refuse the prayer of the conciliating
affection, then beginning to act within him in rebuke. Speaking through his teeth, as if he dreaded that he should want firmness, he resolutely
reiterated what he had said; and, while the sad
girl listened, silently, as one thunder struck, he
went on to give a glowing description of the
wonderful discoveries in store for him during the
proposed voyage. Mary sunk back upon her stool,
and the spinning wheel went faster than ever; but
never in her life had she broken so many tissues.
He did his best at consolation, but the true hearted girl, though she did not the less suffer as he
pleaded, at least forbore all complaint. The thing
seemed irrevocable, and so she resigned herself,

like a true woman, to the imperious necessity.
Ned, after a while, adjusted his plaited straw to
his cranium, and sallied forth with a due importance in his strut, but with a swelling something
at his heart, which he tried in vain to quiet.

XII.

And what of poor Mary — the disconsolate, the
deserted and denied of love. She said nothing,
ate her dinner in silence, and then putting on her
bonnet, prepared to sally forth in a solitary ramble.

"What ails it, child," said old Jones, with a
rough tenderness of manner.

"Where going, baby?" asked her mother, half
asleep.

" Out again, Mary Jones — out again," voci-
ferously shouted the antique aunt, who did all the
family scolding.

The little girl answered them all meekly, without the slightest show of impatience, and proceeded on her walk.

The " Branch of Sweet Water," now known
by this name to all the villagers of St. Mary's,
was then, as it was supposed to be his favorite

place of abode, commonly styled, " The Branch
of Logoochie."   The Indians — such stragglers
as either lingered behind their tribes, or occasionally visited the old scenes of their home, — had
made the white settlers somewhat acquainted with
the character, and the supposed presence of that
playful God, in the region thus assigned him ;
and though not altogether assured of the idleness
of the superstition, the young and innocent Mary
Jones had no apprehensions of his power.   She,
indeed, had no reason for fear, for Logoochie had
set her down, long before, as one of his favorites.
He had done her many little services, of which
she was unaware, nor was she the only member of
her family indebted to his ministering good will.
He loved them all — all but the scold, and many
of the annoyances to which the old maid was subject, arose from this antipathy of Logoochie.   But
to return.

It was in great tribulation that Mary set out for
her usual ramble along the banks of the " Sweet
Water."   Heretofore most of her walks in that
quarter had been made in company with her lover.
Here, perched in some sheltering oak, or safely
doubled up behind some swollen pine, the playful
Logoochie, himself unseen, a thousand times looked upon the two lovers, as, with linked arms, and

spirits maintaining, as it appeared, a perfect unison, they walked in the shade during the summer afternoon. Though sportive and mischievous, such sights were pleasant to one who dwelt alone; and there were many occasions, when, their love first ripening into expression, he would divert from their path, by some little adroit art or management of his own, the obtrusive and unsympathising woodman, who might otherwise have spoiled the sport which he could not be permitted to share. Under his unknown sanction and service, therefore, the youthful pair had found love a rapture, until, at length, poor Mary had learned to regard it as a necessary too. She knew the necessity from the privation, as she now rambled alone; her wandering lover meanwhile improving his knowledge by some additional chit-chat, on matters and things in general, with the captain, with whom he had that day dined heartily on codfish and potatoes, a new dish to young Johnson, which gave him an additional idea of the vast resources of the sea.

10*

XIII.

Mary Jones at length trod the banks of the
Sweet Water, and footing it along the old pathway to where the rivulet narrowed, she stood
under the gigantic tree which threw its sheltering
and concealing arms completely across the stream.
With an old habit, rather than a desire for its re-
freshment, she took the gourd from the limb whence
it depended, *pro bono publico*, over the water, and
scooping up a draught of the innocent beverage,
she proceeded to drink, when, just as she carried
the vessel to her lips, a deep moan assailed her
ears, as from one in pain, and at a little distance.
She looked up, and the moan was repeated, and
with increased fervency. She saw nothing, however, and somewhat startled, was about to turn
quickly on her way homeward, when a third and
more distinct repetition of the moan appealed so
strongly to her natural sense of duty, that she
could stand it no longer; and with the noblest of
all kinds of courage, for such is the courage of
humanity, she hastily tripped over the log which
ran across the stream, and proceeded in the direction from whence the sounds had issued. A few

paces brought her in sight of the sufferer, who
was no other than our solitary acquaintance, Logoochie. He lay upon the grass, doubled now
into a knot, and now stretching and writhing himself about in agony. His whole appearance indicated suffering, and there was nothing equivocal
in the expression of his moanings. The astonishment, not to say fright, of the little cottage maiden,
may readily be conjectured. She saw, for the
first time, the hideous and uncouth outline of his
person — the ludicrous combination of feature in
his face. She had heard of Logoochie, vaguely;
and without giving much, if any credence, to the
mysterious tales related by the credulous woodman,
returning home at evening, of his encounter in the
forest with its pine-bodied divinity ; — and now,
as she herself looked down upon the suffering and
moaning monster, it would be difficult to say,
whether curiosity or fear was the most active principle in her bosom. He saw her approach, and
he half moved to rise and fly ; but a sudden pang,
as it seemed, brought him back to a due sense of
the evil from which he was suffering, and, looking
towards the maiden with a mingled expression of
good humor and pain in his countenance, he seemed to implore her assistance. The poor girl did
not exactly know what to do, or what to conjec-

ture. What sort of monster was it before her. What queer, distorted, uncouth limbs — what eyes, that twinkled and danced into one another —and what a mouth. She was stupified for a moment, until he spoke, and, stranger still, in a language that she understood. And what a musical voice, — how sweetly did the words roll forth, and how soothingly, yet earnestly, did they strike upon her ear. Language is indeed a god, and powerful before all the rest. His words told her all his misfortunes, and the tones were all-sufficient to inspire confidence in one even more suspicious than our innocent cottager. Besides, humanity was a principle in her heart, while fear was only an emotion, and she did not scruple, where the two conflicted, after the pause for reflection of a moment, to determine in favor of the former. She approached Logoochie — she approached him, firmly determined in her purpose, but trembling all the while. As she drew nigh, the gentle monster stretched himself out at length, patiently extending one foot towards her, and raising it in such a manner as to indicate the place which afflicted him. She could scarce forbear laughing, when she looked closely upon the strange feet. They seemed covered with bark, like that of the small leafed pine tree ; but as she stooped, to her

great surprise, the coating of his sole flew wide
as if upon a hinge, showing below it a skin as
soft, and white, and tender, seemingly, as her
own. There, in the centre of the hollow, lay the
cause of his suffering. A poisonous thorn had
penetrated, almost to the head, as he had suddenly leaped from the tree, the day before, upon the
gun being fired from the " Smashing Nancy."
The spot around it was greatly inflamed, and Logoochie, since the accident, had vainly striven, in
every possible way, to rid himself of the intruder.
His short, inflexible arms, had failed so to reach
it as to make his fingers available ; and then,
having claws rather than nails, he could scarce
have done any thing for his own relief, even
could they have reached it. He now felt
the evil of his isolation, and the danger of his
seclusion from his brother divinities. His case
was one, indeed, of severe bachelorism ; and,
doubtless, had his condition been less than that of
a deity, the approach of Mary Jones to his aid,
at such a moment, would have produced a decided revolution in his domestic economy. Still
trembling, the maiden bent herself down to the
task, and with a fine courage, that did not allow
his uncouth limbs to scare, or his wild and monstrous features to deter, she applied her own small
fingers to the foot, and carefully grappling the

head of the wounding thorn with her nails, with
a successful effort, she drew it forth, and rid him
of his encumbrance. The wood-god leaped to
his feet, threw a dozen antics in the air, to the
great terror of Mary, then running a little way
into the forest, soon returned with a handful of
fresh leaves, which he bruised between his fingers,
and applied to the irritated and wounded foot.
He was well in a moment after, and pointing the
astonished Mary to the bush from which he had
taken the anointing leaves, thus made her acquainted with one item in the history of Indian pharmacy.

XIV.

"The daughter of the white clay — she has
come to Logoochie, — to Logoochie when he was
suffering.

"She is a good daughter to Logoochie, and
the green spirits who dwell in the forest, they love,
and will honor her.

"They will throw down the leaves before her,
they will spread the branches above her, they will
hum a sweet song in the tree top, when she walks
underneath it.

" They will watch beside her, as she sleeps in the shade, in the warm sun of the noon-day, — they will keep the flat viper, and the war rattle, away from her ear.

" They will do this in honor to Logoochie, for they know Logoochie, and he loves the pale daughter. She came to him in his suffering.

" She drew the poison thorn from his foot — she fled not away when she saw him.

" Speak, — let Logoochie hear — there is sorrow in the face of the pale daughter. Logoochie would know it and serve her, for she is sweet in the eye of Logoochie."

XV.

Thus said, or rather sung, the uncouth god, to Mary, as, after the first emotions of his own joy were over, he beheld the expression of melancholy in her countenance. Somehow, there was something so fatherly, so gentle, and withal, so melodious, in his language, that she soon unbosomed herself to him, telling him freely and in the utmost confidence, though without any hope of relief at his hands, the history of her lover, and the new project for departure which he had now got in his head. She was surprised, and pleased, when she saw that Logoochie smiled at the narrative. She was not certain, yet she had a vague hope, that he could do something for her relief; and her conjecture was not in vain. He spoke — "Why should the grief be in the heart and the cloud on the face of the maiden? Is not Logoochie to help her? He stands beside her to help. Look, daughter of the pale clay — look! There is power in the leaf that shall serve thee at the bidding of Logoochie; — the bough and the branch have a power for thy good, when Logoochie commands; and the little red-berry which I now pluck from the vine hanging over thee, it is strong with a spirit which is good in thy work, when Logoochie has said in thy service. Lo, I speak to the leaf, and to the bough, and to the berry. They shall speak to the water, and one draught from the branch of Logoochie, shall put chains on the heart of the youth who would go forth with the stranger."

As he spoke, he gathered the leaf, broke a bough from an overhanging tree, and, with a red berry, pulled from a neighboring vine, approached the Branch of Sweet Water, and turning to the west, muttered a wild spell of Indian power, than threw the tributes into the rivulet. The smooth surface

of the stream was in an instant ruffled — the offerings were whirled suddenly around — the waters
broke, boiled, bubbled, and parted, and in another
moment, the bough, the berry, and the leaf,
had disappeared from their sight.

XVI.

Mary Jones was not a little frightened by these
exhibitions, but she was a girl of courage, and
having once got over the dread and the novelty
of contact with a form so monstrous as that of
Logoochie, the after effort was not so great. She
witnessed the incantations of the demon without
a word, and when they were over, she simply listened to his farther directions, half stupified with
what she had seen, and not knowing how much of
it to believe. He bade her bring her lover, as
had been the custom with them hitherto, to the
branch, and persuade him to drink of its waters.
When she inquired into its effect, which, at length,
with much effort, she ventured to do, he bade her
be satisfied, and all would go right. Then, with
a word, which was like so much music — a word
she did not understand, but which sounded like a
parting acknowledgment, — he bounded away

into the woods, and, a moment after, was completely hidden from her sight.

XVII.

Poor Mary, not yet relieved from her surprise, was still sufficiently aroused and excited to believe there was something in it ; and as she moved off on her way home, how full of anticipation was her thoughts — pleasant anticipation, in which her heart took active interest, and warmed, at length, into a strong and earnest hope. She scarcely gave herself time to get home, and never did the distance between Sweet Water Branch and the cottage of her father appear so extravagantly great. She reached it, however, at last ; and there, to her great joy, sat her lover, alongside the old man, and giving him a glowing account, such as he had received from the Yankee captain, of the wonders to be met with in his coming voyage. Old Jones listened patiently, puffing his pipe all the while, and saying little, but now and then, by way of commentary, uttering an ejaculatory grunt, most commonly, of sneering disapproval.

"Better stay at home, a d — d sight, Ned Johnson, and follow the plough."

Ned Johnson, however, thought differently, and it was not the farmer's grunts or growlings that was now to change his mind. Fortunately for the course of true love, there were other influences at work, and the impatience of Mary Jones to try them was evident, in the clumsiness which she exhibited while passing the knife under the thin crust of the corn hoe-cake that night for supper, and laying the thick masses of fresh butter between the smoking and savory-smelling sides, as she turned them apart. The evening wore, at length, and, according to an old familiar habit, the lovers walked forth to the haunted and fairy-like branch of Logoochie, or the Sweet Water. It was the last night in which they were to be together, prior to his departure in the Smashing Nancy. That bouncing vessel and her dexterous captain were to depart with early morning; and it was as little as Ned Johnson could do, to spend that night with his sweetheart. They were both melancholy enough, depend upon it. She, poor girl, hoping much, yet still fearing — for when was true love without fear — she took his arm, hung fondly upon it, and, without a word between them for a long while, inclined him, as it were naturally, in the required direction. Ned really loved her, and was sorry enough when the thought came to him,

that this might be the last night of their association ; but he plucked up courage, with the momentary weakness, and though he spoke kindly,
yet he spoke fearlessly, and with a sanguine temper, upon the prospect of the sea-adventure before him. Mary said little — her heart was too
full for speech, but she looked up now and then
into his eyes, and he saw, by the moonlight,
that her own glistened as with tears. He turned
away his glance as he saw it, for his heart smote
him with the reproach of her desertion.

XVIII.

They came at length to the charmed streamlet,
the Branch of the Sweet Water, to this day known
for its fascinations. The moon rose sweetly above
it, the trees coming out in her soft light, and the
scatterings of her thousand beams glancing from
the green polish of their crowding leaves. The
breeze that rose along with her was soft and wooing as herself; while the besprinkling fleece of the
small white clouds, clustering along the sky, and
flying from her splendors, made the scene, if possible, far more fairy-like and imposing. It was a
scene for love, and the heart of Ned Johnson

grew more softened than ever. His desire for adventure grew modified ; and when Mary bent to the brooklet, and scooped up the water for him to drink, with the water-gourd that hung from the bough, wantoning in the breeze that loved to play over the pleasant stream, Ned could not help thinking she never looked more beautiful. The water trickled from the gourd as she handed it to him, falling like droppings of the moonshine again into its parent stream. You should have seen her eye — so full of hope — so full of doubt — so beautiful — so earnest, — as he took the vessel from her hands. For a moment he hesitated, and then how her heart beat and her limbs trembled. But he drank off the contents at a draught, and gave no sign of emotion. Yet his emotions were strange and novel. It seemed as if so much ice had gone through his veins in that moment. He said nothing, however, and dipping up a gourd full for Mary, he hung the vessel again upon the pendant bough, and the two moved away from the water — not, however, before the maiden caught a glimpse, through the intervening foliage, of those two queer, bright, little eyes of Logoochie, with a more delightful activity than ever, dancing gayly into one.

11*

XIX.

But the spell had been effectual, and a new nature filled the heart of him, who had heretofore sighed vaguely for the unknown. The roving mood had entirely departed; he was no longer a wanderer in spirit, vexed to be denied. A soft languor overspread his form — a weakness gathered and grew about his heart, and he now sighed unconsciously. How soft, yet how full of emphasis, was the pressure of Mary's hand upon his arm as she heard that sigh; and how forcibly did it remind the youth that she who walked beside him was his own — his own forever. With the thought came a sweet perspective — a long vista rose up before his eyes, crowded with images of repose and plenty, such as the domestic nature likes to dream of.

"Oh, Mary, I will not go with this captain — I will not. I will stay at home with you, and we shall be married."

Thus he spoke, as the crowding thoughts, such as we have described, came up before his fancy.

"Will you — shall we? Oh, dear Edward, I am so happy."

And the maiden blessed Logoochie, as she uttered her response of happy feeling.

"I will, dear — but I must hide from Doolittle. I have signed papers to go with him, and he will be so disappointed — I must hide from him."

"Why must you hide, Edward — he cannot compel you to go, unless you please; and you just to be married."

Edward thought she insisted somewhat unnecessarily upon the latter point, but he replied to the first.

"I am afraid he can. I signed papers — I don't know what they were, for I was rash and foolish — but they bound me to go with him, and unless I keep out of the way, I shall have to go."

"Oh, dear — why, Ned, where will you go — you must hide close, — I would not have him find you for the world."

"I reckon not. As to the hiding, I can go where all St. Mary's can't find me; and that's in Okephanokee."

"Oh, don't go so far — it is so dangerous, for some of the Seminoles are there!"

"And what if they are? — I don't care *that* for the Seminoles. They never did me any harm, and never will. But, I shan't go quite so far. Bull swamp is close enough for me, and there I can watch the 'Smashing Nancy' 'till she gets out to sea."

XX.

Having thus determined, it was not long before Ned Johnson made himself secure in his place of retreat, while Captain Doolittle, of the " Smashing Nancy," in great tribulation, ransacked the village of St. Mary's in every direction for his articled seaman, for such Ned Johnson had indeed become. Doolittle deserved to lose him for the trick which, in this respect, he had played upon the boy. His search proved fruitless, and he was compelled to sail at last. Ned, from the top of a high tree on the edge of Bull swamp, watched his departure, until the last gleam of the white sail flitted away from the horizon ; then descending, he made his way back to St. Mary's, and it was not long before he claimed and received the hand of his pretty cottager in marriage. Logoochie was never seen in the neighborhood after this event. His accident had shown him the necessity of keeping with his brethren, for, reasoning from all analogy, gods must be social animals not less

than men. But, in departing, he forgot to take
the spell away which he had put upon the Sweet
Water Branch; and to this day, the stranger,
visiting St. Mary's, is warned not to drink from
the stream, unless he proposes to remain; for still,
as in the case of Ned Johnson, it binds the feet
and enfeebles the enterprise of him who partakes
of its pleasant waters.

JOCASSÉE.

A story of the old-time Cherokee,
Of a true-love, that, like an angel's breath,
Hath a sweet fragrance, still surviving death,
And a bloom Time can touch not — won from high;
A flow'r — for such is true love — of the sky.

JOCASSÉE.

I.

"Keowee Old Fort," as the people in that quarter style it, is a fine antique ruin and relic of the revolution, in the district of Pendleton, South Carolina. The region of country in which we find it, of itself, is highly picturesque and interesting. The broad river of Keowee, which runs through it, though comparatively small, as a stream, in America, would put to shame, by its size, not less than its beauty, one half of the far-famed and boasted rivers of Europe ; — and then the mountains, through and among which it winds its way, embody more of beautiful situation and romantic prospect, than art can well figure to the eye, or language convey to the imagination. To understand, you must see it. Words are of little avail when the ideas overcrowd utterance; and even vanity itself is content to be dumb in the awe inspired by a thousand prospects, like Niagara, the ideal of a god, and altogether beyond the standards common to humanity.

It is not long since I wandered through this interesting region, under the guidance of my friend, Col. G———, who does the honors of society, in that quarter, with a degree of ease and unostentatious simplicity, which readily makes the visiter at home.   My friend was one of those citizens to whom one's own country is always of paramount interest, and whose mind and memory, accordingly, have been always most happily employed when storing away and digesting into pleasing narrative those thousand little traditions of the *genius loci*, which give life to rocks and valleys, and people earth with the beautiful colors and creatures of the imagination. These, for the gratification of the spiritual seeker, he had forever in readiness; and, with him to illustrate them, it is not surprising if the grove had a moral existence in my thoughts, and all the waters around breathed, and were instinct with poetry. To all his narratives I listened with a satisfaction which book-stories do not often afford me. The more he told, the more he had to tell; for nothing staled

"His infinite variety."

There may have been something in the style of
telling his stories ; there was much, certainly, that
was highly attractive in his manner of doing
every thing, and this may have contributed not a
little to the success of his narratives. Perhaps,
too, my presence, upon the very scene of each
legend, may have given them a life and a *vraisem-
blance* they had wanted otherwise.

In this manner, rambling about from spot to
spot, I passed five weeks, without being, at any
moment, conscious of time's progress. Day after
day, we wandered forth in some new direction,
contriving always to secure, and without effort,
that pleasurable excitement of novelty, for which
the great city labors in vain, spite of her varying fashions, and crowding, and not always innocent indulgences. From forest to river, from
hill to valley, still on horseback, — for the moun-
tainous character of the country forbade any more
luxurious form of travel, — we kept on our way,
always changing our ground with the night, and
our prospect with the morning. In this manner
we travelled over or round the Six Mile, and the
Glassy, and a dozen other mountains; and sometimes, with a yet greater scope of adventure,

pushed off on a much longer ramble, — such as took us to the falls of the White Water, and gave us a glimpse of the beautiful river of Jocassée, named sweetly after the Cherokee maiden, who threw herself into its bosom on beholding the scalp of her lover dangling from the neck of his conqueror. The story is almost a parallel to that of the sister of Horatius, with this difference, that our Cherokee girl did not wait for the vengeance of her brother, and altogether spared her reproaches. I tell the story, which is pleasant and curious, in the language of my friend, from whom I first heard it.

II.

" The Occonies and the Little Estatoees, or, rather, the Brown Vipers and the Green Birds, were both minor tribes of the Cherokee nation, between whom, as was not unfrequently the case, there sprung up a deadly enmity. The Estatoees had their town on each side of the two creeks, which, to this day, keep their name, and on the eastern side of the Keowee river. The Occonies occupied a much larger extent of territory, but it lay on the opposite, or west side of the same river.

Their differences were supposed to have arisen
from the defeat of Chatuga, a favorite leader of
the Occonies, who aimed to be made a chief of
the nation at large. The Estatoee warrior, Toxaway, was successful; and as the influence of
Chatuga was considerable with his tribe, he labored successfully to engender in their bosoms a
bitter dislike of the Estatoees. This feeling was
made to exhibit itself on every possible occasion.
The Occonies had no word too foul by which to
describe the Estatoees. They likened them, in
familiar speech, to every thing which, in the Indian
imagination, is accounted low and contemptible.
In reference to war, they were reputed women, —
in all other respects, they were compared to dogs
and vermin; and, with something of a Christian
taste and temper, they did not scruple, now and
then, to invoke the devil of their more barbarous
creed, for the eternal disquiet of their successful
neighbors, the Little Estatoees, and their great
chief, Toxaway.

" In this condition of things there could not be
much harmony; and, accordingly, as if by mutual consent, there was but little intercourse between the two people. When they met, it was
either to regard one another with a cold, repulsive
distance, or else, as enemies, actively to foment

12*

quarrel and engage in strife.   But seldom, save
on national concerns, did the Estatoees cross the
Keowee to the side held by the Occonies; and
the latter, more numerous, and therefore less reluctant for strife than their rivals, were yet not often
found on the opposite bank of the same river.
Sometimes, however, small parties of hunters from
both tribes, rambling in one direction or another,
would pass into the enemy's territory; but this
was not frequent, and when they met, quarrel and
bloodshed were sure to mark the adventure.

"But there was one young warrior of the Estatoees, who did not give much heed to this condition of parties, and who, moved by an errant spirit, and wholly insensible to-fear, would not hesitate, when the humor seized him, to cross the
river, making quite as free, when he did so, with
the hunting-grounds of the Occonies as they did
themselves.   This sort of conduct did not please
the latter very greatly, but Nagoochie was always
so gentle, and at the same time so brave, that the
young warriors of Occony either liked or feared
him too much to throw themselves often in his
path, or labor, at any time, to arrest his progress.

"In one of these excursion, Nagoochie made
the acquaintance of Jocassée, one of the sweetest

of the dusky daughters of Occony. He was rambling, with bow and quiver, in pursuit of game, as was his custom, along that beautiful enclosure, which the whites have named after her, the Jocassée valley. The circumstances under which they met were all strange and exciting, and well calculated to give her a power over the young hunter, to which the pride of the Indian does not often suffer him to submit. It was towards evening when Nagoochie sprung a fine buck from a hollow of the wood along side him, and just before you reach the ridge of rocks which hem in and form this beautiful valley. With the first glimpse of his prey, flew the keen shaft of Nagoochie; but, strange to say, though renowned as a hunter, not less than as a warrior, the arrow failed entirely, and flew wide of the victim. Off he bounded headlong after the fortunate buck; but though, every now and then, getting him within range, — for the buck took the pursuit coolly, — the hunter still most unaccountably failed to strike him. Shaft after shaft had fallen seemingly hurtless from his sides; and though, at frequent intervals, suffered to approach so nigh to the animal that he could not but hope still for better fortune, to his great surprise, the wary buck would dash off when he least expected it, bounding away in some new direction, with as much life and vigor as ever. What to think of this, the hunter knew not; but such repeated disappointments at length impressed it strongly upon his mind, that the object he pursued was neither more nor less than an Occony wizard, seeking to entrap him; so, with a due feeling of superstition, and a small touch of sectional venom aroused into action within his heart, Nagoochie, after the manner of his people, promised a green bird — the emblem of his tribe — in sacrifice to the tutelar divinity of Estato, if he could only be permitted to overcome the potent enchanter, who had thus dazzled his aim and blunted his arrows. He had hardly uttered this vow, when he beheld the insolent deer mincingly grazing upon a beautiful tuft of long grass in the valley, just below the ledge of rock upon which he stood. Without more ado, he pressed forward to bring him within fair range of his arrows, little doubting, at the moment, that the Good Spirit had heard his prayer, and had granted his desire. But, in his hurry, leaping too hastily forward, and with eyes fixed only upon his proposed victim, his foot was caught by the smallest stump in the world, and the very next moment found him precipitated directly over the rock and into the valley, within a few paces of the deer, who made off

with the utmost composure, looking back, as he
did so, to the eyes of the wounded hunter, for all
the world as if he enjoyed the sport mightily.
Nagoochie, as he saw this, gravely concluded that
he had fallen a victim to the wiles of the Occony
wizard, and looked confidently to see half a score
of Occonies upon him, taking him at a vantage.
Like a brave warrior, however, he did not despond, but determining to gather up his loins for
battle and the torture, he sought to rise and put
himself in a state of preparation. What, however, was his horror, to find himself utterly unable
to move ; — his leg had been broken in the fall,
and he was covered with bruises from head to foot.

" Nagoochie gave himself up for lost ; but he
had scarcely done so, when he heard a voice, —
the sweetest, he thought, he had ever heard in his
life, — singing a wild, pleasant song, such as the
Occonies love, which, ingeniously enough, sum_
med up the sundry reasons why the mouth, and
not the eyes, had been endowed with the faculty
of eating. These reasons were many, but the last
is quite enough for us. According to the song,
had the eyes, and not the mouth, been employed
for this purpose, there would soon be a famine in
the land, for of all gluttons, the eyes are the greatest. Nagoochie groaned aloud, as he heard the

song, the latter portion of which completely indicated the cause of his present misfortune. It
was, indeed, the gluttony of the eyes which had
broken his leg. This sort of allegory the Indians
are fond of, and Jocassée knew all their legends.
Certainly, thought Nagoochie, though his leg
pained him wofully at the time, — certainly I
never heard such sweet music, and such a voice.
The singer advanced as she sung, and almost
stumbled over him.

" ' Who are you ?' she asked timidly, neither
retreating nor advancing ; and, as the wounded
man looked into her face, he blessed the Occony
wizard, by whose management he deemed his leg
to have been broken.

" ' Look ?' was the reply of the young warrior,
throwing aside the bearskin which covered his
bosom, — ' look, girl of Occony ! 'tis the *totem*
of a chief ;' and the green bird stamped upon his
left breast, as the badge of his tribe, showed him
a warrior of Estato, and something of an enemy.
But his eyes had no enmity, and then the broken
leg ! Jocassée was a gentle maiden, and her heart
melted with the condition of the warrior. She
made him a sweet promise, in very pretty language, and with the very same voice, the music of
which was so delicious ; and then, with the fleet-

ness of a young doe, she went off to bring him succor.

III.

" Night, in the meanwhile, came on ; and the long howl of the wolf, as he looked down from the crag, and waited for the thick darkness in which to descend the valley, came freezingly to the ear of Nagoochie. ' Surely,' he said to himself, ' the girl of Occony will come back. She has too sweet a voice not to keep her word. She will certainly come back.' While he doubted, he believed. Indeed, though still a very young maiden, the eyes of Jocassée had in them a great deal that was good for little beside, than to persuade, and force conviction ; and the belief in them was pretty extensive in the circle of her rustic acquaintance. All people love to believe in fine eyes, and nothing more natural than for lovers to swear by them. Nagoochie did not swear by those of Jocassée, but he did most religiously believe in them ; and though the night gathered fast, and the long howl of the wolf came close from his crag, down into the valley, the young

hunter of the green bird did not despair of the
return of the maiden.

"She did return, and the warrior was insensible.
But the motion stirred him; the lights gleamed
upon him from many torches; he opened his eyes,
and when they rested upon Jocassée, they forgot
to close again. She had brought aid enough, for
her voice was powerful as well as musical; and,
taking due care that the totem of the green bird
should be carefully concealed by the bearskin,
with which her own hands covered his bosom, she
had him lifted upon a litter, constructed of several
young saplings, which, interlaced with withes,
binding it closely together, and strewn thickly with
leaves, made a couch as soft as the wounded man
could desire. In a few hours, and the form of
Nagoochie rested beneath the roof of Attakulla,
the sire of Jocassée. She sat beside the young
hunter, and it was her hand that placed the pure
balm upon his lips, and poured into his wounds
and bruises the strong and efficacious balsam of
Indian pharmacy.

"Never was nurse more careful of her charge.
Day and night she watched by him, and few were
the hours which she then required for her own pleasure or repose. Yet why was Jocassée so devoted to the stranger? She never asked herself so

unnecessary a question ; but as she was never so
well satisfied, seemingly, as when near him, the
probability is she found pleasure in her tendance.
It was fortunate for him and for her, that her father was not rancorous towards the people of the
Green Bird, like the rest of the Occonies. It
might have fared hard with Nagoochie otherwise.
But Attakulla was a wise old man, and a good ;
and when they brought the wounded stranger to
his lodge, he freely yielded him shelter, and went
forth himself to Chinabee, the wise medicine of
the Occonies. The eyes of Nagoochie were turned upon the old chief, and when he heard his
name, and began to consider where he was, he
was unwilling to task the hospitality of one who
might be disposed to regard him, when known,
in an unfavorable or hostile light. Throwing
aside, therefore, the habit of circumspection, which
usually distinguishes the Indian warrior, he unco-
vered his bosom, and bade the old man look upon
the totem of his people, precisely as he had done
when his eye first met that of Jocassée.

" ' Thy name ? What do the people of the
Green Bird call the young hunter ?' asked Attakulla.

" ' They name Nagoochie among the braves of

the Estato : they will call him a chief of the Cherokee, like Toxaway,' was the proud reply.

" This reference was to a sore subject with the
Occonies, and perhaps it was quite as imprudent
as it certainly was in improper taste for him to
make it.　But knowing where he was, excited by
fever, and having — to say much in little — but
an unfavorable opinion of Occony magnanimity,
he was more rash than reasonable.　At that moment, too, Jocassée had made her appearance,
and the spirit of the young warrior, desiring to
look big in her eyes, had prompted him to a fierce
speech not altogether necessary.　He knew not
the generous nature of Attakulla ; and when the
old man took him by the hand, spoke well of the
Green Bird, and called him his ' son,' the pride of
Nagoochie was something humbled, while his
heart grew gentler than ever.　His ' son !' that
was the pleasant part ; and as the thoughts grew
more and more active in his fevered brain, he
looked to Jocassée with such a passionate admiration that she sunk back with a happy smile from
the flame-glance which he set upon her.　And day
after day she tended him, until the fever passed
off, and the broken limb was set and had reknit-
ted, and the bruises were all healed upon him.
Yet he lingered.　He did not think himself quite

well, and she always agreed with him in opinion.
Once and again did he set off, determined not to
return, but his limb pained him, and he felt the
fever come back, whenever he thought of Jocassée; and so the evening found him again at the
lodge, while the fever-balm, carefully bruised in
milk, was in as great demand as ever for the in-
valid. But the spirit of the warrior at length
grew ashamed of these weaknesses ; and, with a
desperate effort, for which he gave himself no little credit, he completed his determination to depart
with the coming of the new moon. But even this
decision was only effected by compromise. Love
settled the affair with conscience, after his own fashion, and under his direction, following the dusky
maiden into the little grove that stood beside the
cottage, Nagoochie claimed her to fill the lodge
of a young warrior of the Green Bird. She
broke the wand which he presented her, and seizing upon the torch which she carried, he buried it
in the bosom of a neighboring brook, and thus,
after their simple forest ceremonial, Jocassée became the betrothed of Nagoochie.

IV.

"But we must keep this secret to ourselves, for as yet it remained unknown to Attakulla, and the time could not come for its revealment until the young warrior had gone home to his people. Jocassée was not so sure that all parties would be so ready as herself to sanction her proceeding. Of her father's willingness, she had no question, for she knew his good nature and good sense ; but she had a brother of whom she had many fears and misgivings. He was away, on a great hunt of the young men, up at Charashilactay, or the falls of the White Water, as we call it to this day — a beautiful cascade of nearly forty feet, the water of which is of a milky complexion. How she longed, yet how she dreaded, to see that brother ? He was a fierce, impetuous, sanguinary youth, who, to these characteristics, added another still more distasteful to Jocassée ; — there was not a man among all the Occonies who so hated the people of the Green Bird as Cheochee. What hopes, or rather what fears, were in the bosom of that maiden !

"But he came not. Day after day they looked for his return, and yet he came not; but in his place a runner, with a bearded stick, a stick covered with slips of skin, torn from the body of a wolf. The runner passed by the lodge of Attakulla, and all its inmates were aroused by the intelligence he brought. A wolf-hunt was commanded by Moitoy, the great war-chief or generalissimo of the Cherokee nation, to take place, *instanter*, at Charashilactay, where an immense body of wolves had herded together, and had become troublesome neighbors. Old and young, who had either taste for the adventure, or curiosity to behold it, at once set off upon the summons; and Attakulla, old as he was, and Nagoochie, whose own great prowess in hunting had made it a passion, determined readily upon the journey. Jocassée, too, joined the company, — for the maidens of Cherokee were bold spirits, as well as beautiful, and loved to ramble, particularly when, as in the present instance, they went in company with their lovers. Lodge after lodge, as they pursued their way, poured forth its inmates, who joined them in their progress, until the company had swollen into a goodly caravan, full of life, anxious for sport, and carrying, as is the fashion among the Indians, provisions of smoked venison and parched grain, in plenty, for many days.

13*

" They came, at length, to the swelling hills,
the long narrow valleys of the Keochee, and its
tribute river of Toxaway, named after that great
chief of the Little Estatoees, of whom we have
already heard something. At one and the same
moment, they beheld the white waters of Charashilactay, plunging over the precipice, and the
hundred lodges of the Cherokee hunters. There
they had gathered — the warriors and their women — twenty different tribes of the same great
nation being represented on the ground ; each
tribe having its own cluster of cabins, and rising
up in the midst of each, the long pole on which
hung the peculiar emblem of the clan. It was
not long before Nagoochie marshalled himself
along with his brother Estatoees — who had counted him lost — under the beautiful green bird of
his tribe, which waved about in the wind, over the
heads of their small community.

" The number of warriors representing the Estato in that great hunt was inconsiderable — but
fourteen — and the accession, therefore, of so
promising a brave as Nagoochie was no small
matter. They shouted with joy at his coming,
and danced gladly in the ring between the lodges
— the young women, in proper taste, and with

due spirit, hailing, with a sweet song, the return
of so handsome a youth, and one yet unmarried.

"Over against the lodges of the Estatoees, lay
the more imposing encampment of the rival Occonies, who turned out strongly, as it happened, on
this occasion. They were more numerous than
any other of the assembled tribes, as the hunt was
to take place on a portion of their own territory.
Conscious of their superiority, they had not, you
may be sure, forborne any of the thousand sneers
and sarcasms which they were never at a loss to
find when they spoke of the Green Bird warriors;
and of all their clan, none was so bitter, so un-
compromising, generally, in look, speech, and action, as Cheochee, the fierce brother of the beautiful Jocassée. Scorn was in his eye, and sarcasm
on his lips, when he heard the rejoicings made by
the Estatoees on the return of the long-lost hunter.

"'Now wherefore screams the painted bird to-
day? why makes he a loud cry in the ears of the
brown viper that can strike?' he exclaimed con-
temptuously yet fiercely.

"It was Jocassée that spoke in reply to her brother, with the quickness of woman's feeling, which
they wrong greatly who hold it subservient to the
strength of woman's cunning. In her reply,
Cheochee saw the weakness of her heart.

" ' They scream for Nagoochie,' said the girl;
' it is joy that the young hunter comes back that
makes the green bird to sing to-day.'

" ' Has Jocassée taken a tongue from the green
bird, that she screams in the ears of the brown
viper? What has the girl to do with the thought
of the warrior? Let her go — go, bring drink to
Cheochee.'

" Abashed and silent, she did as he commanded,
and brought meekly to the fierce brother, a gourd
filled with the brown beer which the Cherokees
love.   She had nothing further to say on the subject of the Green Bird warrior, for whom she had
already so unwarily spoken.   But her words had
not fallen unregarded upon the ears of Cheochee,
nor had the look of the fond heart which spoke
out in her glance, passed unseen by the keen eye
of that jealous brother.   He had long before this
heard of the great fame of Nagoochie as a
hunter, and in his ire he was bent to surpass him.
Envy had grown into hate, when he heard that
this great reputation was that of one of the accursed Estatoees; and, not satisfied with the desire
to emulate, he also aimed to destroy.   This feeling worked like so much gall in his bosom; and
when his eyes looked upon the fine form of Nagoochie, and beheld its symmetry, grace, and

manhood, his desire grew into a furious passion
which made him sleepless. The old chief, Attakulla, his father, told him all the story of Nagoochie's accident — how Jocassée had found him ;
and how, in his own lodge, he had been nursed
and tended. The old man spoke approvingly of
Nagoochie ; and, the better to bring about a good
feeling for her lover, Jocassée humbled herself
greatly to her brother, — anticipated his desires,
and studiously sought to serve him. But all this
failed to effect a favorable emotion in the breast
of the malignant young savage towards the young
hunter of the Green Bird. He said nothing,
however, of his feelings ; but they looked out and
were alive to the sight in every feature, whenever
any reference, however small, was made to the
subject of his ire. The Indian feeling is subtlety,
and Cheochee was a warrior already named by
the old chiefs of Cherokee.

V.

" The next day came the commencement of the
great hunt, and the warriors were up betimes and
active. Stations were chosen, the keepers of
which, converging to a centre, were to hem in

the wild animal on whose tracks they were going.
The wolves were known to be in a hollow of the
hills near Charashilactay, which had but one
outlet; and points of close approximation across
this outlet were the stations of honor; for, goaded by the hunters to this passage, and failing of
egress in any other, the wolf, it was well known,
would be then dangerous in the extreme.   Well
calculated to provoke into greater activity the jea-
lousies between the Occonies and the Green Birds,
was the assignment made by Moitoy, the chief, of
the more dangerous of these stations to these two
clans.   They now stood alongside of one another, and the action of the two promised to be
joint and corresponsive. Such an appointment, in
the close encounter with the wolf, necessarily promised to bring the two parties into immediate contact; and such was the event.   As the day advanced, and the hunters, contracting their circles,
brought the different bands of wolves into one,
and pressed upon them to the more obvious and
indeed the only outlet, the badges of the Green
Bird and the Brown Viper — the one consisting
of the stuffed skin and plumage of the Carolina
parrot, and the other the attenuated viper, filled
out with moss, and winding, with erect head,
around the pole, to the top of which it was stuck

—were at one moment, in the indiscriminate hunt, almost mingled over the heads of the two parties. Such a sight was pleasant to neither, and would, at another time, of a certainty, have brought about a squabble. As it was, the Occonies drove their badge-carrier from one to the other end of their ranks, thus studiously avoiding the chance of another collision between the viper so adored, and the green bird so detested. The pride of the Estatoees was exceedingly aroused at this exhibition of impertinence, and though a quiet people enough, they began to think that forbearance had been misplaced in their relations with their presuming and hostile neighbors. Had it not been for Nagoochie, who had his own reasons for suffering yet more, the Green Birds would certainly have plucked out the eyes of the Brown Vipers, or tried very hard to do it; but the exhortations to peace of the young warrior, and the near neighborhood of the wolf, quelled any open show of the violence they meditated; but, Indian-like, they determined to wait for the moment of greatest quiet, as that most fitted for taking away a few scalps from the Occony. With a muttered curse, and a contemptuous slap of the hand upon their thighs, the more furious among the Estatoees satisfied their present anger, and then addressed themselves more directly to the business before them.

"The wolves, goaded to desperation by the sound of hunters strewn all over the hills around them, were now, snapping and snarling, and with eyes that flashed with a terrible anger, descending the narrow gully towards the outlet held by the two rival tribes. A united action was therefore demanded of those who, for a long time past, had been conscious of no feeling or movement in common. But here they had no choice — no time, indeed, to think. The fierce wolves were upon them, doubly furious at finding the only passage stuck full of enemies. Well and manfully did the hunters stand and seek the encounter with the infuriated beasts. The knife and the hatchet, that day, in the hand of Occony and Estato, did fearful execution. The Brown Vipers fought nobly, and with their ancient reputation. But the Green Birds were the hunters, after all; and they were now stimulated into double adventure and effort, by an honorable ambition to make up for all deficiencies of number by extra valor, and the careful exercise of all that skill in the arts of hunting for which they have always been the most renowned of the tribes of Cherokee. As, one by one, a fearful train, the wolves wound into sight along this or that crag of the gully, arrow after arrow told fearfully upon them, for there were no marksmen like the Estatoees. Nor did they stop at this weapon. The young Nagoochie, more than ever prompted to such enterprise, led the way ; and dashing into the very path of the teeth-gnashing and claw-rending enemy, he grappled in desperate fight the first that offered himself, and as the wide jaws of his hairy foe opened upon him, with a fearful plunge at his side, adroitly leaping to the right, he thrust a pointed stick down, deep, as far as he could send it, into the monster's throat, then pressing back upon him, with the rapidity of an arrow, in spite of all his fearful writhings he pinned him to the ground, while his knife, in a moment after, played fatally in his heart. Another came, and in a second, his hatchet cleft and crunched deep into the skull of the hairy brute, leaving him senseless, without need of a second stroke. There was no rivalling deeds of valour so desperate as this ; and with increased bitterness of soul did Cheochee and his followers hate in proportion as they admired. They saw the day close, and heard the signal calling them to the presence of the great chief Moitoy, conscious, though superior in numbers, they could not at all compare in skill and success

with the long-despised, but now thoroughly-hated
Estatoees.

"And still more great the vexation, still more
deadly the hate, when the prize was bestowed by
the hand of Moitoy, the great military chief of
Cherokee —when, calling around him the tribes,
and carefully counting the number of their several
spoils, consisting of the skins of the wolves that
had been slain, it was found that of these the
greater number, in proportion to their force, had
fallen victims to the superior skill or superior daring of the people of the Green Bird.   And who
had been their leader? the rambling Nagoochie
— the young hunter who had broken his leg
among the crags of Occony, and, in the same
adventure, no longer considered luckless, had won
the young heart of the beautiful Jocassée.

"They bore the young and successful warrior
into the centre of the ring, and before the great
Moitoy.   He stood up in the presence of the assembled multitude, a brave and fearless, and fine
looking Cherokee.   At the signal of the chief,
the young maidens gathered into a group, and
sung around him a song of compliment and approval, which was just as much as to say, — 'Ask,
and you shall have.'   He did ask; and before
the people of the Brown Viper could so far re-

cover from their surprise as to interfere, or well comprehend the transaction, the bold Nagoochie had led the then happy Jocassée into the presence of Moitoy and the multitude, and had claimed the girl of Occony to fill the green lodge of the Estato hunter.

VI.

"'That was the signal for uproar and commotion. The Occonies were desperately angered, and the fierce Cheochee, whom nothing, not even the presence of the great war-chief, could restrain, rushed forward, and dragging the maiden violently from the hold of Nagoochie, hurled her backward into the ranks of his people; then, breathing nothing but blood and vengeance, he confronted him with ready knife and uplifted hatchet, defying the young hunter, in that moment, to the fight.

"' *E-cha-e-cha, e-herro—echa-herro-echa-herro,*' was the warwhoop of the Occonies; and it gathered them to a man around the sanguinary young chief who uttered it. ' *Echa-herro, echa-herro,*' he continued, leaping wildly in air with the paroxysm of rage which had seized him, — 'the brown viper has a tooth for the green bird. The

Occony is athirst — he would drink blood from the dog-heart of the Estato. *E-cha-e-cha-herro, Occony.*' And again he concluded his fierce speech with that thrilling roll of sound, which, as the so much dreaded warwhoop, brought a death feeling to the heart of the early pioneer, and made the mother clasp closely, in the deep hours of the night, the young and unconscious infant to her bosom. But it had no such influence upon the fearless spirit of Nagoochie. The Estato heard him with cool composure, and though evidently unafraid, it was yet equally evident that he was unwilling to meet the challenger in strife. Nor was his decision called for on the subject. The great chief interposed, and all chance of conflict was prevented by his intervention. In that presence they were compelled to keep the peace, though both the Occonies and Little Estatoees retired to their several lodges with fever in their veins, and a restless desire for that collision which Moitoy had denied them. All but Nagoochie were vexed at this denial; and all of them wondered much that a warrior, so brave and daring as he had always shown himself, should be so backward on such an occasion. It was true, they knew of his love for the girl of Occony; but

they never dreamed of such a feeling acquiring
an influence over the hunter, of so paralyzing and
unmanly a character. Even Nagoochie himself,
as he listened to some of the speeches uttered
around him, and reflected upon the insolence of
Cheochee — even he began to wish that the affair
might go over again, that he might take the hissing viper by the neck. And poor Jocassee —
what of her when they took her back to the
lodges? She did nothing but dream all night of
Brown Vipers and Green Birds in the thick of
battle.

VII.

"The next day came the movement of the
hunters, still under the conduct of Moitoy, from
the one to the other side of the upper branch of
the Keowee river, now called the Jocassée, but
which, at that time, went by the name of Sarratay.
The various bands prepared to move with the daylight ; and still near, and still in sight of one another, the Occonies and Estatoees took up their
line of march with the rest. The long poles of
the two, bearing the green bird of the one, and
the brown viper of the other, in the hands of their
14*

respective bearers — stout warriors chosen for this purpose with reference to strength and valor — waved in parallel courses, though the space between them was made as great as possible by the common policy of both parties. Following the route of the caravan, which had been formed of the ancient men, the women and children, to whom had been entrusted the skins taken in the hunt, the provisions, utensils for cooking, &c. the great body of hunters were soon in motion for other and better hunting-grounds, several miles distant, beyond the river.

" The Indian warriors have their own mode of doing business, and do not often travel with the stiff precision which marks European civilization. Though having all one point of destination, each hunter took his own route to gain it, and in this manner asserted his independence. This had been the education of the Indian boy, and this self-reliance is one source of that spirit and character which will not suffer him to feel surprise in any situation. Their way, generally, wound along a pleasant valley, unbroken for several miles, until you came to Big-knob, a huge crag which completely divides it, rising formidably up in the midst, and narrowing the valley on either hand to a fissure, necessarily compelling a closer march for all parties than had heretofore been pursued. Straggling about as they had been, of course but little order was perceptible when they came together, in little groups, where the mountain forced their junction. One of the Bear tribe found himself along side a handful of the Foxes, and a chief of the Alligators plunged promiscuously into the centre of a cluster of the Turkey tribe, whose own chief was probably doing the proper courtesies among the Alligators. These little crossings, however, were amusing rather than annoying, and were, generally, productive of little inconvenience, and no strife. But it so happened, there was one exception to the accustomed harmony. The Occonies and Estatoees, like the rest, had broken up in small parties, and as might have been foreseen, when they came individually to where the crag divided the valley into two, some took the one and some the other hand, and it was not until one of the paths they had taken opened into a little plain in which the woods were bald — a sort of prairie — that a party of seven Occonies discovered that they had among them two of their detested rivals, the Little Estatoees. What made the matter worse, one of these stragglers was the ill-fated warrior who had been chosen to carry the badge of his tribe ; and there, high above their heads — the heads of the Brown Vipers — floated that detestable symbol, the green bird itself.

"There was no standing that. The Brown Vipers, as if with a common instinct, were immediately up in arms. They grappled the offending stragglers without gloves. They tore the green bird from the pole, stamped it under foot, smeared it in the mud, and pulling out the cone-tuft of its head, utterly degraded it in their own as well as in the estimation of the Estatoees. Not content with this, they hung the desecrated emblem about the neck of the bearer of it, and, spite of all their struggles, binding the arms of the two stragglers behind their backs, the relentless Vipers thrust the long pole which had borne the bird, in such a manner between their alternate arms as effectually to bind them together. In this manner, amidst taunts, blows, and revilings, they were left in the valley to get on as they might, while their enemies, insolent enough with exultation, proceeded to join the rest of their party.

VIII.

" An hundred canoes were ready on the banks of the river Sarratay, for the conveyance to the opposite shore of the assembled Cherokees. And down they came, warrior after warrior, tribe after tribe, emblem after emblem, descending from the crags around in various order, and hurrying all with shouts and whoops and songs, grotesquely leaping to the river's bank, like so many boys just let out of school. Hilarity is, indeed, the life of nature ! Civilization refines the one at the expense of the other, and then it is that no human luxury or sport, as known in society, stimulates appetite for any length of time. We can only laugh in the woods — society suffers but a smile, and desperate sanctity, with the countenance of a crow, frowns even at that.

" But down, around, and gathering from every side, they came — the tens and the twenties of the several tribes of Cherokee. Grouped along the banks of the river, were the boats assigned to each. Some, already filled, were sporting in every direction over the clear bosom of that beautiful water. Moitoy himself, at the head of the

tribe of Nequassée, from which he came, had already embarked ; while the venerable Attakulla,
with Jocassée, the gentle, sat upon a little bank
in the neighborhood of the Occony boats, await-
ing the arrival of Cheochee and his party. And
why came they not? One after another of the
several tribes had filled their boats, and were either
on the river or across it. But two clusters of
canoes yet remained, and they were those of the
rival tribes — a green bird flaunted over the one,
and a brown viper, in many folds, was twined
about the pole of the other.

"There was sufficient reason why they came
not. The strife had begun ; — for, when gathering his thirteen warriors in a little hollow at the
termination of the valley through which they came,
Nagoochie beheld the slow and painful approach
of the two stragglers upon whom the Occonies
had so practised. When he saw the green bird
— the beautiful emblem of his tribe — disfigured
and defiled, there was no longer any measure or
method in his madness. There was no longer a
thought of Jocassée to keep him back ; and the
feeling of ferocious indignation which filled his
bosom was the common feeling with his brother
warriors. They lay in wait for the coming of the
Occonies, down at the foot of the Yellow Hill,

where the woods gathered green and thick. They were few — but half in number of their enemies — but they were strong in ardor, strong in justice, and even death was preferable to a longer endurance of that dishonor to which they had already been too long subjected. They beheld the approach of the Brown Vipers, as, one by one, they wound out from the gap of the mountain, with a fierce satisfaction. The two parties were now in sight of each other, and could not mistake the terms of their encounter. No word was spoken between them, but each began the scalp-song of his tribe, preparing at the same time his weapon, and advancing to the struggle.

" ' The green bird has a bill,' sang the Estatoees ; ' and he flies like an arrow to his prey.'

" ' The brown viper has poison and a fang,' responded the Occonies ; ' and he lies under the net for his enemy.'

" ' Give me to clutch the war-tuft,' cried the leaders of each party, almost in the same breath.

" ' To taste the blood,' cried another.

" ' And make my knife laugh in the heart that shrinks,' sung another and another.

" ' I will put my foot on the heart,' cried an Occony.

" ' I tear away the scalp,' shouted an Estato, in

reply; while a joint chorus from the two parties, promised —

"'A dog that runs, to the black spirit that sleeps in the swamp.'

"'*Echa-herro, echa-herro, echa-herro,*' was the grand cry, or fearful warwhoop, which announced the moment of onset and the beginning of the strife.

IX.

"The Occonies were not backward, though the affair was commenced by the Estatoees. Cheochee, their leader, was quite as brave as malignant, and now exulted in the near prospect of that sweet revenge for all the supposed wrongs and more certain rivalries which his tribe had suffered from the Green Birds. Nor was this more the feeling with him than with his tribe. Disposing themselves, therefore, in readiness to receive the assault, they rejoiced in the coming of a strife, in which, having many injuries to redress, they had the advantages, at the same time, of position and number.

"But their fighting at disadvantage was not now a thought with the Little Estatoees. Their blood was up, and like all usually patient people, once aroused, they were not so readily quieted. Nagoochie, the warrior now, and no longer the lover, led on the attack. You should have seen how that brave young chief went into battle—how he leapt up in air, slapped his hands upon his thighs in token of contempt for his foe, and throwing himself open before his enemies, dashed down his bow and arrows, and waving his hatchet, signified to them his desire for the conflict, *à l'outrance*, and, what would certainly make it so, hand to hand. The Occonies took him at his word, and throwing aside the long bow, they bounded out from their cover to meet their adversaries. Then should you have seen that meeting — that first rush — how they threw the tomahawk — how they flourished the knife — how the brave man rushed to the fierce embrace of his strong enemy — and how the two rolled along the hill in the teeth-binding struggle of death.

" The tomahawk of Nagoochie had wings and a tooth. It flew and bit in every direction. One after another, the Occonies went down before it, and still his fierce war cry of ' *Echa-mal-Occony*,' preceding every stroke, announced another and another victim. They sank away from him like sheep before the wolf that is hungry, and the dis-

parity of force was not so great in favor of the
Occonies, when we recollect that Nagoochie was
against them.   They were now, under his fierce
valor, almost equal in number, and something
more was necessary to be done by the Occonies
before they could hope for that favorable result
from the struggle which they had before looked
upon as certain.   It was for Cheochee now to
seek out and to encounter the gallant young chief
of Estato.   Nagoochie, hitherto, for reasons best
known to himself, had studiously avoided the
leader of the Vipers ; but he could no longer do
so.   He was contending, in close strife, with Okonettee, or the One Eyed — a stout warrior of the
Vipers — as Cheochee approached him.   In the
next moment, the hatchet of Nagoochie entered
the skull of Okonettee.   The One-Eyed sunk to
the ground, as if in supplication, and, seizing the
legs of his conqueror, in spite of the repeated
blows which descended from the deadly instrument, each of which was a death, while his head
swam, and the blood filled his eyes, and his senses
were fast fleeting, he held on with a death-grasp
which nothing could compel him to forego.   In
this predicament, Cheochee confronted the young
brave of Estato.   The strife was short, for though
Nagoochie fought as bravely as ever, yet he

struck in vain, while the dying wretch, grappling his legs, disordered, even by his convulsions, not less than by his efforts, every blow which the strong hand of Nagoochie sought to give. One arm was already disabled, and still the dying wretch held on to his legs. In another moment, the One-Eyed was seized by the last spasms of death, and in his struggles, he dragged the Estato chief to his knees. This was the fatal disadvantage. Before any of the Green Bird warriors could come to his succor, the blow was given, and Nagoochie lay under the knee of the Brown Viper. The knife was in his heart, and the life not yet gone, when the same instrument encircled his head, and his swimming vision could behold his own scalp waving in the grasp of his conqueror. The gallant spirit of Nagoochie passed away in a vain effort to utter his song of death — the song of a brave warrior conscious of many victories.

X.

" Jocassée looked up to the hills when she heard the fierce cry of the descending Vipers. Their joy was madness, for they had fought with — they had slain, the bravest of their enemies. The in-

toxication of tone which Cheochee exhibited, when
he told the story of the strife, and announced his
victory, went like a death-stroke to the heart of
the maiden.   But she said not a word — she uttered no complaint — she shed no tear — but,
gliding quietly into the boat in which they were
about to cross the river, she sat silent, gazing, with
the fixedness of a marble statue, upon the still
dripping scalp of her lover, as it dangled about
the neck of his conqueror.   On a sudden, just as
they had reached the middle of the stream, she
started, and her gaze was turned once more backward upon the banks they had left, as if, on a sudden, some object of interest had met her sight, —
then, whether by accident or design, with look still
intent in the same direction, she fell over the side,
before they could save or prevent her, and was
buried in the deep waters of Sarratay for ever.
She rose not once to the surface.   The stream,
from that moment, lost the name of Sarratay, and
both whites and Indians, to this day, know it only
as the river of Jocassée.   The girls of Cherokee,
however, contend that she did not sink, but walking ' the waters like a thing of life,' that she re-
joined Nagoochie, whom she saw beckoning to
her from the shore.   Nor is this the only tradition.

The story goes on to describe a beautiful lodge, one of the most select in the valley of Manneyto, the hunter of which is Nagoochie of the Green Bird, while the maiden who dresses his venison is certainly known as Jocassée."

THE CHEROKEE EMBASSAGE.

————

———— " Where go these messengers —
These untamed lords of the forest, — whither speed
Their barks o'er unknown waters — to survey
What land of blue delight, what better shore,
More grateful to the hunter than the last ?"

THE

CHEROKEE EMBASSAGE.

It was deemed prudent, soon after the close of a trying war with the savages, to conciliate the Cherokee nation, then one of the largest in the colony; and Sir Alexander Cumming, himself an ostentatious person, was fitly chosen for this purpose. Charged with proposals of alliance, and amply provided with gifts, more imposing than valuable, to the several leading chiefs and sages, this gentleman, in the beginning of the year 1730, set forth for the Apalachian mountains, in the neighborhood of which the principal towns of the Cherokees were situated. He was attended on this occasion, as well by several voluntary travellers, as by a numerous military retinue; and no circumstance was omitted, of display or pomp, which could impress upon the abo-

rigines an idea of the vast power of that foreign
potentate, whose representative was then to appear
before them. Every expense called for by the deputation was cheerfully conceded on the part of
the royal government, as the king well knew the
great military strength of the people, whom it was
the object to conciliate. The Cherokees inhabiting
South Carolina at this time, were as numerous as
they were brave. The inhabitants of thirty-seven
regular towns, were computed to amount to twenty
thousand. Of these, six thousand were bowmen,
ready, on any emergency, to take the field. In
addition to this force, which may be considered
the regular force of the nation, the roving tribes
were supposed to reach several thousand more ;
not so easy to be brought together, but, if possible, far more dangerous to an enemy when once
collected, as, from their continual habit of wandering, they grew even fiercer than the wild beasts,
in whose pursuit only they seemed to live.

It was some time before Sir Alexander reached
Keowee, a distance of three hundred miles or more
from Charleston. His way, for the most part,
lay through a wilderness, seldom, if ever before,
trodden by European footsteps. It was a dreary
pilgrimage, and it was no small satisfaction to the
English, when, as they attained the outskirts of the

Cherokee territory, the chiefs of the lower town, hearing of their approach, came forth to receive and to guide them still further on their way.   *Eefistoe*, the chief of the Green Birds or Little Estatoees, Chulochkolla, the sachem of the Occonies, and Moitoy, the Black Warrior of Telliquo, the most renowned of all their braves, thus joined the jaded cavalcade.

Sir Alexander Cumming hailed them with a flourish ; and, having disposed of his retinue, before their approach, in such a manner as to show them to the best possible advantage, he was pleased to think that he had made a favorable impression. He was not deceived.   The wondering savages — themselves ostentatiously decorated, according to their sylvan fashion, in all the rich plumage of their native birds, contrasted strangely with the hideous paint, and rugged skins, which formed so large a part of their ceremonial equipment — were nevertheless overcome by the more imposing splendors of the deputation.   The glittering armor — the gorgeous uniform of the English, shining in gold and scarlet — the lofty plumes — the plunging and richly caparisoned horses — together with the thrilling military music of an English band — all combined to overpower their imaginations, and to impress the deeply excited senses of the Cherokees; and though, like the Roman Fabricius, they were not to be surprised, and suffered neither awe nor irreverent curiosity to appear upon their faces, or in their gesticulation, they were all nevertheless strongly wrought upon by both these emotions.

Sir Alexander lost no time in securing the friendship of the chiefs, as they severally came forth to meet him. He received them in great state, and to each gave some particular present, so carefully chosen as to avoid all chance of showing a preference to any one, thus giving offence to the rest. This caution had its due results. The chiefs were all well satisfied, and Moitoy, the Black Warrior of Telliquo, not to be outdone in these respects, brought from Tenassee, the principal town of the nation, the crown of the Great Keowee, the old chief and reigning sovereign — a monarch too potent, according to his own and his people's estimation, to be even looked upon by strangers. The policy of the suspicious savage had much to do with this strange seclusion. His person, like that of Montezuma, was considered sacred, and a proper watch was maintained over it accordingly. Thus, though able to have annihilated the entire force under Cumming in a single effort, it was yet thought advisable to risk nothing, by the exposure of a commodity so susceptible to injury as a reigning sovereign; and with the first annunciation, therefore, of the approach of the English, Keowee, a decrepid and almost blind old man, was hurried bodily away from the contiguous country, more deeply than before into the thick forests, and among the impassable barriers of rock, which girdled in and covered their extended territory. To Moitoy, and the other chiefs or kings, was entrusted the task of receiving and providing for the strangers; and, to do them all justice, the reception was such as became a brave and honorable people. The fruits and flesh, the maize and provisions, to which they were themselves accustomed, were all freely provided; and five eagle tails, and four scalps from slaughtered enemies, were also among the presents brought by Moitoy. These had a signification which, through the interpreter, the dusky warriors explained to the satisfaction of their European visiters. The feathers of the eagle marked the strength and the glory alike of Cherokee, and the scalp of their enemies announced the unerring certainty of Cherokee victory and vengeance. These were presented to the English, in token that henceforward their course should be trodden on the same war path, in close affinity, and against the same enemies.

Thirty-two chiefs, each paramount with his own tribe and section, appeared at the solemn council which followed. A great deal of pompous talk was uttered, and Moitoy of Telliquo, the Black Warrior, found such high favor with Sir Alexander, that he nominated him as the commander-in-chief of the Cherokee armies, and presented him with a rich robe as a badge of his new office. The chiefs present agreed to recognise him as such, provided that there should be a like accountability to him, (Sir Alexander,) on the part of Moitoy. Every thing went on amicably, and, emboldened by the friendly disposition which the savages evinced, the English ambassador proposed that some of them should accompany him to England, in order, with their own eyes, to behold that great king, of whom he had given them a most flaming description.

"Your brother, King George," said he, in a speech which was well remembered by the attentive chiefs, "will be glad to see you. He will load you with presents, with hatchets and knives, with rich clothes, and beautiful feathers. He will bind you to his heart with a bright gold chain, which will last unbroken for a thousand years."

"He is our brother," replied the chiefs with one

voice, dazzled by the glorious promise — " he is our brother — we will go to our brother George."

There was no difficulty in getting the proposed deputation ; the only difficulty, indeed, was in making a selection from the number of those offering. Unconscious of the length of the voyage, of its dangers, and the new and unaccustomed scenes and circumstances through which they would have to go before realizing the prospects set before them, the simple savages, each a king in his own country, were readily persuaded to undertake the embassage which promised them so much enjoyment. The gold and the glitter — the fine armor like that which Sir Alexander wore — the pomp and the display, which, through the interpreter, the Englishman dwelt upon in the most glowing language — were irresistible ; and, full of the splendors of their brother George, they threw the bear skins about their shoulders, filled their quivers with fresh arrows from the canebrake, and kissing the sunny side, one after the other, of the broad tree that covered them during the progress of the council, they bade their farewell to the green forests, and the wild free country, their eyes might never again behold.

Six of them accompanied Sir Alexander to Charleston, and thence, having been there joined

by another chief who followed them after a brief
delay, they embarked with him for Europe.   The
eldest of these chiefs, or kings, was Tonestoi,
prince of Nequassée, a once formidable, but now
decayed warrior, and a good old man.   He was
renowned among the Cherokees for his wisdom.
The next in order was the famous orator, Skiajagustha — a man whose eloquence performed wonders in the councils of his people, and of whose
speeches, some occur upon our own historical re-
cords, not unworthy to appear in any collection.
Next came Chulockholla, another orator, neither
so old nor so well renowned as Skiajagustha.   The
chief of the Occonies, or Brown Vipers, Cenestee,
was the fourth of this delegation — a chief only
remarkable for the reckless audacity of his valor.
The fifth was a gallant young warrior of the Little
Estatoees, or Green Birds, Ee-fistoe — a warrior
intelligent as valiant, and not any thing less amiable because of his acknowledged bravery.   Occo-
nostota made the sixth.   He was the king of Echotee, and could himself bring three hundred warriors into the field ; but he was something of a
tyrant, and was deposed the very year after his return from Europe.   The seventh, who joined the
deputation in Charleston, was a chief also, but

his name does not appear in our history.   He was probably of no great renown.

These were the Cherokee kings, who, consenting to the invitation of Sir Alexander Cumming, sailed with him in the Swallow Packet, for London, some time in the month of May, 1730.   Seduced by the glowing pictures spread before their minds by the English agent, full of expectation, and flushed with the promise of so many novelties, the wild men of the woods, wrapped in their hunter garbs, gorgeously covered with fresh paint, and armed to the teeth, after the fashion of their people, fearlessly went on board the little vessel that awaited them, and, with favoring breezes, were soon lost to the sight of land, and plunging steadily over the bosom of the Atlantic.

The sea — a new element to the Cherokees — exacted its dues, and it was not many hours before the warriors grew heartily sick of their unusual undertaking.   Much would they have given to be once more in their native forests, but they were too brave, and too well taught in the stoical morality of the savage, to confess to any such weakness. They had long before learned, that, to conquer, it is first necessary that we should bear with, our fate, and they withstood, accordingly, as well as they could, the storms and the tossings of the waters, in

16*

a manner by no means discrediting their creed or
nation.   They grew, in a little time, familiar with
their new abiding place, and, as the initial sickness
passed away, soon began to contemplate, with
comparative steadiness and a growing appreciation, all the various objects and aspects of their
new domain.

All was strange — all was wonderful around
them.   Their own complete isolation — the absence of the woods and wilds to which only they
had been accustomed — their initiation into a world
so new and strange, as to them was that of ocean
— the singular buoyancy of their ship — the as-
tonishing agility of the seamen, moving about with
ease and dexterity, where they could scarcely
maintain the most uncertain foot-hold — these were
all matters of profound astonishment and curiosity.
But these were all as nothing, after the first blush
of novelty had passed away, in comparison with
the queer tricks and uncouth antics of one of the
ship's company.   This was no less than a monkey,
belonging to one of the sailors, named Jacko — a
creature of habitual trick and mimicry, continually
provoked to its exercise by some one or other of
the seamen.   He ran along the ropes and rigging
in pursuit of them.   He mounted the spars, and
sat in uncouth shapes in the most dangerous

places. He carried off the caps of the sailors, then pelted them down upon those who walked the deck. In short, nothing in the semblance of mischief was omitted by Jacko. Tonestoi, the venerable elder of the Indian chiefs, was absolutely ravished by the tricks of the sportive monkey. He had no thought for any other object than Jacko. He watched his movements by the hour, provoked their exercise by continual stimulating affronts, and laughed, in despite of the grave looks of his brother chiefs, as immoderately as if such had been his continual practice. Tonestoi was an ancient chief, renowned as much for wisdom as for valor, and he presumed upon his reputation. He therefore gave vent to his merriment without any fear of losing either his own or the general respect of his people. The other chiefs, who were all younger, were either differently situated in rank, or were not altogether so secure in the estimation of their people ; and, though equally delighted with Tonestoi, were yet prudent enough to preserve a greater degree of gravity. They looked on with composure ; and, while watching closely all the sports of Jacko, they yet forebore to take any part in the merriment. But the old chief had no such scruples, and his laughter was without reserve. He played with Jacko like a child — rolled with him about the decks — hallooed him on to all manner of mischief — clapped his hands and cheered him in his performance, and then, in his own language, pronounced a high eulogy upon his achievements. He called him " Hickisiwackinaw," or " the warrior with a tail ;" and at length, when he saw Jacko swing by his hind legs from a rope, and, with his paws, grapple and take fast hold upon the bushy poll of one of the sailors as he walked beneath, he called him " Toostenugga," after the celebrated leader of the Cherokee hobgoblins — — this being one of the favorite modes by which Toostenugga, suspending himself from a tree, laid hold of, and punished, those who offended him, as they walked beneath.   Nothing could divert the attention of Tonestoi from the monkey.   Sir Alexander Cumming, whose sense of dignity was greatly outraged by such unbecoming levity, tried his best to attract the mind of the Cherokee to more dignified amusements ; and, in his vexation, was with difficulty restrained from tumbling Jacko overboard, hopeless of any other means of obtaining his object.   He made a show of anger towards the monkey, but, upon beholding the sudden gravity of Tonestoi as he comprehended this design, he thought it only wise to forbear, as it was his policy, as well as his orders, to avoid all manner of offence. His dernier resort then was in his liquors, and once made acquainted with their potency, the old chief, Tonestoi, was soon taught to prefer the intoxicating cup to the antics of his more innocent companion. Jacko, or, as he called him to the last, Toostenugga, ceased to attract so much of his attention, and, to the shame of all parties be it said, the good old warrior, after this, had scarcely a sober hour until they reached the haven of their destination.

Their arrival in London was the signal for much bustle and exhibition. Apart from the desire to impose greatly on their senses by shows and splendors, to which, in their wild abodes, they had never been accustomed, the better to acquire dominion over them, they received a thousand attentions as the last new lions in the metropolis. Lords and ladies thronged the hotel at which the Cherokee kings were lodged, and the beautiful squaws of London, as was more recently the case in our own country, submitted joyfully to the salute of the Indian warriors for the sake of its novelty. Feasts were given them in profusion — frolics conceived on purpose to make them actors; and from the day of their arrival to that of their departure, all was uproar and exultation. In all these junkettings, it need scarcely be said that our Cherokees preserved happily their usual equanimity of character. They were grave and composed, and behaved, for all the world, as if they had been accustomed all their lives to such honors and indulgences. Tonestoi, alone, of all the deputation, gave way to the garrulous good humor of the aged man. He laughed and joked freely with his visiters, and nothing gave him such profound pleasure as when his great cheek bones and painted lips came in contact with the velvety skin of his lady visiters. Never had Cherokee warrior so given way before to all the practices, and so many of the evidences, of *la belle passion.* So much was this the case, that his more youthful companions began to have doubts as to the tenacity of that superior wisdom in the ancient chief which had been a proverb in his own country.

But if the general acquaintance with the Indians, and their usual deportment, prevailed with and gave satisfaction to the English nobility, their conduct in the interview with the king completed the merriment, and furnished a fitting climax to the whole proceeding. Seized somewhat with the spirit of the fashion in reference to them, and desirous of securing, by a proper policy, the affections of these people, the British monarch desired, and determined to do them particular honor. An especial drawing-room was appointed them, and, in the presence of a most brilliant and imposing assemblage, he prepared to receive his distinguished visiters. Sir Alexander Cumming, who had the chiefs in charge, attempted, before going to court, to give them certain instructions as to their behavior in the presence of majesty ; but they either did not, or would not, understand him. They comprehended sufficiently his object, however, and the native pride of an aboriginal chief rose in arms at his suggestion. Skiajagustha, the orator, was the first to take fire at what seemed an indignity. Wrapping his bear skin around him with a majesty which George himself, in all his career, and with the best teachers, never could have emulated, he looked scornfully upon his would-be tutor, while he replied :

"Skiajagustha is the great mouth of Cherokee — he has stood before his nation when Keowee, the red arrow, was there. His words are good."

The interpreter explained ; but, as similar sentiments were uttered by nearly all the party, Sir Alexander saw that it would not only be idle, but most probably offensive, were he to endeavor to teach them farther. As they approached the chair of state, in which sat the monarch, the aged Tonestoi took the advance. The king rose as he drew nigh, and came forward, extending his hand for the usual salute, as he did so, to the approaching Indian. But Tonestoi, remembering his own dignity, and what had been said to him on the score of the relationship between them, prior to his leaving his own country, to the great horror of the courtiers, and of Sir Alexander Cumming in particular, grasped the extended hand of the English monarch with his own, and, giving it a squeeze that none but a bear could well have equalled, shook it heartily and long, exclaiming, in the few words of courtesy which he had committed in broken English,

"Huddye-do, Broder George — huddye-do — glad to see you" — and, continuing with a smile as he looked round upon the women — "You got plenty squaws."

The court was convulsed and shocked beyond measure. All were astounded except the king himself, and the savages. George, with his usual good nature, withdrawing his hand, though with some difficulty, from the powerful gripe of his brother monarch, smiled pleasantly, and, amused with the familiarity, responded in similar style, giving the cue to those around him. Nothing then could exceed the hilarity with which the business of the conference was carried on and finished. The kings made long speeches through the interpreters, satisfactory on all sides, and a treaty of alliance was then and there agreed upon between them, to be valid and binding upon the Cherokees and English in America, as they were avowed to be so by both parties present then in England.

We quote portions of this treaty, as it not only presents us with much of the eloquence employed by the several contracting parties, but also gives us some idea of the various topics of trade and communion, rendering such a treaty between people so dissimilar essential to the mutual good. It will be found, however, that the performance of duties devolves much more frequently upon the Indian than upon the white man, and that his rewards, estimated by our standards of use and value, are quite inadequate to the services required at their hands. Doubtless, however, they were such as were best calculated for the uninstructed savage.

The preamble to this treaty recites,

"That whereas the six chiefs, [without naming them, and without any reference to the chief who unquestionably joined the embassy at Charleston, when about to sail,] with the consent of the whole nation of Cherokees, at a general meeting of their nation at Nequassée, were deputed by Moitoy, their chief warrior, to attend Sir Alexander Cum-

ming to Great Britain, where they had seen the
great king George, and where Sir Alexander, by
authority from Moitoy and all the Cherokees, had
laid the crown of their nation, with the scalps of
their enemies, and feathers of glory, at his majesty's feet, as a pledge of their loyalty; — and
whereas the great king has instructed the lords
commissioners of trade and plantations, to inform
the Indians, that the English on all sides of the
mountains and lakes, were his people, their friends
his friends, their enemies his enemies; that he took
it kindly that the great nation of Cherokee had
sent them so far to brighten the chain of friendship
between him and them, and between his people
and their people; that the chain of friendship between him and the Cherokee is now like the sun,
which shines both in Britain and upon the great
mountains where they live, and equally warms the
hearts of Indians and Englishmen; that, as there
is no spot or blackness in the sun, so neither is
there any rust or foulness on this chain; and, as
the king has fastened one end to his breast, [suit-
ing the action to the word, in George's best and
bluffest style,] he desired them to carry the other
end of the chain and fasten it to the breast of Moitoy, of Telliquo, and to the breasts of all their

wise old men, their captains and people, never more to be made loose or broken.

" The great king and the Cherokees being thus fastened together by a chain of friendship, he has ordered, and it is agreed, that his children in Carolina do trade with the Indians, and furnish them with all manner of goods they want, and to make haste to build houses and plant corn from Charleston towards the towns of the Cherokees behind the great mountains. [Vague enough, and, like most treaties with the Indians, carried on through dishonest or imperfect interpreters, not understood by one of the parties, and a frequent source of mischief afterwards.] That he desires the English and Indians may live together as children of one family —that the Cherokees be always ready to fight against any nation, whether white men or Indians, who shall molest or hurt the English—that the nation of the Cherokee shall, on its part, take care to keep the trading path clean—that there be no blood on the path which the English tread, *even though they should be accompanied with other people with whom the Cherokees may be at war—* [what an exaction—how is it possible that the Cherokees should have understood this charge, or, understanding, that they should have complied with it ?]—*that the Cherokees shall not suffer their people to trade with white men of any other nation but the English*—[here is monopoly with a vengeance!]—nor permit, [mark this,] *nor permit white men of any other nation to build any forts or cabins, or plant any corn among them,* upon lands which belong to the great king."

Such was the morality of these selfish traders. They actually excluded the savages from the exercise of those wonted rites of hospitality to white men, and to christians like themselves, (for the French and Spaniards were contemplated by this clause,) which the Cherokees had freely accorded to the British, and which they must otherwise have extended freely to all others. The treaty goes on to provide, that, if any such attempt shall be made by the white men of any other than the British nation, the Cherokees must not only acquaint the British government of the fact, but must do whatever he directs, in order to maintain and defend the " great king's right to the country of Carolina." The treaty further provides, " that if any negroes shall run away into the woods from their English masters, the Cherokees shall endeavor to apprehend them, and bring them to the plantation from whence they ran, or to the governor."

Hitherto the contract has been all on one side, and the English king has never said " Turkey," once, to his Cherokee brother; but, at this stage of the treaty, he seems to have recollected himself, and, accordingly, we find him promising, that, " for every slave so apprehended and brought back, the Indian that brings him shall receive a gun and a watch coat; and *if, by any accident*, it shall happen that an Englishman shall kill a Cherokee, [an event only possible, it seems,] the king or chief of the nation shall first complain to the English governor, and the man who did the harm shall be punished by the *English laws* as if he had killed an Englishman; and, in like manner, if any Indian happens to kill [by any accident is entirely wanting here] an Englishman, the Indian shall be delivered up to the governor, to be punished by the same English laws as if he were an Englishman."

This was the substance of the first treaty between the British and the Cherokee nation; and a precious specimen it is, of cunning beguiling simplicity, and of unfair relationship between parties originally contracting on an equal footing of advantage. The Cherokee chiefs heard it first from the lips of George, who paused at every sentence, and, as the interpreter explained it, clause by clause, a nobleman presented to the expecting chiefs a rich present of cloths or ornaments.

17*

When the king had got through his task, he suddenly withdrew through a private door, glad to escape any farther embrace from his Cherokee brethren.   The further business of the treaty was then concluded by Alured Popple, secretary to the lords commissioners of trade and plantations, on the one side, and by the marks of the Indian chiefs on the other.   The secretary, at the same time, addressed them in a speech confirming the words of the great king whom they had just seen; and, as a token that his heart was true and open to the Cherokees, a belt was given the warriors, which the king desired them to show to their children and children's children, to confirm what was now spoken, and to bind this agreement of peace and friendship between the English and the Cherokees, " as long as the rivers shall run, the mountains shall stand, or the sun shall shine."

Such was the glowing termination of the secretary's speech.   When he had concluded, the old chief Tonestoi gave way to Skiajagustha, the famous orator, who seemed to know his own claims to reply for the rest.   Gathering his robe over his left shoulder, so as entirely to free the right arm, he began his reply, the greater portion of which is preserved as follows.   It will be found to contain quite as much good sense, dignity, and beauty, as was called for by the occasion :

" We are come hither from the mountains, where there is nothing but darkness. But we are now in a place of light. We see the great king in you-- we love you as you stand here for him. We shall die in this thought. The crown of Cherokee is not like that in the tower ; but, to us, they are the same — the chain shall be carried to our people. The great king George is the sun — he is our father — the Cherokees are his children. Though we are red and you are white — yet our hearts and hands are tied together. We shall say to our people what we have seen, and our children shall remember it. In war we will be one with you — your enemies shall be ours — we shall live together as one people — we shall die together. We are naked and poor as the worms that crawl — but you have all things. We that have nothing must love you. We will never break the chain that is between us. This small rope we show you is all that we have to bind our slaves — You have chains of iron for yours. We will catch your slave that flies — we will bind him as strongly as we can, and we shall take no pay when we bring him back to you. Your people shall build near ours in safety. The Cherokee shall hurt them not — he shall hurt nothing that belongs to them. Are we not children of one father — shall we not live and die together ?"

Here he paused, and one of the other chiefs coming forward at a signal from the speaker, presented him with a bunch of eagle feathers. Taking them in his hand, Skiajagustha presented them to the secretary with these words :

" This is our way of talking, which is the same thing to us as your letters in the book to you. These feathers, from the strong bird of Cherokee — these shall be witnesses for the truth of what I have said."

Thus discoursing eloquently together, the parties contracted to their mutual satisfaction, and however unequal were the general advantages obtained, there was certainly no dissatisfaction expressed among them. The terms were agreed upon without discontent or difficulty, and it will not be premature or anticipative, in this stage of our narration, to say, in the language of the historian, Ramsay, that in consequence of this treaty, the Cherokees, for many years after, remained in " a state of perfect friendship and peace with the colonists, who followed their various employments in the neighborhood of these Indians, without the least terror or molestation."

But the nine days' wonder was now over in the British metropolis. The Indian chiefs began to lose their importance in the sight of their European brethren. Some new monster soon occupied their place, and Sir Alexander Cumming being now prepared to return to Carolina, and the vessel ready to depart, they had little reluctance at leaving a land, where, though every kindness and courtesy had been shown them, they had found so few objects and features at all like or kindred with their own. They set sail from England on the 23d September, 1730, and, under favoring aspects of wind and weather, were soon out upon the comprehensive world and void of ocean.

But the second voyage was more tedious to the chiefs than the first. That had novelty to recommend it — the strange mass of all objects at sea, relieved, in the first instance, its general monotony. But the second brought all this home to them ; and, what added to their dulness still more, was the absence of Jacko — the monkey was no longer one of their fellow passengers. The sailor who owned, had sold him, while in London, and nothing could exceed the dissatisfaction of old Tonestoi, on hearing of the circumstance. The first thing he did on coming aboard the vessel, was to call aloud for Toostenugga. But he called in vain, and was with difficulty made to understand, that his goblin acquaintance was left behind them. He refused consolation, and chafed and almost quarrelled with those who offered it. He drank with Sir Alexander Cumming ; but that was all, in the way of relief or amusement, that he could be persuaded to do. In a state of moody absence, as soon as his fit of sea sickness was well over, he roamed about the ship, tumbling from side to side, and, in his own language, muttering continually of Toostenugga. Dreadfully, indeed, did he suffer from blue devils, and, in this mood, shooting with his arrows wantonly at little spots in the sails, he soon exhausted all his quiver, as the flying shafts would generally, after a few discharges, find their way into the bosom of the ocean. The other, and younger, chiefs bore the voyage with far more philosophy than their ancient comrade ; and with that aptness which belongs to man in all situations, and which we have erringly denied to the Aborigines, they, at length, began to accommodate themselves to the novel employments of the sea. Skiajagustha, the great orator himself, was the first to set an example of this discipline. He seized upon the ropes on one occasion, and began to tug away lustily along with the sailors. His companions followed him, all but old Tonestoi, and, from a sport at first, it grew to be a common resort for exercise among them. Sir Alexander Cumming, however, thought such practices unbecoming in those who had royal blood in their veins; but, as there was no alternative, he could suggest no objection. To Tonestoi, alone, he could address himself; and, as the old chief took no part in the amusements of his companions, he was the more ready to sit gloomily and gravely over the lengthened glass with the Englishman. But his ennui continued to increase, and, at length, to the great consternation of Sir Alexander, the poor savage grew sick, and his free habit of drinking only made him worse. The liquor was then withdrawn from him; and this seemed to increase his malady. The attack was a very severe one, and, unhappily, but few precautions had been taken against such an occasion. There were scarcely any medicines on board; and even these, the old chief, with all the fretful obstinacy of a spoiled child, could not be persuaded to take. Day by day he grew worse, and it now became evident to all that the danger was alarming. The younger chiefs assembled about him, and Sir Alexander, with deep concern, strove, through them, to persuade him to the adoption of those remedies which he proposed. He resolutely rejected all their suggestions, and tossing about in his fever, from side to side, he exhibited a feeble peevishness to all around him — his own people not excepted. Several days passed over in this manner, and it was evident to all that he had sunk amazingly. At this stage of his illness, and while he was chafing querulously with all of them, Skiajagustha approached him where he lay. The brow of the orator was stern and full of rebuke, and the first words which he uttered, in his own sweet but solemn and emphatic language, rivetted the attention of the dying warrior. He ceased to tumble upon his couch — he ceased to chafe and chide those about him. The appeal of Skiajagustha had been made to his manhood — to his sense of the dignity and the courage of a brave of Cherokee:

"Shall Tonestoi go to the Manneyto with the word of a child on his tongue? Shall he say to the Master of Life, wherefore hast thou called me? The brave man has another spirit when the dark spirit wraps him.

"Tonestoi — it is the word of the Cherokee — is a brave among the braves. He has taken scalps from the light-heeled Catawba — he has taken scalps from the cunning Shawanese — he has taken scalps from the Creek warrior that rages — he has taken scalps from all the enemies of Cherokee.

He should have a song for his victories, that the Great Manneyto shall be glad to receive him."

"Achichai-me!" cried Tonestoi in reply — and, in his own language, proceeded as follows:

"It is good, Skiajagustha — it is good what thou hast spoken. But I heard not before the words of the Great Manneyto. I hear them through thee. He has called me — I hear him speaking in the heart of Tonestoi — I am going to the land of spirits — to the plum groves where my fathers journey on the long hunt. I am not afraid to go. The Master of Life knows I am ready."

"Ha! ha!" he sang a moment after —

"Ha! ha! I laugh at my enemies. The Catawba could not take the scalp — he could not drink blood from Tonestoi. Ha! ha! *That* for the Shawanee — *that* for the *Creek* that rages — *that* for all the enemies of Cherokee. The Master of Life only can kill, and Tonestoi is ready for him.

"Bring me arrows, Skiajagustha — bring me arrows, young Ee-fistoe of the Green Birds — bring me arrows, young braves of Cherokee — the arrows shall speak for my victories."

They brought him arrows at his request, and he separated the bundles, laying each shaft by itself. The younger chiefs curiously gathered around

him, as they well knew they were now to hear a
chronicle of his own and his country's achievements; and for every arrow, he had the story of
some brave adventure — some daring deed. One
of them stood for his first battle with the Chicka-
saw, when, yet a mere boy, he went forth with his
old father, Canonjahee, on the war path against
that subtle nation. Another arrow was made to
signify his escape from a band of roving Shawanese who had made him a prisoner while hunting;
a third told the affair with the Creeks, for his bravery in which his countrymen had made him a
chief — feather chief and arrow chief; a fourth
recounted his long personal combat with Sarrata-
hay of Santee, the big boned chief from that river,
who had come up on purpose to contend with him,
at the lower town of Chinebee. Tonestoi was the
victor after a long struggle, and this he dwelt upon
the most emphatically of all his victories. And
so, with a dozen other events, he associated the
arrows. For an hour his strain proceeded, and
the Indians listened with unrelaxing attention.
Sir Alexander Cumming, apprised of the nature
of the scene, hung over the dying chief with the
deepest interest; and even the sailors, several of
them came as nigh to listen as they well might

without manifest impropriety. The old man lay
silent for some time after his song was ended. But
his chosen arrows had all been carefully gathered
up by Skiajagustha, who tied them closely together with the sinews of the deer. Towards evening the chief grew much weaker, and he muttered fitfully, and started every now and then like
one from sleep. When the sun was about to set,
its faint delicate light streamed through the little
aperture in the cabin just where the dying man
lay. He started and strove to raise himself up to
behold the orb now sinking like himself. But failing to do this, he only raised his right hand and
waved it towards the bright object which he could
not see. Skiajagustha bent towards him, and uttered two or three words in his own language, at
which all the other chiefs rose and bent over him.
Tonestoi gave each of them a look of recognition,
and, while muttering a brief sentence, probably one
of parting, his lower jaw suddenly dropped, then
caught up as in a spasm, then as suddenly again
relaxed and fell, never again to move. The light
grew dim in the eyes which yet opened upon the
spectators.

Skiajagustha laid the bunch of arrows upon the
breast of Tonestoi, where they remained until the

next day, when his body was committed to the deep. They were then carefully preserved by the survivors, as witnesses of the whole transaction, and received as such by the people. They form one of the tokens of Cherokee valor, and are preserved to this very hour, among the trophies of the nation.

THE END.

www.ingramcontent.com/pod-product-compliance
Lightning Source LLC
Chambersburg PA
CBHW020227110726
47898CB00004B/1183